JUST ONE DAY

JUST ONE DAY

Hannah Nelson

Copyright © 2013 by Hannah Nelson.

Library of Congress Control Number: 2012920758
ISBN: Hardcover   978-1-4836-1195-2
        Softcover   978-1-4797-4514-2
        Ebook   978-1-4797-4515-9

This book was printed in the United States of America.

Rev. date: 04/24/2013

To order additional copies of this book, contact:
Xlibris Corporation
1-888-795-4274
www.Xlibris.com
Orders@Xlibris.com
120821

ACKNOWLEDGMENTS

Thanks to Grandma Nelson. Without your love and support this wouldn't have been possible.

You are the best mentor and grandma a person could have.

Mom and Dad thanks for the patience, love and moral support I needed to turn a hobby into a fantasy. Thanks to my sister, Olivia, for providing me with inspiration and ideas without realizing it. I am so glad God blessed me with a sister as amazing and understanding as you. Thank you for being there for me when I needed you.

A special thanks to Lauren Macke and Mackenzie See, who taught me dreams really can come true if you want them enough. Also, for teaching me anything is possible. You are great friends; I couldn't have done this without you.

To Vicki Foley thanks for your fantastic editing skills and strong encouragement throughout this whole process.

It's almost funny how everything can change in just one day. How everything you've ever known and loved can be taken away from you and you won't have any say in what happens. You just have to learn to live with it, but the truth is you never learn; it always creeps up on you again, like a song stuck in your head or drama you never expected. There's plenty of that in life, trust me. And that's another thing trust is not real, at least not for me. Trust is defined as the trait of believing in honesty and reliability in others. Yeah right, you can't rely on anyone but yourself because you will end up getting hurt, and even though you may not know it, your loved ones are the ones that hurt you the most.

BOOK ONE

Hayden

CHAPTER ONE

"The fifteen missing teenagers from Lakota were found dead in Riverelli early this morning. The children were suspected to be kidnapped and abused until their death. The killers are still loose and could be anywhere. It isn't likely they will find you, but take extra precautions. This is Heather Launter, Channel 8, saying good night everyone." I click off the television, immediately overcome with fatigue. I've been very tired lately. Between track, soccer, and homework, I barely have time to think, let alone sleep. I slink over to my bed and crawl in, letting the cool silk of my sheets surround me. It's been crossing the ninety-five-degree mark on the thermometer, and the air conditioning in my house isn't really helping, considering it's broke. I turn on to my side and close my eyes. I don't toss and turn or even have a dream, and that's rare for me. Morning comes too quickly and my alarm goes off.

Just in case I don't wake up, Ozalee checks on me. Today she doesn't need to wake me up a second time; I roll out of bed and slip on a pair of shorts and a tee shirt. My hair is actually manageable this morning; all I have to do is run my fingers through it. I'm lucky, compared to most girls, when it comes to hair that is. My brown waves fall past my shoulders in locks, and it's easy for me to handle. Most girls have to throw theirs in ponytails or put straightening spray in it, but that's rare because hardly anyone can afford that type of spray now. As much as I'd love to just sit here for the rest of the day, I gather up the motivation to stand and make my way into the kitchen.

The smell of bacon and eggs make my mouth water. My mom always cooks breakfast for Ozalee and I in the morning since she is never around any time else to do anything for us. She is always working at one of the three jobs she's had to take on since my dad died. I don't know when she sleeps, if ever, and when she does, she usually wakes up screaming from her

---

13

nightmares. Ozalee and I get nightmares too, but we comfort each other or cry ourselves to sleep. Again, it's the same dream over and over—my dad sailing his boat. The boat hits a reef and starts to sink. The forty-foot high mast breaks in half and lands on him, forcing him to inhale only water. Then the sea swallows him and he never resurfaces. This is what my mom and I was told happened to my dad, and this is the nightmare that visits my precious dreams almost every night.

If it weren't for Ozalee, I wouldn't be here anymore, in Villa, I mean. If I didn't have to take care of her and her friends, I would be long gone by now, probably living in Tibbet or somewhere like that. Anywhere past the river valley is fair game, so why not? But I know I would never be able to leave her so I stay.

My mom loads my plate, and I start to eat, blowing carefully on each bite before I put it in my mouth and allow it to go down my throat. I can see Ozalee out of the corner of my eye doing the same thing.

"Thanks for breakfast, Mom."

"You're welcome," she says amiably.

Everything about my mother screams nice and caring. Her dark hair, her big brown eyes, even her soft tan skin. I don't understand why such a terrible thing could happen to her, and I resent the fact that she has to live with it.

I trudge through the kitchen into the garage where I get in the car. I wait over five minutes before my family makes their way to the car, and in no time, I'm getting dropped off at the high school. "Have a good day. I love you," my mother says as I get out of the car.

"Love you too." I then say to Ozalee, "Coach will pick you up from school at four forty-five, so be ready." My track coach picks her and four of her friends up from school because he has to pass the elementary school and my house to get to his house anyway.

The first three periods of school are the same every day. First period: learn about the history of Gipem, a nation built as a result of the Third World War. Second period: learn about the twenty-five blocks of Gipem. This period is my least favorite, not because it's boring but because we virtually learn the same stuff in first period. The country of Gipem has twenty-five blocks; our teachers taught us the blocks used to be called states back when Gipem was called America. But it is way different now. And blah, blah, blah, so on and so forth. Third period: learn about the economy, military, and Gipem's Center. The Center is the capital of Gipem; we call it the Center because that's where it is located, smack dab in the middle of Gipem, pretty obvious. Our country is led by President York and his followers. He is the reason my father was killed, well, not him personally but my dad was sailing his marine ship when it sank. President York was the person who recruited him to the marines, and I despise him for it. At fifteen, I shouldn't be concerned about the economy or the well-being of the country, but since I practically raise thirteen other people, some even my own age, I have matured fast and it is essential I know what is going on in the world around me.

The day goes by in a blur. I talk to my friends, go to the rest of my classes, and somehow, I manage to get all of my homework done before the last bell of the day rings. My friends wait for me outside my last period before we change in the locker rooms for track. I open my locker and try to catch all of the books as they fall to the ground with a thud. Most of my friends disappear down the steps before I bend down to pick them up. I rub the energy back into my face with a loud sigh, and my stomach twists into knots. Pete hands me my books, "You can smile every once in a while," he says.

I slam my locker shut. "I'm done with this. I hate school. I hate the people in school. I hate track. I just want to go home."

He pats my shoulder. "Good thing I'm here to make you seem somewhat enjoyable because if I weren't, you'd have no friends."

I let a small giggle; Pete always knows how to make me a tiny bit happier. "Yeah, that would be such a shame. Maybe it's because of you I have to put up with half these people."

We split at the locker rooms, meeting back up in the typical circle our group always forms to converse in.

Coach summons the track team and separates us into sprinters, distance runners, and the very rare people who can do both, which doesn't include me. I'm a sprinter, an average placement for someone with a muscular lower body and only a medium endurance level. Lakuna, on the other hand, is different. She can sprint and run distance. I come in after Lakuna in any race, every time, no matter how hard I try. I've never said anything about it, but I'm jealous of her. She's good at everything she does, and she is twice as beautiful as me. I try to do different things, but it seems she always one-ups me, so I have learned, over time, to push my thoughts to the back of my mind. Sometimes I can't help it, and my jealousy creeps into my brain again. I try to ignore it. Nothing to complain about.

"Go?" Coach questions as I stand there mindlessly while everyone else is already at the finish line. I missed the whistle.

I wave my hand at him. "Whatever. I'm done for today."

"Be here at three sharp tomorrow for team pictures. See you all then!" Coach yells to the team.

As soon as all of the runners are done with the workout, the track starts emptying of students in a matter of minutes; soon the only people left are my group. "Come on, kids. We have to get Ozalee," says Coach. We hurl ourselves up the steps and pile into his black Escalade. We still have to smush together as there are only six seats in the car including the driver's seat and nine people need a ride. The banter starts up as the car rolls to the elementary school.

"How was school?" I greet Ozalee. "Good," she says.

"Any drama?" I ask.

"Tinley and Ariel got in a fight. Hixel was on Tinley's side, but they all made up by the end of the day." Ozalee has a little square of four best friends she absolutely adores. Ozalee, Tinley, Hixel, Ariel, and Broppin grew up together. They are inseparable. But when they fight, Tinley and Hixel always team up against Ozalee and Broppin because Tinley and Hixel are cousins as well as Ozalee and Broppin. Pete's younger sister, Ariel, is always the peacemaker. Ariel, Hixel, Tinley, and Broppin come home with us every day of the week except Thursday because they have after-school tutoring sessions; unlike her friends, Ozalee is abnormally smart for her age. I like Thursdays because I only have to cook dinner for ten people instead of fourteen. Then again, her friends are like my little sisters as well, and I like it better when they stay at my house so I know they're safe.

"Did you get any test scores back?" I ask.

"Yes, I got a 101 percent on my science test," she says excitedly. "That's great. What are you learning about?"

"Survival skills. Like what to do if you ever get lost or get stuck in a storm without shelter."

"I wouldn't doubt you'd ace a test like that." A smile crosses Ozalee's face, and she weaves her fingers through Lakuna's blonde ponytail. "Do you have homework?" I ask Bree just to make conversation.

"Ummm, I forgot to bring it home."

"You can copy mine," I say.

"Okay, thanks. Did you hear what Cam won today?"

Cam looks like he hasn't slept in days. He probably hasn't. I bet his nightmares have flared up again, as mine so often do. His father was on the same ship mine was. He didn't make it either. The accident happened only about a year ago when I was fourteen.

"No, what?" I ask.

"Best smile for our year in the schoolbook."

I look at Cam to see if he'll flash the smile I love so much, but he just gives a faint twist of his lips. "How do you know he won?" I question. She hands me the schoolbook I forgot to order, and I flip to the Best section. I expect what lies under the male section. Best overall looks: Griff Malrook. Best personality: Pete Girth. Brint and Spence are not recognized. I turn the page to the female section. Best overall looks: Lakuna Crest. Most likely to become a model: Mazi Seedar. Most athletic: Bree Uley. It is not surprising to me my name is not on the list—I'm not anything special.

The Escalade pulls into my driveway and reaches my indecent-looking house. My dad left all of his money to us, and my mom works three jobs, but hardly is it enough. We used to have money to spare, but after paying the bills and purchasing clothes and school books for my friends, our money is running dangerously low. Right before my dad died, he made my mom's dream come true and bought her a house in the country and built her a barn, which put us in more debt. My mother has to make all of the money herself, we struggle to keep up with it all.

We hop out of the car as Coach says, "See you tomorrow and remember to bring your uniforms."

I type the code into my garage, and it opens noisily. I enter the house, and a cool wind rushes across my face. The air conditioner must have gotten fixed. I want to unarm the security system and notice it has already been disarmed. My stomach twists again, a nauseating feeling that makes me want to curl into a ball and lay on the floor. My friends stack in the house and head straight for the kitchen, opening every cupboard and cabinet which holds food. "What do you guys want for dinner?" I ask. I'm usually the one who makes dinner because no one else can cook well. I picked up the cooking trait from my mom who is a very skilled with food. Hence, the reason she's a chef. They all want something different, so I decide on spaghetti because it's easy to make and we haven't had it in a while. I begin to make dinner while everyone but Pete retreats from the kitchen to their own floors.

As I boil the water on the stove and add the hard noodles, I notice those blue eyes staring at me, the deep pools of bright blue. He knows can get me to do almost anything he wants; they're like a spell I can't get out of. "What?" I ask.

"What's wrong?" he asks.

My eyes flit away from his. "I have this weird feeling, and it's bad."

"Are you sick?" he wonders, his voice turning into that when he has to care for me rather than the other way around.

"No, anxious maybe."

"About?"

"I haven't got that far yet."

When I finish making dinner, we all sit around the huge dining table and gorge ourselves on salad and spaghetti until I decide it's getting late and Ozalee needs to finish her homework. "Hurry up. I want to run the dishwasher," I say.

Ozalee leads the group to the kitchen, willingly taking everyone's dishes and putting them in the dishwasher. "Just relax Hayden," she says, "I'll do it."

I give my homework to Bree and plop down on the couch, clicking the television on. Some stupid cartoon pops up, but I don't feel like looking for the remote, so I just watch it.

When books start to shut, I know everyone is done with their homework. "What do you want to do?" Brint asks.

"We could watch a movie?" Griff mentions. All of us march down the steps into the theater in our basement. It's a big room with two large couches forming an L-shape. Spence and Mazi sit hand in hand on one couch along with Lakuna, Bree, Griff, and Brint. Pete, Cam, Ozalee, and I take the smaller couch. Just as the movie starts playing, Ozalee gets up.

"Where are you going?" I ask. "To make popcorn," she says.

I hear her light footsteps on the stairs and the cabinet opening. I get up to help her; she can't reach the microwave anyway. It's when my foot hits the second step I hear the petrified scream of a nine-year-old girl. My feet fly up the steps so fast, they don't even touch them. I'm all the way up before I feel the vibrations of eight pairs of legs bounding after me. I turn the corner to the kitchen only to find my sister surrounded by six monstrous men in masks. They turn with their hands curled by their shoulders, all in black capes, like the slaughterers in horror movies. My body freezes, and my muscles turn to ice, my breath unable to catch. The knot in my stomach lurches against my body, pushing me forward to protect Ozalee. Within one step, a buzz of shock tells me to run away, save yourself, and that's what Ozalee is screaming, "Hayden, run!"

One moment I'm next to her, feeling her trembling, and the next my hands are pressed behind my back and a gun at my head. Two of the men carry a thick metal bar through the garage door, shove it into the wall, and hang Ozalee and I from it by our hands. All at once, I realize these people are the same as the ones who got the teenagers from Lakota. The reason for my uneasiness earlier becomes apparent.

The men whip their heads around at the sound of more people running up the steps; they bolt around the corner to catch them as well. "No, don't come—" I start. The only masked man remaining to watch Ozalee and I holds his gloved hand over my mouth, very effectively cutting my voice off. I struggle against the strength of the man, but I am simply overpowered. His hand is the size of my entire face. Two men come back with two of my friends squished in each massive arm, Mazi and Lakuna and Brint and

Bree. They squirm against the pure strength of the men, but as much as they fight, they know they're trapped. In seconds, they are dangling from the metal bar, shaking their heads. The turn of events is quick; it takes a very ignorant person not to notice how wrong everything felt. Almost as quick as everything changed, I realize this is my fault. I glance at Ozalee as she looks at me with her puppy eyes. "I'm so sorry."

Tears spill onto her skin. "Are we going to die?" she cries.

"No, I promise. I won't let anything happen to you." I look at Mazi and Lakuna for support, but they can't seem to hold their heads up and make eye contact with me. I sense it. Someone is already hurt.

Griff appears next. He is being detained by one of the men with his arms twisted behind his back in a fashion that makes him wince. He has a wide gash over his left eye, and his lip is busted horribly. Pete is in another's arms, his mouth, temple, and nose all gushing. Griff and Pete can't seem to resist. The man slides Griff onto the bar first and then Pete. A couple minutes pass. No one talks. All I hear is Ozalee's sniffing, Griff's hard breathing, and the whispers of the people who are doing this to us. Then the last two of the men walk into the kitchen dragging Spence and Cam into our view, out cold. They put handcuffs on them even though it's unnecessary and leave them lying on the floor. "Okay," one of them says in a raspy voice as he lights a scented cigarette. "I'm saying this once, so listen. My name is Darious. This is the rest of my gang." Darious is the only one who removes his mask. His skin is pale white with a scar running from his chin to his ear. *Why would he tell us his name?* "We are from the Center." *So they are from the Center. Of course, they are.* "Our job is to collect the specified people on our list. Each person on the list will be put through a survival test. You ten are on our list. We have decided a punishment for what you have done, and the punishment will be carried out as planned. Your actions will decide your fate. We did the same thing with the fifteen from Lakota, but as most of you know, their engagements weren't clever enough, and as an effect, they are dead."

It takes me a moment to process what Darious has said. We have a chance to survive. If we are smart, we will live. If we are stupid, we will die. I bite the man holding my mouth shut.

"What did we do?" I ask.

He thinks the question over for a minute and then answers carefully as if trying not to reveal too much. "When you were young, you were observed by a special person. This person has decided to put you all through this test. Only a certain number of people were special enough to be put on the list. Therefore, I'm here to dispose of you. Every person on each list has been killed or is being put through the same thing you are. Most have not survived their challenges because of their incapabilities. The people put through these tests are given special tools for their survival."

What? I am lost. Okay, think, think. We will be put through a test, and if we survive, then what?

"What happens if we survive?" I ask.

"You will be checked off of our list as a survivor. We have no further information to give you."

I have so many questions. What did we do? What tools will we be given? When does the test start? Where are we going? What about my mother? Why is my sister involved in this? All of a sudden, I am scared, not for me, but for what will happen to my friends. Out of the corner of my eye, I see one of the men grab something from a black bag they must have brought with them. He trudges over to already-insensible Spence and sticks a needle in the bend of his arm; he does the same with Cam. I can't tell what the effect of the needle has on them. The man moves on to Pete, but what good would it be sticking him with a needle when he's already hurt? Then he walks to Griff and shoves the needle in his arm; Griff is close enough for me to see there is a cloudy white liquid in the shot. It takes only a moment for him to slump to the floor. I fight against the handcuffs; I know I can get my arms out of if I only had a minute! But I can barely get out a scream before the man jabs the needle into my arm. I try to overpower the soporific; my knees go weak, my eyelids gain weight, and my mind gets foggy and white. Rapidly I slide away.

It is too hot. My bed is slipping away from my touch with every wave that approaches me. Wait. Waves? My eyes flutter open. I have to close them instantly because of the bright light shining in them. I open them slower and gently push myself into a sitting position. I'm lying on a sandy coastline. Crystal clear water is coming up to my waist with a tiny splash. I stand up and look around me. Down the beach to my left is nothing but more beach. Down the beach to my right are more beaches, but in the distance are some cliffs. In front of me there is only water, no islands, no boats, and no civilization. This is clearly the test Darious has thought of—survive on a deserted island, and we live. Not being able to survive with natural resources, we would die. I turn around and am stunned by the huge dense-looking jungle. In front of the jungle is a stack of something and the rest of my friends.

Brint is the only one awake; I guess the drug hasn't worn off for the rest of them. He is in the shade of the trees, sitting on a rock with his head lying on his knees. "Where are we?" I ask. Dumb question.

"I don't know. I woke up, and everyone was still sleeping or whatever you call it. I dragged them over here out of the sun. I saw you open your eyes, so I just let you go."

"What happened to Spence, Cam, Pete, and Griff last night?"

"Griff and Cam tried to keep two of those guys from handcuffing Bree and Lakuna, but that didn't go so great. One of the guys punched Cam in the eye, and it all went downhill from there."

One by one, my friends wake up. First Spence then Cam, Griff, Lakuna, Bree, Pete, Mazi and Ozalee. We decide this is the test the gang has chosen for us. My friends take time to observe their surroundings, and then we go over to the stack of stuff Darious left for us. There is a bow and a sheath of twelve arrows, an ax, a knife, goggles, a one-liter container, some rope and a blanket, a box of matches, a flashlight, and a first-aid kit. The first-aid kit includes a profuse amount of bandages, tweezers, a needle, string, fever-reducing medicine, an empty shot-type thing, and eight lost pills. Why would we need lost pills? We use them back home to knock someone out when they're in pain. We call them lost pills because almost the second it hits your stomach, you're gone. A full pill can knock a person out for four days and that's why every pill is breakable.

There's a note in the first-aid kit. Pete picks it up and reads, "If you can survive on this island for thirty days, you pass." Great, thirty days on a deserted island with no food and no fresh water. I look at my friends, their faces, their expressions. Cam, Griff, Pete, and Spence! All of their wounds are gone. How? It's not even possible!

"We have to find water," says Ozalee, pulling us to the reality this is actually happening, and we have to get it together or we'll end up like the kids from Lakota.

"Spence, Lakuna, and I will hunt for food. Brint, Mazi, and Griff, go find water," I say. "Ozalee, Cam, Bree, and Pete, set up a camp or build a fire or something." No one objects to my authoritarianism. This is real. I grab the bow and the sheath of arrows and sling them over my shoulder. Spence leads the way through the dense jungle, stopping only to make sure we are still safely behind him. There are beautiful flowers, eye popping and vibrant—orange, yellow, red, blue, green, and purple. The trees have plentiful fruit that hangs with ease. I feel a poke on my back, and I turn to find Lakuna walking toward a tree. The lowest branch of the tree is ten feet high, so she looks at me and whispers, "Get Spence."

I turn back around and grab Spence's shirt. He stops and turns to me. "Give Lakuna a boost." He nods and walks to her, picks her up; she grabs onto the tree limb and uses her gymnast skills to flip onto the branch. She climbs up the tree until she reaches a branch containing fruit. I hadn't realized what the yellow pod was until she uses the knife she grabbed from the pile to cut it down. The bananas fall perfectly at my feet. I pick them up and give them to Spence since he isn't carrying anything.

He insisted he take the bow and arrows, but we both know I'm a better shot than him. My dad taught me how to shoot a bow when I was young. I am a better shot with a gun, but Darious obviously decided a gun was too easy of a weapon to use. Lakuna continues to cut fruit from the treetops, and Spence picks them up.

"I'll be right back," I whisper. Lakuna swoops down on a vine and stands right in my way. "The last time you left, we were drugged and brought here. We're coming with you." I begin to tell them they will only scare off prey, but I know the attempt is useless. They're coming whether I want them to or not. We walk deeper in the woods trying to be as quiet as possible. As we wander deeper in the jungle, the trees grow more eastern woodland than tropical escape. The palms convert into oaks, and the fruit transforms into nuts, leaves, and berries. Since we live in Villa, the woodsy part is more familiar to us than the jungle portion, but it's still very different than home. Most of the trees I do not recognize. The plants appear dangerous and prickly like it would be risky to walk on the ground without shoes. They seem deadly to touch and definitely unsafe to eat, some even have thorns dripping with blood-red goo. I am careful to avoid those. I find a maple tree with low enough branches so Spence doesn't have to help me get up. I climb higher up than normal in case the animals here have a more vivid sense of smell than the animals back home. Spence and Lakuna scurry up after me, cracking sticks and crunching leaves, for sure scaring off every creature in a three-mile radius.

We wait for any sign of life to walk by us, but nothing appears. The world is completely quiet. "I'm thirsty," whispers Spence. Come to think of it, I'm thirsty too. I haven't had a drink since dinner, and I have no idea how long the sedative lasted, so as of right now, I don't know when my last drink was. I can tell it's been some time because the signs of dehydration have been working on me for a while. My head hurts, my tongue is dry, and my saliva is sticky. I hope Brint, Mazi, and Griff found some water.

Just as we're about to get down from the tree, I pick up the sound of leaves crunching in the underbrush. I turn my body around in a position to shoot, and right in front of me stands a tiny deerlike creature. I draw back on my bow and let the arrow fly. It pierces the deer right behind the rib cage, but it's a good enough shot to bring it down. Spence, Lakuna, and I drop from the tree, already observing this odd creature. It's at least five times smaller than an average deer and weighs thirty pounds at most.

Spence uses Lakuna's knife to skin and field-dress the deer. He cuts the edible meat from the carcass, and we use the deer pelt to carry the meat back to the beach.

I know how to skin a deer. After my dad died last year, I found a method to get away, to forget for a small moment the sorrow of it all. I cleaned my father's rusty gun until the silver of the barrel shone through. I thought of how happy my mother would be to have fresh meat. I called my horse, Girl, from the barn and rode her across the grass plain in front of my home into the field of Tibbet. Since anywhere after the river valley is free to do what you want, Tibbet is legal land to hunt. We crept through the grass until her hooves hit the water of the river; I watched her ears tilt forward and knew prey was close. I looked through the scope, spotting the deer yards away looking a different direction. The bullet hit the deer in the upper part of its body, breaking its back. I cut the deer carefully, slicing around the bullet hole and carving out the good meat. I tied the carcass on Girl's back, and she took me home. From that point on, I've been able to cope with his death by shooting his gun and bringing home needed meat for my family every week. It helped me remember he's never coming back and taught me to fend for myself.

The temperature is reaching almost 110 degrees, it feels like, and the hike back is miserable. Uphill is a long way when you're dehydrated and you're lugging around leer (a mix of little and deer) meat, but in time, we all reach the beach. Ozalee, Cam, Bree, and Pete did their job in setting up camp. Somehow they assembled a shack with only the rope Darious left us and bamboo from the jungle. It has a roof, three sides and a floor. The side of the shack facing the ocean doesn't have a wall. All you see are the waves crashing on the beach. The rock Brint was sitting on is located to the right side of the shack, and someone was smart enough to construct a fire pit to the left of the shack. Mazi, Griff and Brint found their way back with the container Darious left us filled with water.

"How long have you guys been back?" I ask anyone who's listening. "About three hours," says Griff.

"How long were we gone?"

"About four," he says as he hands me the container of water. I chug it thirstily until it's gone, realizing I didn't save any for Spence or Lakuna. Mazi takes the container from me. "I'll get it." I know Spence would go with her. However, when I look for him, he's stretched out in the shack already sleeping. Dehydration must have taken its toll on him. What has it been since we've been here, five hours? Six? And someone's already dehydrated. It's going to be a long month.

It's only a few moments later when Mazi comes back to the beach with the container of water and hands it to Lakuna. "Where is the water? How long did it take you guys to find it?" I ask.

"It's not far. There's a steep hill and a waterfall. It took us awhile because we couldn't hear it over the waves," she answers.

Ozalee is showing Bree, Cam, Griff, and Pete how to light a fire with a single match. Not wasting a good match just to show them how to light a fire, she cooks the raw leer meet. Ozalee doesn't seem as worried as the rest of us about our situation, but then again, we do have six years on her. She's just a kid. She shouldn't be here. I know all of us won't survive; one of us is destined to die. But it won't be her; I won't let it be her. I promised her.

"Hayden, come eat with us!" shouts Pete.

"I'm not hungry!" I yell back. I know I should eat, but I just can't bring myself to think of food right now. I crawl over to the group around the fire, not even looking for Lakuna. I saw her curl up next to Spence. "I'm sorry for getting us in this mess guys," I apologize. I hold my knot in my stomach. Stupid, that's what I am. I watched the news the night before. Lakota is right next to Villa, and I didn't even think to take extra precautions. I should've known the second I walked in the house something was wrong. The air conditioning in my house was fixed, and the alarm wasn't even on!

"It's not your fault, Hayden. You didn't do anything wrong. It was someone else's, and they're probably dead, so it doesn't matter," Cam says. He waves me off like I'm trying to feel sorry for myself.

"Who do you think put us on the list?" I wonder. Once again, I'm ignored.

"I'm going to bed," says Mazi when the sun sinks down over the horizon. I watch her walk over and lie down on the other side of Spence. She and Spence have been together ever since I can remember. She's his and he's hers, and it will never change no matter what because just as they've been together ever since I remember, they've loved each other ever since I can remember. They're in each other's pocket. The rest of my friends eventually follow her. I wander over to Ozalee; she looks at me with those puppy-dog eyes and crawls into my arms.

"I'm scared," she murmurs.

"You're doing a good job," I whisper.

"Just think about it. Darious said it was a test. We're not all going to make it," she chokes.

"We'll do our best. You know I promised." I wipe the water from her eyes. "Everything will go back to normal. It's like a vacation."

"Hayden, I don't want you to die," she says. "Don't worry about me."

"Mom is all alone," she cries.

All I can get out of my mouth is, "I know." I feel her shaking in my arms. I start to sing her favorite song. "Walking alone is hard to do, so take my hand. I'll stay by you. Forever and always, I'll be here. Never worry, I'm always near. You're so precious, little dove. I'll never leave my sweetest love." Her quivering slows gradually. I put her down, and seconds later, she drifts off.

Ozalee's favorite song is old. My great-grandparents taught it to my grandparents, my grandparents taught it to my parents, and my parents taught it to us. It's been her favorite song ever since she's learned it. I sing it to her and her friends when they are sad. Ozalee's friends, my so-called sisters, Ariel, Tinley, Hixel, and Broppin are also alone. When Coach drops them off at our house tomorrow after school, they'll see the blood on the floor, the metal bar in the wall. They'll see my mother sitting on the fireplace with her head in her hands crying, "Where are my daughters? Where are my children?" Broppin will crawl in her lap and say, "I'm right here," and my mother will say, "What about the other two?" Then they will cry together. They've seen the news too, and they know we've been kidnapped.

Broppin will be missing two of the three people left in relation to her. She'll wonder what she did to deserve this, everyone in her family dying other than her aunt. Broppin, Ozalee, and I are blood. Her mother was my mom's sister. She died giving birth. Broppin's father left them before Broppin was born. I can see Broppin lying on her and Ozalee's bed, rubbing Ozalee's blankets on her lips, holding on to her. Broppin's brown eyes will close, and she'll dream we were there next to her, then she'll wake and we won't be there.

Ariel, Pete's sister and Ozalee's best friend, will not cry. She doesn't ever cry. She'll go on as usual until she finds out Pete is gone too. Then she'll be put in another orphanage with Tinley and Hixel. And they'll stay there because my mother won't be able to afford them. Broppin will beg, and my mother will apologize, but in the end, they'll be split up. With no Pete to bring them together and no me to house them, they'll amount to nothing but unloved orphans. I'm glad today was Thursday when Ariel, Tinley, Hixel, and Broppin stay the night at Ann's house, Cam and Griff's mother. If not, they'd be here with us, with us, yes, but safe, no.

The exact day Pete turned sixteen, he signed those four out of the orphanage and came to live with me so the younger girls could be together. Now that Ozalee is here, my mother will keep Broppin, Ariel will be put in one orphanage, and Tinley in Hixel will be put in a different place. They'll be kept in an orphanage where family members are always held together. They'll be split for life.

I let the waves leak over my toes. Will I ever see my mom again? Will my mom ever see Ozalee again? Will Pete ever see his sisters again? Will I ever see them again? Why did we have to be put on this list? What list?

I get frustrated with these unanswered questions really quick. I grab the flashlight and the knife and trudge into the jungle; it takes me only a minute to find a coconut tree and scale up the flaky, bumpy trunk. I saw through the stem of the coconuts, and they drop to the ground with a clunk. I slide down the trunk and take the ten coconuts back to camp, putting them with the rest of the supplies we have. I make a mental checklist of what we have to work with—a bow and a sheath of twelve arrows, a knife, a blanket, a flashlight, a first-aid kit, a one-liter container full of water, a box of matches, an ax, goggles, ten coconuts, a bunch of fruit, plenty of leer, and a shack. It might not be hard to survive. We're doing pretty well so far, but then again, it's only been a day and a half.

I walk back to the beach and look for shells. I try to find ones that have a big enough dip to hold water, and I'm in luck because I find two. I add those to the pile of supplies we have to work with. The sun has just started to rise. I sit on the rock Brint was sitting on yesterday when I woke up, and I watch the fiery ball climb into the cloudless sky. The contrast between the orange sphere and blue sky makes the heavens around the sun a purple pink color, amazing.

I eat a banana and drink the rest of the water; I'll get more in a bit. I'm surprised I haven't felt tired yet. Does stress make you restless? Because if so, I'm not going to be able to sleep for a full year. I gather some long, thin vines and large, fat leaves from the jungle and attempt to weave a basket to carry water or fruit with. I've never done this before, and it's as hard as I thought. While I sew the leaves together with the vines, I hum Ozalee's song. I got my voice from my grandmother. She could make the frogs croak, crickets chirp, and bees buzz with that voice. It was creamy like milk and soft even in the highest of notes. It sounded like a bell that continued ringing. It was harmonious like a piano key.

"It's Ariel's favorite song," Pete says.

I jump, and the basket goes flying. "It's been Ozalee's favorite ever since I can remember, and I know." I pick up the basket and begin to weave again.

"Did you stay up all night?" he asks. I nod my head. "I can tell. What are you doing?" He plops down next to me on the sand.

"I'm trying to make a basket to hold water, but as you can see it's not going well," I answer.

"May I?" he asks. I hand the messy basket, the vines, and the big leaves over to him, and he starts lacing. His brows crease in concentration as he works his magic on the hideous basket I tried to make. In a matter of minutes he hands the basket back to me, and I look at it stunned. It's almost a perfect bowl with no frays.

"How did you do that?" I ask astounded. "I'm just that good."

"Do you know where the waterfall is?" I ask. "Yeah, do you want to see it?"

"Yes," I say. He stands up and holds out his hand, I grab on to it, and he yanks me to my feet in one swift motion. I take the basket, and he leads me past the shack where everyone is still sleeping. Right before we walk past the fire pit, we turn into the jungle. We only have to walk a short distance before the ground slopes steeply down to the left of us.

"Do you want to walk down or go by vine?" he asks, raising his eyebrows.

"Whichever one gets us there faster."

He grabs me around the waist and pushes off the ground. We fly through the air. I know I shouldn't look down, but I do anyway. Sweat runs down my face. I'm only scared of a couple of things in life, and one of them is definitely heights. I close my eyes. "Pete, we have to get off." Before he responds, I feel the wind of the ride stop. I open my eyes only to find his feet planted firmly on the ground. He puts me down and walks forward. I follow him through the jungle, only a couple of yards, and then he pushes away some bushes with orange and yellow flowers, and I for the first time see the waterfall.

There is a wide stream with plenty of rocks to stand on in the middle, then it gracefully flows into a small waterfall. The waterfall ends in a large pond. It has another stream coming from it which leads who knows where. I'm taken aback by the beauty of the waterfall. Like a movie, it has a perfect rainbow when it starts to fall, and when it ends, there are no rocks. Instead there is misty, watery foam. "It's pretty, isn't it?" he says. We stand there in silence, looking at it. "We should probably get back," he says as he fills the basket with water and walks in the direction of the camp.

"Wait," I say. I take off my shoes, socks, shorts, and shirt. "Go stand behind the tree." I point to a tree with a wide trunk. "And don't look!" I take off my sports bra and underwear and jump into the stream. The water is cool and refreshing; I swim to a spot shallow enough for me to stand up. I hadn't realized how dirty I was until I start scrubbing myself with my fingernails and layers upon layers of sand wash away from my skin. I take in a big breath of air and go under the water, cleaning my hair. Once done bathing, I get out of the stream, put back on all of my clothes, and sweep my wet hair into a braid down the side of my head. "You can come out now."

He steps out from behind the tree. "It's my turn," he says. I walk behind the tree and sit down. I hear his shoes hitting the ground and then him splash into the water; I listen to the birds chirping and the bugs buzzing. *Darious, is this seriously the best you can do?* is the last thing I think before I fall asleep leaning against the tree.

I feel Pete pick me up and put me on his back but I just let him carry me. He is more than strong enough. "What happened to Hayden?" I hear Ozalee ask just as Pete reaches the beach.

"Nothing, she's just tired," he answers. I think he puts me down on the shack's floor, but I can't tell because I'm already sleeping again.

As usual, I have nightmares, but they aren't the normal ones. In these nightmares, I'm alone on the island; I'm alone in my kitchen when Darious and his band of creeps break in my house, and I'm alone when I watch a masked figure kill my sister. This is the nightmare that awakens me; I sit up with a sudden jolt. I'm trying to catch my breath, but it just isn't happening. I put my hands on my head and desperately try to breathe slower, then a tear rolls down my face and I realize I'm crying. I wipe the water off quickly, hoping nobody sees, but of course, Griff is there watching me. Griff knows how I have nightmares and what they are about, but I don't remember if he's ever seen me cry.

"Want to talk about it?" he asks.

I give a fast no, walk out of the shack, and run down the beach. My legs are stiff from their lack of movement, but I push them into a sprint anyway and let my tears flow. *It's not real. It's not real,* I tell myself this over and over again. I'm not alone, and I will never ever let anything happen to Ozalee. *I mean, what could possibly happen to her when she has nine people here willing to risk their lives for such a lovable girl?* As soon as I calm myself down, I jog back to our camp only to find our group sitting in a large circle. I join in, squeezing myself between Bree and Mazi, careful not to make eye contact with Griff.

"Finally awake, Sleeping Beauty?" says Brint. He licks his chapped lips and spits the sand off his tongue. Everyone is covered with beach. We decide to eat the rest of the fruit and the leer meat. Spence uses the ax to chop off the tips of the coconuts and then we drink the sweet water from their insides. Now we have absolutely no food. I will have to go hunting again soon.

We agree to go to the waterfall to get more water and to wash off; even though it's not necessary for Pete and me, we go for the fun of it. Without being seen, I grab the knife and stick it under my shorts and cover it with my tee shirt—I might be able to catch a fish or something. Lakuna and Bree bring the container, the shells, and the basket to fill with water since the supplies have been drained of liquid. Spence, Brint, Mazi, Pete, Ozalee, Bree, Cam, and Griff swing to the waterfall by vine. Lakuna and I just run down. I'm surprised by how quick and somewhat noiseless we make our way through the jungle.

"Do you think we'll get off this island, Hayden?" Lakuna asks.

"Yes."

"How?" she continues.

"I don't know. We'll probably be taken to the gang. Darious said if we live, we pass."

We make it to the pond where the waterfall flows into before the rest of the group. We hurry and strip down to only our shorts and sports bras and dive into the water. Just as we begin to scrub our bodies, the rest of our group flies in on their vines. Spence and Mazi come first followed by Bree and Ozalee, Pete and Brint, and Griff and Cam. Mazi and Bree strip down to their shorts and sports bras just like Lakuna and I did and jump into the water with smiles on their faces. Ozalee hops in with her shorts and tee shirt on. Pete, Brint, and Spence take off their shirts and jump in, seeing who can make the biggest splash; Spence wins because he is the biggest. We play water tag until I notice Cam and Griff are still on the pond bank, reluctant to completely immerse themselves in water that could so easily swallow them as it did their father. I paddle over to the edge. "Ozalee and I are swimming, and nothing bad is happening to us."

They take off their shirts, which reveal their perfectly sculpted abs and dive in.

"You're it." Brint calls as he tags Ozalee's shoulder. She giggles and disappears under the water with a thrash. I expect her to pop up by me so she can tag me and rub it in my face, but when I look underwater, she's just floating there. I poke her stomach playfully; she looks at me with her big brown puppy-dog eyes and lets out the most awful noise I've ever heard. Her scream is blood curdling. Even though I'm underwater, I can hear the agony in it. *Why is she doing this? Is she trying to be funny? Because it isn't.* I grab her arm and pull her closer to the surface. It's then I realize I'm not pulling only her. A long fish creature with its teeth buried in the other side of her stomach slides out of the murky bottom as I pull her to the surface. Fear instantly takes over my muscles, my body, and my thoughts; she's not going to make it. I cannot move anything.

I regain sense after all of the oxygen is drained from my lungs; I pull her to the surface. "Get out of the pond!" I cough. "Go!" I spit the excess water from my lungs. Ozalee lets out another scream. This cry isn't just noise. Blood trickles out of her mouth and tears spill from her eyes. My friends just stand there, stunned. "Help!" I scream. Griff pulls me to the bank. The pond fills with blood as I climb up on shore. He grabs Ozalee under the arm and begins pulling her out of the pond then stops when he realizes she's not alone. I push him off her. "Move!" I wrench the rest of her and the monster fish out of the blood-filled pond and grab my knife.

Pete, Brint, Spence, and Cam kick the monster fish, and Mazi, Lakuna, and Bree try to comfort my sister as her death so quickly approaches. I frantically slice at the fish with my knife until it releases its jaws from Ozalee's torso. Spence kicks the creature far enough away from my sister so it can't latch on to her anymore, but it simply sinks its teeth into Mazi's hand, and she hardly notices. I bend down and try to put Ozalee's stomach muscles and skin back together. "Come on. Work! Work!" The flesh falls off her blood-slick body. "No!" I grab my shirt, pressing it to her body to staunch the blood flow. She presses her hands to her stomach. I push them up to her face to cover her eyes. She can't see this. She looks at the blood on her fingers, the bits of flesh caught in the fish's teeth, then she grabs my face and stops me short.

"Hayden," she whispers, "please stop." And I do. "Hayden, you have to get off this island," she gasps.

"You're getting off it too!" I yell at her.

She curls around her stomach. The blood gushes out of her with every breath she takes. "Not alive, I'm not. Don't give up no matter what. Promise?"

"Yes, I promise." I caress her face in my bloodstained hands and lay her head on my lap. "I'll tell dad you said you love him," she murmurs.

"Please . . ." I beg, "don't do this." "Tell mom I love her," she says.

"I will." A tear falls off my face onto her cheek.

"Remember to tell Ariel, Broppin, Tinley, and Hixel I said bye."

"I will."

"Don't forget Ariel. Don't forget," she drones. "I won't."

"I love you," she whispers.

"I love you more," I say. "Please don't do this. I promised I wouldn't let anything happen to you! I promised." She closes her eyes and draws in her last breath. Then I watch my baby sister die in my arms. "No." My fingers fumble over her lips where warm breath should be coming, then they move to her heart where it should pound against my fingers. "No, don't go. Please. I promised."

CHAPTER TWO

Unable to move, I sit on the jungle floor with Ozalee's head in my lap. It's night when Bree tells me they have to go back to camp. "Why?" I ask without any emotion.

"Mazi's hurt. We need to bandage it before infection sets," she replies.

I look down at Ozalee's lifeless face, and her song pops into my head. *Walking alone is hard to do, so take my hand. I'll stay by you. Forever and always I'll be here. Never worry, I'm always near. You're so precious, little dove. I'll never leave my sweetest love. You're not here anymore.* "You guys can go back. I'm staying," I say.

"Are you sure?" she asks.

"Yeah," I answer, and my friends disappear into the darkness of the jungle.

Seconds later comes, "She was special," from Pete's mouth. He whispered as if not to wake her. "I thought you went back to camp," I say quietly.

"I stayed to make sure you were okay."

I gently lay her head on the ground and stare at her. I feel Pete's warm, sturdy arms embrace me as he sits down. "You know she's with your dad now. She'll always love you."

"It was her song, not mine," I whisper. Then it hit me; my sister is gone forever. She is never coming back. I will never hear her giggle, her cry, or her voice again. She will never push my hair back from my head; she will never see her friends; I will never hear her say I love you to me again. The emptiness takes over, and all of the sudden, my world crashes down around me. "We were all in that pond. Why couldn't the fish have bitten me? Why couldn't I save her like she would have saved me? I hope whoever observed her is dead. They deserve it. I hope Darious is dead. I hope they're all dead," I say as my sobs rack my body.

"It was her time," he says.

"She was only nine! Her time is supposed to be ninety years from now!" I yell at him. "She didn't even get to say bye to her friends—she's making me do it."

"I know," he says. He pulls me closer to him, and I lean my head on his shoulder and let my tears stain his dark green shirt.

Pete stays with me by the pond all night, then when morning comes, he asks me if I want to go back to camp. "Why not?" I answer, and we start walking.

When we get back to camp, Pete veers straight over to Griff and fills him in on the most awful night of my life. Maybe even his too. Ozalee and Ariel were best friends. Were. Pete saw Ozalee more than any other one of my friends. She was his sister as well, more or less anyway. I look around and see Mazi in the shack sleeping and Spence sitting next to her. "Is she okay?" I ask, not really caring.

"Her hand needed stitches. I tried to give them to her, but she was in a lot of pain, so I gave her a little piece of a lost pill." Her hand has at least thirty stitches in it. They start at the middle of the back of her palm and work their way all the way around to the other side.

Griff brings me the first-aid kit. "Can you do this?" He takes the bandage off the deep cut on his forehead.

"Did I do that?"

He hands me the needle and grips Lakuna's hand when I poke back and forth to sew the slash shut.

CHAPTER THREE

"Hayden, it's been two days. We have to do it sooner or later," Cam says. I stand up and walk to the pond without any word from anyone else. They follow with half of the blanket and the shovel. They cut the blanket in half with the knife. It will take only that much to cover her tiny body. I find her in the same position I left her in. I watch as Pete and Cam lift her off the ground and place her on the soft blanket. We put flowers around her unmoving body, weave them through her golden hair, and make a flower crown trying to make her look like as much of her normal self as possible. She always loved to clip fresh flowers and put them in her hair.

Brint, Spence, Pete, Lakuna, Griff, Cam, Mazi, and Bree plant kisses on her forehead. They leave me to go last. I situate each blossom so it looks as perfect as she was. Every color of flower surrounds her face and body; I place extra petals on her fish bite, making sure her angel will never have to look at her wound. I sing to her her song and touch her with a gentle kiss on her forehead for the last time. Pete and Cam fold the blanket over her so none of her skin shows and tie her up with vines covered in her favorite colored flowers, pink. We find an opening in the jungle floor that has just sand and dig her grave. Pete and I carefully place her body in the three-foot-deep hole, and I slowly put each shovelful of sand in the correct place until my little sister is no more.

Lakuna, Bree, and Mazi cry over the loss of my Ozalee. Their tears are somewhat of a joke to me. She wasn't their sister—she was mine. I'm the one that should be crying now, but I can't. I cannot bring myself to produce any more tears. I study the dead monster fish that took my sister's life from her. The monster is as long as me with wicked barbs on its back and tail. It is the color of mud and that's probably why none of us saw it before it grabbed her. I open its mouth. Its teeth have to be at least three inches long; I'm surprised Mazi's hand isn't torn off. After a while, the fish is too much to soak in, so I go to the tree I fell asleep on and use vines to work my way up to the lowest branch. I use the thickness of the jungle tree's branches to walk from the waterfall to camp.

No one else is here; they're still down there, comforting each other like wimps. I relax down onto the shack's floor. I haven't really slept since I've been on this island, and we've been here for about five days. I'm hungry too. Come to think of it, I haven't eaten much either. The banana, some leer meat, and some fruit, then again that was three days ago. My stomach and my torso have gotten smaller. What little abs I had are almost gone, and my ribs and hips bones are more visible than they've ever been. My friends have been making sure I've had enough water, so I'm good. The breeze blows on my hot skin, and I fall asleep.

I'm the first one awake in the morning. The sun is hidden behind large gray clouds; I can smell the rain approaching, fresh and revitalizing. I grab the knife, the bow, and the sheath of arrows and head into the jungle. I find the tree Spence, Lakuna, and I went to the first day on the island and climb up. It takes only small amount of time for a herd of leer to walk by. I easily take two down. I shoot the first leer in the leg, and it can't go anywhere. I shoot it again in the heart. The second leer dies with only one arrow to the rib cage. I shimmy down the tree, skin and field-dress the leer, and lug them back to camp where everyone is still sleeping. I put the leer down in our pile of supplies and go back into the jungle to get some fruit. I scale up a coconut tree and cut down only nine coconuts this time. They fall to the ground, and I leave them there. I walk over to a tree that has fruit dangling from it and cut some down. Once done, I gather the fruit and coconuts and head back to camp.

I wait until everyone wakes up then use a single match to start a fire, just like Ozalee taught me. We cook the leer meat but don't eat it; instead, we eat some fruit and our coconuts. By the time we're done, I'm stuffed. I guess it's from having nothing to eat for so long. "For the first time since we've been here, we are all full, hydrated, and none of us are tired," Lakuna says. I want to tell her this is true. However, my sister did die, so it shouldn't make any of us happy. But I know Ozalee wouldn't want me sulking around all the time.

"Do you guys see those cliffs over there?" I say pointing to the right. "Yeah, what about them?" asks Griff.

"We should see what's there." "I'm in," says Griff.

Cam, Lakuna, Brint, Pete, and Bree agree to go. Mazi and Spence probably want some time alone. We take the knife with us just as a precaution; we don't want anyone else getting eaten by a giant fish. It takes us a long time to get to the base of the cliffs; nonetheless, we make it in one piece. The cliffs are tall, and they stand straight up. We walk around the back and hike up the shortened ledge to get on top, then we climb on the big rock. On top of the cliff, there are small tide pools filled with sea life. I sit next to one and observe the delicate sea creatures inside. The pool is illuminated with tiny pink sea anemones, crabs, sea urchins, and fish. I try to catch a small yellow fish in my hand, but it's too fast, so I give up and just stare at it. The water starts to circle and small drips float into it.

I stand up and look at the sky; the raindrops are big water splashes falling from the clouds in waves that range from tiny to huge. I walk to where the cliff is only about twenty feet up, and I start jumping from rock to rock, edge to middle. This is the most fun I've had since we been here! Lakuna and I spin in circles, dancing in the rain; I'm pretty sure the rest of the people here are staring at us, but I could care less. Lakuna is spinning so fast, I know she is going to fall over soon. We laugh at each other, tripping over the rocks; we even push each other onto the smooth rocks and empty tide pools. She tips me into a small pool, smothering me in cool water. I sip a huge gulp, spitting it in her face the same time I grab her ankles. She begins to fall before I see the rock sticking out of the cliff.

"Watch out for that—" is all I get out before she plummets over the edge. "Lakuna!" She's dead. I killed her. I didn't mean to, but I did. I wait what feels like hours for any noise from her, silence. My friends stop in their tracks and listen with me.

"Help!"

I run to the edge and peer over; Lakuna hangs on an outcrop of rock, out of my reach. I toss my legs over the edge, holding tightly on to the solid rock above. I lower myself until I can put one shoe into a hole in the cliff. I feel someone get a good grip on my shirt. "Get off me!" Whoever it is pulls me up and holds my arms behind my back. "Get off!" I scream, squeezing my eyes shut, wishing this wasn't happening. "She's gonna fall!"

"You're going to get yourself killed," Cam says.

"I don't care. Let go!" I open my eyes long enough to see Griff dip down below the edge of the cliff. I elbow Cam in the ribs and watch as Griff reaches the ledge Lakuna is hanging from. He pulls her up and lifts her above his head to Pete. Pete flings her onto the rock about a second before I dive on top of her. She squeezes me back. "I thought you were going to fall." I feel a tear roll down my face and mix with the chilled rain. Then Griff screams. I squint over the edge and, through the downpour, see a crumpled figure lying on the ground holding his leg and the rock ledge in shards next to him.

Cam takes off around the back of the cliff, and I'm not far behind him. We reach Griff first, and the rest of the group forms a circle around him.

He looks fine except for the fact the bone in his left leg is bent forward when it's supposed to be straight. Cam and Pete get under his arms and hoist him to his feet; he can hop on one leg all the way back to the shack.

As soon as his head is under the roof, he collapses. I honestly think he uses every curse word in the book at least twice before the lost pill kicks in, and he loses consciousness.

"Get the first-aid kit," I order Bree. "Lakuna, go get a stick we can use as a splint," I instruct them. When they get back with the supplies, Pete and I go to work on his leg. "Pete, on three, push his bone back in place. Make sure it's straight," I say. "One, two, three!"

Pete shoves down on Griff's bone, and it pops back in place. Apparently, the other half of Mazi's pill wasn't enough because Griff comes to with a vicious word we both know he doesn't mean. Cam quickly shoves half of another pill into his mouth, and the drugs pull him back under. I put the splint on the front of his leg so the bone doesn't pop back out, wrap it in bandages, and tie it with vines. He looks so young and innocent when he's out; in person, he has the same outlook on life I do. Pointless, just another thing to get you stressed over. Harsh things find you, not the other way around. Everyone is stupid even yourself. Everything is your fault. No matter what. He's exactly like me but in male form, my twin brother of sorts. I can't imagine me being twins with Griff though because that would mean I'd be Cam's twin too and that just wouldn't work.

"What happened to Griff?" asks Spence as he and Mazi walk into the clearing.

"Lakuna slipped off the edge of the cliff, and Griff went down to get her. After he got her up, the rock he was standing on broke, and he fell. I guess he landed on his leg wrong because it's broke. We gave him a full dose of a lost pill," says Brint.

"Oh, great," Spence utters under his breath. "He's going to be in a great mood when he wakes up," he continues sarcastically.

I hadn't even noticed the rain has stopped; it looks like it just got dark outside. Lakuna, Bree, and I walk over to the campfire. I squeeze myself between Pete and Cam. Brint and Lakuna get some leer meat for each of us and the basket of fresh rain water.

"How's Griff?" asks Bree.

"Good, I think. The lost pill won't wear off for a couple of days. Those things are strong," says Cam.

Bree and Lakuna are talking about something I can't quite hear. Mazi looks sad; I can tell Spence is unsuccessfully trying to cheer her up. How it goes from a partially good day to horrible, I don't know. "I'm going to bed,"

Lakuna says. We all follow her; I lay next to Pete and Griff. Their body heat rubs off on me. I stare at the moon. I am going to see her tomorrow.

I wake up in the middle of the night twice. The first time I awaken, I find myself lying in the same place as I was. This is a definite surprise. Pete's face is turned toward me, and his light breathing is peaceful in my ear—in, out, in, out, in, out. I shake his shoulder.

"What's wrong?" he whispers.

"I'm going to her grave tomorrow," I tell him. "Do you want me to come with you?" he asks. "No."

He wraps his arm around me. "Night."

I hope this is a dream. I see my dad and Ozalee on his boat. I know what's going to happen, but I can't move. Why can't I move? I just start to shout their names so I can tell them to jump, but a hand covers my mouth. I look up at the person holding me back. It's Darious. He forces me to look forward at the boat and watch the mast come down on my family; they fall into the water and don't come back up. I struggle in his arms, but he starts shaking me.

"Hayden. Hayden," says Pete. "What?" I mumble.

"You were having a bad dream."

I look at his face, and his nose is bleeding. "Sorry." I grab a small piece of blanket and hand it to him.

He holds the rag up to his nose and lies back down. He pulls me down with him, "What was it about?"

"She was on the same boat my dad was on. I watched them die." I yawn.

It's sunrise when I finally wake up. Only Griff and Spence are still sleeping. Cam is lying next to Griff, watching him. "How long have you been awake?" I ask making him jump.

"Awhile," he replies. I sit up and crawl over to Griff whose pill still hasn't worn off yet. I yell for Pete. "We have to change his bandages." Pete unwraps the sandy bandages, and we carefully change the old ones. It is so much easier to work with an unconscious Griff than a cussing one.

The girls of the group want to wash off in the ocean since I ban the waterfall for any use except for drinking, so all of the guys go hunting except for Griff, obviously. We strip down into our undergarments and dive into the clear water. I scrub my body down with my fingernails, and then I work with my hair. I hadn't noticed how knotty and matted it was until I try to run my fingers through it. *Ouch.* I rake my hands through the rat's nest on my head until I get it untangled, then I put it back in a braid on the side of my head. "Let's wash our clothes." Before I reenter the water, I strip Griff, grabbing his socks, shirt, and shorts. I skip back over to the ocean and emerge myself in its salty water. I swish mine and Griff's clothes around until they are free of any dirt and grime. We make our way out of the water and hang our drenched clothes up on a tree's branch. We sit around the fire pit talking about things we haven't been able to lately.

I've hardly talked to any girls for the past ten days. Mazi's been with Spence, and Bree's had a hard time coping with the whole situation, especially Ozalee. They were close. Bree always made Ozalee laugh. As soon as she'd appear in the same room as Ozalee, she would giggle. It was a reflex for Ozalee after a while. Now her voice isn't here to laugh at Bree, and she's not managing it well. Lakuna, on the other hand, has herself worried sick over Griff. I keep telling her he'll be fine, it's just a broken leg, and the lost pill will wear off soon, but she's having some sort of withdrawal, I guess. Griff and Lakuna are a silent duo, very protective of each other. They mesh well together, both with movie-star good looks while Lakuna's effervescent personality tones down Griff's sweltering disposition. Since he dropped off almost a day ago, Lakuna hardly wants to leave his side.

"I haven't hit my monthly yet. I usually start by now," Mazi says.

"Me either, and my limb hair is gone and hasn't grown back." Bree shows.

I run my hands over my legs and underarms, totally smooth. "The guys don't have stubble either," Lakuna says.

"Probably some type of beauty drug Darious gave us to ensure they don't have to watch kids that look like apes; for sure, they're watching us on camera. How else do they know how we're doing on the test?" I say. "They're probably laughing at us right now. We can't even get ten days without a major injury and a deadly catastrophe."

I leave my friends at the campfire. This is the first time I've been down here since her funeral, but the place looks duller. Dead. I sit next to her by her grave. "I miss you." There is no response, only silence. "We've been here for ten days. I'm trying to keep myself together, Ozalee. You don't have to worry about me." More silence. "I know you're thinking that up there, and you're probably saying I should always think about you but try not to mope. It is what I would say to you if I was gone. I just came down here to make sure you know you'll always hold a special place in my heart, and you'll never be forgotten." I look up to the sky and blow her a kiss, knowing she will catch it and hold on to it forever.

I feel a lot better when I get back to camp, like a huge burden has been lifted off my shoulders. The guys still aren't back. At least I hope they're not because Lakuna, Bree, and Mazi are running around in their underwear. I put my clothes back on; I'm not the one who's going to be caught running around undressed. As Mazi, Lakuna, and Bree get dressed, I grab Griff's clothes off the tree. He being bigger than me makes it way hard to get his clothes on. Eventually, Lakuna has to help because he's simply too heavy. "He's getting sick," Lakuna says. He's dehydrated, breathing hard, and has oven-hot skin with absolutely no sweat.

"The pill will wear off soon. He's just dehydrated," I say although I decide to leave his shirt off so he doesn't overheat. I get the small rag Pete used for his bloody nose and rinse out the blood. Once clean and saturated with cool ocean water I lay it on Griff's head. I make sure his matted black hair is drenched in water before I run my fingers through it to get the knots out. He looks almost unrecognizable without his crystal blue eyes showing against his skin.

The guys come back with only fruit and coconuts. "I'm not a good enough shot to bring down a leer," Spence apologizes as he hands me the bow and arrows.

"We will go hunting now, and you guys can wash off. We already cleaned Griff's clothes, so you just have to do the rest." He smiles and strips off his shirt. "Mazi, Bree, Lakuna, we have to go hunting. The guys can't do it themselves." They laugh, and we take the bow and arrows into the jungle. We walk into the more eastern woodland part of the forest and scale a tall tree to get out of the scent range of the leer. Minutes pass and, by the sun's movement in the sky, maybe even hours. We haven't seen or heard anything. The wind is chilling, preparing itself for the night. Evening bugs begin singing even though the daylight is still here.

"Listen," Lakuna whispers.

A herd of leer run into my sight but disappears into the trees almost as soon as they come out of them. I must be deaf if I couldn't hear that.

"Let's go get them," Bree says. We quietly work our way down the tree trunk and stalk the way the leer went. Lakuna leads, followed by Mazi and Bree. I take the back since I have the weapon. We walk until we're close enough to the leer, making sure we are completely out of sight. I load my bow with an arrow. I'm just getting ready to shoot when the leer take flight again.

They disappear into some thick underbrush woven with those red dripping flowers. I drop the bow to my side. "Why do they keep running?" Faintly to my right, a twig snaps. I turn to holler at the boys for scaring off our prey, but nothing is there, just those poisonous-looking plants. "Did you hear that?" I ask Mazi before her eyes go big, dilating with fear.

"Hayden, run!" Lakuna yells.

"What?" I ask only a second before a hidden black panther sinks its teeth into my calf. The pain doesn't hit, but the blood flows from the puncture wounds. I feel the panther's tongue lapping the hot blood out of my veins. Its eyes meet mine, green and glowing, craving for bigger prey and for sure deadly. The arrows are pulled out of my hands.

"Lakuna, don't!" Bree shouts. Leaves crunch behind my head. Suddenly, the panther unlocks its fangs from my leg. I roll over, using my good leg and my free hands. Lakuna has the arrows pointed straight at the cat's throat, at a stalemate of sorts. If the cat attacks, it gets shot. If it runs, it starves. As Lakuna moves her fingers about the arrow to aim, the panther lunges, tackling her with a piercing roar. The feline stares at her for a moment, deciding where to bite, the throat or the face. The last look of death. I grab its tail and yank it backward as hard as I can, throwing off its aim so it lands its fangs in her shoulder rather than her throat. The panther's hair stands on end. It hisses, pulling its gums over its incisors and scrapes its claws over my ribs, not deep enough to lose feeling but just profound enough to create an excruciating sensation. Instantly, I pull my hands over the wound. The salt from my skin scorches the cut. My flesh feels like raw meat under my palms. The pain is blinding.

Back in Villa after every deer I killed, my mother would barbeque us the ribs. The grease ran down our fingers when we bit into the meat between the bones. A gamey tender taste with heaps of fat and juice fed our growling stomachs. Ribs. The panther turns its attention to Mazi, a noticeably smaller and easier target.

At the first twist of her head, the panther swipes. "Spence! Spence!" she screams while the panther works away at her back. Certainly, he can hear her! Her back arches on the ground as she tries to keep the gashes out of the dirt. Bree throws the bow over her shoulders. I know what she's thinking; all she needs is to get out of the panther's reach to deliver a fatal shot. The second she grabs on to the first limb of the nearest tree, the cat flips and grabs her hip. I can see the layer of Bree's flesh hanging from the panther's teeth after she falls to the ground. No one moves. All I can think about is us dying together. When the boys come and search for us, the panther will be gone, and they'll see us like this.

I jump to my feet. I think my ribs rattle from the extensive amount of skin and muscle damage between the bones. I take off toward camp as fast as I can go, screaming for Cam and Pete. They can pick my voice out of a crowd of hundreds of people, much less a desolate island. I notice the eerie silence of the jungle around me and then the panther's lax treads as it jumps on my back. It digs its claws down my spine just as it did to Mazi, but I feel as if mine are abysmal. I keep running. Just a few more feet! The panther continues ripping at my skin with its razor-sharp talons. I am familiar with the area I'm in now, closer to camp. "Cam! Help! Pete!" I cry. I hear them talking through the greenery.

Faintly Cam's voice seeps through the trees, "Grab the ax." I glance backwards to see how far I can get before another round of grating begins. I have no time. The panther grips me with its paws, and a vine takes my feet out from under me. The cat and I stumble head over heels onto the beach. The feet of the guys run by me, and the ax swings past my chest. Pete hoists me off the ground where my blood soaks into the sand.

"Hayden?" Pete's voice is unclear as it reaches my eardrums. "Where are they?" My sweat seeps into my gashes. I can't seem to catch my breath. The world spins around me. "Look at me," he says. "Just look at me." I face him, then Cam is there holding me up.

"Oh no," Cam whispers.

"Is it dead?" I ask. Spence and Brint disappear into the woods. "I killed it," Cam says. And everything goes black.

"Don't that probably hurts," Cam says viciously.

"You know I wouldn't be doing this if I didn't have to," Pete snaps. They're pressing on the ripped skin of my back and holding my leg together. My weight is applying firm pressure on my ribs.

"Ouch. Stop," my voice slurs. I feel for Cam, for some sense of security around my grated body. He takes my hand. "It'll be all right."

"Where are they?" I whine. "Sleeping."

"Alive?" I ask.

"Yes." Pete shoves a lost pill into my mouth and then covers my airways until he sees I have swallowed.

"Those don't work on me," I say. Because they don't.

A couple months ago, Pete and I were fishing in the river that runs through Tibbet. After a long afternoon of skunking, we decided to check the trap in the shallows. When I pulled the trap out of the water, the load of the fish and me toppled the slippery rocks on the bottom of the sandbars. One of the base stones landed on my ankle, and Pete carried me all the way home. My mother gave me a bit of a lost pill just long enough to ease the pain; Pete sat on the couch with me until I fell asleep. Well, what was supposed to be a three-hour soporific only lasted ten minutes. My mother said it was because of the dreams I had although I don't remember them. I have refused every lost pill I've been offered since.

"Just until we get the stitches in," Pete says.

For the next three days, I doze in and out of consciousness, wanting Pete and Cam by my side at all times for refuge from the nightmares and pain. I watch my dad's death replay over and over again in my dreams only to wake crying and slick with sweat and fresh blood. I crave Pete's cerulean eyes. And when I have nothing to do but writhe in pain until the pill takes affect again, all I want is Cam's smile to tell me everything will work out. I desire the warmth of Pete's skin or the chilled feeling of being around Cam. But never together. I cannot tell if it's only in my dreams they fight or if I'm actually hearing them.

On the second day, Cam disappears. When I surface, Pete is there. He wipes the tears streaming from my face. "Are you in a lot of pain?"

Through the gasps of air I take, I manage, "Where is Cam?" Pete touches my sore cheeks, then there is more blackness.

"It's been days. When do you think they'll wake up?" Spence asks as someone gently turns me over.

"What are you doing?" I ask.

"Do you want another pill?" Pete. "No," I sigh.

"We have to change your bandages," he says. "We didn't have enough stitches to sew up your back, so we wrapped you in bandages. We had to stitch up your leg because you were losing too much blood." He hands me the container of water. "Has the pill worn off?" he asks.

"I think. I'm so sore." My body is aching from not moving for so long, it takes all I have to even turn my head a little so I can see what's around me. Lakuna, Bree, Mazi, and I are spread out across the width of the shack with enough room between each of us to fit another body, so I'm guessing I'll be sleeping next to the guys tonight.

Spence fidgets a little. "When is Mazi going to get up?"

Pete checks her bandages. "She's smaller, Spence. Give it time."

Spence lays a wet towel over her forehead. "She'll get too dehydrated." Spence leaves with the water basket.

"How long have we been on the island?" I ask. "Fourteen days," Pete says.

"Great," I breathe.

"Do you mind if I rest for a little bit?" Pete asks.

"Go ahead." It's midnight by the looks of it. The stars are well up in the sky, and the guys appear drained. Pete's blonde hair has lost its natural curl and lies almost smooth on his head. His abnormally long eyelashes have tangled together, and although his skin is a deep bronze, the bluish shadows are visible. Cam seems to have made himself so concerned over my injuries he's contracted some sort of illness. Supposedly since the second day, he's done nothing but worry, and today when I fully woke up, he has just slept. All day.

"How are you guys feeling?" I ask Mazi, Lakuna, and Bree. Periodically through the night, they've woken up too.

"Could be better," Mazi whimpers.

Lakuna doesn't remember the attack. She has four puncture wounds to her shoulder, and she's all wrapped up with bandages and vines. Bree has a chunk of skin gone from her hip. Pete put moss in it and tied it with vines. Mazi was more serious. The claw marks to her back are deep, and she has trouble breathing. I am the worst, or so I was told. My back is one big cut by now, my ribs are hollow, and my leg is permanently numb.

Cam is right next to me, the discs under his eyes a deep purple. He has a slight frown on his lips, not his smile. His breathing is quiet but fast. He must have used his shirt to help staunch the blood flow from my back because it's hanging on a nearby tree limb. His abs are still there, but his ribs are also prominent; it doesn't look like he's been eating much, and he's sweating worse than I've ever seen. I turn away from the streak of morning light in my eyes. I want to sleep so badly. Even though sleeping is all I've been doing, I am drained. I am nodding when a hand slaps down on my back.

I gasp as the intense pain makes its way to my brain. My breath catches in my throat, and I choke on nothing desperately trying to find air that isn't there. "Pete," Lakuna wakes him shortly after she notices my face is purple.

The pressure comes off of my back, and his soothing voice in my ear, "Hayden, calm down. Just breath." I inhale deeply, hold it, and exhale. Repeat. My hyperventilating slowly converts into a quick pant, but the searing pain in my back is still there. I know who slapped me, but it's not his fault. I can't help but thrash when I have bad dreams either.

"Sorry," Cam whispers. Sweat pours off of his forehead by the buckets even though he's shivering.

"It's fine," I gasp. He lies back down but scoots closer to the wall.

"Lay on this, will you?" he asks as he holds out his arm. I lean my head up, and he slips his bicep under it.

"When was the last time you've eaten anything?" I ask.

He thinks over my question. "I can't remember," a slight smirk forms on his lips.

Brint brings the blanket to Cam and spreads it out across his body, but he is already sleeping again to notice. I gently touch his forehead; it feels like I've just stuck my hand in an oven. His body temperature has to be at least seven degrees over what it should be. I hate the fact I have to do this, but since I can barely move without crying, I have no choice. "Brint, can you bring the first-aid kit over here?"

"Yeah?" he says curiously. As he hands it to me he asks, "Why do you need it?"

This is absolutely the dumbest question I've ever heard. "Are you kidding me?"

"No."

"Look at him!" I yell to Brint and point my finger at Cam's face. "What about it?"

"Oh my gosh, you're going to let him die. Feel his forehead!"

Brint bends down and touches Cam's forehead, pulling away quickly afterward. "Oh," he mumbles.

"Yeah," I add in a mocking tone, "Moron."

"Cam?" I push his dark brown hair back from his forehead. No answer. I give his shoulder a shake.

"Hm?" he mumbles, never opening his eyes.

"Can you take these?" I ask. "No," he answers.

"Please?" I beg.

"I'm not hungry," he says.

"It's not food." His eyes flutter open, and I notice his pupils are way too dilated and completely bloodshot. He glances down at my hand, which holds four tiny pills.

"What are those?" "Fever fighters," I say.

"I don't have a fever," he mumbles.

"Yes, you do," I argue.

His green eyes close again, and his other arm comes up to his head. "My head hurts." "I know," I say. "You'll feel better if you take these."

Brint grabs the basket of water. "Here," he says as he hands me the basket and walks back to the ocean.

"Cam. Here," I whisper as I gently shake his shoulder again because he has dozed off. He goes to grab the basket. I guess he forgot I was lying on his right arm because he moves it, and my head bashes into the shacks floor. "Ouch," I groan, but he doesn't notice. He props himself up on his elbow, but he is so wobbly that his what-used-to-be-strong arm gives out. "Brint," I shout to the ocean.

"What?" he hisses.

"Just help me for a second, okay?" "Fine."

"Push him up." Brint gets behind Cam and thrusts his back up. I put the pills in Cam's hand, and he tosses them in his mouth. I hold the basket up to his lips, and he takes a couple of sips. "Just drink four more gulps," I tell him, and he actually listens. Brint softly puts Cam back on his back. Cam turns himself to his stomach and spreads out.

"I don't want the blanket anymore," he whispers.

I rip it off his overheated body. His light, hurried breathing starts up again instantly. "Pete, get over here!" I yell at him. His blonde hair bounces as he trots over to me. "Are you trying to kill him? You know what you're doing? Why is he like this?" I ask him angrily.

"I can't help it! He refused to eat. He refused to sleep. He wouldn't drink anything," he answers innocently.

"Why couldn't you have used a pill and gave him water?" I hiss.

"For one, we have to save the pills for something important like a broken bone, and for two, he still couldn't swallow if we tried to feed him when he was under it."

I know Pete is right, but I can't stand the fact of admitting it, so I just say, "Go away." And he does.

The sun has just started to set, and the waves crashing on the beach are soft; the breeze blows and I let the tropical air run through my nostrils. This is actually pretty nice except for the fact Ozalee is dead, Cam is practically dying, Mazi, Bree, Lakuna, and I can't get up, and Brint is being a complete jerk, and for the first time in years, I do not want anything to do with Pete. Every time I think about Ozalee, her song pops into my head. The song is an old passing hymn we played at our father's funeral. I have no clue who sings it or who wrote it, but I have a feeling I would like them. I know Ozalee did. My sister, the girl whose laugh always brought joy to my life. The girl whose golden curls and brown eyes looked up to me. The girl who was one of the few people I loved. Gone forever.

Griff offers me some fruit, but I deny it. I'm not in the mood for eating. The sun finally sinks down under the sea, and the moon appears along with the stars. Pete lies between Bree and Lakuna, and Griff takes his place between Lakuna and me. He woke up a few short minutes after Spence and Brint found them in the jungle. He didn't get to talk to her before Pete gave her the lost pill. "You know Cam is sick?" I ask.

"No. Why?" he looks to me concerned.

"Because you idiots didn't make him sleep or drink or eat anything for the past four days. His temperature is high. If we were home, he would be in the hospital," I snap.

"But we're not home, Hayden. We are trapped on a deserted island. If we were home, none of us would be like this!" he yells, and he turns over, putting his back to me.

It takes a minute for his words to register in my brain, but when they finally click, I realize he's right. I feel like we are trapped here because of me. We are hurt because of me. My sister is dead because I couldn't save her.

I stand up in one quick motion. My calf throbs, and I hear the stitches rip. Hot blood runs down the skin of my bandaged back, but I don't care. I limp past the rest of the shack and to the boundless beach, which probably ends nowhere. I'm not coming back. Why should I? My friends are either sick or mad at me, and I don't even know if we are going to survive on this island or off of it. So there is really no point for me to stay if we're all going to fight anyway. I can fend for myself, and they will get on just fine without me. I'm nothing special to them anyway. Especially Brint, I'm sure he would be happy to see me leave. We never got along well in the first place, and now with something to fight about, I'm sure it will get worse, so why not make it easier for him and leave?

I get just out of sight from the shack when I have to sit down because I can hardly breathe; my injuries have taken their toll. It's not like after I just woke up when I could barely move at all. This time, I forced my body to do what I don't even think it's capable of. I'm glad I did to because now, instead of me aching everywhere, only the direct cuts sting. A couple of seconds pass before I hear footsteps behind me. I turn defensively. "What do you want?" I snap.

"I just wanted to talk." Lakuna's voice surprises me. I thought she was sleeping and Griff was chasing me, but how could he because of his leg?

"I thought you were Griff."

"Oh," she says quietly with a slight laugh and takes a seat next to me. "He is being a little harsh, isn't he?" she asks.

"I deserve it," I answer. "No, you don't."

"I really do. You don't need to argue. You're never going to change my mind." Redness leaks through the bandages on her shoulder. "Why did you follow me?"

"Because I knew you wouldn't come back," she says. "How?" I ask.

She laughs a real laugh, not a forced one. "Hayden, I've known you since we were little. I can practically read your mind. Ozalee was the only thing keeping you here, not here on the island, but like mentally. There is no way you would be staying with us if it weren't for her," she says.

"You guys would be fine without me."

Her mouths drops suddenly. She pretends to smack my face. "You don't get it. I can't let you leave. I won't be able to handle it." Wow, Lakuna Crest not being able to handle something. She has coped with everything her whole life, my family's deaths and even her parents leaving her at age ten.

One day her parents got into a big fight. Lakuna tried to stop them. Her dad hit her and left. Her mom chased him out, and they never came back. They've sent her letters with money, explaining her dad was sorry about hitting her, but he couldn't bear to look at her anymore. Her mom picked her dad over her and left Lakuna to fend for herself. She has practically lived with me ever since. My dad was like a second dad to her. His death affected her life too, and I never even noticed. Ozalee was a little sister to her, and she's gone. I am all she has other than Griff.

"I never knew you needed me that much. I'm sorry."

"It's okay. You're trying and that's all that counts. You've had to deal with so much in the past year." She says, waving off everything she's been through and turning the conversation back on how unstable I am.

She helps me up, and we start hobbling back to camp. "How are you handling this?" I ask.

She takes a second to think and then answers, "Pretty good. Most of the people I love are here except for Tinley, Hixel, Ariel, and Broppin, but I have a good feeling they are safe. I'm not going to lie though. My shoulder hurts really bad." She giggles at her own discomfort.

"I'm happy for you then," I joke. It takes us longer to get back to the shack than it did getting away from it. Every so often, we stop and point out star formations in the sky, like we used to do when we were young.

When we get back to camp, we head straight for the supply stack. I grab a shell full of water, and Lakuna picks one up eagerly. The water is soothing when it floods down my throat. I eat a banana, and she peels a purplish fruit and takes a bite. Juice dribbles down her chin. It has to be at least three in the morning before we finally return to our sleeping spots. "Night, Hayden," she whispers.

I watch her crawl under the protection of Griff's arms. "Night." I thought I would fall asleep fast, but the sense of peace never comes. "Lakuna, are you awake?"

"Yeah," she says.

"Can you sleep?" I ask. "No."

An idea pops into my head. "Remember when we used to watch the stars and fall asleep in the grass.

"Yes," she says. We walk around to the side of the bamboo shack. Gallons of sweat and hours later, we reach the top of the shack. We tease each other about the faces we make every time a piece of bamboo rips a stitch. The roof of the shack is sturdy; it can hold us both up with no problem. Well, I hope this is the case because if not, our friends are going to get hurt. We lie stretched out next to each other and look at the stars. Eventually, I fall asleep.

"I think I can walk now," Mazi whispers. This statement brings me back to reality from my dreamless sleep. I knew I was a light sleeper, but this is ridiculous. I woke up from every tiny noise last night, the crash of a wave, Lakuna's soft breathing, and I swear I could hear the wings of the jungle bugs flapping. Maybe I've lost it, or maybe I never had it, but I hope I get better sleep tonight. I crawl to the edge of the roof and peer over; Brint, Griff, and Pete have disappeared into the ocean, and Mazi and Bree are standing up. Bree gets behind Mazi and carefully unties her wrapped back. Mazi's back is definitely infected, but the open wound has crusted over. If she takes it easy, I don't think it will break open again. Bree's wound is much deeper than Mazi's, still bloody. Mazi puts clean bandages over it and ties it with a vine.

Cam and Spence are still sleeping. Cam doesn't look any better. I'm not close to him, but he appears to be getting worse. "Lakuna, wake up." I give her a shake.

"What?" she complains. "It's morning," I say. "So?" she argues.

"Griff is up," I tell her. Her eyes fly open, and a smile crosses her face. I know we should climb down, but we are so excited to be able to move again without bleeding we decide to jump off the top of the roof. It can't be more than six feet. "One, two, three!" I whisper, and we jump. I expect us to land with a thud, but instead we float to the ground and plant our feet firmly in the sand. Mazi and Bree almost knock the back of the shack off as they run into the wall screaming in their high-pitched girl voices. Griff, Pete, and Brint run back from the ocean. Griff whips the knife from his shorts and looks around for any oncoming danger. Cam and Spence jolt awake too. Lakuna and I can't help but laugh.

"You two are so stupid," Mazi says embarrassingly as she throws her old bandage to the ground. "What is your problem!" Brint yells; the question directed at Bree and Mazi.

"They scared us," Bree says defensively. Her finger flicks toward Lakuna and I.

He glares at us. "Don't you two know you're only supposed to scream when you're in trouble?" He snarls as we back away from him.

I don't know what we did, but he is starting to frighten me. At the same time, I hate getting yelled at, so I shout, "We didn't scream! They did! And I don't like the fact you're yelling at us either!" Lakuna and I separate as we walk backward slowly. I am scared now.

Brint's knuckles go white and his jaws clamp together. His hand rises behind his shoulder. He's going to hit one of us. Almost in sync, we bolt and hide behind Spence and Cam. They are standing now, and their muscular frames cover most of our bodies. Cam reaches back and grabs my hand. I honestly don't know how long he can stand without passing out.

"Chill, Brint," says Spence.

"No," he hisses and lunges between Spence and Cam to get to Lakuna and me. Their body wall's gap was too big, and Brint grabs my and Lakuna's throat. His strength is unbelievable as he slams us against the shack's wall, tightening his grip on our throats and blocking my airway. I look past Brint's red face, trying to find the help from one of my friends. I can feel the air draining from my head and the purple color taking over.

For just a quick second, my vision blurs. My eyes do all the work for me, pointing out to Griff the drinking shell lying on the floor. He picks it up and bashes it into Brint's skull with a sickening thud. Brint slumps to the floor unconscious. Lakuna and I slip to the ground gasping for air, and without even examining my throat, I know something is wrong.

Brint wouldn't normally do this; he doesn't get violent when he gets mad. My curiosity crests. I crawl over to him. Cam grabs my shoulder, and I yank it away reflexively. I lift up Brint's shirt. His stomach is normal with no sign of anything I suspect. I roll him onto his back and rub my hands across his skin. Aha, I knew it. Directly under his shoulder blade, I find a lump the size of an apple. Puss drains out of it, and a black stinger is wedged in the tip of the disease-ridden bump. I grab hold of the stinger and try to pull it out, but it's stuck. I yank harder with all of my strength. A barb on the stinger pops out; I keep pulling until the stinger, which is longer than my pinky finger, is all of the way out. Just touching the lethal-looking stinger makes my fingers numb; this is probably why Brint didn't feel the insect sting him.

I try to tell my friends what I think happened, but nothing comes out. I turn to Lakuna, and her eyes are locked on mine. My hands go up to my throat. My fingers rub my neck. Tears drain from her eyes. It hurts. Bad. We open our mouths and try to talk, but again, nothing comes out. My throat stings on the inside and has a type of pain I've never experienced before on the outside. I honestly don't know if I'll be able to talk again. It feels as if the lump in your throat you get when your cry is stuck there and won't come out.

Pete taps my shoulder; he drops to his knees in front of me. "You're hurt?" Lakuna nods her head. Pete uses his middle finger to guide my chin up until I'm looking at the sky. His hands probe the spot where Brint grabbed. He stops when I begin to make the noises that happen when I cry. He wraps his arm around me. "I'm sorry." Griff won't let Pete touch Lakuna.

"Do you know what happened to Brint?" asks Bree. I flap my arms up and down until Bree guesses a bug stung him. "How do you know?" she continues.

"Bree, her mom is a nurse, and we live in Villa. People get stung by bugs every day," Pete says.

"Well, that explains why he kept getting mad at the stupidest things," Griff says. "What do we do?" asks Bree.

"I say we tie him up and wait until the venom drains out of his system," Spence says. Pete and Griff drag Brint to the coconut tree next to the shack and tie his hands around the trunk with a vine. His head falls downward; he will have a massive headache tomorrow.

I walk over to the ocean. I sit just deep enough so when the waves come, they cover my legs. After a while, I take off my shirt because of the heat. As I lie down, I put my hands behind my head and close my eyes. I think my wounds make my thoughts get all topsy-turvy because I find myself organizing them again. Lakuna, Bree, Mazi, and I can walk again. Griff has a broken leg. Cam and Spence are sick. Brint is crazy. The only normal one here is Pete. We have been on this island for sixteen days. We have a bow, twelve arrows, a basket full of water, a container, two shells, an ax, a knife, goggles, bandages, a little over three sleeping pills, fruit, a needle, some string, tweezers, a flashlight, and a blanket left to work with. Judging by the sun, I would say it's about noon. Ozalee is dead. My stomach churns. I have to curl up in a ball and hold it.

"Hayden?" Griff's voice surprises me. I uncurl from my ball and open my eyes. The up and down movement of my head is slow, but it gets the job done. "Look. I'm sorry about last night. I just haven't really taken in our situation yet, and me yelling at someone helped me do that. You just happened to be the closest person to me at the moment." It sounds reasonable. I smile at him and close my eyes again. I hear the footfalls of six of my friends coming toward Griff and me.

"We should probably wash off," Spence says.

Pete, Spence, Griff, Lakuna, Bree, Mazi, and I walk toward the ocean. Cam isn't coming to the ocean. He can barely stand up, much less swim. He went to go lie down again. Mazi just gave Spence some fever fighters that should bring him back to normal. When we get to the water, the boys take off their shirts and shorts. I hadn't noticed until now they have the same clothes on. The guys wear dark green tee shirts, black shorts, and black boxers. The girls have on tighter dark green tee shirts, black sports bras, black underwear and black shorts. All of us have on black socks and black shoes that go up past our ankles to give us extra support. The shoes have a rubber sole built for running and tiny holes on the side to air out our feet. Darious and his crew must have changed us while we were under the sedative. Violation! They were like forty years old!

I stomp over to Mazi. Mazi and I have this thing where we know what each other is thinking without saying anything. This only happens sometimes, but I desperately hope now is one of those times. I have or had this with a couple of people. One of them used to be Ozalee. Now only with Lakuna and Mazi. Other than Ozalee and I, Lakuna and I have this best, but since she can't talk, she is no use to me. I point to Pete and my shoes and that is all it takes. As soon as she realizes what I'm telling her,

her hands fly up and cover her chest. "They changed us," she whispers, not loud enough for Pete and Spence to understand.

"What?" asks Pete.

"They changed us!" she yells. Mazi and Bree glare down at their matching outfits; they instantly hold their hands over their girl parts.

Mazi starts to speak for me; she goes on the rampage she knows I would go on. "What right do they have to see me naked? I don't care if they did kidnap us. They shouldn't have done this!" she screams as she points to her stomach.

"Mazi! Calm down. Sure, they saw us naked. What's the big deal?" Griff asks. It's not surprising to me Griff asks this. He is so obsessed with himself. He knows he's the best-looking guy in our group, and he definitely shows it off. He flirts with every girl in school, and they all fall for it. His comment was arrogant. It angers Bree, and she throws sand at him.

"The problem is you don't have breasts, that's the problem!" Bree screams at him. "Well, we can't help it now, so just forget it," Griff says.

The guys are already in their boxers. They dive into the ocean waves. Lakuna, Bree, Mazi, and I strip down into our bras and underwear more reluctantly. Once we get our clothes off and tear off our bandages, we trudge into the water. The waves are cool and refreshing but painful. The salt of the water gets in my cuts, and it stings them. I know it's helping disinfect them, but I wish it was less agonizing. The guys float on their backs, riding the waves like nothing is wrong. I walk until the water is to my shoulders, then I scrub my blood-caked skin. It takes a long time to get my skin and gashes clean. Once done, I go to work on my matted-down hair.

I can't get the knots out by myself, so Bree rips her fingers through my tender scalp until my hair is smooth. I put my hair in a ponytail down the side of my head and help Mazi untangle her hair. I move my attention to Bree and Lakuna, but they don't need help with their knots since their hair isn't that long. I wade out of the water and onto shore. It doesn't take long for me to grab my clothes and head back to the ocean. I swish my clothing around in the water and see the clouds in the sea as dirt and blood wash off. My friends do the same thing I do. As soon as I'm done, I wade out of the ocean and drip dry. Pete, Spence, Lakuna, Bree, Griff, and Mazi crowd around me, and we stand there drying off, trying not to get sandy all over again.

"Since we're clean. We should probably try to rebandage ourselves," insists Griff. He is probably dying for a bandage change. He hasn't had one since he was under his lost pill.

We walk over to the supply stack to aid ourselves. We help Bree first; her hip isn't scabbed over or even a little better. The gash is at least five inches across and a half of an inch deep. I wrap it in fresh bandages. Griff is next. His leg isn't any better, and I don't think it will heal for a long time. Pete and I unwrap his leg. The cuts from the rock shards are scabbed over, but that's it.

"Can you feel your leg?" Mazi asks.

"It's uncomfortable but not painful. It would be if I didn't have a splint."

We can't do anything else for him, so we move on to Lakuna. Her shoulder and chest are infected and swollen. The wound is crusted over with a yellowish liquid. Pete glances at me with a worried look and mouths, "I don't know what to do."

I think about what we have to work with—bandages, tweezers, string, needles, and an empty shot-type thing. The empty shot? I open the first-aid kit and rummage through it until I find what I'm looking for. The empty shot will do the trick, I think. I stand up with it in my hand, and Lakuna looks at me suspiciously. I walk to the coconut tree closest to the shack and bang the needle part of the shot on the trunk until it pops off; I grab the needle and limp back over to the group. As I drop the needle into the first-aid kit, I grab Lakuna's arm and pull her closer to me. I grab the knife from the ground and hold it up to the top of Lakuna's wound and press down on the blade until it cuts through the yellowish crust. I was right—it did hurt. Her eyes are still closed, but a fat tear rolls down her cheek. I stick the empty shot into her gash and pull the end of it. The yellowish infection recedes from her bite and gets sucked up in the shot. I have to empty the shot eight more times until all of the puss is drained from her bite holes. I wrap her whole chest and shoulder in bandages until her bite is entirely covered.

Pete and I go to work on Mazi next. Her hand is healing well; she has had the stitches in for about fourteen days, so all Pete has to do is rebandage it. Her back is a whole other story. It's exactly like Lakuna's. I do the same thing I did to Lakuna's, and just like Lakuna, Mazi cries. I have to empty the shot seventeen times until the puss is gone. Lakuna takes the shot from me. For some reason, I don't want to be next. I'm perfectly fine with my oozing infectious wounds, and I'm in no mood to have her poking at me with a knife. I step behind Pete like a small child shying away from a new teacher. She crosses her arms impatiently as if to say, "Seriously, just get it over with." She stomps her foot in the sand, points to me, then pretends to slit her throat with the knife. Right when the blade crosses the width of her neck, I notice the indigo five fingers and a palm of a hand showing through her skin. I wonder if I have those too. Pete wraps Mazi's back and turns to me.

I lie down on the sand while Pete pokes the knife into the slivers of infected flesh; the pressure of the blade squishes my lungs to such an extent I have to focus more on breathing than crying. To pass the time, I count to sixty and add a minute on my fingers. When they finish, all of my fingers and seven of my toes are taken with a minute, and I couldn't come up even one tear. *I'm no wimp*, I think to myself sarcastically. I don't think I could produce a tear if I tried. I've cried so much since we've been here I don't know if I'll ever cry again. They wrap my back and move to my leg. The skin is ripped, and the stitches have torn open to form an alligator mouth across my calf; Pete ties the stitches back together tight and bandages my leg again.

Spence unties Brint, and he drops to the ground. Pete washes his clothes in the ocean while Bree cleans him with a piece of drenched blanket. Lakuna and I look at his insect sting. I use the empty shot and suck all of the puss out, needing only two emptyings. She blots his bloodied head until the crimson is gone, and she bandages the wound caused by the impact of the shell. Spence ties Brint back up to the tree, and we step back and look at him. He is as clean as he'll get, and his clothes are somewhat dirtless. His wounds are cared for, so I think he's good to go. "When do you think the poison will drain out of his system?" Bree asks to no one in particular.

"Maybe a day or two or as soon as he goes to the bathroom or throws up. Whichever comes first," Pete says nonchalantly.

Now for Cam. Stretched out sleeping on the floor like he always used to do back home. Everybody stares at me, even Griff and Pete. Why are they staring at me? What do they want me to do? I can't even talk. I touch my fingertips to his forehead, scorching. Except this time, he isn't sweating, which means his fever broke and then got worse and he's still shivering. He rolls onto his back. "What?" His pupils are a little less dilated than yesterday but still not normal. What used to be the white in his eyes is bloodshot. I've never had to deal with anything like this. I don't know what to do. He looks dead. Like someone who got drunk, passed out on the street, and got run over by a couple hundred cars. My face breaks to sweat.

Griff kneels down next to Cam, "Do you feel any better?" "No," Cam says.

"You don't look good either. Um, we are just gonna clean you up a little," Griff's voice quivers. He knows. He's not stupid. He's holding himself together pretty well. If my twin looked like this, I'd be throwing fever fighters down his throat left and right. Mazi and Spence wash Cam's clothes in the ocean. I dunk the tiny piece of blanket in the water and scrub him with it. The sweat, dirt, and grime are hard to get off his body, but in time, I get him clean and recognizable.

The only thing we can do to help him is give him four more fever-fighting pills and make sure he stays hydrated, so we do. Griff hands me four tiny blue pills, and I hold them out to Cam. He puts them in his mouth and swallows them with the water we keep in the shack. "How do you feel?" Cam asks, then he looks at me. When he sees my neck, which must have very bright bruising, his eyes bug out of his head. "What happened? Who did this?"

Pete pulls me away. "Brint got stung by something. He lost his temper for only a second. Don't worry. We've got it under control."

"Are you hungry?" Griff asks, quickly switching the focus of the conversation.

"No," Cam slurs.

Lakuna, Bree, Griff, Mazi, and I sit on the hot sand by the fire pit. Spence and Pete went to get more water. It's dark now. The stars are shining bright in the clear sky, and the moon is full. Ozalee would have loved this. We always used to get out on our roof and stare at the night sky. We used that as our time. Now I will use Broppin for a night like this. She's no Ozalee, but she's the next thing to a sister I have. Cousin is close enough. Broppin has no patience to look at stars or to listen to the poems I wrote on bad nights. That's what Ariel is for—to do what Broppin won't. And what Ariel won't do Tinley will, and what Tinley won't Hixel will. Maybe I can make this work.

"I'm hungry," Mazi says, breaking into my train of thought. She brings the basket of fruit to the firepit.

I peel a banana and stick it in my mouth. The sweet taste of the yellow fruit explodes on my tongue, and I savor it until I have to swallow. I start the swallowing process, but the pain is so unbearable, I choke my food back up. My friends are staring and laughing at me until Lakuna tries to swallow her food and spits it all over the ground. Then they realize we can't swallow. Griff grabs the ax out of the supply pile and marches into the jungle. Minutes later, he comes back with an armful of coconuts. He uses the ax to chop the tip of the coconut with one easy swing and hands one to Lakuna and the other to me. I drink the water from the nut and throw it to the ground; that is not going to hold me over. I try to chop off another coconut's top, but I'm not strong enough, so eventually Pete steps in and does it for me. I wish I was strong like them. I grab the coconut eagerly and sip it until it's dry.

They get done eating, and we drink the whole container full of water. Mazi grabs Spence's hand and starts walking toward the shack. I guess she is tired. Before they get there, Spence scoops her up in his arms and carries her the rest of the way, leaning in for a kiss when they reach the entrance.

As much as I hate to admit it, they are a cute couple. Lakuna, Griff, and Bree follow Mazi and Spence and leave Pete and me to check on Brint. He sits straight up. When we get close enough to him where he can identify our figures, he tenses up. We inch toward him until we are a safe four feet away.

"Hey," Pete says to him reassuringly.

"Why is she here?" he asks harshly. His forehead furrows over his brows.

It rubs me the wrong way. I trudge over to him. It's a good thing he has his hands tied behind his back because I grab hold of his hair and slam his head into the tree. I ignore the words he starts calling me and limp back to the shack.

"Brint, come on! She's just trying to help," Pete explains. "I don't want her help."

"Give her a break. You broke her throat!" Pete yells in my defense. "What?"

"You got stung by some kind of bug thing." "When?" asks Brint.

"We don't know, but I think it was when you were walking to Hayden from the ocean. She called you over because she needed help with Cam, Mazi and Bree were sleeping, and Lakuna and Hayden were the only ones awake, so you saw them first and that made you want to go after them first. Maybe," Pete answers.

"Oh," mumbles Brint.

"Yeah, you definitely owe them an apology." "Sorry, I can't help it," Brint says.

"Don't apologize to me. Say sorry to them. Do you want any food or water?" "Yeah."

I hear Pete's footsteps walk to the supply stack, and then I stop listening. I don't think I was supposed to hear that conversation, but I can't do anything about it now. My exertion on the stuff I did today was extremely tiring. I lie down between Lakuna and Cam and close my heavy eyelids. Pete's soft footfalls come closer to the shack and stop on the other side of Lakuna.

A boom of thunder wakes me up a little after I fall asleep. When my eyes adjust to the light, I see the sky is pouring rain and bright lightning strikes are filling the air. I sit up and rub the sleepiness from my face. The waves from the ocean are throwing themselves around violently, and the wind is making the trees' branches slash at each other. I stand up and walk out of the shack; the rain and wind immediately pierce my face, leaving a stinging sensation. The items in the supply stack are drenched with water, so when I try to pick up the knife, it slips from my hands. I bend down and pick it up again but with a tighter grasp and head to the tree Brint is tied to. He is sitting straight up, cringing from the rain. He jumps when I graze his arm with my shorts, not knowing anyone was standing in front of him because of the loud wind and blinding rain. I walk behind the tree and slice the vines that are restraining him. They fall to the ground in pieces, and he stands up, flexing is hands to regain movement in them.

I lead him back to the shack, kicking Pete's back on the way in. I don't know how the storm hasn't woken anybody up yet, but Pete must be so ridiculously exhausted I'm surprised he's lasted this long. For the past four days, he has been taking care of seven of us! "Hmmm?" he groans. He rolls over and see's Brint standing beside me. "Why is he untied?" Pete asks worryingly.

The lightning bolt that strike's Brint's tree and ignites the branches in flames answers his question. Brint's tree is close enough to the jungle where it can catch the other trees on fire, and that's just what it does. In a matter of seconds, the jungle is in flames.

CHAPTER FOUR

My first instinct is to run, but that is not an option. Before I can even think, Brint is yelling, "Get up! Wake up!" Pete is on his feet; he grabs my arm and yanks me out of the shack. We run to the supply stack. "Grab as much as you can!" he screams at me.

I bend down and pick up the blanket, throwing it onto the ground so it spreads out when it lands. He piles the supplies on the blanket. I shove the knife and the ax between my shorts and my underwear, and I sling the bow and arrows over my shoulder. Pete picks up the bundle of supplies and sprints back to the shack. I follow him like a dog.

Living is more important than my stupid throat. "Spence, get Brint! Lakuna, help Griff!" This is the first time I've spoken since Brint tried to strangle me. The words are extremely agonizing to get out. Crackles of something choke me and make my voice hoarse. A dull aching accompanies a harsh cutting but the safety of everyone overcomes the pain. Spence ties Brint's hands behind his back with some extra vines Pete collected and wraps the end around his waist and knots it. Lakuna takes Griff's arm and puts it over her shoulder; he will not be able to walk right until he gets real medical attention. Pete and I look at the blazing jungle, assessing the situation. To the right are all flames. The fire is even hiking up the cliffs. *How can a fire spread this fast?* To the left of the fire pit is open jungle just starting to ignite. "What do we do?" I ask Pete, hoping he'll be able to understand me through the deafening rain.

"Let's take to the beach!" he answers.

Bree and Mazi have Cam between their shoulders and are hoisting him up by his arms. Even petty movement makes him fall sideways. It's a good thing they're holding him up.

"Run!" I scream, and we take off down the beach.

I'm glad Coach had us running a ton in track practice; I never knew it would come in so handy. My stitches in my leg have ripped open again. I can feel my adrenaline coursing through my veins, giving me a jittery boost of energy. Lakuna tried to help Griff, and it worked for a short time, but his weight overpowered her athletic figure. She hands him off to Pete when she can't tow him any longer. Spence and Brint are making good time; they don't need me to help. Lakuna and I now lead the group through the thick smoke to an unknown somewhere.

Every inhale I take sets my lungs on fire, filling them with the black ash that could so easily kill me. After a while of breathing in smoke, my stomach, lungs, and heart are rejecting any further movement without fresh air. The smoke seems to be affecting everyone. When I physically feel my heart burning in my chest, I know we have to stop. We slow for a brief moment. The flames have almost caught up to us. We're just getting ready to move on when my stomach erupts and bile spews from my mouth. My eyes are so watery, I can hardly make out anything, but when I look, everyone is keeled over with stuff dripping off their tongues. I bend over trying to catch my breath, but all I draw in is smoke.

"We have to go. Now!" I yell. The looks of incoherence are what answer me. "We *need* to move!" I scream.

The firestorms are only yards away, and we are standing too close to the jungle. The beach is so slim here, I couldn't even lie down without getting wet. We can't turn back because the trees have already fallen, blanketing the shack and everything around it in infernos. I turn my attention to my friends. "Seriously, we need—" But I am interrupted by the falling of a flaming tree that cuts Lakuna, Mazi, and me from the rest of the group.

The look on Mazi's face is unforgettable. Her mouth immediately opens in the shape of an *O*, and her brows crease with worry. "Can't help them now! We'll find them again!" Lakuna yells then pukes by our shoes. The flames have caught up to us and are engulfing the shore; we only have one choice. Go deeper into the jungle.

I grab Mazi's hand. "Run! They're smart! Run!" I pull until I get to the wall of flames and then stop and look up at the sky. *Ozalee, Dad, everyone I've ever known and loved who's up there, please help us through this,* I think and sprint into the flames.

The wall of fire is thin, but it's enough to set my clothes aflame. It's hard to think of the pain you feel when your skin is melting. I don't have to think of it—I feel it. I cover my face with my hair, but the fire burns my shoulders and knees. The smell of dead skin enters my nose; I'm scared to look if my skin is dripping off me like melting wax.

My mom always told me if you ever catch your clothes on fire, stop, drop, and roll. As of now, all I can think is to pull Mazi and Lakuna through the flames. All on fire. Stop, drop, and roll. My knees lock, and I fall to the ground, thrash around like a wild person, and roll as if I were an alligator. Soon the burning sensation is extinguished from my shoulder and knees, leaving a penetrating throb. I feel to see if it's wrinkled like it would be if it melted, but gory ooze stains my fingers. Lakuna yanks me sideways, digging her uncut nails into the burns on my shoulders. I have a millisecond to catch a breath before we're running again. Running from the falling debris, running from the red and black flames, running from the burn, running to find them.

The flames lose themselves behind us, but the smoke continues to fill the air with thick darkness. We make sure to stay closely attached to one another so we don't get separated. I pull my shirt up over my mouth and nose and cough until I'm positive my lungs are on the ground. I feel around in front of me to make sure I don't smack my face on a tree or limb, especially a smoldering one. Mazi, Lakuna, and I work this way until Mazi's burned feet won't take her another step. "Please. I have to stop."

Who am I to object? We can't see. We can't breathe. I am in desperate need to analyze a much-burned shoulder and kneecap of my own. We sit by the base of a tree, or what I think is a tree.

"Mazi, Hayden, what if they got trapped? What if they burned to death?" Lakuna asks.

I feel around for her. "Pete wouldn't let that happen. They got out. I know they did." *Brint. Spence. Griff. Bree. Cam. Pete. All dead in one night? No! Impossible.* I know Pete will get them out of it. I know he will! He's my best friend. Cam, no matter how sick, won't let Griff die. His heart is too big. I know him too well to recognize he won't go like that. And there is no way Spence and Griff will die without telling Mazi and Lakuna they love them. It's so obvious they do.

I must've fallen asleep some time during the night because when the first light of morning streaks through the foggy leftovers of the smoke, I wake with aching muscles and red skin discharging thick liquid stretched so tight against my bones, I can't stand up without help. We were sitting on a soft bed of moss, which now shows the imprints of our bodies huddled together to keep the ash out of our faces. Lakuna and I have to almost carry Mazi. The fire burned straight through the top of her shoes on to the tips of her feet. The cinder has completely covered the olive skin of her legs and has fallen all over and inhaled the glossy ringlets on her head. She, although in the back of the group, has taken the fire on full force. I know every step we take is an enormous effort on her part, but Lakuna and

I simply aren't strong enough to carry her especially when I have all of the weapons shoved down my pants. We go left, the direction we ran from and the direction everyone else should be.

We barely talk. My throat is constricting, swollen from Brint's hands, and stinging from the smoke that every word sends a jab of pain down my esophagus. The only part of Lakuna the fire burned was her throat. I don't know how it managed to throw a flame at any angle to reach a location like that, but she now has one of her socks pressed against it to keep out infection until we can get to water. For Mazi, avoiding infection looks impossible, and even worse, we don't have the first-aid kit. As we walk deeper into the island, the jungle disappears entirely, leaving a deciduous forest like back home. Dirt and sticks rather than moss and sand. Maples, oaks, and pines rather than bamboo and palms. Even nuts and berries substitute for the fruits and flowers. The temperature cools the farther we walk, and the burnt jungle that was the night before is no more.

I hear it before I see it. The sound of water running through a creek. Such a recognizable sound for me considering I can see the river valley and the creek from my bedroom window back home. We push through a wide bush with tiny red berries and step into the calm water. Ah. I hold handfuls of water to Mazi's mouth before mine; she needs it way more than I do. "Let your feet soak," I choke getting caught on my own words. The water runs over my burns, and I take gulp after gulp until I feel it swishing around in my stomach.

"We should look for them," Lakuna says.

"If they made it, they'll be looking for water," I say.

Mazi looks every which way and screams as loud as I've ever heard her. Birds from nearby trees take flight. Her voice echoes throughout the island, "Spence! Bree!"

I want to yell so badly for Pete and Cam. They'd hear me too, pick my voice out, I mean. But my throat is so incredibly tight I can barely talk. "If they're anywhere, they are upstream. They couldn't come downstream. They wouldn't make it. So we're going that way." I point to the left. Mazi's face drops.

"We'll only go a little bit," Lakuna says. "Just keep screaming."

The creek is wide with many twists and turns, and thank goodness, it doesn't have a pond connected to it. After the first ninety-degree bend, taking us deeper into the island, the creek bed grows one, five, ten feet on both sides towering above my head with rocks. Not flat rocks, big boulders. On my right, the boulders continue to grow as we walk, but my left still allows me to walk back into the woods instead of climbing. We stop to rest. "Mazi, try yelling again," I say.

"Bree! Spence!"

"Now we wait. A few minutes max," Lakuna sighs.

My stomach growls from lack of food, and I can't seem to stop jittering. I wait anxiously. I have it! The feeling I get when I know what's there, what will happen next.

"Shhh!" Mazi says although we're not saying anything. "Spence!" Mazi roars one more time. Seconds later, he bounds around the corner half naked with his shirt wrapped tightly around his arm.

"Spence! You're alive! I knew I heard you," Mazi shrieks.

"Quiet!" he whispers as he strides through the water. "He just fell asleep, but I'm glad you're all right! I've been worried sick," he says softly. He looks at Mazi's feet, kisses her cheek, and picks her up like a baby.

"What do you mean he just fell asleep?" I ask. "Did everyone make it?"

"Follow me," he says, "Quietly."

We trail him around the next twist and into a small cave made by three fallen boulders smashed together. The second I place foot in the cave, I see him. His shirt ripped away, his chest burned from his hip bone to his chin, and his arms spread out wide to keep from touching his stomach. My heart sinks. "No." Pete's stomach looks like his skin was put on a stove and boiled. Large bulbs of skin bulge out in blisters, and sticky clear stuff runs throughout the streams of blackened flesh. "What do you mean he just fell asleep?" I ask in a low voice.

"He was in so much pain, he couldn't even talk much less sleep," Griff says. I see how a flame licked his forehead.

"What about the lost pills? We still have the supplies right?" I ask.

"We do, but he's just too bad. We didn't know if he'd make it through the night."

I soak his shirt in water and lay it over him. His skin sizzles under the chill.

"Here." Bree hands me the container of water. "I think this will help."

I tilt the canteen, setting a steady drizzle over the blanket. "Does anybody have suggestions?" I ask, badly hoping I get help with this. They look at one another; I slide down the wall as the silence lengthens. I put my head between my knees because I think I might throw up. The mere thought of any of us dying, particularly Pete, makes me incredibly ill. Out of all of my friends, Pete and Lakuna are my best, one a guy and one a girl. A perfect equation, but with no guy and one girl, I am thrown to one side. It doesn't work. "I'm not a doctor; I don't know what to do. Pete is the medic here, not me! I don't take after my mother. That was Ozalee," I say.

Bree shoots up. "I know what to do!"

"Shhh," Griff snaps. "Seriously, guys, be quiet. He needs to sleep."

We move our conversation across the creek so we can talk openly without unsettling Pete. "Mazi, remember when we were stuck in traffic because an electrician was injured by a power line which fell on the road?" Bree asks.

Mazi nods. "Of course. I'll always remember. We were late for school!"

"So when that electrician on the side of the road got burnt by the wire, what did he use before he covered his burn?" Bree urges.

"Oh!" Mazi squeals. "Why didn't we think of that before?"

"Think of what?" I ask.

"Because we're brainless." Bree begins throwing the rocks off the bottom of the creek and digging through the dense mud on the bed. Mazi flings mud everywhere, granting my burns the slimy coating of the mud. Although it's spelling infection for them, it feels so good.

"What are you looking for?" I ask impatiently.

"This! A lipper plant!" She yanks a white bulb off a purple leaf hidden in muck.

"That will help Pete?" Griff asks.

Bree tosses the baseball-sized tuber to Mazi. "Probably. The electrician said it had some type of chemical that caused cells to grow back faster. He said it numbs the pain." Mazi shrugs as if she was a genius, which we all know she's not.

"So I rub this goo on his chest, and it will heal him?" I ask.

"Not only will it help him recover, but it also sets on top of the skin, so when we bandage him, the wrapping won't directly touch the burns," Bree says.

The goo switches from purple to blue when I pour it on his stomach. I smear it all over his abs and neck, careful not to apply too much pressure through my fingertips. I set the first bandages in place; I'll have to finish the rest when he's able to stand. I wrap his legs in the blanket. The temperature has dropped significantly from the jungle to the forest. I'd guess about thirty degrees or so, plus the sun is still high in the sky.

Cam, who I've mindlessly ignored since I've been reunited with everyone, seems to be deteriorating. He interchanges with dozing and babbling about stuff I have never even heard of. "I was wondering about your horse. If she grew wings, she would be called a Pegasus. Did you know that?" he says. I feel his forehead and give him six fever fighters instead of four. He's lost his mind.

"Cam, Girl doesn't have wings."

He pokes the burn on my shoulder. "What's that?"

I yank away. "Ouch! It's a burn from the fire."

Griff drags him to the wall of the cave. "Stay here. Rest and don't touch her burns." Griff shakes his head at me. "He's dying. I know it." That's what he wants to say, but he doesn't.

Lakuna wraps her arms around him. "Don't think like that."

Cam's hair was brown, so shiny the sun glinted off of it on a rainy day. Now it's puffed out of color, lying tangled on top of his head. And his old suntanned skin is a sickly greenish grey, the color of people lying in a coffin. "And remember that cat?" Cam says. "It made you look disgusting. Your back, ew."

"Shut up, Cam," a voice croaks from behind me.

"Pete! Did I wake you?" I ask. "You're alive," he says.

"Of course I am."

He looks down at his chest. "Nice, almost as good as my tape job on you."

I roll my eyes. "Thanks to you I can't even bend over." My bandages keep me from bending my back so far in every direction, but they did keep my skin from being burnt in the fire. He tries to laugh, a few smalls coughs and a major wince. "Are you in pain?"

"A lot. My ribs and my throat." His voice is raspy like someone who's smoked for twenty years. "How are Lakuna and Mazi?" he asks.

"Fine, stop worrying. We've only been here a few hours. We're not going anywhere. You can sleep."

He rests his head on his arm, and moments later he's gasping, "Can't." A sheen of sweat coats his forehead, and his fingers rake down the hard-packed dirt for something to squeeze until the pain stops. I dig through the supplies until I find a tiny piece of a lost pill. "I don't want it," he says.

I put it in the container of water. "It will knock you out for an hour tops, just long enough for the lipper to take effect, then you'll wake up and feel better."

He sips at the water slowly. As he fades away, the container slips out of his fingers. I push his curls out of his face; his eyes follow me carefully until his eyelids become too heavy for him to keep open. Even after his eyes close, he mumbles something hardly interpretable, "Don't go."

I take his hand. "Never."

My stomach grumbles. Food is gone. Spence said he and Brint went looking earlier today. Apparently they found plenty of nuts and berries, but when they ate them, they wound up puking violently. The fruits from the jungle are gone, burnt to a crisp. When Pete and Cam are well enough, I will go hunting, but for now, I won't risk them dying while I'm trying to find food they won't touch. The protest of my middle against the emptiness is enough for me to drink container after container full of water to have something to hold on to.

The sun dips below the tree line, sending the temperature plummeting. After only minutes, we have no choice but to light a small fire. Everyone bunkers down for the night, getting ready for bed at dusk because the smoke inhalation took a huge toll on the amount of physical activity any of us can do. The cave isn't big enough for all of us to fit, so in the end, everyone is lying on one another with random limbs spread out, and all of us are careful not to touch Pete or lay on Cam to keep him cool. Mazi looks so young when she's sleeping. Her deep brown ringlets fall over the tan of her face, covering the dark beauty mark above her lips. Her body is like a small child's, taking up only half of Spence's. She is dangerously skinny now. She was small before, but now it's unhealthy. Pete's pill has worn off, leaving the aftereffects—drowsiness, drowsiness, and more drowsiness. "You feel better though, don't you?" I ask. He smiles a crooked forced smile against the impacts of the pill.

I don't sleep all of the way through the night, as usual. The howling wind is what wakes me up. The fire has gone out, and every bone in my body feels frozen. I stand up and walk to the mouth of the cave. I want to go get more firewood, but I am not in the mood for the cold water touching my skin. I stand there for a little bit, and then I suck up the that fact I'm going to be cold either way, so I splash into the creek and trudge through the water and into the woods. As soon as I step onto the forest floor, I hear the twigs under my feet crunch. Gathering up the sticks is effortless as well as starting the fire. I do this more for my friends than for me because I won't be back until morning.

I run the way we came to camp for a long way when I hear light footfalls a couple of yards away. I pull up short. *Please don't be a panther. Please don't be a panther.* The only thing I can think of is the unbearable pain of the black cat ripping its claws down my back and sinking its razor-sharp teeth into my leg and ribs. My body tenses. My breathing stops. *Maybe if it doesn't hear me, it'll lose my scent.* Something grabs my shoulder.

"Hayden, what are you doing?" Lakuna asks.

I let out my breath. "I thought you were the panther! I was just going to see Ozalee. I wanted to make sure she was there. I feel like the fire destroyed everything, and I needed to make sure it didn't." Lakuna doesn't say anything. "And I wanted to get warm again, so I'm going to the jungle," I continue.

"I'm coming with you," she says.

The closer we get to the beach, the more the forest turns to jungle, and the blacker and ashier it gets. We reach Ozalee's grave, and I sit on the burnt sand. "Ozalee, I'm sorry we couldn't take you with us, but we had to get out. I know you'll understand. But we all are alive, at least." I feel a slight breeze blow and smell the scent of flowers—she is happy for us. I know she wants me with her but not dead.

"We all miss you. I wish you were here with us. No, not here, I wish you were at your house with your mom," Lakuna whispers.

"Well, that's it. I love you," I say then I stand up and start toward our old camp. I'm pretty sure Lakuna says, "I love you too," but I'm not positive.

Lakuna catches up to me, and we walk in silence to our old camp. Every tree, vine, and leaf is scorched. Nothing lived through the fire. Lakuna groans as our shack comes into view. There is nothing left but a pile of ashes. "I don't get how one lightning bolt can make a whole jungle burn down," Lakuna says.

"Me either."

Lakuna and I decide to cut straight through the jungle to our camp instead of taking the long way from the waterfall. We haven't been through this part of the woods yet, but you'd have to be an idiot to get lost. "If you were home and you could be doing one thing, what would it be? It can't be anything that deals with the people on this island," Lakuna asks. That was random.

"I'd be riding Girl," I answer.

Behind my house in Villa is a barn. My dad built it when we moved there. He knew I had always wanted a horse, and he promised me when we moved to the country he would build a barn and get me a horse, and that he did. The barn he built was good looking, had a red exterior, twelve stalls, and a hay loft. But the barn was nothing in comparison to Girl, the beautiful chestnut horse my dad bought me. She doesn't have any markings on her, and she looks like she was dipped in caramel. When I got her, she didn't have a name, so I decided to name her Daddy's Girl, Girl for short. She has the best personality of any horse I've ever seen, and she glides through the air like a bird. Other than Girl, we have seven horses living in our barn, Lakuna's, Mazi's, Bree's, Brint's, Broppin's, Tinley's, and Ozalee's. I miss Girl's free spirit. I miss her sweet nature. I love riding Girl more than almost anything in the whole entire world, and frankly, I would give a lot right now to do something I like. I mostly think I just miss home. "I want to go home," I say as I pull Lakuna closer to me and give her a hug.

We walk with our arms linked at the elbow until we hit woods again. Then ground disappears from my feet with one quick lurch.

CHAPTER FIVE

I am upside down. I look up and find my feet tied next to Lakuna's, and we're hanging from a tree. This is definitely not normal; this thing was built by someone who knows how to catch prey. The word *someone* lingers on my tongue. We've been snared like a rabbit. Like game. We're going to be eaten. Someone else is on the island! "Lakuna! Someone else is on the island!" Her cheeks are turning red, filling with blood. Not good. My pulse thumps in my temple. I scrunch up and tighten my abs to reach the vines that are holding Lakuna and me. I just need to cut one vine, and then we'll be able to get loose. That's when I feel the dart enter my neck.

My muscles freeze up in my legs then in my arms, and my whole body goes numb. I hang helplessly and watch as someone puts a blindfold over my eyes. I hear the sound of a knife cutting the vines and then the wind on my face as I fall to the ground and land on my back. I can't move at all. I don't know what was in that dart, but whatever it was, it was paralyzing. The ground's hardness leaves from my back, and I feel the up-and-down motion of someone walking. I think I'm being carried. This motion continues for a long time, and the coolness of the deep forest returns to my body. I hear the voices of the people who have kidnapped Lakuna and me, but I can't understand a word they're saying. They sound like a mix between aliens and monkeys. Just then, the blindfold is ripped from my face, and I see our kidnappers.

There are about thirty of them. These are easily the ugliest things I've ever seen in my life. They are only about three feet tall, and their skin is a purplish grey color. They have piercings in their noses and giant holes in their ears. The piercings in their noses don't hold rings but some sort of bone from an animal, and they wear nothing but leaves that cover only their private parts and breasts. *What in the world goes through their minds to make them look like that?* My arm swings down from on top of my chest and

---

smacks one of them in the face. They throw me to the ground and push my hands and legs to the floor. I don't know why I can't move anyway. They shove some bad-tasting thing in my mouth so I can't talk, which is useless. A guy with a headdress yells some gibberish to his followers, and they prop me up and tie my hands with a vine. I guess the guy in the headdress is the chief of the tribe or something. They drag me over to a tree, and we're left alone.

Escape doesn't look easy. They have a large circular area cleared of trees and a fire pit in the center of it. Small huts line the edge of half of the circle, and a patch of what look like spears are next to a big ditch next to one of the huts. A lady with shells tied in her hair lights the wood in the fire pit, and the whole thing ignites in flames. I push myself closer to the tree. Small black-haired children stand in front of Lakuna and I and throw pebbles at our faces. Drool spills from my mouth. I spit the talk blocker from my mouth. "St-stop." I move my tongue around my jaw bone. "Get away." They take off screaming. I don't think they have ever seen a normal person before. Five of the Uglys run over to me and stick a spear at my neck.

I've decided to call the small people the Uglys because every time I look at one of them, I want to throw up. Lakuna and I have been sitting here for a long time; it was morning when we got kidnapped for the second time, and now its sunset. Ten of the Uglys take spears from the patch of weapons and disappear into the forest, probably going hunting. The rest of the Uglys gather around the circle and start singing songs and dancing. I've seen weird stuff like this on television, but I didn't think people actually did it.

"What are we going to do? Do you think they're going to hurt us or something?" she asks.

"Listen. We're going to wait until it gets dark, and then we're going to run," I whisper.

"Let's wait until they go to sleep." By now Griff, Spence, Brint, and Bree will be looking for us. Bree will know we went to Ozalee's grave. I only hope they won't come this way.

It hasn't even been ten minutes when the hunter Uglys return with a full-sized deer on their shoulders. Why couldn't we kill that? We didn't even see one. The Uglys around the fire stop dancing and singing and run over to the deer, ripping it apart and shoving raw meat and fur into their mouths. That is disgusting. I'm next to starved, and I still wouldn't act like that. Thinking of food brings water to my mouth. The Uglys have completely stripped the deer of all meat and fur in a matter of seconds, and they throw the stinking carcass in my and Lakuna's direction. The deer's bloody bones land on our legs. I spit at them. The chief marches over to me. He stares at me, bends down, and slaps my face. No one has ever done that to me. Who does he think he is? I don't even know how to react to something like this. I don't stand up or say anything because I know that will get Lakuna or I hurt, so I just stick my tongue out at him. The chief stares at me some more and then stalks away and yells something at his tribe. They quickly retreat into their huts and leave only two of them outside armed with spears.

It's dark now; this is when Lakuna and I were going to run. We didn't plan for the Uglys to have guards with spears. I look at Lakuna. She has a crease between her eyebrows. "I don't know what to do," she whispers.

Okay, think, think. I push myself into a standing position and run the other way of the giant ditch with a patch of spears. I stop when I reach the first tree of the woods. The ugly guards run over to me and point their spears at my neck; I look past their shoulders. Lakuna gets up and does something I'd never believe. I mean I knew she was a gymnast but not that talented. She places her feet firmly at the edge of the hole and then springs backward into the air, her hands out first. Just when she goes to land, one of the spears cut through the vines tying her hands together, and then she sticks her jump on her feet. How in the world did she manage? I have no idea.

The Uglys heard her thud; one of them turns to her and points the spear at her face. While the ugly guarding me is distracted, I grab the spear from his hand and quickly cut my arms apart. He starts screaming in his alien-monkey voice, and a swarm of Uglys burst out from the shacks. It's common sense to get the heck out of here, so I do. I take off for the woods at a dead sprint. It's too dark outside to see the upcoming trees, and every couple steps or so, one of their branches whip across my face, slicing my already-tender skin. I saw Lakuna jump out of the spear pit and run into the woods. I know it's a waste of my precious time, but I cut her way. I know I'll never catch her, but I just have to make sure I don't find her dead on the forest floor. My eyes scan back and forth for any signs of my friend, and that's when I see the spear coming at me.

In one quick motion, my body flattens to the ground, and the spear that could've ended my life flies over my head. I know the Uglys have found me. If they catch me, I can't even imagine what they'd do to me. I swiftly push myself into a running position and dash toward the closest tree I see. Thank goodness the first branch is low enough for me to pull myself up. One by one, I climb each branch, and one by one, the spears glide past by body, sticking into the tree. It doesn't take me long to get high enough to the point where the Uglys can't throw any further. The branches are dangerously thin where I sit, but I don't dare get lower.

I find a fork in the twigs of the tree and lay my upper body on one limb and my legs on another limb. This is comfortable enough, I guess. There is no sign of Lakuna, and I was wrong—a spear did find my body. Not find exactly, more like graze. The middle of my forearm bleeds heavily, and I have to rip of one of my sleeves to try and stop the blood flow. I tie it in a knot over the gash, not tight enough to form a tourniquet but tight enough where I don't lose too much blood. My wound isn't even that deep, but I'm feeling lightheaded already. I don't know if it's from how much blood I've lost since I've been on this island or if it's from dehydration.

The night winds pick up, and it feels like the temperature drops to below forty degrees. I was cold the other night even with the body heat of eight other people around me and a fire. Now that I don't have either of those, I'm chilled to the bone. Can you get hypothermia when it's forty degrees outside? I think it's a definite possibility; there is no way I can stay here all night. I study the ground below me, making sure the Uglys have disappeared completely. Not positive of the dangers that await me on ground level, I decide to stick to the thicker branches and tree-jump. I do this for a couple of trees then decide its safe enough to get down. Ever so carefully, I make my way to ground level. With not much energy left in my battered body, I start back to our cave.

It takes me the rest of the night and most of the afternoon to get into familiar surroundings. My easy walk has turned into a slouched drag of my feet, and every muscle in my body is screaming for help. My eyelids droop to the point that I can barely hold them open, and my hands are shaking so bad that if someone gave me a glass of water, the liquid would be out of the cup before I could even bring it to my lips. I stare at the ground and try without success not to trip over the ruble in my way. A smile creeps on my face when my feet splash into the water in front of our cave.

"Hayden!" I look up just as Lakuna's arms wrap around my neck. "I thought you were dead," she cries. Tears make their way out of her eyes, which are so blue they appear purple, and run down her ashy cheek.

"I'm good," I mumble. "When did you get back?" I continue. "Late last night," she says.

"How?"

"All of those things went after you, and I knew if I tried to find you, they would come after me. So I didn't. I'm sorry," she sobs.

"It's fine."

She lets go of my neck and studies my face. "Hayden? You're sick," she says.

Duh. I'm not literally sick. I don't have a fever or anything, just dehydrated and tired. Lakuna has cuts on her face from running into trees and bags under her eyes. "Did you sleep today?" I ask.

"How could I?" Lakuna helps me into the cave.

"You're back! By the way, Lakuna made it sound you were dead," Mazi says. "It's a long story," I say. "Where is everyone?"

"Looking for you," Pete says. Just as I called earlier, Bree, Spence, Griff, and Brint are nowhere to be found. "What happened to your arm?" Pete asks.

"A spear happened."

"They got you?" Lakuna asks. She hands me the small piece of blanket. The fire in the cave is burning bright, warming my frozen bones. I untie the knot covering my spear wound and slip down the side of the cave. I lean my head against the fire-warmed stone; I wrap the blanket around my whole body. I want to examine my arm some more, but I'm so, so tired and hungry. Someone has pulled Pete against the side of the cave and sat him up. He examines my arm, and I drop off, thinking for some reason we're back home.

A chill runs up my body and makes my hair rise. I reach for the blanket to pull it back on when Griff says, "Hang on a sec'."

My eyes don't open, but I feel a hot cloth sitting on my forearm, and every time the cloth moves, a stinging pain rises on my limb. I try to move my other arm, but it's too heavy for me to lift. I'm almost positive my friends didn't give me a lost pill, but I can't comprehend why I am unable to move—*is my body too exhausted?* "Are we at the hospital?" I ask. I'm lying on a pillow, and warmth is all around me. I'm still hungry.

"I wish," Griff says.

Why is he taking care of me?

When I awaken fully, the cave is bright with sunlight. How long has it been? The rest of that day and night? My arm is still outstretched from when Griff was working on it, but the rest of my body is covered with the blanket. When I sit up, a wave of black rushes to my head. Lakuna, Mazi, and Bree are awake and sitting in a circle, taking tiny bites of those nuts that are supposed to make you sick. "What are you doing?" I ask.

"We're just so hungry, we don't have another choice."

I crawl to Cam. "Has he been drinking?" I ask. He's so skinny now.

"He hasn't been awake for two days. We can't get him to wake up," Bree says. "He's fading." "Cam," I say. Nothing. "Cam!" I shake his shoulder so hard, he'd pull out of a lost pill. Still nothing. I put my head on his chest and feel the quick up and down of his breathing and the light beat of his heart. My lungs drop into my stomach, and wet drops well up in my eyes.

I pull up his eyelid with my pointer finger, and what used to be a pupil the color of grass in the summer is now a black ball of emptiness. Looking at nothing, lost in the world of unconscious delirium. His head feels like I've just stuck my hand on a stove. I feel so helpless. I do the only thing I can think of, push his hair off his forehead and press his burning lips to mine. "Come on," I say. I shake his hand. "Come on!" I even resort to smacking him. Nothing.

A choke escapes my throat, and in no time I'm crying. Mazi caresses me in her shrunken arms. "He's going to die. I don't know what to do. I can't just watch him go like this," I say. Sobs rack my body. Cam . . . His perfect smile always made me melt. I could tell him anything, and he could trust me with his life. Every time I had a nightmare, his strong arms would wrap around me and keep me safe. When I got attacked by the panther, he was there. He said everything was going to be fine; he caught me when I fell. He saved my life. Now it's my turn to keep him safe, to tell him everything will be okay, to save his life. Only I can't.

My mom once told me everyone brought into your life has a specific purpose and a special place in your heart. I had no idea Cam's place was so big. I had no clue what his purpose was. But now I do. His purpose is to stay with me and keep me safe, not disappear forever.

"I know," Mazi whispers, and I bury my head in her curls. I feel like I'm six again. Every time I got scared, my father would cradle me in a cocoon of warmth. But now I'm wrapped in a girl's arms, and to make it even worse, a girl who's smaller than I am.

I wiggle myself away from Mazi and crawl outside the cave. I slide down the bank of the creek and dip my head in the icy water. I try to massage a bruised spot on my head before I remember my hair is in a braid and rip out a chunk of my scalp. I slip over the edge of sanity and lose it. Cursing and splashing, I roll the rest of my body into the water. I slam my legs into the creek bed, purpling my heels, and put my hands over my eyes. *Keep calm, Hayden.* I focus on my breathing in, out, in, out. *Okay, it's day twenty, only ten more days left, and then you'll be off this godforsaken island. I just have to keep his heart beating for ten more days. Just ten . . .*

The water in the creek makes my body heat drop within minutes, and I have no choice but to get out. I sit on the edge of bank, drawing pictures in the clay with my fingers. I draw a flower, and it looks pretty good, so I add a head and body to it. Soon enough, a poorly illustrated Ozalee is looking at me.

Hang on! My body heat dropped from being in the water. I've got it! In an instant, I'm in the cave and giving orders. "Spence, help me." I am almost positive this will work.

"What?" he says.

"I have an idea. Get Cam."

Spence picks Cam's limp body off the ground and heaves him out the entrance. Spence lays him on the muddy bank of the creek and stands there until I whisk him away. If this doesn't work, I don't want everyone to get there hopes up. I strip Cam of his shoes and shirt and grab hold of his feet. Dragging him is a harder task than it seems. Even though he's lost a lot of weight since we've been here, he weighs way more than I do. I get him into the creek and lay his head on my lap so his nose doesn't flood with water.

"What are you doing?" Griff asks in alarm.

"I was just lying in this a couple minutes ago, and I got chill bumps, which means the water brought my body temperature down. And maybe it will bring his down too," I say with uncertainty. I can't keep this from him. His brother is dying. It's either he gets his hopes up or Cam dies.

Griff hands me a rag. I dip it into the stream and place it on Cam's head. I feel the hair on the back of his neck stand up, and I pull his arm above the water—bumps have risen. This is a good sign. Five minutes pass. Fifteen. Then twenty. No sign of health. I let his arm splash into the water; Griff falls to his knees on the bank.

"I'm sorry, I tried," I whisper.

"He's not going to make it, is he?" he pleads to me.

I shake my head. "I don't know. I'm not a doctor like my mom. I only know the basics."

Griff hunches against the rock. His hands grip his hair. "Pete told me he's been shoving fever fighters down his throat."

"And?" I ask.

"He gave up. He said there was no point on wasting the medicine if he's using it for something that's going to die."

I can't imagine a world without Cam. A world that would leave Griff twinless. A bond of a sibling is something that can't be broken, not through poverty or disaster or even death. The bond is forever. Like you're bound by an unspoken oath you will never leave each other. And when one does leave the other, they are never really gone. You'll always feel them around you, in the wind or the fragrance of your home, the dreams you can't control. They will find a way to get to you again just to tell you they are doing well. And to say they love you. I want to tell him this, that he will never really be gone. But I can't. My throat is tight with tears. I know how he feels. I've been through it. I knew Ozalee wasn't going to make it the second I saw her wound, and Griff knows now. Cam is lost. I lay Cam's head on the pebbles in the bottom of the creek, letting the water flow over him. Speeding up the process of his death. Griff looks over me; he can sense I have no control over what happens now. His neck jerks back, and his eyes grow big. I spin my head around and stare at the thing in the water. Ever so slowly, it opens its eyes.

A grin sweeps across my face; I bring his face out of the water. He chokes the fluids out of his lungs with the help of me holding his head up. His hollow eyes look around for any sign of his friends, and the moment he finds mine, he flashes his smile, my smile. I never thought I would see his dimples again. "I thought you weren't gonna come back," I say. To some people, my words wouldn't make sense, but even with his fever, he understands me.

"Psh, are you kidding me?" he laughs and then coughs. "Shhh, someone get me some fever pills," I say.

Griff slides down the bank slick with mud, his face enlightened. Before he knows what he's doing, he yanks Cam up and hugs him. I can hear the sniffles he tries to hold in. Once he lets go, Cam's head bashes into my lap, and his hands come up to squeeze his temples.

"Griff, I know you were scared for him, but he can't really hold himself up yet, so please don't do that!" I say. My voice cracks at the end of the sentence. I'm crying.

"I'm sorry," he gasps as he hands me the pills. We give him more than double his normal dose. Griff and I help Cam back into the cave and sit him on chilled stone, away from the fire.

Everyone smiles. Pete looks at me in disbelief. "I didn't do it," I say. I put Cam's saturated clothing on top of him, trying to keep his temperature down.

"Yes, she did!" Griff squeezes me until I yelp.

Now that Cam is with us again. Everyone gets back to more serious business. "We're starving," Lakuna says.

"I'll go deeper to see if I can find a different kind of nut or berry. If not, we'll all have to go. Maybe to the other coastline, we can't go ten days without food," Bree says.

"I'll come. It's not a good idea to go by ourselves anyway with those ugly things out looking for Lakuna and Hayden," Brint says. They don't even bother to take the bow, considering neither of them has ever shot, but before they leave, I see Brint shove the knife down his shorts. I would volunteer to go, but frankly, I'm still worn from my fleeing from the Uglys, and I'm not leaving Cam now.

Pete's chest is improving; the lipper plant goo has stopped the bleeding and replaced it with white blisters. He's strong enough to stand by himself now; I've wrapped the bandages around his back to make sure they stay in place. He says he's had no appetite, but he's been drinking. He refuses to take any more lost pills, and he will not let me get his water for him anymore because he knows I'll drug him. I have no tolerance to see him in such pain. I'm not one to run from blood and wounds, but I cannot tolerate watching someone in ongoing pain. He can't sleep. Maybe after twenty hours of being awake, he'll nap for an hour or so only to be woken up by a new surge of agony. I sing him Ozalee's song to calm him down, and from what I've observed, it is the only thing that will get him to rest upon request.

I watch Pete as he dozes off before I turn my attention to Cam. He's still in bad condition but getting better. His black eyes have turned to their original emerald color, and he is sweating, which means the fever has broken. I offer him water, and he drinks willingly. Not being able to do anything else for him, I lean against the wall across from Pete and Cam. I place my body around the curve of our makeshift home and pull my shirt up, letting the coolness of the wall sooth my scabbed skin. I lean my head on my hand and watch the fire, the orange, red, and yellow dancing in an array of beauty. I see random images of things with every flame that flares up and dulls down again. I stare at this for a long time before I am even able to break away my gaze.

"You know you've been staring at that for over an hour?" Cam says. "Huh?"

"The fire, you've been watching at it for over an hour."

"It's kind of hard not to if you really look at it." he says.

He tries to see the intriguing point of the flames but loses interest in no time. "I'm not seeing it,"

"Your loss." He smirks and closes his eyes. There is no way on earth I'm letting him go to sleep. It's not that I don't want him to be well rested. It's the fact that if he goes to sleep, I'm scared he won't wake up. He's better than he was, but by the feel of his forehead, he's still on death's door. "Are you hungry at all?" It's not like I'm going to give him food because there is none at the moment, but asking him doesn't hurt. He doesn't say anything, but instead, he wrinkles his nose and pretends to gag.

Just then Lakuna walks in the cave, her body still glistening from the creek water. Her shirt, shorts, and shoes have been removed. I notice how Cam's eyes move up and down her body, taking her in. Blonde hair that falls to her shoulders, purple blue eyes, and a perfectly proportioned frame. Her good attitude adds to the jealousy I feel about her. I'm envious of Mazi too, but not in the same way. I mean, she's beautiful with her dark curls, black eyes, and bronze skin, but her attitude is so abnormal compared to everyone else's. She doesn't care about anything, and she takes nothing seriously. It's a kind of attitude you try to put up with, not have.

I don't stand out in the looks category. I don't have the blonde hair or the perfect ringlets that so many people notice. I have normal brown waves, eyes that change from blue to green depending on the clothes I'm wearing, and a muscular frame I honestly hate. Lakuna can get a guy with a snap of her finger. I've seen it a million times and sat idly by staying silent like usual. I've never been much of a talker especially to the opposite sex, but conversation from me is natural when it comes to Pete, Cam, Griff, Spence, and Brint. Mazi, on the other hand, is a huge talker, and although her looks seem to be working to attract guys, she's never grabbed one until Spence.

Mazi and Spence are a rarity though. Living in Villa, a more moderate block in Gipem, people under the age of sixteen don't usually have a paramour. In places such as Riverelli, a poor block, deaths are common because of starvation or pitiable medical treatment. Hence the reason people start trying to find a mate at age thirteen. Since most citizens there die before they turn fifty, that's the only way to keep the population up. Since Mazi will be sixteen next year and Spence is already sixteen, their relationship is permitted. At least one person of a relationship has to be sixteen or older. Any younger and the relationship is strictly prohibited. Some stupid rule President York made up to "sustain a substantial race."

I pick up splashing in the creek and assume it's Spence, Griff, and Mazi, but that's when Bree and Brint burst in to the caves entrance yelling, "We have to leave here now!"

"What? Why?" I ask. Their faces are bright red, and their breathing is abnormally fast. They have been running for a long time.

"Those things that had you and Lakuna, they saw us! We ran here to get you guys. We have to go now," they pant.

"Why wouldn't you just hide in a tree like I did?" I scream at them. "You have to use your heads out here!"

They ignore me and throw all of our supplies in the blanket, and Bree hauls it over her shoulder. I grab the basket and the container Darious left us and fill them up in the stream just in case we can't find any more water. Brint has recovered from his insect sting. He helps Pete up and half carries him out of the cave. Spence grabs Mazi who still has a hard time walking because of her burns. I put Cam's arm over my shoulders, and Lakuna helps Griff with his leg. I throw the remains of our fire into the creek.

We take flight around the bend of the creek and out of the canyon. In the distance, we hear the alienlike screams of the Uglys, and we push our reckless jog into a run. It's hard not to trip over the sticks and leaves of the forest floor with all of the people and supplies we have to deal with, but we manage to keep a steady pace for a little while. As I run, I notice the temperature has gotten colder, and my breath comes from my mouth in giant puffs. The cracking of sticks and leaves turns into soft crunching of the ground. I stop and listen for any signs of pursuit, and there are some, barely. The screams have almost transformed into a whisper. I decide its safe enough to stop. Plus, it's getting dark, and who knows what kind of predators lurk in the shadows of the forest?

They slow to a stop, and that's when I notice my surroundings. What used to be a woodsy forest is now a vast expanse of overly sized trees, trees I don't have a name for. They look like pines, but the roots curve in every which way to form a shelter of a sort. And the ground! Oh, this is not my type of atmosphere. The ground is covered in a thin layer of snow! Mazi gasps as she realizes the fact that we have to sleep here tonight—she doesn't take to cold well either. Even in the midst of summer, when the air conditioning is blowing in my house, Mazi and I are bundled up in sweatshirts and sweatpants. But here, we're dressed in thin shirts, one blanket, and no way to keep warm. "Well," Bree sighs, "I guess we can make camp here." She points to a large domelike structure made of roots.

"Why don't we go a little further to see if it gets warmer, or we can find food?" I ask. I'm ravenous, beyond starving; I'm weak because of lack of food. She points to Pete keeled over in pain and Cam massaging his own temples and Griff limping with Lakuna's help.

It would be dangerous to light a fire in a tree, but since it's below thirty-two degrees, we have no choice. The dome is large enough that I can stand up straight; everyone else has to bend their head. Sometimes being the shortest of the group has its advantages. Thankfully, the giant tree has blocked the snow from our makeshift home, leaving a soft bed of pine needles in its place. Instead of lighting one fire, we light two. I'm kind of glad because the chills bumps on my body are the biggest they've ever been, and I'm shivering so bad it takes me at least five minutes to get out the sentence, "We have to cover our tracks."

Lakuna and I slip out of the roots run in the same direction of the tracks we left before. We cover at least a mile, sweeping brush over our footsteps to hide what direction we came from, and then take to the trees, making sure not to leave any signs of our return to our dome. Our shelter is easy to tell from the other trees because of the steady flow of smoke coming from the top of the tree. *Marvelous, what is this?* Lakuna and I climb higher up the tree to the very tip. Right on the point of the trunk is a giant hole. This is no doubt manmade. Nothing this helpful is natural, and holes aren't on tops of trees. Amazed with our new discovery, Lakuna and I slide down the trunk and squirm through the roots. "The coolest thing is up there,"

Lakuna says, no chattering of her teeth at all. She is always hot. "This tree's trunk opens at the top so the smoke can get out," she says.

"Good, we won't burn to death," Pete says through clamped teeth.

My friends lie down for the night all huddled in a big group. Spence's stomach is pressed against Mazi's back with her feet curled up in a ball. Bree stuck on Mazi's belly and Lakuna is hunched against Bree. I cover them with the blanket and thank god Darious gave us a huge one. Brint still sits by the fire with Griff by his side. I pull my hands inside my sleeves and tuck my feet under the blanket. Cam leans against the wall and offers his lap as a pillow for me. I just close my eyes when I feel his hot fingers start to write letters on my cheek. The same way he did the first day we met.

When I was ten, such a small naive girl at the time, President York had to draft men from Villa into the Center's navy. Gipem has just started war with the nation directly south of us. In school, we are forbidden to learn about any country other than our own, so that is all of the information I ever got. The night my father was drafted, our family was invited to a feast in honor of the brave souls going into war the following week. Of course I was a mess, but I tried to stay strong for my mom and Ozalee. At the feast, the families were assigned tables to sit and eat. I sat in the seat labeled *Hayden Kolter*. My family sat on one side of the table, and another family sat on the other side of the table. The name tag across from mine read *Cam Malrook*. This name sounded familiar, but I couldn't quite put my finger on it. When he sat down, I immediately recognized him. He was in my year at school, but I never talked to him. He was always surrounded by a big group of people, and I was never one to start a conversation, so I just stuck with Mazi, Bree, Lakuna, and Pete most of the time. His eyes were red and puffy, showing he'd been crying, so I decided not to make eye contact with him. Partially because I didn't want to make him feel bad and somewhat because I would never know what to say to someone of such a social status, schoolwise that is.

"I look pretty awful, don't I?" he said, directing his question at me. "You could look better."

He laughed and smiled, a smile I reluctantly returned. He presented me to his family, and I introduced him to mine. Ozalee was intrigued by Griff the moment she met him, not his looks but his talent. He took her hand and told her to think of a number between one and five. She told me her number, and then Griff fiddled with her hand for a little bit and then said the number she told me out loud, getting it right every time. I don't know, but he couldn't do it with me or Cam. Griff took to Ozalee pretty well too. It was impossible not to.

When we were waiting for our meal, I had my face pushed into my hands, bored out of my mind. My mom had braided my hair down my back, giving me nothing to play with. "Would you like to play a game?" Cam asked.

"Sure," I said.

He placed his finger on my cheek and drew something. "Guess what letter that is," he said.

"Do it one more time," I said, not because I didn't know the letter but because every time his finger ran along my skin, I tingled. It felt so good. We played this game the rest of the night, and I didn't get bored once. At dessert, he asked me why I got bumps on my skin every time he drew a letter, and I told him it was because it felt good. He smiled my dimpled smile, and that's when it clicked. I had a new friend. After that, Cam introduced me to Spence and Brint, and within one day, there was our group.

I wake with a jolt when a huge gush of wind sweeps through our new home. Immediately my body convulses with shivers. My teeth are chattering, and I feel them nipping my tongue, but I'm too cold to care. After a minute or two of this, my abs begin to hurt from shaking so bad. The fire is still burning, and Cam has turned his letter drawing into a movement he knows I like. He starts at my forehead and traces my facial features down to my neck and then back up. At the moment, it only makes me shake harder. He looks down on me. I raise my neck off his lap, and he lies down next to me. He fashions some pine needles into a lump, and I rest my head on them. Since his shirt is loose enough, I squeeze myself into it, keeping my hands under my top as well. With him blocking the wind from my body and my face buried in his chest, I fall asleep.

"You know what, Spence? Shut up. I'm so sick of hearing you complain. We're all going through the same stuff here, not just you! And you don't even have parents to worry about. You know where mine are? Not here! The people you love are standing right in front of you!" Brint yells.

This is a great thing to wake up to in the morning. I'm still snuggled up against Cam; he must feel my ribs expand when I take a deeper breath because he tightens his hold on me. I turn to see Spence's jaw flex, and I can tell he's debating whether to turn Brint into raw meat. I know he has the power to; he clears six foot four, and his muscles bulge every time he moves. He's at somewhat of a disadvantage though. Yes, he is strong, but Brint is quick and armed. Cockily, he swings the ax around his ring finger.

"You two are acting like a bunch of two-year-olds," Pete snaps. "Brint, put the ax down. We all know you're not going to use it. And, Spence, he's right! Stop complaining. You're in the best shape here, and Mazi is right there, so shut it!"

"I love more people than Mazi," Spence whispers.

"And where are these people, Spence?" Brint hisses through his teeth.

Spence looks away. Spence used to love other people, but that was a long time ago. He had just turned eight when his father was diagnosed with cancer. His mother had his father sent to the Center for medical treatment, and she went with him. They were forced to put Spence in the children's home. They promised to come back, but after four years of waiting, he gave up all hope and forgot what trust was. He hasn't seen them since.

Pete rips the ax from Brint's hand and throws it across the dome, sticking it into a root. I wiggle out of Cam's shirt and try to stretch my limbs, which are completely and utterly destroyed. My head aches from malnourishment and lack of fluids. The cuts on my face have scabbed over, but the bruises on my throat are still painful. The claw marks on my back and ribs are unhealable without doctors, and the burns on my hands and knees require medical handling. As for my forearm and calf, I have a sense they are done. I've lost feeling in both, and I highly doubt I'll ever regain it. And to top it all off, I'm filthy.

Our supplies are growing limited. A blanket, an ax, a knife, a bow and nine arrows, matches, the empty shot thing, a needle, string, bandages, a little over three sleeping pills, an empty basket, and a container full of water, which will deplete fast if it has to keep nine people alive. Through the fire and fleeing the Uglys, we have managed to lose the flashlight, the goggles, two shells, and three arrows. No food.

Bree hands me the container of water, and I take a sip, careful not to drink too much and save some for my friends. "There is no water here. We'd have to backtrack. We tried, but we heard those Uglys still yelling," she informs me.

"How would you know?" I say. "We looked. No food either."

"Who's we?" I ask. They couldn't have looked hard enough.

"Spence and I." Darn, Spence has enough hunting experience to find food, animals, or plants.

"May I?" I ask, reaching for the bow.

"Be my guest. Know-it-all," Bree says. I've been putting food in her belly for the past twenty days, and if she hasn't figured out I have enough sense to keep myself and them fed, she is highly mistaken.

"And when your stomach is empty tonight and everyone else's is full, don't come crying to me! By the way, you could melt the snow over the fire, genius!" I yell as I grab the knife, one arrow, and stomp out. My exit would've been more prevalent, but I had to stop to get around the stupid roots.

I search for a useable tree to hunt in and scale the branches with ease. After an hour or so with no luck of animal life, I start to cut away at the bark. I slice past the hard outer layer, and soon my knife is chopping off the soft, tender innards of the tree. I've eaten bark before when I've hunted. If I got hungry, I would just chew on the bark of the tree I was sitting in. It's not harmful to your body. My friends won't be happy about my coming home empty handed, but bark is better than nothing. Just as I'm about to climb down, I see a movement in the corner of my eye. I look to my left to find a huge bird of brown and green flying out of its nest. If the bird has a nest, then maybe it has eggs. In a matter of seconds, I have my hands on four large eggs.

"I see you found food," Spence says. I jump so high, I'm scrambling to keep hold of all of my newest treasures. It's disturbing how he can appear out of nowhere without a sound. "Did I scare you?" he laughs.

"No, I like to randomly jump. That's my favorite hobby, you know?"

"I'll be sure to keep that in mind."

"I'm a big girl. I can hunt by myself. You can keep that in mind too," I say.

"That's not going to happen when I have seven people in my ear telling me to go find you," he says.

"Well, you tell those seven people I can handle myself."

The walk back to camp takes some time, but I don't mind. I mean, the weather is freezing, but it gives me time to clear my head and get away from things. I don't ask Spence why Brint was yelling at him this morning; it's not hard to figure out since Spence tends to complain a lot. Most days his presence annoys me because of his extreme immaturity. I'm not one to judge because I'm pretty immature myself, but he just doesn't know when to stop! I can be both—mature and not. But being here on this island is the first times I've ever seen him pull himself together and stay calm for more than two seconds.

"I know this isn't much, but it's better than nothing," I say to my friends, handing them each a piece of bark, careful to avoid Bree's hands. I pass out the eggs and tell everyone to split them in half.

"But they're uneven?" Pete says.

"Oh, Bree's not eating," I say and shoot her a look. She doesn't make eye contact with me. She's sitting against the tree, holding her stomach. I can't say she's been through more than me, but she has been through a lot.

"Never mind, give her mine." I toss her a piece of bark. No one has been through more than me—that's a fact. My dad gone, mothering thirteen people at times, being stranded on an island, Ozalee dead. On occasion, I find myself huddled in a corner, holding my chest, afraid at any moment my heart will burst. An irreversible feeling of hate crosses my mind; I don't know what I hate yet. As of now, I hate myself for letting them take us, for letting my friends get hurt, for letting Ozalee down.

"Did you hear that?" whispers Griff. "Here what?" Mazi says.

Griff puts his hand up to silence us. *Crack*. I hear it. Branches cracking. But we're all here? Leer, they could make sticks crack. These sticks are breaking on accident though. Leer aren't careful enough. They don't try to be quiet. These footsteps are precise, common to me. These are hunter's feet. I cover my mouth to hide my gasp. We are being hunted. Ever so carefully, I pull my bow and arrows closer to my body and position myself on my knees.

"What are you doing?" Cam panics. And just like that, the roots smash into a million pieces, and I'm staring into the jaws of a beast.

CHAPTER SIX

I don't have time to load my weapon before the monster pushes my shoulders to the ground. It opens its mouth, revealing long fangs dripping in saliva. I try to throw it off me, but it's no use. The creature is too heavy. I squeeze my eyes shut and wait for the searing pain that came with the panther bite except it never comes. Instead, I am pulled to my feet and running. The woods fly by me. I hear the snarls behind me and push my legs faster. My lungs seem to burst with every breath I take. And while fleeing once again, I have made a conclusion: when your life is on the line, you don't get tired. One hundred percent true.

I don't know who I'm following or where I'm going, but I keep running. The second I begin to cross from winter to spring, the rabid snarls of the beasts die down. As it has three times already, the world alters before my eyes. The overly sized trees and snow have disappeared. In their place a beautiful meadow of flowers, blossoming at all different colors and sizes over my head or below my feet. I can smell the springtime in the air, sweet and pure. A shallow stream of water trickles from a distant mountain and into a small clear pool at the end of the meadow. This is a place that reminds me of home, my dream home, Tibbet. And if this reminds me of home, I'm almost certain a new nightmare will await me here because as I have come to learn in the past twenty two days, everything beautiful is deadly.

The breathing of my friends comes in loud huffs; I wait at the edge of a meadow as my group gathers around me.

"I think they're gone." Her voice rises at the end of her sentence as she sees the creature leap out of a tree, directly on top of her. Before it can bury its teeth in Lakuna's skull, I shoot an arrow down its throat. I twist around to see if there are more, but none come into sight. Lakuna lies gasping on the ground, chest ripped open by the beast's claws. Not a death blow, but it will require stitches.

"Give me the first-aid kit!" Pete shouts. He completely forgets about his chest. Spence scrambles to give him the needle and thread.

Humpty Dumpty fell off a wall. Humpty Dumpty had a great fall. All the king's horses and all the king's men couldn't put Humpty together again. But Pete is more handy than the ignorant king and his men. Pete can put Lakuna together again. With stitching utensils in hand, Pete tears off her shirt and surprisingly doesn't pay attention to her breasts. Bree and Mazi have to pull Spence and Brint away, knowing Lakuna wouldn't want observers, and it annoys them they are so attracted to her. For once, they know how I feel all the time. Griff grabs her hand. "It's just a cut. The panther was worse."

"It's cut over the bite, Griff," Lakuna cries.

Pete works quickly and steadily, securing the ripped skin in place. Her gasping gradually dies down to panting. I push the beast away from her face so its blood stops running down her spine. I know it's dead but it still frightens me. It looks like a badger excluding its feet turning outwards instead of straight, milky red eyes and fangs that hang over its muzzle. A possessed badger. Impossible, just like everything else in this manmade hell. I've officially decided this island isn't natural, the animals too dangerous, the environment too different, the feel of the place, too haunting.

Lakuna pushes Pete away from her. She seems to totally overlook the pain in her chest. She grabs hold of her foot. She winces at the touch then screams an awful sound coming from the very pit of her stomach. "What is it?" Griff asks.

"My foot! It's burning!" she screeches. Pete looks over it but finds nothing. He probes the bones to see if there is a break, but he can't catch one. All of the sudden Lakuna turns to me. "This is your fault," she accuses. "You knew we were being hunted. This whole thing is your fault," she says.

"But I—" I start.

"I don't want to hear it. Stop trying to blame everyone else. We wouldn't be here if you used your brain, if you even have one." She's yelling now horrible things at me, and with each word comes a stab to my heart. Pete forces the rest of the fourth lost pill down her throat. Not because she's in pain but because I am. He knows I'm barely holding myself together as it is, and she's not helping. The pill wears in, and she slips away, her eyes trained on me, hating me. She should. So should everyone else here. But they don't, not yet. She has cracked; I thought she would last longer than Mazi or Bree. She was so good at controlling herself, getting over things. She was a best friend of mine until now.

I see myself in sections, sections that my life consists of. Section one: hobbies. Section two: survival. Section three: love. I have exactly fourteen people left I love; only thirteen love me back. The part of me that was hers flows from my body like the heat did in the winter woods leaving bitterness and cold in its place. Leaving me missing her already.

The sun has long past gone down, and the stars have popped up in the night sky. I fill my lungs with the scent of flowers and warm air. I know my friends are around here somewhere. I don't bother looking for them. I don't even care what supplies we have left or how we use them. I just want some sleep. I slept last night, but my endless shivering woke me up consistently. I find a patch of red flowers that tower above my head and create a little nest out of them, pushing down the sides so they cocoon me in a soft bed.

"You should see yourself. You look horrible," Cam says. He somehow found me in the middle of the night and took up half of my tiny nest.

"I know. I can feel it," I say. My eyes have swelled up, and an itchy rash covers my skin. I should've taken more precaution; I've always been allergic to pollen. I push myself out of the nest and trudge to the little creek. I strip off my shirt, shoes, and socks and submerge myself in the water. I use the tiny pebbles at the bottom to scrub the dirt, dead skin, and pollen from my body. When I let the water flow over my face, I immediately feel the relief of the pollen washing away. I snort the water in and out of my nose and mouth to clear my sinuses. Then I put my hands behind my head and just lie there.

Cam joins me; he sits on the gravel that surrounds the creek. "Do you feel better?" he asks. "Better than I did," I say.

"Here, I picked you something," he says and holds out his hand, revealing an aqua blue flower. "Thanks." I sniff the petals and sneeze.

"Maybe you shouldn't have it," he laughs and reaches for it.

"No! I want it!" I pull it out of his grasp. I look around the field, trying to find any blue flowers, but there are none.

"How did you find this?" I ask. "It took a while."

"Why blue?"

"It's your favorite color, isn't it?" "Yeah. How did you know?" I test.

"It's not hard to figure out. Your room is blue, and you always paint your nails blue," he answers.

My room is blue. I painted it the year we moved in, and my nails are usually painted blue. I do that because I think it shows a little part of me. "I didn't think you noticed that kind of stuff," I say.

"I notice more than you think," he smiles my smile. "Like what?" I ask.

"Like how you always chew gum when you play soccer." I do chew gum when I play soccer—it brings good luck. He continues, "Like how you only roll the window down enough to stick your fingers out in Coach's car because you hate the wind in your face. Like how you clean the bathroom every night because it aggravates you when people's toothbrushes stand crooked. Like how you can sit at the kitchen table for hours and write random quotes and poems. Like how you're always playing with something in your left hand." He points to my left hand where I'm knotting and unknotting the stem of my flower. I always have something in my left hand because I don't write with that hand, and I can't stand sitting still. And he's right—I hate the wind in my face, crooked toothbrushes irritate me, my dream is to become an author, hence the writing.

The look on my face must show something because he steps closer to me and wraps his arms around me. For a moment, I just stand there, not knowing how to react, and then I hug him back. I've hugged him before, but this time is different. Something stirs inside of me. I don't know what it is. It makes my insides tingle. I don't want to let go. He pushes my chin up so I am forced to meet his gaze. I feel my eyes fill with tears. "It's going to be okay, Hayden."

"You always say that, but it's never true. You almost died. I almost died. And look at Pete! He can't even walk," I whisper.

"What if I promise?" he asks. "People break promises," I say. "I swear," he counters.

"On what?" I ask.

"My life." That's a definite no; I won't let him swear on his life. I decide to take his swear but on my life instead. Of course I don't tell him this because he'll just take it back.

"Okay," I mumble.

A look of pain crosses his face, but he still shakes his head. He takes my beat-up face in his cool hands and smashes his lips to mine.

I am so shocked I yank away. "Cam!"

His eyes grow large. "I-I-I'm so sorry," he stutters.

I can feel the question cross my face. "No don't be." I felt something. Something little, a burning in the pit of my stomach the second his lips touched mine. He gets closer and, gently this time, kisses me. The flames shoot up inside me, and I try with all I have not to pull away. The only boy I've ever kissed is Pete, in times of loss and pain. When he or I needed something soothing, it was him. But now the only two people in the world are me and Cam. His kiss is forceful. Not with strength, but passion. Neither one of us stops. We keep our lips locked, wanting to hold this moment for always. But that doesn't happen. As soon as I see Pete looking at us, I push Cam away, and he knows it's time to stop.

"Well, we better get back to the group." "No! Lakuna hates me," I whimper.

"Like I said, it will be okay." I hesitate, so he grabs my hand and yanks me forward. Even though he's weak from his fever, he's still stronger than I'll ever be. I trudge forward, and we quickly find our group.

They have made a camp on the base of the creek. Before the pebbles start, they have created eight flower nests, and in the pebbles is one leaf bed. It has no part of flowers but leaves from the winter woods.

"That one is for you," Mazi says, "because we know you're allergic to flowers." "Thanks," I say.

Lakuna's eyes track me down through the crowd that is my friends. I see Griff tap her shoulder and then say something to her, and she looks away. I bury my face in my knees. Why did she instantly start hating me? I don't know. I peek out of my little ball and see my friends are sitting in a circle, including me. They make attempts at bringing me into their conversation, but I whisk them away with only a couple words. Mazi hands me a handful of Dandelions, "They're edible," she says, so I take a bite. They are bitter and sweet. They taste awful, but they're still food so I get over it.

The most exciting thing any of us do today is eat dandelions and leaves and fill our bellies with much-needed food. Even though we use most of the day to catch up on sleep, we've decided we're going to have a person keep watch round the clock just in case the Uglys find us or a panther or the mutated badgers. We only have to keep watch when everyone else is sleeping, and we'll switch shifts so we can all get a chance to nap. Mazi filled me in on the whole badger story because I was still kind of fuzzy about it. Apparently, the badger pinning me down got an ax to the back. Once we started running, they took to the trees and tried to jump on us, but Spence, Brint, and Griff killed the ones that tried to attack us, and of course, I killed the one that attacked Lakuna. The rest of the badgers trailing us wouldn't come into the meadow for some strange reason.

I've avoided Lakuna today. I hate that she's mad at me; I honestly don't know what I did. I've accepted the fact this whole thing is my fault. What does she want me to do about it? Apologize? My mother always said to be the bigger person but that's not me. That's not who I am. I stick to how I feel, and no one can ever change that.

I pull Pete away from Griff. "I don't know what I did," I tell him. "Me either." He doesn't make eye contact with me.

"What? Did I anger you too?" I ask. "No." He stands up.

"Wait. What's wrong then?" "Nothing."

"Pete, please tell me."

He turns to me. "You and Cam, huh?" "What?"

He wipes the sweat from his forehead. "I saw you kiss." "It was in the moment," I say defensively.

"But you like him," he says.

"No, I don't." I can't tell whether I'm lying or not. "Pete, you're my best friend. I love you. You know I do."

He gently wraps his arms around my waist. "I know. You realize Cam and I do not get along, right?"

I laugh, "It's hard to share Griff, isn't it?"

Night comes quickly, and Cam and I are conveniently assigned first watch. We start by sitting back to back, all supplies at our side, but only a couple minutes through, I crawl into his lap. "So what else have you figured out about me?" I ask and look up at him.

"Hmmm . . . you absolutely hate it when people tell you what to do. You like to be your own person."

"And that bothers you," I whisper. "What? No. I like everything about you."

"Hardly. Am I perfect? Not even close," I say. Pete. Pete. Pete. His name thumps in the back of my head. What am I doing? I can't have conversations like this with Cam; I can't hurt Pete that way.

"You don't think highly of yourself at all. You don't see yourself the way others see you." The way others see me? Others see me as a normal teenage girl whose dad died. And if they don't see me like that, they see nothing at all.

Cam keeps talking about school and other stuff that I don't pay attention to. I'm having an extremely hard time keeping my eyes open, and my head drops every couple of minutes. Once in a while, he'll say something louder, and I'll drift back into consciousness but lose it again. When I prop my head up on my hand, he notices. Without a word, he leans back on his elbows, letting me rest my head on his chest. He continues with what he was saying, but after his fourth word, he's talking to himself.

"Cam, we can take over now," Spence and Mazi say to him.

Spence laughs when he sees me curled up on Cam's chest. "I guess assigning her first watch wasn't the smartest idea," he says.

"It's cool," Cam says. He starts to pick me up, but I tell him I can walk. "Good night," he says.

I cuddle up next to Pete by the gravel. It's not comfortable, but I want him to know he's still my number one. Even in his sleep, the instant he feels my body heat next to him, he wraps his arm around me protectively, and tonight I fall asleep feeling perfectly safe.

CHAPTER SEVEN

I wrestle my way out of Pete's arms and plant a kiss on his forehead. Griff and Lakuna have fallen asleep on guard duty; I wake them and tell them to go to bed. I take the knife and walk upstream to where it widens. It takes some time and a lot of patience, but I finally get what I came for. Nine fish. I gather dandelions, some sunflower seeds, and nine flat rocks. I haul my new findings back to camp.

"I got food," I tell Bree and Mazi, the only ones awake. I place the rocks down and put the dandelions on top, covering each with a fish and sunflower seeds.

Mazi laughs, "Salad?"

"One of my specialties," I say.

Bree takes a bite of hers. "Not bad. The ones you make at home are better."

I smile and give my salads to my friends as they wake up.

By the position of the sun in the sky, I can tell it's around noon. Ever since morning, all we've done is gorged ourselves on dandelion salad and washed off in the creek. I decide to keep my recently washed hair down instead of putting it in a braid. I'm scrubbing my clothes clean when Lakuna approaches me.

"Hayden?"

"What?" I snap.

"I'm sorry," she says.

"There is nothing to be sorry about," I say because there isn't. My mind has been made up. This is my fault. No one or nothing can change that.

"There is. I was wrong. To be mad at you, I mean."

Just to humor her, I mumble, "Okay." I don't truly mean it. I just don't want her thinking I'm mad at her.

88

Halfway through our conversation, the sky fills with dark clouds, and it starts to drizzle. As if on cue, the meadow overloads with butterflies and rabbits. I grab my bow and load it with an arrow, blistering a rabbit in the side. The rain turns into torrential downpour, and my clothes are drenched faster than I can say my own name. Spence, Griff, Brint, and Lakuna refuse to go back into the winter wonderland in fear of the badgers. The mountain is at least a day's hike, but as of right now, that is the only choice of shelter we have. Another forest is on the other side of the meadow, but it's a way longer hike than the mountain, and who knows what type of predators lurk in there. The steady stream of water expands to a river in no time. We urgently gather our belongings and head toward the mountain.

The butterflies flutter all around us, flapping their wings in my ears and face.

"Look at that one!" Bree shouts and points her finger at a giant silver butterfly. The glorious creature lands on Mazi's wrist. Her breath catches in awe. Even though she has so many things to be sad about, Mazi somehow finds the joy of the silver gift and lets out a giggle. "It's so pretty," she chirps. The butterfly points its back end closer to her wrist, looking like it's going to lie down and rest; instead it sticks its butt against her skin and opens a flap in its abdomen. A gold needle pokes out and buries itself in her skin.

Her scream pierces through the air and rings out in the meadow. "Get it out! Get it out!" she panics.

Spence rips the golden stinger out of her skin. "Are you okay?"

"I'm fine. It just scared me." "You sure?" he presses.

"Yes! I'm fine," she says in an aggravated tone.

"Okay then, let's keep going," Brint says. "I'm getting soaked."

"Too late for that," Griff says.

We trudge through the flowers, getting closer to the mountain. I'm completely and entirely intrigued with a tiny red moth when I'm yanked to the ground. "What the heck?" I say irritated. I turn to find Mazi lying on the ground holding her wrist. "Mazi?" I ask.

"What?" she cries.

"I thought you said you were okay?"

"I'm just a little dizzy." She tries to stand up but falls back down. Her efforts go from barely trying to thrashing frantically to get up. She flops on her back and gasps for air. *What is she doing?* In a matter of seconds, her breathing slows and her eyes go blank.

"Mazi!" I kneel down beside her and press my head to her heart. *Thump . . . Thump . . .* and no more. Spence pushes me out of the way and checks the pulse on her neck.

"Mazi? Mazi!"

Pete's face automatically takes on the look of concentration he has when working on complicated projects. Then he presses his lips to hers.

"Pete! Quit it! She has a boyfriend!" I say. He doesn't even care. He clamps her nose shut. Her chest rises and falls. *What is he doing? Sucking out her lungs?* "Stop!" I yell at Pete. I don't know what he is doing, kissing her, killing her maybe. It angers me no one is stopping him and particularly after we had that conversation last night. Then I lunge for him. I knock him off her and push my hands to his throat, pinning him down. "Quit it! You're going to kill her!" I shout, and then I'm shoved off him.

Griff and Brint are holding me down, one sitting on my shoulders and one on my feet.

"Get off! No! He's killing her!" I'm screaming my head off, throwing my body weight around to get away. They're telling me she's dead, and he's trying to save her. "She's not dead!" I yell. "Butterflies don't sting!" I hear Spence's cries in the background of my screaming, and then I go still. Everything here stings. Whether it's physical or emotional, it hurts. It's deadly. That's when I realize, Mazi really is dead.

CHAPTER EIGHT

With one burst of strength, I fling Brint and Griff off of me. There she is, lying in the meadow; her chest rising and falling with every breath Pete takes. My vision becomes blurry because of the salty water filling my eyes, running down my cheeks and into my mouth. I spit the tears from my tongue, and they land in a puddle at my feet. The puddle circles at the middle and shines my reflection back at me. Abused, scared, alone. Of course I'm not alone, but that's how I feel. Abandoned.

Spence pulls Mazi close to him, his dark hair is black from the rain. A steady stream of water drips from the tip. Their skin is the same color, his and Mazi's. Both dark. But now, even through the rain, his hazel eyes are wet with tears.

She's dead. Mazi is gone. I think it. They say it but it will not click. It doesn't bother anyone other than Spence. That's because it's not real. Mazi is immortal. She can't die.

"We need to get to that mountain before we drown," Pete whispers. Spence picks Mazi up off the ground. Her head falls slack. Pete finds his way to me automatically, "Hayden?"

"I'm fine," I tell him. That's when I start coughing.

I take deep breaths in and out before I realize I'm not the one making the noise. Spence leans over and sets Mazi on the ground. He rocks back on his heels and wipes the rain from his face, smiling. And Mazi opens her eyes.

I take her up in my arms. "I knew you couldn't die."

"Don't touch those silver butterflies," she chokes and smiles.

I can't describe how I feel right now. I don't know whether to cry or laugh. She's not gone. Mazi is alive. Ha, I called that! She doesn't have the capability to die. It's Mazi, for heaven's sake! My friends gather around us and hug her, a group hug. Forgetting about the storm, we drop all of our supplies and sit in our hug. I don't know how long we sit. The rain keeps coming, and the rabbits and butterflies become more plentiful, making me uneasy. "As much as I want to stay here, I think we better get moving."

Spence's eyes float around, and he notices the multiplying butterflies. "Good idea." He takes Mazi on his back; we grab our supplies and head for the mountain.

Our trek lasts the rest of that day and late into the night. The rain has gotten worse. On the "bright" side, I've managed to bring down six more rabbits. By the time we get to the base of the mountain, we are dragging. I don't even have the strength left to carry the bow and arrows much less climb a mountain. We find elevated land with an overhanging rock formation branched over it and decide to stay here until tomorrow. As much as I want to join my friends and sleep, I have to cook the rabbit meat before it goes bad. I light a small fire with dead flowers from the meadow and skin the furry creatures. It feels like it takes an exceedingly long time to cook the meat, skinning and waiting, skinning and waiting. Seven times over! I put the roasted meat in the water container's lid and settle down for tomorrow which comes all too quickly.

Morning light sweeps into my eyes, barely. The rain has turned into nonstop walls of water. When I step into the waves, I literally can't see my hand in front of my face. Somehow the sun has found its way through the rainstorm and into the meadow. My friends and I huddle along the base of the mountain to escape the wetness; I sit smashed between Pete and Bree. We easily consume the seven rabbits I shot, and I can tell it's going to be one of those days. One of those days where no matter how much you eat, you're never full; in this case it's not much. One of those days you don't feel like talking and practically everything gets on your nerves. It's going to be a bad day.

"How long have we been here?" Brint asks me. "Too long," I say.

"In days?" he asks impatiently.

"Ummm, twenty-three, I think." Only seven days left, just seven. I like that number although thirteen is better. Everyone thinks it is an unlucky number because of Friday the thirteenth, but it's my number for every sports team I play on. It was the day Ozalee was born, December 13.

"Do you see that?" Lakuna says frantically. "See what?" Mazi says.

"The badgers. They're there," she murmurs and points directly to her left.

I squint my eyes and look to my left, and only a couple feet from me is a pack of possessed badgers. "Shhh!" I whisper. "Maybe they won't see us!" But they aren't looking for us. They are running. They fly past us and head toward the woodsy forest to our right. It would take a human days to get there, especially in this rain, but the man-eating animals crash into the forest in only a couple of minutes. I see leer and panthers and even some normal-sized deer fleeing from the winter wonderland. *What are they running from? Is there a bigger threat here? One that could even bring down a badger?* And there is.

CHAPTER NINE

It takes me seconds to realize the presence of a giant wall of water throwing itself at me. Griff yanks me from under the outcrop of rock and yells for me to run. *Am I always the last person to notice lethal things?* It must be because most of my friends are already running, and then there is Griff trying to gather the little belongings we still have. He shoves the ax in his shorts, wraps his arm around the first-aid kit, and sticks a small box in his mouth. "Just leave it!" I yell at him and put his arm around my shoulder. He tries to run, but we aren't getting anywhere, and I'm not strong enough to carry him. The wall is now on our heels and about to crest. "Swim!" I scream. We take to the air just as the wave crashes over the top of my body.

The water flings me every which way, mashing my face to rocks, burying my head in mud. I feel as if the world slows, my lungs inhaling water, just as my father's did. So this is how I'm going to die. Trapped on an island, young and innocent. I never accomplished anything I wanted to—writing a book, living in Tibbet, all of that is ancient history now. Dying seems like it would be painful or scary, but it's not. I suck up my last breath of water and close my eyes, thinking death will come. But of course it doesn't. My head bobs above the water, and I start to swim, throwing up liquid and rabbit, thrashing around in what must be forty feet of water.

The wave has effortlessly whisked me into the woodsy forest; I didn't even think to grab hold of a tree until the force of the water slams my face into a trunk. I climb up, out of the reach of the water. My stomach continues to heave up liquid and rabbit. I sit on a branch and watch the waves to see any sign of life. Seconds pass, minutes, hours, days, years. That's how long it feels anyway.

It takes a lot of screaming for him to hear me. The moment he lays his eyes on a familiar face, his expression brightens with hope. It takes all of the strength he has to make it to my tree. He has a summer job as the head lifeguard at Villa's community pool, and he's an amazingly good swimmer, but I guess he's been going for so long. I pull him up on my branch and pat his back as he vomits the water and rabbit. Brint's pale skin is bloody with cuts, his brown eyes are bloodshot, and his chocolate-colored hair is dripping in his face.

"I don't know where they're at," he gasps.

I think it will be awhile before we have company again, I think silently. "We'll, wait here until the water goes down, and then we'll go find them," I say reassuringly. I can feel him shaking beside me, not of cold but fear. He thinks our friends are dead—I don't doubt that. I would rather them be dead than stuck here for seven more days and have to face whatever comes after we get rescued.

Brint tells me he'll watch for our friends or any of our supplies while I rest. But I don't. I finish retching excess water from my stomach. I hear Brint gasp and shoot myself upward, "What?" I ask.

"Oh, nothing," he says sheepishly. He's lying. He sucks at lying. I memorize the landscape and try to find what he's worried about. I see a school of fish jumping out of the water, but that's it. I do a double take as when I realize what they are. Huge fish. *Huge* fish. Monster fish. I squint to get a better view of the fish; they have barbed backs and tails the color of mud. I squeeze my eyes shut, desperately trying not to picture one of those ripping my sister apart, but it's no use and the unwanted flashback slips into my view. My arms automatically pinch my insides, holding them together so they don't fall apart like the rest of my world.

I hold my fetal position and rock back and forth. *It's over. It's finished. She's gone. Get over it. Get over it!* But it can't be done. I'm about to go completely mad when Brint pushes my shoulder. I lean closer to the water and latch onto the branch before I can fall off.

"Look!" he steadies himself on the branch. "Spence! Cam! Pete!" he shouts as they float under our branch.

I swoop down, grabbing the tree limb they're clinging to before they can float away. Brint shoves his elbow into my knee and mouths, "*Hurry, fish.*" The school of barbed fish swims toward our tree, sensing the vibrations of the boy's blood in the water.

I hear the snarls and hisses of the death machines and start to panic. "Guys get up here." Cam leaps onto my branch. Their makeshift boat splashes in the water. The fish flop and scrunch together in a bloodthirsty frenzy. Spence lifts an unconscious Pete up to Cam, and he lays him on the branch. Pete's limbs drop into the water, but Brint quickly scoops them up.

"Cam, the fish are coming," Brint whispers. "The fish?" Cam asks.

"Get higher!" Brint climbs to an upper branch, and I help Cam drag Pete up to a safe height. Spence tries to jump onto the branch like Cam. The first time he misses and falls into the water. He curses and scurries onto the lowest branch of our tree. The fish have disappeared from the surface. Spence lets his feet dangle in the water mindlessly.

"What happened to Pete?" I ask Cam.

"I don't know. We found him like that, just floating there. I think he hit his head on a rock or something. We listened to his heart not like we would know what to do or anything. It seemed fine though. Every time he breathed, his lungs made a swishing sound. There might be water in them."

"He's going to be fine," Brint says as he puts his ear to Pete's chest. He knows what to do in cases like this.

I hear Spence splashing his feet in the water. "Get up here, Spence." However, it's too late. The water ripples under his leg and then goes still. A few moments pass before the water explodes in a deadly abruption. The fish fly out of the shadows in the wave, snapping their jaws down on the branch Spence is sitting. He starts to climb, grabbing the branches but getting no grip. "Spence, come on!" I yell.

One of the monster fish sinks its teeth into Spence's calf. He cries in pain and kicks it off with his other foot. The fangs of the fish rip all of the way down his leg. I grab the back of his shirt and pull him up higher. The second his feet leave the lower branch, it breaks off the tree and lands in the middle of the death trap that is fish. With every drop of Spence's blood that falls into the water comes another fish trying to reach us, but they never will.

"I need a bandage," Spence says queasily.

I rip off my last shirt sleeve and tie it in a knot over the bite wound. "Don't worry," I say. "After a couple hours, you'll lose feeling. That's what happened to me anyway."

Spence lies on the tree limb gasping in pure agony. All I can do is sit here and watch hoping for it to stop. His blood soaks through my shirt, but I don't have anything else to stop it. "You can stick it out until we find the first-aid kit." Brint stops pushing on Pete's chest. Water spews from his mouth, and he coughs so hard he makes himself throw up.

We sit on the branch exhausted. I volunteer for the first shift of watch dog. We decided to call the new position watch dog because we are guarding others from danger, or on the better hand, we are spying for companions. Three of my friends breathing slows out like lights. "I wish I had a lost pill right about now. I can feel my heartbeat in my calf," Spence says.

"Yeah. Only for a little while, enjoy it while it lasts," I say.

His brows come together questioningly. "You can't feel it at all?"

I stick my finger in the cut on my calf and spread it out so it starts bleeding again. He winces. Instead of crusted-in scabs, the edges of my deep wound are stretched tight with shiny pink skin. "Not at all," I say. "You should get some sleep. You're our next watch dog."

He smiles, and in seconds, his light snoring starts up.

When I start dozing off I figure it's time to wake Spence for his watch.

"Spence, get up," I whisper.

His tired eyes meet mine and he unwillingly takes my place as watch dog. "Find anything?" he asks.

"No," I mumble and fall into oblivion. In the midst of the night, the rain starts up again, and I have to pull my shirt up over my face. The wind blows in colossal gusts, swaying the trunk of the tree, swishing it so hard in fact Cam, the watch dog of the hour, has to wake my friends up, and we have to hold on to the branches so we don't fall off. No other sleep comes that night; Brint and Pete are lucky though. At least they got a full four hours.

I'm relieved when morning comes. The water has gone completely down, leaving the ground mushy and wet. Spence managed to find our knife when we were sleeping, but the rest of our friends and supplies were nowhere to be found. Cam is on the borderline between insanity and hysterics because he doesn't know what has happened to Griff. And Pete and Spence are just plain spent. The wind blows so hard, it pushes me over every time I try to stand up. Cam and Brint have to hold me down so I can walk. We trudge deeper into the forest instead of back to the meadow because we know if we have any chance of finding Mazi, Bree, Lakuna, and Griff, we have to search where the wave would have washed them.

My stomach has caved in on itself. I ate plenty of rabbit yesterday, but it all came up again, and we only have a knife to get food with. My shorts, which fit snuggly when we first got on the island, now, have to be held up with a vine from the jungle. We yell for our friends, a pointless act because they will never be able to hear us. But what if they could see us? I stop dead in my tracks. Pete runs into the back of me. "I have an idea," I say. "We need to light a fire to signal them."

Cam's face perks up. "That might work." We gather some dry leaves off of a branch high above the waterline. I put the leaves in a pile as Brint tries to hit two rocks together to form a fire. After a while, he gets frustrated and shoves the stones into Cam's chest. "You do it."

Cam curses at him under his breath and clacks the rocks together. His jaw clenches with anger, and he smashes the rocks with such great force splinters of stone fly off. His nostrils flare, and he chucks the stones into the woods, "Useless!"

I try to think back to when Griff was gathering up supplies. What did he grab? He stuck the ax in his shorts, wrapped the first-aid kit around his arm, and he put something in his mouth. What could fit in his mouth? The container? No. Definitely not the bow and arrows. What else did we have left? We lost the goggles, and Spence has the knife. Nothing else would fit! Different words linger on my tongue—*fire, earth, water, air*. The four basic elements. I hate fire and water. Fire? Hmmm. Aha! Griff has the matches! I look around high above the tree line and low to the ground. The rain is blinding. I wipe the water from my face with a dirty hand. And there it is in the distance. Just as I had thought.

A smile forms on my face before I can stop it. "They're alive?" Spence, Pete, Cam and Brint turn their heads toward the direction of the smoke and we start "running." We have to join hands and slog through the blistering wind and rain to get to them. I faintly hear them screaming our names, and we yell back. Some of the trees have begun to crack and fall, but we don't let that stop us. We tumble into the clearing and are immediately greeted by hugs and kisses. Spence grabs Mazi around the waist and brings her close. Griff and Cam hug, a tight longing union formed between two brothers. The rest of us are just glad to see each other. Lakuna plants a playful kiss on my cheek and shakes me until I'm dizzy. I guess she forgives me.

We stand in our normal circle position, Pete on my left, Griff on my right, Cam and Lakuna across from me. They tell us how they escaped the flood. Lakuna and Bree held hands through the whole thing and grabbed onto a tree without getting hit in the face. Mazi swam through the water until she found a point she could touch the bottom, and she just stood there until she saw the signal fire Griff made. She spent all night alone. Lakuna and Bree found the fire later that night; they were closer than we were. The trees around us shake, and their branches crack, tumbling all around us.

"We should get out of here! It's too dangerous!" Griff shouts over the wind. Understatement. Just as he finishes his sentence, the tree across from Lakuna and Cam shatters and creeks. The wood around the center splinters and throws itself in our direction. It leans toward them, slowly at first and then it speeds up. All they can do is bring their hands up to cover their faces before the thick tree crushes their bodies.

CHAPTER TEN

But it doesn't hit them. It crushes me instead. Only a split second before it smashed them, I sprang, knocking them out of the way. Two more of the people I loved gone was undoable. I would rather die. I lie face up, the massive trunk covering every part of my body except my head, knees, and shoulders. I can't feel the unbearable pain on the lower half of my body, and I know without a doctor I have a broken spine. When I open my eyes, rain stings them. Unrecognizable people are staring at me.

I jolt back when I realize the people looking at me are Cam and Lakuna. I cannot forget them. I cannot forget them. No matter how hard I hit my head. They are leaning over me, yelling my name, for me to stay with them. My eyesight becomes foggy; I can only make out the outlines of their bodies. The air has been pressed from my lungs; it doesn't leave the burning feeling it usually does when you stay underwater too long. It feels like I never needed it in the first place. At first, their voices were loud. "HAYDEN!" they scream. But they're fading. They become quieter, distant.

I slip from the girl I was into something new. The people around me have smiles on their faces. They dance in a meadow. In the beginning, I'm staring at them from ground level, and then I float up into the clouds. Pink clouds, the color of the sunset. I drift down so my feet touch the soft pillows in the sky; I push my way past the golden gates keeping me outside the place I want to go. As soon as I step inside, they are there, waiting for me. "I told you I'd tell him you loved him," Ozalee says. She and my father wrap me in their heavenly arms, holding on to me *forever.*

BOOK TWO

Cam

Book Two

Can

They appear only seconds after the tree squished her like a bug. A bunch of them. They say they are from the Center, and they are here to help. A clean-faced black-haired man, I'd say about fifty years old, tells me he was assigned to me. His name is Yanish. I do not speak to him or go near him. Every time he gets close, I back away. He is from the Center, and that means he is not to be trusted. He pulls a square box from his pocket and mumbles something into it. I search for any familiar faces. Griff? Spence? Anyone? I find them lying on the ground with clear masks strapped to their faces. They just stare into the air with dazed looks on their faces. Bunches of other people are fluttering around me, talking in soothing voices, even though no one is listening. I run to Griff and rip the mask off his face; he sits up and coughs. "That's a drug dude."

We go down the line of our friends and take their masks off before Yanish pops up in front of me. I jerk backward into someone else's arms. I struggle to free myself, but he smacks one of those clear masks on my face and presses a button. The mask fills with a pungent smelling air, and my knees give out. It's not a sedative, I don't think. I've been under this stuff before, at the dentist when I had to get my tooth pulled, but this gas is stronger. The dentist's gas makes you loopy. This stuff is numbing. I know Hayden is dead, and I'm being kidnapped again, but I don't care.

The guy puts me on a stretcher and loads me into a tiny plane. On the outside, the plane is miniature. The inside is huge. It seemed to have multiplied in size. At first I'm put in a tan room with red couches and people in white uniforms sitting everywhere. They load my friends on to the plane and then ten more people march on. A guy in a black suit starts giving orders, "Get the girl to the CCH! Hook them up." A gurney is wheeled by my head and disappears behind a door. They pick up my stretcher and take me to the opposite end of the plane through a different door.

The medical room is bright. White walls, white floors, white beds, and white uniforms. I squeeze my eyes shut in hopes the blinding light will be closed out, but it just makes the back of my eyelids red. I am placed in a cubby, all by myself, blocked from the sight of my friends by a thick curtain. An older man with gray hair comes in and sits in the chair next to my stretcher, which has been transformed into a bed. "Hello, Cam Malrook," he says. I look at him and he smiles. "Well, you've been through quite a lot, haven't you, kiddo?" he asks. He slips on a pair of rubber gloves, cuffs my hands and feet to my bed, and removes my precious gas from my face, bringing me back to reality.

"How do you know my name? What are you going to do to me?" I snarl.

"I'm just helping you out." He pinches the skin on my bicep and sticks a needle into it. "This puts some fluids back in your system."

"I just went through a flood. I think I've had enough fluids," I hiss. He rolls his grey eyes and tells me even though I've swallowed more water than I should, I'm still dehydrated. The liquid kicks in, and my head stops spinning and returns to feeling normal.

"Told you it would help," he chuckles. "Take this," he says and shoves a pill in my mouth. I spit it out. "It's a fever fighter." He pushes it back in my mouth; I chew the thing up and barely hold back my vomit.

"That's disgusting."

He shines a flashlight in my eyes and tells me to follow his finger. He sticks a different light in my ears. "Ears look good." My mind starts to crowd with the past days' events. I recognize this feeling though.

"What else does that pill do?" I ask. "It makes you drowsy," he says.

"And this is why I don't listen to doctors. They never tell you enough. How do you know my name?"

"Don't worry. I'm here to help."

"Doubt that. Where's Griff?"

"He's safe." The fever fighter tingles my tongue. The doctor takes off my shoes and socks and puts them in a plastic bag, then he uses his pocket knife to cut away my shirt and shorts.

"Why?" I ask.

"I cut them in case of injury." When he attaches the gas to my face again, that's when I finally zonk out.

I come to in a small clear cupboard with Lakuna sitting next to me. There are four closets arranged like a four-square court. Each one has a door on the nonsee-through side, and of course, the door doesn't open from my side. The piece of tape under the handle reads *Cam Malrook, Lakuna Crest*. In the cupboard next to us sits Griff and Pete. The tape says *Griff*

Malrook, Pete Girth. Crossways from them is Brint and Bree. The writing on their tape reads *Brint Turner, Bree Uley.* And then there's Spence and Mazi's tape reading *Spence Leadmen, Mazi Seedar.* I can't hear what any of my friends are saying except Lakuna. I rub the sleep from my eyes.

"How do you feel?" she asks.

My body aches with bruising, and my burns have been bandaged. The light is too bright, and my head thumps to the beat of my heart. All of us have been changed into spandex maroon shirts and silky black shorts. We have no shoes on, just black socks that come to our ankles. "Great. You?"

She shows me her shoulder; the stitches have been newly done. Her burns have been cared for; however, the bruises around her neck are darker than ever. "Awful."

I want to hug her and tell her she has to grasp the fact her best friend just died for her. For us. I know she knows, and I know she cares more than I can even imagine. It's one of those things no matter how much you want it to be a lie, it's true. There's a knock on our door. "Please move out of the way of the door. We're coming in," says the voice of a very recognizable man. The door flings open.

I look out the door to see if escape is possible. Here is dangerous. Two armed guards stand on each side. "Don't even think about it, Cam," the man says.

"How do you know my name?" I can't bring myself to look straight at him.

"You are well known, Mr. Malrook," he says. Yanish stands on one side of him, and the man Lakuna was assigned to stands on the other side. In the middle is President York. I've seen him before, a short plump guy with a balding head, but only on television. They introduce themselves as if we don't already know them; well I know two of them anyway.

"I'm President York," he says and holds his hand out for me to shake. I just stare at it until he eventually puts it down. He introduces the other two men, "This is Yanish and Bolt." Bolt is a younger guy with silver hair slicked back into a ponytail and a shiny lightning bolt tattooed around his left eye. Weird. "We are here to explain your predicament."

Supposedly, Darious lied to us. He was from the country we're at war with right now, the nation directly south of us. The whole kidnapping party was from there. The country is called Duxia. Apparently, all of the kids that ever enrolled in any school in Gipem were marked down on a list. The list was for future reference of some of the children that would be drafted to war later in the years. The teachers in Gipem schools would observe the children and pick specific kids who were talented enough to go to war and survive. In all of the other schools in Gipem, the lists were destroyed, but being the largest block, ours was kept to see how well we would turn out.

The Duxians got hold of this list, and anyone who was marked was put through a survival test. We were the only kids from our school who were marked; *all* of the other kids who were marked in Villa have died. The Duxians had never planned for our survival; they put masses of threats on the island to see how many would survive until they decided to kill us off with a bomb or something. They wanted to see how strong the future fighters would be defending our country so they could kill the soldiers off easier. The Center has been looking for Duxia's survival headquarters, the place where they kept all of the lists, cameras, and the buttons to activate the threats. They could do all of that with a push of the button! Some of the Center's undercover spies found their headquarters and invaded it, taking the Duxians prisoner and saving us, the last marked kids on the list.

"Any questions?" President York asks.

Yes, I have so many, I can't keep them straight.

"How did you find us?" Lakuna chokes out, horrified.

"They implanted tracking devices in your feet. We got them out. They videoed your whole time on the island. You can watch it when you're ready," Bolt says. "In addition to the tracking devices, they were using something else also. Each of the devices had three bubbles, a red, a blue, and a green. When a Duxian pressed a certain button, the bubble of their choosing would pop. The bubbles could control how someone felt toward another person. That is why Lakuna got mad at Hayden so suddenly. A member had pressed the red hatred button, and Lakuna hated the first person she saw."

"And Brint?" she questions. "He almost killed me."

"No, that was no bubble. One of the members let a genetically altered bug sting him. That was an actual sting."

Lakuna continues testing them. "Will we be going into war?"

"You are a very special group of kids who have a lot of talent. It is a big possibility. You children could help end the fighting," President York informs us. End the war? This comes as a shock. How can a group of minors end a war?

"Last question," she says. "Is Hayden alive?"

A look of mercy crosses Yanish's face, but he recovers quickly. It is all too obvious he has watched the video of us on the island. "She is in very bad condition. We're doing all we can," York says, and they leave the room. I see him enter the next cupboard with two new men to speak to Griff and Pete.

After a while of waiting for President York to finish explaining, Bolt opens our door and tells us they have a room made up for us. Our assistants, along with armed guards, lead us to our room. Seven assistants, all male. They walk us down a long white hallway and into an elevator where one of them pushes the button that has a thirteen written on it. Thirteen floors. Wow.

"Where are we?" I ask.

"You're in the Center, the military headquarters. The president's mansion is connected to the north end. You'll be seeing him a lot," says one of the assistants I haven't met yet. As soon as the elevator door opens, they lead us directly across the hall and into a giant bedroom.

"Would the females prefer to stay in the same room as the males?" Yanish asks.

Bree, Mazi, and Lakuna look at each other and nod their heads. "Well, we're not going anywhere without them," Mazi snaps as she grabs hold of Spence.

"Ground rules," Bolt says. "There are surveillance cameras around this room, none in the bathrooms. One bathroom is designed for girls." He points to the one on the right. "And one is designed for boys." He points to the one on the left. "You are required to bath every night and report for supper at approximately six-thirty every night. That is the only meal you must attend. Any other food can be ordered through this." He walks us to the wall that the bathrooms are buried in; between the powder rooms is a white box with too many buttons. "Everything you need can be delivered to you. Your curfew is eleven. Meals will be provided if you want to come. At eight in the morning, you will report to the main office to be given your schedule for the day. The doctors will be in to check on you shortly." The assistants form a crooked line and file out the door.

"Just to remind you, we have security everywhere. If you have any questions, just call," Yanish says and places a small box, one like he talked into on the island, on the table beside the door.

"This place is different," Bree says.

"Yes, because we're not accustomed to difference yet," Brint mumbles. The room is an oversized square. The wall with the door has a table, a water fountain, a temperature-changing gadget, and a closet. When you open the closet, it is labeled in sections CAM, SPENCE, BRINT, GRIFF, PETE. Our sizes of clothes are in our section, but all of the clothes match, the same thing we're wearing now. There is a pair of shoes, black tennis shoes. *How original,* I think sarcastically. The back wall is lined with eight beds, not nine. The far wall is the same as the wall with the door except it has a large window overlooking a field where the troops train and has no water fountain. The next wall has the bathrooms, the order box, and a television. All of the walls are painted a sky blue color, and the carpet and bed covers are snow white.

We sit on the beds awkwardly waiting for the doctors, but none come. "Well, since they are here, why don't we use them?" Mazi asks. "Everyone, get clean clothes and get off this fancy carpet. You never know the president could get mad that we're ruining his million-dollar decorations." She rushes around and throws our clothes in our faces and pushes us into our assigned bathrooms.

Our bathroom contains a bath, five showers, a toilet, five sinks, and a urinal. I strip off my clothes and jump in the shower. As soon as my feet hit the floor, the water squirts on. I don't even have to use the control panel on the side to pick the settings because it's already perfect. I let the water rinse over my body. It feels so good. I press a couple buttons on the control panel until shampoo spills onto my hand. It takes no time for me to scrub my hair clean and wash the blood, dirt, and mud from my body. I step out of the shower and start searching for a towel, but there's no need because a gust of hot air fills my shower space and I'm instantly dry. I feel twenty pounds lighter without the muck and body fluid matting my hair down and clinging to my skin.

I hop on the first bed in the row and sink into the mattress. Spence takes the bed right next to me; Griff takes one but leaves one for Mazi between himself and Spence. Pete leaves a bed for Lakuna next to Griff, then Pete and Brint get the beds next to Lakuna and leave the last for Bree. Spence's calf is stitched up. A lot. There must be hundreds of those little suckers in there. Well, that's no surprise. By the time the plane arrived, he could bear no weight at all. Griff's leg is held by a thick black cast and a walking boot; the stitches over his eye were removed, leaving a ragged scar. Pete had to take the bandages off his chest to get in the shower; his burn has turned into a bunch of white pussy blisters. Disgusting!

The girls come out of the bathroom, spotless and almost unrecognizable without the sand and leaves entangled in their hair. Their tresses shine in the bright light from the ceiling as they walk to their beds. The clock reads 6:16. "Don't you think we should try to find the dining room?" I say to no one in particular.

Like clockwork, the door to our room flies open, and two doctors walk in. A guy and a girl. The guy is the one who worked on me earlier today. "I forgot to introduce myself to you, boys. My name is Dr. Ezzard. I am the guys' doctor," he says.

The woman starts to speak, "You can call me Kanga. I'll be the girls' doctor." So the girls get a girl and the guys get a guy, fair enough.

Dr. Ezzard starts with me. He makes me get off the bed, and he takes my height and weight. "Five-eleven and 124 pounds?" He shakes his head in disappointment. He tests my eyes again, takes my temperature, which has hiked up, then tells me to take off my shirt. I do what the old man says, and he traces his fingers over my visible ribs and hip bones, then he puts burn ointment on my burns, gives me an ice pack for my bruises, and moves on to Spence. I sit on the edge of my bed and wait for the doctors to finish examining my friends. He has to rewrap Pete's chest and put the ointment on each person.

"Some fire," he says as he rubs the medicine on Griff's shoulder. "I'm surprised all of you lived through that. You're lucky, Brint. You would've turned into a human torch."

"I know," Brint says. The old man decides to shut it. I'm glad too because he was about to hear an earful. We all know Hayden saved our lives, and now we can't save hers. Typical.

The doctors take a long time to study their observations.

"Well," Kanga says, "you all have lost a lot of weight, an unhealthy amount. You will be put on a special diet to gain your weight back. Other than that, you should be fine. We'll be in to check on you every day until you're notified otherwise. See you tomorrow." They close the door behind them. I hear it lock from the outside, and then the ceiling of our room starts beeping.

"Your supper will be brought to you tonight. Do not leave your room," a lady with a stern voice says. There's a knock at the door and the click of a lock unlocking; Bree opens it and tell us to come get it. I hear the lock click shut again. Each of us has a small tray with a bowl filled with a red-colored mush, a cup of milk, a spoon, and a napkin. I take a bite of the mush and swallow unwillingly; the steaming stuff runs down my throat and plants itself in my stomach. I drink the milk and get halfway through the bowl before I can't eat anymore. I guess the days of having so little food have shrunk my stomach or something.

A nurse pushes her way in the door. She doesn't tell us her name, but instead she hands us circular black stickers about the size of a can. "What are these for?" Mazi asks.

"Put them on your stomachs. They help you gain weight. Be careful. Put them on before you go to bed. They are for nighttime." At least she gave us a hint these would make you tired, unlike Dr. Ezzard, drugging me up without telling me, real nice.

"Will we be seeing you again?" Lakuna asks. "Every once in a while," she answers politely. "Your name?"

"Wyllie," she says and then leaves.

There is no way I'm going to remember all of these names, but I think I can keep hers straight. I walk to the table next to the door and pick up the tiny box thing Yanish put there. I press the button that has a question mark, and the stern voice that said we didn't have to go to dinner picks up. "Yes?" it says.

"What is this thing?" I ask stupidly. "A teletalky."

And that is? I don't bother asking because I don't really care. "Can I have the update on Hayden Kolter in the CCH?" When Lakuna and I were in the cupboard, I asked Yanish what *CCH* stood for. He said Critical Condition Headquarters.

"She has undergone surgery on her spinal cord today. The medical staff removed the splintered pieces of her spine and pinned the break together. Her ribs are poor. Her internal bleeding has stopped, but her left lung has been punctured." It takes me a moment to regain my speaking ability.

"Um, tha-thanks."

A broken spine? Punctured lung? Worse. She is worse than I thought. I knew she died; the medical staff had to restart her heart with those shocky things. I thought she had a broken arm or leg or something, but her spine? What if she doesn't make it through the night? What if she does make it, and she's paralyzed? She'll never be able to walk again, run again, play softball, and play soccer! For as long as I've known her, she's always loved to run, not competitively but for fun. She hates track. She just does it to get in shape for soccer. But if she's paralyzed, she won't be able to play soccer. That will break her heart. That will break her already broken heart. I mean, how much could one person take?

Lakuna touches my back. I jump. I can tell by the redness of her eyes she heard what the lady on the teletalky said. Her voice is shaky, barely holding back sobs. "We did this." If we weren't standing in the way, she wouldn't have jumped, and she wouldn't be like this now. I've never cried in front of a girl before, but there's always a first time for everything. Tears flood my face. Mazi's tears pour from her eyes. Lakuna's are running in her mouth. Bree catches hers in her hands. Soon everybody in the room is crying, even Spence and Brint. Pete ends up curled in the corner. My insides start trembling; Griff puts his arm around my shoulders. He leads me to the bed and looks at me questioningly.

"Mom cried this way when she heard dad died. Hayden cried this way when Ozalee died . . . You love her, don't you?"

He already knows the answer.

CHAPTER ELEVEN

Ding! Ding! Ding! Ding! Ding! The alarm goes off at seven this morning. I roll out of bed and rub the sleeplessness from my eyes. I put the patch on last night. It took me out for a little bit, but the rest of the night was awful. I rotated between staring at the ceiling and silently watching TV. I trudge into the bathroom, change my clothes, wash my face, brush my teeth and hair, and wait for the others to get ready. Everything looks so odd and out of place, so incredibly clean that it's sickening. Even in Villa where there is moderate wealth, our home is a dump compared to this.

I stretch my hand out in front of my face and look at my palm. It looks abnormal without being caked in blood and dirt. I grab the teletalky and shove it in the pocket of my shorts; we were told to bring it everywhere. Lying under the teletalky was a map of the military base; we are supposed to report to the main office first.

We peek our heads out the door. Silent and unspoken, we have decided staying here another night is not happening. We are going back to Villa, packing up all of our belongings and hiding somewhere in the Tibbett. No one would ever find us for two reasons. One, we have survived on an island for thirty days—we can go the rest of our lives with supplies, no problem. And two, we could probably outsmart these Center people any day. No guards are in the hallway. We creep to the nearest window. Pete and I are just about to unlatch the lock when a voice booms from the ceiling. "Don't even think about it." It's that same stern woman.

"How do we know we can trust this place?" Pete asks the air. "If we wanted you dead, we wouldn't have rescued you."

I'm a pretty smart kid, and that is a darn good excuse to me. We head to the main office on the west wing of the base without breakfast. We get lost many times before we make it to the office.

"You're late," the lady with the strict voice says. Her grey hair spikes out in every which way, and her nails and lips are painted red to match her eyes. Does she think red contacts are attractive? Creepy.

"Sorry. We got lost in the maze you call a military base," Brint cracks. Pete laughs at him and gets a stare down from the woman.

Yanish and the other assistants walk out a door behind the desk. They look at us. "If you leave your room or come to get your schedule without eating one more time, we will personally shove food down your throats," one of them says. Speaking like this to a group of kids who have been stranded on an island for the past month is not that great of an idea.

"Don't even try to threaten us," Griff snarls.

"What right do you have to talk to us like that? Your our assistants, not our bosses," Mazi hisses.

"Assistants?" Bolt laughs. "We're your personal mentors."

A fifty-year-old was assigned to me to be my *mentor*? Pathetic.

"Whatever you call yourselves, don't threaten us," Pete snaps. They exchange nervous glances and nod in approval, no more threatening.

Our "mentors" give us our specified schedules for the day. The first assignment on my schedule says "Questioning." "What is questioning?" I ask Yanish.

"You'll be questioned about your time spent on the island. You all will be questioned at different times for personal reasons."

The lady with the red eyes stands up. "Your group, meaning, Pete Girth, Spence Leadmen, Cam and Griff Malrook, Brint Turner, Bree Uley, Hayden Kolter, Mazi Seedar, and Lakuna Crest will be referred to as the Rescue Squad when needed as a group." She hands the rest of my friends a teletalky. "Emergencies only," she states.

We split up with our mentors and reluctantly head our different ways. I walk through the hallway looking down at my feet. "I'm sorry. She's strict," Yanish says to me.

"Who is she?" I ask, taking his apology even though it's not necessary.

"Cocoa Labush. The head secretary. She's in charge of most of the information given to the base and scheduling. You get the point." I don't say anything. "Hungry?" he asks and pulls a protein bar from the tiny pack he carries. I peel the wrapper and bite into the sweet granola. As soon as the bar hits my stomach, it disagrees and comes back up on the floor.

"I guess I should stick to the meal plan," he mumbles and pulls out his teletalky. "Clean up in H1."

"Sorry," I mumble.

He grimaces. He leads me through the tunnel of hallways and into a grey room with three chairs and a table. "Take a seat. It will only be a minute," he says and sits in one of the chairs behind the table. Lied to again.

Almost a half hour later, a woman in a business suit steps into the room and takes a seat in the other chair behind the table. She puts her laptop on the table and presses a button. "Hello, Cam," she says in a proper tone. "My name is Rae. Just answer my questions as honest as possible," she continues. Her hair is dark red. She is straight to the point and very upfront. It catches me way off.

"Uh, um. I don't—"

But she begins anyway. "When you first landed on the island, did you think you were going to survive?"

That's an easy one. "No. I mean the supplies were helpful, but we didn't know what to expect." I pause a moment. "Can I ask you a question?" I say.

"Of course."

"Why were we given supplies if they were going to kill us anyway?"

"The Duxians thought you should have the supplies we would send you with if you were to go into war," she says.

"You would send us to war without guns?" I ask so appalled, my brain almost stops working.

"No! They knew a gun would be too easy of a weapon and wanted to see what you could accomplish without one.

"Next question. We saw how fearless you were to kill the panther when it was attacking the girls. You weren't afraid?"

The black cat ripping its claws down their skin and it's knifelike teeth buried in their flesh, I was all but reluctant to pound the ax into the cat's back. "No."

"Can you tell me why that is?" "It would have killed them."

"Interesting. So you would rather have the panther kill you than kill them?"

"Its back was turned. It didn't know I was coming."

"Pete Girth gave the girls sleeping pills because they were in pain. You stopped eating, sleeping, and drinking. What was going through your mind?"

"Ummm, well, I don't really know." "Think," she says.

"Uh, if I slept, they could've died, and I wouldn't be able to help them. I never got hungry, and I needed to save the water for Pete. He was working so hard. And Griff, he couldn't walk yet."

"Why didn't you go get the water then?" she asks. "What could've happened to them when I was gone?"

"I see. That's enough for today. I'll see you soon, Mr. Malrook."

Yanish leads me to the cafeteria where the rest of my friends are already sitting. He takes me through the line and tells the lunch lady my name. She flips through the packet labeled Rescue Squad, and instead of giving me the pizza everyone else eats, I get the same red mush I did last night. I sit at the table with my friends, and Yanish disappears out the cafeteria door. I eat the salty mush and drink my milk.

"Did everyone get questioned?" Bree asks. "Yes," Brint says.

"How many questions did they ask you?" she asks. "Four, but it took a while."

A beeping starts on the ceiling of the cafeteria. "Rescue Squad, please report to CCH. Rescue Squad to CCH." We haven't finished our lunch, but none of us care. We leave our trays on the table and rush out the door. We start at a quick walk until Spence pulls out the map, and we see where we're going, and our pace immediately turns into a run. We go through the hallway I know as H1 because there's a WET FLOOR sign the exact spot where the power bar came up.

"That was me," I say and point at the sign.

"Nice," Griff chuckles. We burst in the room door labeled CRITICAL CONDITION HEADQUARTERS WAITING. Everyone I've met since I've been in the military base is here except for President York.

"Is she okay?" Mazi panics. A group of five male doctors push their way out of the white medical room. They tell us to sit on the couch of the waiting room; I try desperately to prepare myself for the worst.

"Is she okay?" Lakuna repeats impatiently.

A doctor with a white mask on his face pulls it down. "Hayden is improving. We've had her on medication for over a week, sleeping meds. Today is the first day she's been awake. We took her off the medication."

"You put her on a sleeping pill for a broken spine and ribs and punctured lung?" Griff yells. "When I first broke my leg, I could still feel it under those stupid pills!"

"Hold on. Hold on. I was using less-advanced terms so you could understand better. I promise she didn't feel a thing," the doctor defends himself while the others nod in agreement.

Lakuna lets out a loud huff and shakes her head. "You should've started out like that." "Over a week? We've only been here for two days?" Bree asks.

The doctors look at our mentors questioningly. "You've been here for ten days."

Ten days? What is he talking about?

"What?" Spence asks.

"The first eight days you were here, you were in the hospital. We took care of your major medical needs, such as burns, cuts, and breaks."

"I don't remember that," Mazi says.

One of the mentors steps forward. "That's what we hoped would happen. Dr. Ezzard and Kanga gave you the same type of medication Hayden has been on for the past ten days. Dr. Ezzard and Kanga performed emergency treatment on the plane ride here then handed you over to these five." He points at the doctors.

"So what are we here for?" Pete asks.

"We told Hayden everything we told you, about Duxia and why you were put on the island. We gave her a chance to ask questions, but she never talked. At first, we thought she was incapable of speaking. We ran tests and concluded she chooses not to talk. We want you to get her to speak to us," the doctor says and points toward the medical room. "Go right in. Room 17."

As soon as I walk into the medical room, the smell of antiseptic leeks into my nose and makes it burn. We stroll past room 1, room 2, room 3, and so on until we reach room 17. I grab the handle of the door.

"You can't go in there," one of the nurses roaming the halls says in a country accent. "Let them."

Everyone in the waiting room followed us here and stands a few feet behind us. The nurse nods her head at the order and walks away. I turn the handle of the door and hold it open for my friends as they walk in the room. I put the door stopper down and follow them.

One of her hands grips the mattress under the stationary bar that keeps her from falling out of bed; the other is clenched in a tight fist. Her body looks shrunken down under the thin hospital gown the doctors have put her in. Her rib and hip bones end in sharp points under the cloth of the gown. Her exposed skin is a sickly pale color, and the shadows under her eyes are such a dark purple, they appear black. This is the worst improvement I've ever seen.

Brint quietly knocks on the wall, "Hayden?"

She opens her eyes and a smile engulfs her face. "Guys? Is that really you?" "Who else would it be, silly?" Mazi asks.

"So I've heard you won't talk to the doctors?" Spence asks. "I don't trust them."

"I do. They fixed my hand and my back," Mazi says. She shows Hayden her recovering injuries.

She thinks about it. "What do they want?"

Lakuna sits on Hayden's bed; Hayden catches her breath and squeezes her eyes shut. "Are you in pain?" I ask.

"No. I'm fine," she says.

Lakuna wraps an extra gown around Hayden's feet. "You're so cold."

Pete's jaw clenches, and he stomps out of the room. I hear him trying to stay quiet while yelling at the doctors. "You call yourselves doctors? You don't have her on any pain medicines, and you can't even give her a blanket!"

"She wouldn't take any of it," one of them says.

"What do you mean she wouldn't take any of it? Do you mean to tell me you can't hold a ninety—pound girl down and put her on some medication?" I can tell by the tone in his voice that he's about to strangle someone.

"Every time we attempted to give her something, she would try to get away. She would rebreak another rib or poke another hole in her lung."

"So if we can get her to hold still, you'll fix her?" he hisses.

"Yes."

Pete walks back in the room. "Hayden, can you please hold still while the doctors help you. You can trust them. I promise," he says.

"People break promises," she whispers. I've heard that before. Pete rolls his eyes and smiles at her. "Yeah, I'll hold still," she says.

The doctors pile in the room and order us out. Our mentors take us back to the waiting room. "It might be a while," one of them says. *Yay.*

I can't keep calling all of them the mentors; I know two of them. Only seven more names to learn. "What are your mentor's names?" I ask. Pete's is Simone. Spence's Byron. Griff's Fabien. Brint's Cyrus. This is only one of the mentors that makes me wonder if they're normal in the head. His cut—down afro is dyed a dirty blonde and stands out against his dark skin. His eyebrows and eyelashes are died to match his hair, leaving his irises pitch black. Bree's mentor, Bronte, has long red hair braided down his scalp but somehow swoops up so it ends at his ear lobes. His sideburns form a braid down his face that melts into his beard and ends at his chest. But Fallon, Lakuna's mentor, is by far the strangest. His auburn hair spikes up over his forehead and ends in curved points to resemble eagle's talons. His hair contrasts against his milky skin tattooed with trees and an occasional bird. And then there's Hayden's mentor, Gibson, a middle-aged man with hardly any hair and soft blue eyes.

Wow, that's a lot of tags. I create a mental checklist to make sure I remember the entire list of name's I've learned so far: Ezzard, Kanga, Rae, Wyllie, Cocoa Labush, Yanish, Bolt, Simone, Byron, Fabien, Cyrus, Bronte, Fallon, and Gibson. Fourteen names, plus the guy in the black suit on the plane. All of my friends are being smart and catching up on sleep in their chairs. I lean my head against the wall and decide to be clever too. The next thing I know, Yanish is shaking my shoulder telling me we're allowed to go back and see Hayden now.

Her room has been dramatically altered in only the two hours we were waiting. The lights have been flipped down from bright to dim, the thermostat turned up way higher, and the bed moved to the center of the wall to fit all of the stands attached to Hayden. On her left, the side furthest away from the door is a metal stand with a bag of dark red connected to it. Blood. Next to the blood is a clear liquid, an IV. On her right is a breathing machine that runs through her gown and up her nose. Next to the breathing machine is a stand containing a bag labeled MORPHINE. This is the only bag not connected to her. The IV and blood run through a tube inserted in her arm. From her chest down is covered with thick blankets. One of the doctors comes in and asks if we want to say anything to her before they hook her up to the morphine.

"Do you need anything?" I ask her.

"No," she whispers. I notice how her mouth is speckled with dust from the island.

"Please do not lie to me," I say.

She sighs. "I am a little hungry."

The doctor pulls her blanket down, lifts up her gown, and sticks a patch on her stomach. I look at him curiously. "We would prefer not to give her solid food now," he says.

"Anything else?" I ask.

"No." The doctor connects the morphine to her arm, and her face relaxes almost immediately. She looks at us. Her eyes get big for only a second, and then they go back to normal. "Spence, what happened to your leg?"

He glances at his calf. "Huh?"

"Hayden, you were there. You saw it happen?" I say.

"What? I um. I don't—"

The doctor steps in now. "She doesn't recall most of it. Her concussion was very bad." "None of it?" Pete whispers.

"Only some."

"You know the only reason they didn't have to reset my bone was because of you," Griff says.

She yawns. "Really? Well, that's good." Her voice is more quiet now. She is shot. She squeezes her eyes shut. "It's not my fault, is it? Not Griff's leg, I mean the island?"

All at once, we tell her no and don't think that. "You saved my life Hayden," Brint says.

"And ours," Mazi adds, pointing to Lakuna and Bree.

"How? Wait, Lakuna, they told me you hated me because of a bubble. What bubble?" Her voice trails off, and her breathing turns heavy trying to avoid using the breathing tubes as she sleeps.

Wyllie steps into the room and walks over to Lakuna, Bree, and Mazi. "She had me write you girls something. She's been thinking of it for a couple hours. She said it reminds her of all of you."

"Where is it?" Lakuna asks.

Wyllie glides to Hayden's bedside table and lifts up a book. "Hm? It was under here. Maybe she moved it." She lifts up a picture frame. "Not here either. I'm sorry, girls. I don't know where she put it." She leaves the room.

"What's that?" Brint says. He points to Hayden's hand. I pull the cream piece of paper from her hand, and it falls off her chest to the side of her bed. She winces. As I bend up to hand the paper to Mazi, I notice the picture on Hayden's bedside table. It's a picture of Ozalee and her horse, Fancy. I pick up the picture. Ozalee's golden hair is curled in this portrait, pinned back by a pink flower. She seemed to have somehow covered Fancy's halter with pink flowers too, lining the horse's face. How did she get this? I pass the picture to the closest person by me and hand the paper to Mazi. Lakuna and Bree lean over Mazi's shoulder and skim the letter. Tears fill their eyes. Once they finish reading it, Mazi folds it up and slips it in her pocket.

"I hope she does become a writer someday," Lakuna says. "Can I see?" I ask.

Mazi grabs the paper from her pocket and holds it out to me. I unfold it.

The Lock and the Key
The lock is what keeps me going
I am the key
I could never work without my lock
It's impossible
When I am bronze, she makes me golden
We are meant to be friends
Sisters even
If I shines, she shines
If I'm dull, she's dull
We work in sync
Always together
The lock and the key

A beeping gets faster on one of the monitors connected to Hayden, and a doctor rushes in and scans the screen. He opens the side of her bed and pulls out a clear mask, straps it over her face, and then connects it to one of the stands. "It gives her more oxygen," he says.

I make sure Hayden is completely out before I ask. "Is she going to be able to walk again?" "It's hard to tell. She can't really move anything right now. She'll be sore for a couple of days from the surgery," he says. And that does it for Mazi; she rips the poem out of my hands and runs out of the room crying. Spence and Bree follow her out to make sure she'll be all right.

"We'll see you guys later," Spence calls from down the hallway.

Brint and Griff have been relieved of the rest of their schedule for today, so they decide to check out the rest of the military base, leaving me, Pete, and Lakuna with Hayden.

CHAPTER TWELVE

Pete sits on the cushioned windowsill, looking out the glass and watching the troops train in obstacle courses. Lakuna clicks on the TV and turns the volume down to almost nothing; she and I pull the sofa that was against the wall closer to the bed.

"What if she can't play sports again?" I say to Lakuna. "That would be my fault."

She looks at me. "I am so tired of everyone blaming themselves for this. It's none of our faults," she explodes.

"Except mine," I whisper.

"I'm holding myself together by a string that is this big"—she holds her fingers a millimeter apart—"so if you don't mind, shut up." She snaps and buries her face in her hands.

Simone, Fallon, and Yanish make Pete, Lakuna, and I leave CCH for a meeting with the rest of the mentors and our friends. They lead us to a room called the Council Room. Our friends and their mentors are sitting around a giant wooden table in cushiony chairs. The guy in the black suit from the plane stands in the hole lining the inside of the table, still in a suit except this time it's light grey. We take our seats, and the guy in the suit snaps his fingers. The table opens in seventeen spots, and glasses of ice water pop up in front of us. The guy in the suit goes around and shakes each of the mentor's hands; they obviously already know each other.

"Hello. I am the president of the military base, the commander if you may. My name is Chipolaux Donovan." He looks at us and smiles with pleasure. "I have seen the video of you eight on the island. A very smart group!" If he's not careful, he might start dancing with joy. "Cam, Griff, Mazi, and Brint, we have contacted your legal guardians and told them what has happened to you and that you are perfectly safe here. Lakuna,

Spence, Bree, and Pete, your parents were not reachable. You were legally signed over to your mentors."

"You mean to say we've been adopted without our permission?" Spence growls.

"Not adopted per se. You will have someone to look after you, make sure you don't get into trouble, and make sure you're healthy. Other than that, you're free to do as you please." Bree and Pete don't seem too upset. Their parents died when they were young, car accidents. They've been passed around their whole life; they've been adopted and then abandoned so many times, I'm sure they've lost count.

"What about Ariel?" Pete whispers. Ariel is his younger sister and was Ozalee's best friend. Hayden met Pete before I met either of them. She introduced me to him. Ariel met Hixel, Tinley, and Broppin at one of the many orphanages they were sent to. Pete kind of took them all on as little sisters.

"That is why we called you here," Chipolaux says. "Since you will be staying here for quite a while, we want the base to feel as much like home as possible. We are giving you the choice to bring your families here."

They want us to bring our families into this mess? My mom? Ariel? Tinley? Hixel? Broppin? I mean, I know I'm not, in any way, related to those girls, but I still care about them. I don't want them to get hurt like we were. Ozalee dead is bad enough. She wasn't marked on the list for our school. She was too young. Was she marked on the elementary school list, or was she just put on the island with us because she was conveniently there when we were abducted? "When we were marked on that list, what were the standards?" I ask.

Chipolaux turns to me wondering what is going on inside my head. "I'm not sure I'm following you, son," he says.

"Were all of our ages marked on that list?"

"Oh, no, no. Just high schoolers. We only marked the children who were the closest in age to joining our military forces."

Ozalee was only in the third grade, so they must have taken her for the convenience of her being there, which means if Ariel, Tinley, Hixel, and Broppin were there, they would've got taken as well, and they could've died. If they didn't die, they would be here where some people would be debating on sending them into war.

"No. I do not want any of them here. You will not use them like you're using us," I say assertively. Chipolaux smiles. "Clever. Tell your friends your theory of me and my usage of you."

I tell them if Ariel, Tinley, Hixel, and Broppin were to come here, how easily the Center just earned four more children to go into war, to help end the war.

"Absolutely not. Don't even think of making Ariel into a soldier. There is no possibility I will let you do that," Pete says.

"We haven't decided any of you will be going into war, and if you do, you will go through training that will make it almost impossible for you to get killed. We assure you, none of the younger girls will be put into battle unless we have permission to do otherwise."

I don't trust them this time. Medical care is fine, but when it comes to these girls, no way. "No," Pete says, and his fist slams on the table.

"What if it was the only way to keep them safe?" Chipolaux says.

CHAPTER THIRTEEN

The Duxians sounded an alarm before the undercover spies attacked their headquarters. The spies who worked with the Duxians knew who they were going to kill next, us. They stole all traces of our existence from hospitals and school. The only place that has our remaining records is the Center. The people who worked with the gang now know who we live with, who we're related to, who we have history with (the younger girls), and our medical history. They practically know everything about us, and now they're after them. They're after Ariel, Tinley, Hixel, Broppin, and our parents.

"You swear they will not be put into war?" Pete asks in a hushed tone, defeated with what might happen.

"They will not be put into battle unless we are given permission," Chipolaux confirms. "All right then," Pete whispers.

Chipolaux is delighted with his new agreement. "Get those girls here within twenty-four hours!" he shouts to the random people lining the walls. They burst into a firework of excitement.

We and our mentors have to stay in this part of building as the people I don't know come in and out of the room. "As for education, you will be taught here at the military base. On the bright side, you will be excused for a while longer while you recuperate and whatnot." At least we'll be able to do something normal, eventually. Chipolaux goes on about how lucky we are the undercover spies got to the Duxians before they killed us and how we should be thankful the Center is welcoming to us. Bree gets so frustrated she walks out of the room, muttering it was their fault in the first place for saving the list of the kids in Villa.

Chipolaux finally figures out we're getting impatient with him. "Is there anything else you wish to have here to make you stay more comfortable?"

What is he, a hotel manager?

"Anything?" Mazi asks. "You'll give us anything?" "Anything reasonable," he answers.

Spence automatically says, "I want a guitar." And boy, can he play. I love to listen to him play. He doesn't play off a sheet. He plays as he goes. We always used to sit around a campfire in Hayden's backyard and listen to him. It was relaxing.

"A camera," Mazi says. She likes taking pictures and making collages.

"I want the horses down here," I say. Everyone freezes. "Not for me, I don't even own one. They'll help everyone relax a little. It will be better for Broppin and Tinley too."

"It will be better for everyone," I say. Mazi, Brint and Lakuna agree with me. "Please," Lakuna begs.

Chipolaux sighs. "All right." He speaks into a contraption on his wrist, telling the person on the other end to start building a barn in an unclaimed piece of land close to the base.

I lay my head on my hands, feeling my burning forehead, and wait until Chipolaux releases us.

We make it to the cafeteria at 8:03 p.m., an hour and a half late to our only mandatory meal. I expected Cocoa to be waiting at our assigned table to yell at us, but she's not. Instead there are extra chairs for our mentors. "We are supposed to try to get to know you," Fabien, Griff's mentor, says. That doesn't happen. We eat our red mush in silence and watch our mentors shovel in roasted chicken with some kind of sauce and mashed potatoes. Most of them go back for seconds unlike us because we're not allowed.

"You don't look too good, kid," Yanish says. "I'm fine," I mumble.

"We're trying to get you all to recover, not lie to us and make it worse, c'mon." Yanish and Simone take Lakuna and I to see our doctors. We don't go to the medical center, like we were apparently in the first ten days here. As an alternative, we go to just a small office tucked into a corner. Kanga and Ezzard are already waiting for us. Dr. Ezzard checks my heart rate and blood pressure before he addresses the obvious problem, my fever.

"It's not hard to see what the problem is. You didn't recognize what was happening in the days you've been here, and now with you fully aware of the situation, you've been stressing yourself out. Stress with these injuries will make you sick." He reaches to feel around my throat, but I yank away.

"Don't," I say defensively.

"I just need to check your lymph glands." He reaches for my throat again; my hands clench into fists.

"I wouldn't do that," Yanish says as he rubs my shoulder reassuringly; I shake it off and try not to run at the touch.

"A hundred four is a high fever. All I can do is give you stronger pills than what I've been giving you," Ezzard says and hands me a two bottles of pills, one for the night and one for the day.

We wait in the hallway for Lakuna and Simone. Yanish raises his eyebrows in question.

"It seems my little princess has a worse concussion than we thought," Simone says and pats Lakuna's back.

Lakuna carries a bottle of liquid medicine. "Nasty stuff. They'll be sorry the day they try to get me to take this." She reaches to grab my bottle, and I notice she has a bright orange band on her hand. RESCUE SQUAD, LAKUNA CREST, MUS. I have the same bracelet on my wrist except with my name. This is the first time I've noticed it.

"What does *MUS* stand for?"

Our mentors hesitate. "Mentally Unstable." Before we can say anything, Yanish continues, "It's not that your mentally unstable. It's just to say you can't be trusted yet."

"Whatever," Lakuna huffs and presses the Door Close button on the elevator, blocking them outside.

"So concussion, huh?" I say just to make conversation. "From the panther attack they think."

"What does that feel like?" I've never had a concussion before. I've got knocked around plenty at football, but I've never got hit hard enough to get a concussion.

"Your head always hurts. It's hard for me to think straight. They told me to close my eyes and rub my temples, try to make a list of what I do know. But it's hard because everything I know I wish I didn't," she moans.

"I'm feeling you."

I push open the door to our room and am greeted by the soothing cool air. Someone turned on the air conditioning. The rest of my friends are already showered, and I see they've got what they asked for. Spence sits on Mazi's bed, trying to tune his guitar. Mazi has probably shot one hundred pictures already, taking one of Lakuna and me as we walk through the door.

I strip off my shirt and swing the bathroom door closed before I take off my pants, then I step in the warm shower, immediately turning it to cold. The sweat on my face rinses away. I scrub down with pine-smelling products and get out, letting the puff of air dry me. I put on my clean clothes, walk into the bedroom, and smash my face into my pillow. It feels so good to lie down.

"Don't forget to take your pills," Lakuna says.

"The day you take your medicine is the day I'll take mine," I say.

"Or you'll both take it now," Dr. Ezzard says as he bursts through the door. He throws the pills at me, and they hit me in the side.

"Get me some water, old man," I say. He smiles. I take one of the night pills and start feeling the side effects immediately. He rubs the burn ointment on me, and I just lay there and listen to Spence play. I never put my shirt back on. I want the ointment to seep through my skin and heal my burns. I just want to feel normal again. Somewhere in there, my body and my mind give in to the pill, and I fall asleep.

No alarm goes off in the morning to wake us up. No people knock on our door. We are left to sleep. The clock reads 8:46 AM when I wake up. Mazi takes pictures of my friends sleeping. Lakuna curled up in her usual ball, Griff and Pete spread out, clenching their pillows for security, and Brint tapping his foot on his covers. She snaps me and my messy morning hair. "That's attractive, Cam."

"Thanks, I try to look good when I wake up in the morning," I say. She giggles and goes back to taking pictures. I go to the bathroom and do my usual morning routine, throw on my usual clothes, and go back into the unusual bedroom.

"Breakfast?" I ask Mazi.

"Sure, I bet you can't guess what we're gonna have."

"Yeah. Just stamp a big sticker on my head that says moron and then *maybe* I won't know."

We finish our mush quickly; we both want to see Hayden before everyone else gets in our faces. It takes us less time to reach CCH this morning. After Mazi's meltdown yesterday, she toured the building and got to know it better. The nurses don't try to stop us when we open her door. Hayden smiles when we walk in, and her skin stretches across her face, "You need some lotion," Mazi says. The room is the same as yesterday, but the couch has been pushed back. Mazi and I pull it forward.

"Look," Hayden's voice is so quiet and hoarse. The blankets on the lower half of her body move. "What was that?" I ask. My face moves closer to her bed so I can get a better view.

She does it again, her ankles move in circular motions, and her knees pop off the bed a little. "Oh my gosh. Hayden! That's awesome. How? Does that hurt?" Mazi asks astounded.

"It puts a lot of pressure on my back, but the morphine won't let me feel anything but weight."

The only thing I can say is, "Why?" "What?" she asks.

I say it louder, "Why did you do that?" "Do what?"

"Why did you push me out of the way?!" There are no words, nor will there ever be for how I feel right now. The closest thing I can get to is off the guilt charts. Severe depression maybe?

"Because you swore." "Excuse me?" I say.

"In the meadow, you swore on your life everything would be okay. I took your swear, but I changed it to my life instead. And now everything is okay." She smiles, happy with her answer or that she remembers that specific part of the island.

"Everything is *okay*?" My voice cracks at the end of my sentence, and I try really hard to keep a calm face. "Look at you," I choke. "You can't move. You can't do anything!"

"And you know what? I don't regret it."

I totally forgot Mazi was listening until she asked why.

"I got to see my family. My father and Ozalee. I was with them, only for a little bit, but I was there and they were happy."

I walk out of the room and lean against the wall of the hallway. How in the world can she be happy about this? Would she really take a swear that far, to die for it? The palms of my hands fill with sweat, and my mouth gets the taste you feel before you throw up. I try to swallow the sick feeling, but it sticks, clinging to my tongue. A nurse asks me if I'm all right, and I hold my hand up because I know if I say something, it will come out as yelling, not talking. She sees the bulge in my pocket and reaches her hand in there. She pushes the ringer on the teletalky that automatically connects to my mentor.

"What he doesn't know won't hurt him," I mumble to the wall.

Yanish taps my back. "But it will hurt you." He hands me the fever fighter I never took this morning.

"These don't help." I say, throw it on the floor, and crush it with my shoe.

"Take it anyway." He impatiently shoves the pill and a bottle of water in my hand, then he moseys into Hayden's room and comes out with a small shot filled with a clear liquid. "Do you mind?" he asks. It's not like he cares if I did or not. He sticks the needle in my arm.

The morphine is great; it makes all feeling of any hurt go away. The mental pain dims but doesn't vanish. Either way, I would rather have this than any pill. Yanish doesn't let me return to Hayden's room scared I'll say something I shouldn't because of the drugs. He tells Mazi to come with us; we are to report to the main office anyway. My group and their mentors are there waiting for us. Cocoa leads us through the door behind the desk and into a room called Makeup and Dress. Sitting in a movable chair is a small woman with big black eyes and a sheet of black hair that falls in a straight line just before her shoulders. Everyone exits the room and leaves us standing there with this woman.

"Darlings! Let me take a look at you," she says in a weird accent. She scrambles out of her chair and runs in small circles around us. When she stands on her tiptoes to examine our faces, she still only goes to my chest. "You poor, poor children. I'm going to have to do something about this," she says as she pulls Spence's face down to her eye level.

"Do what?" Lakuna asks.

"You need touch-ups on your looks before your families get here. They would be appalled if they saw you like this!"

She starts with the guys, scrubbing our scalps with different types of shampoo to match our hair color, texture, and other stuff I don't care about. She trims the split ends and burnt hair from our heads and then moves on to the girls. They take at least two hours, but the result is good. Lakuna's burnt hair is completely gone. You can't even tell she went through a fire, and Mazi's tangled curls once again form neat spirals. She makes us get showers that smell of bleach, but we come out with no scent. She says our hair that was removed before we were put onto the island will never grow back, meaning the girls will always have smooth legs and underarms, and the guys will never grow facial hair. Darn, I've always wanted a five'-o clock shadow. She plucks the heck out of our eyebrows, and then puts a yellow liquid where she yanked our hair, making sure the hair won't come back. She scrapes the dirt out from under our nails and toenails then carves them into perfect curves. She dabs make up on our faces to cover up the dark circles under our eyes and applies medicine to our burns, cuts, and bruises.

"All done. You look fabulous," she says and pushes us out the door. "If you ever need a makeover, ask for Edna," she calls behind us.

"Rescue Squad, please report to the main office." Cocoa calls over what I've learned is called an intercom. The color drains from Pete's face, and his eyes turn misty.

"Pete, it's going to be fine. They're not going to hurt them," Lakuna says.

"Yeah, yeah," he mutters under his breath. His joints start moving in a robotic fashion, and every couple steps he stops and someone smashes into his back. Our mentors meet us by the door behind the desk and escort us to another room lined with cushiony couches, chairs, and love seats. President York waits with a camera crew right next to the other door across the room.

"A camera crew?" Brint asks as he plops down on a couch.

"Your story is so miraculous, we thought to film every big event that happens. We might make a movie," President York says.

So that's why we were made over.

Chipolaux lines us up according to height. Spence, Griff, me, Pete, Brint, Bree, Lakuna, Mazi. He makes us stand straight with our feet shoulder width apart and our hands behind our backs. A tiny red light on the camera starts blinking. We look forward. I'm pretty sure the camera does a close-up on each of our faces. The door opens.

CHAPTER FOURTEEN

Cocoa leads everyone in. "Right in here," she says in a nicer voice than she's ever used with any of us. A blonde ponytail pokes out from behind Cocoa's back; big blue eyes peer out from under her arm.

Ariel's head rakes down the line until she finds who she's looking for.

"Petrie!" she squeals, pushes past Cocoa, and jumps into Pete's extended arms. She wraps her arms around his neck, squeezing his chest and his burns, but he doesn't notice. She buries her face in his hair. Tinley and Hixel find him also, grasping his shirt and sides. He moves his hands down to them to push them closer. Ariel stays locked around his neck. I can hear them whimpering, begging him never to leave them again.

"I won't. I won't," he comforts, but it's useless. They're scared to death.

Broppin searches for her cousins without any luck. She sweeps her eyes across us again, looking harder. I can almost feel the lump building in her throat; she slowly walks to Lakuna and whispers something in her ear. Lakuna bends upward, finds my eyes. She doesn't need to say anything. I already know. Broppin wants Hayden and Ozalee. I break off the line and glide toward them. Broppin's ear comes to my mouth, wanting an answer, but I don't have a good one. What do I say, "Oh, Hayden is broke and Ozalee is dead"? No, I lie. "They couldn't make it here, but you'll see them eventually."

She nods her head and gets on with the hugging. She clings to Mazi the longest and then moves down the line.

Eventually the line turns into a giant circle of hugging. The camera light clicks off when Chipolaux begins giving orders. The younger girls have already been prepped for the cameras, and Chipolaux asks them to sit on one of the couches so they can get more footage. Tallest to shortest. Broppin, Tinley, Hixel, Ariel. They wear the same thing we do except their shirts are dark blue instead of maroon. Everyone here is allowed to wear whatever they want, except us, the younger girls, and the troops. This makes me uncomfortable. I understand us and the troops, but not them. The camera's red dot starts up again, and Chipolaux positions us in the same order we were in before, and Cocoa leads in another group. Our parents.

Both of Mazi's parents, both of Brint's parents, Hayden's mother, and my mother. We are greeted by hugs and kisses, tears and smiles. Griff moves next to me and our mother touches our cheeks as a tear runs down hers.

"My boys," she smiles. Wrinkles form around her eyes. "Do you know how hard it was to not know if you were dead or alive? We searched everywhere. You just vanished, no evidence or nothing." She's full out crying by the time she finishes her sentence. I'm glad she's here, but I'm used to having her gone. She cares about us, just not nearly enough. If she really loved us, we would sleep in our own beds more than twice a week. She would take off work before eight to see us before we go to bed. It's not like we go to bed early, but it's when we settle down. I can see Mazi's and Brint's reluctance in their parents too.

My mom's motherly instincts kick in as she holds her hand to my cheek. "Son, you're burning up!"

"I'm fine, Mom," I tell her.

"Don't these people know what medicine is?" she says louder so everyone can hear her.

"Ma'am, I assure you, he's as hopped up as he can get," Chipolaux says. That's definitely true—Ezzard popped two more pills in my mouth right before the cameras started rolling.

She turns to Griff and glares at his black cast. "How?" she whispers. She apparently hasn't seen the video yet.

"I fell off a cliff," he grins, raising his eyebrows making the scar above his eye stand out. "What is this?" she says and rubs his scar.

"That's a long story," he mumbles and looks at his feet.

As Dr. Ezzard informs our parents of all of our injuries, they become more protective. Mazi's mom asks her everything in the world about the panther attack, butterfly sting, and Spence. Brint's dad checks out the stitches on the top of his head from the shell Griff hit him with. Hayden's mom has been removed from the room where the news of Ozalee's death is reported to her and Hayden's recovery is told. And mine, well, she's just a mess.

"Petrie, how come you're not hurt like them?" Ariel asks and points to Griff's leg and Mazi's bandaged hand. He chose not to show her his chest. That would freak her out, and I suppose he hasn't told her about the flood.

"Because I'm smart," he jokes.

Ariel's nickname for Pete makes me laugh. I asked why she called him that once. She couldn't say her *G*s when she was little, and every time she said Pete Girth, it came out as Petrie and it stuck. The camera clicks off, and our mentors introduce themselves to our parents and the younger girls. Cocoa is allotted to look after the girls, joy.

The younger girls are assigned a room with Cocoa, my mother, and Hayden's mom across the hall. Lakuna's and Brint's parents stay in separate rooms down the tower. We meet for lunch in the cafeteria, given a larger table than we had before. The younger girls question about the red mush. We tell them it's to help us gain weight. The steak they eat is mouthwatering. It's extremely hard to resist when Tinley offers me some.

Yanish smacks her fork away from my mouth. "You don't want that to come back up, do you?" he says.

Wyllie barges in the cafeteria with a huge grin on her face. "Rescue Squad is needed in CCH," she chirps, wheels on her heels, and dances out the door. As I anxiously try to dump my tray, my undrunk milk spills all over the table.

"Where are you going?" Broppin asks, worried.

"Um, we need to go see someone," Mazi says, and we run out the door.

We don't make it to Hayden's room. She comes to us. We barely get into her hallway before she, accompanied by four nurses, hobbles down the path. She grips the stand with the morphine bag for her life, might as well be. "We tried to get her to stop attempting to move, but it didn't work and it seemed to be for the better," says one of the nurses.

Has it even been two weeks since the tree hit her?

"It truly is impossible," another nurse says with a smile.

My friends and I gather around her, amazed at her progress. I want to hug her. I can't stop smiling. Chipolaux comes in with the camera crew and films her walking. After she walks around the hallway a couple of times she asks, "Got enough, Chipolaux?" I can tell no matter how little she actually walked, she is exhausted and so, so weak.

"Thank you, Ms. Kolter." He leads the camera crew out the door.

The nurses take her to a different room, a less hospitaly one. The bed doesn't have bars, and there is no ventilator present. The nurses help her into the bed. I notice how her hair is shinier, and the chalk from her skin is gone. I know someone attempted to bath her when we got off the island, but I think Edna worked on her today too. The nurses leave, and we pull the couch closer. Mazi, Lakuna, and Bree take the windowsill. The guys get the couch this time.

"Thanks for the heads-up about my mom, guys," she snaps the second my butt hits the cushion. "She knew about Ozalee. She surprised me. I thought I was hallucinating or something. I asked her if she was real. She started crying. No one even told me she was coming," Hayden says.

We fail to come up with an excuse for not telling her because we should have. Lakuna calls Gibson, Hayden's mentor, so he can explain in more detail how we came to the conclusion our parents should be brought here.

"She saw the video. The only parent that did," Gibson says.

Hayden puts her hands over her eyes and pulls the sheet up to her chest. "Great," she mutters under her breath. "What about the other girls?"

"We were going to show them, not tell them."

"Show them her death or the whole video?" Hayden asks as she tries to understand. "Whichever," Gibson says.

They would see us hurt, coping, and loving. I don't know if I would want them to see our kiss. It was just one, but it meant a lot. Our chemistry is still here but dying, or what chemistry I thought we had. I hoped we had anyway. Would she want them to see us kissing? They don't know we have something going on between us. I love her, but does she feel the same? Can she, or does she, even remember being on the island or the things that happened there?

"The whole thing. I want to see it," she says.

"We can arrange that," Gibson walks out of the room.

The rest of the group follows Gibson out. Pete says they need to explain some things to the younger girls before they watch the video themselves. I tell Hayden about the room we're staying in and what our diet is and how Chipolaux asked us what we wanted. "Spence got a guitar. Mazi got a camera."

"Oh gosh, Mazi with a camera?" she asks. "I wanted the horses," I say.

"Girl is here?" she asks.

"Well, Lakuna and everyone wanted them, and I thought you would too, so I asked. Chipolaux had some people build a barn."

Her smile grows to cover her whole face. "You did that for me?" she asks.

"Well, he said we could have anything reasonable," I say only because I don't want to admit I got them strictly for her.

"Thanks," she holds her icy hand out to me. I press it to my lips. She gasps.

"Did that hurt?" I ask, letting go of her hand. "No, Cam, your lips . . . they are on fire." "Huh?"

"Your fever," she stutters. "You almost died?"

I don't understand her sometimes. She looks like this, and she's worried about a fever. Nice. Just to humor her, I pull another pill from my pocket—Yanish made me carry some—and shove it in my mouth. "All better," I tell her.

She runs her fingers over the makeup-covered circles under my eyes, and I yawn so big my jaw cracks. "You need a nap," she says.

"I need a lot of things." She pats the empty side of her bed. I would truthfully love to sleep just once without being knocked out by a fever pill or a patch. I lie down next to her. She wipes the powdery cosmetics off my face and laughs as it reveals shadows as dark as hers. She pulls the cover up, and I crawl under it. I can feel the bumps on her skin rising, but she doesn't say anything.

She leans on her side and slides her hands under the pillow. "It feels nice to lie on my side." "Can't you feel it?" I ask.

"Nope, they gave me a brace. They said I should be able to come to your room soon," she says. That's the last thing I remember.

I wake up a couple hours later and scramble out of the sweat-soaked sheet. Aw, man, my head spins when I stand up too fast. When I grab the bed for support, I wake her too.

"Please go see a doctor," she gasps as she talks. One of the nurses has unplugged her medication. I watch as her hands clench so tight they turn white. I click her morphine back into place. "Thank you." Her eyes dilate under a layer of opiates. She drifts off. I still can't stop thinking that even though she's talking and whatnot, she is going to die. I yank the teletalky from my pocket and check my missed calls. I ignore the voice messages from Yanish and Chipolaux and go straight to see Ezzard.

I push open the doctor's door. "Ezzard, I don't care what kind of treatment you give me, but please make this go away."

"That bad?" he asks as he pulls the magazine away from his face. I shoot a look at him, and he brings the stethoscope from his neck and presses the cold metal to my chest. He takes my temperature. "A hundred six. That's healthy," he says sarcastically. He finds a long needle from a blue thing hanging on the wall. "It might make you sick for a couple days, but after you'll feel a lot better." He pulls the collar of my shirt down and sticks the needle in my neck.

"Owww!" I yelp. I stomp out of the office rubbing my neck and pick up my teletalky when it rings. "What?" I say agitated.

"Come to the theater," Yanish says and hangs up. I press the map on my teletalky and follow the animated GPS as it guides me through the base.

The theater is a black room with red leather sofas in front of a giant screen. Chipolaux makes us sit in a special order to relive what we've already faced. Brint, Bree, Spence, Mazi, Broppin, Hayden, Pete, Ariel, Lakuna, Griff, Tinley, Hixel, and then me. The younger girls were ecstatic to see Hayden; they keep asking questions about what happened, but Chipolaux tells them to be patient. Our mentors sit directly behind each person they were assigned to. Chip, Cocoa, and all of our doctor's sit in the very back, and our parents sit to the side. Hayden's mother is not present, probably mourning over the loss of her youngest daughter.

"We've only put the important parts in this," Chipolaux says. A nervous lump forms in my stomach as our fears come alive again. They start the video with us awakening on the island and go forth with some events I don't really care about such as us building the shack or the first night.

Chipolaux pauses the tape. "Does anyone want to leave?" he says because we all know what upcoming horror awaits us. I notice how Hayden presses her body closer to Pete's. She winces but she doesn't move back. And then they replay Ozalee's death. How Hayden tries to put her muscles back together but they slip off Ozalee's body because of the blood, how she tells her she loves her more, and how Ozalee's last breath was in Hayden's lap. Chipolaux pauses the tape after Ozalee's funeral.

"Hayden?" Hixel whimpers, her orangish eyes overflowing with tears. "You couldn't save her?" Tinley whispers.

Pain flashes across Hayden's eyes for only a second. "I tried. You saw I tried."

Hixel presses her face into my shoulder; I wrap my arm around her as she sobs. Tinley pushes her cheeks into her hands, and I watch as tears run down her wrists, and her throat makes small noises. That's all of the reaction that occurs. Broppin stares straight forward, her face hard as stone. Ariel moves away from Pete and sits on Lakuna's lap; Lakuna sweeps Ariel's hair away from her face.

"We'll start again tomorrow," Chipolaux says, seeing that's all we can take.

Mazi and Spence take Tinley and Hixel to our room. They're allowed to sleep in our room tonight because Cocoa realizes she's as much help to them as sand was to us on the island. Useless. Brint and his parents help Hayden back to her hospital room. She doesn't need it, but I think it makes them feel better. She has to wash her makeup off sooner or later; I wonder how his parents are going to react when they find out how she got the bruises on her neck. The rest of us decide to go to the cafeteria to attend our only mandatory meal. That's a joke. Out of the days I've been here, I've never went to it.

Pete and Lakuna attempt to coax food into Broppin and Ariel, but they turn their noses. Bushed, we retreat to our room for an early night. That's where Broppin cracks. The mascara Edna put on her runs down her face; it kind of matches the storm outside. Lightning bolts strike the base, sparks of orange and red flutter to the grass, and big booms of thunder shake the floors. Now three of the girls are crying, but not Ariel.

Twin-sized beds are too small to hold four girls, so Spence and I push our beds together so the girls can sleep. Spence will share a bed with Mazi. It's not like that's something new. They've done it every night we've been here. I'll get the floor. The younger girls get showers and sit on the windowsill, listening to Spence play. *Now would be a great time for morphine,* I think to myself. The weeping rubs me in the wrong way. I loved Ozalee just like the rest of us, but I haven't cried over her death, yet. And I would like to keep it that way, but the younger girls are making it hard. Every once in a while, one of us says we have to go to the restroom, but we all know no one actually goes—they cry and try to hide it from the younger girls. Eventually they fall asleep, which gives us a chance to shower without showing them our injuries. I slip on a pair of shorts and steal some of the blankets off of Griff's bed to make a spot for me on the floor.

Pete and I decide to go back to the hospital to see Hayden before the night is over. When we enter the room, Chip, Gibson, Kanga, Rae, and the five doctors are their sitting around her bed. We push through to see what's going on. A tiny thin wire is attached to her forehead just below her hairline. A large television screen is behind the bed. It also connects to the wire. She is not awake.

"What are you doing?" I ask.

Rae scribbles something down on her notepad just as a picture of Mazi pops on the screen. But it isn't the Mazi we know. This one is pregnant.

"These are her dreams," Chipolaux says. He is mesmerized by what is flicking on and off the screen.

"You can actually do that?" Pete asks. "Well, yes. But only with some people."

We sit on the couch in front of the TV and watch the screen. Many pictures are different and strange. The sunset, a bow, the field of Tibbet. And then a picture of Pete's face flashes and sticks longer than all of the others. He is smiling with his hand in his hair and a football in his arm. Then he laughs. I glance at him to see what is so funny, but it's not him. It's the sound on the screen.

"Miraculous," Chipolaux mutters, "this has never happened before. I've never seen dreams so clear. For this to be so, she has to know exactly this noise." Chipolaux's face brightens; he turns to the doctors and tells one of them to laugh. When they do the screen goes black, Rae is frantically writing.

"Laugh, Pete. Not the one you just heard." Pete chuckles a fake, lying laugh and the screen lights up again with his picture and his sounds. "Now talk to her," Chipolaux says. Pete leans close to her ear, moves her hair away, and whispers her name. The screen gets blurry, but Pete is there looking straight at us. The camera moves closer to him, and he whispers her name. Lying on the bed, Hayden squeezes her eyes tighter and breathes heavier.

"Stop, she doesn't like it," Pete says. "What do I do?"

"That was before she passed out from the panther attack. That is how she saw you, Pete," Chipolaux says.

"But she doesn't remember?" he asks.

"She doesn't remember directly. She knows what happened but only in the deepest of her consciousness."

When Hayden starts grasping her stomach Pete quickly whispers, "Sleep now. We will not let anything happen to you." Her hands go still, and then she's on the screen smiling. "Can she hear me?" he asks.

"Somewhat." The dreams go back to the original random stuff—horses, books, school. And then I'm looking at myself, smiling. The picture in the yearbook that says best smile. And I'm there again with her hand on my cheek when I was in the deepest part of the lost world I went to while I was raging with fever. Pictures flash slowly across the screen, her kissing me when I was unreachable, me giving her the blue flower she still has on her bedside table, and then I attaching the morphine back to her arm.

"Now you talk to her," Chipolaux says.

I mumble, almost silently the word *love* in her ear. The younger girls flash first but disappear quickly. Mazi, Lakuna, and Bree creep on to the screen, and then there is us again, Pete and I, in the same picture. The scene moves from just us two to us tackling each other in football to us having our first fist fight over who gets more of Griff's attention and transforms into us holding each other at knife point. The dream is in such detail I have no choice but to look away, a total nightmare. Not because it shows every last image of us killing each other but because it shows she loves me. And Pete. The same exact amount.

Sweat drips down her face, and she mumbles something although the medicine won't allow her to wake up. "Stop. Help," she whispers, trapped in herself.

"How do we make it stop?" Pete asks frantically. Rae searches through her notes; I hear a loud crunch and automatically know one of her ribs has recracked from her thrashing. The sight of Lakuna and I pops up on the screen. It's fuzzy and we are yelling her name. This is when the tree crushed her.

"Chipolaux!" I hiss. "Make it stop! We're hurting her." Just then Pete gets close to her and presses his lips to her temple. It's irritating to me that she automatically connects the touch to Pete because then I know he has kissed her before. She may not have known it, but it has happened. She knows his every touch. As much as it bothers me that Pete is in her dreams again, at least she's not hurting herself over it.

I get to my room late. I flip off the bright lights when there's a knock on the door.

"Since when do you bother to knock, old man," I say to Ezzard as I click the lights back on and open the door. My mother follows him and Kanga into our room, and she sees the full extent of our injuries without our shirts on. She watches in horror as Ezzard rubs burn ointment on my third-degree burns and puts ice packs on the large bruises all over my body. I take the fever pill and stick the patch on my stomach. This usually takes me out straightaway but not tonight. I observe my mother's different expressions as Ezzard moves on to Griff. He does exercises with him to help heal his leg faster, applies the burn ointment, and gives him the patch.

"Get your own blankets next time," he mumbles into his pillow and drops off.

Each patch helps you gain weight, but each of us has a different one. Mine is a fever reducer, Lakuna's a stabilizer. Griff has a pain patch. It burns him out like a light. It's like it uses all his energy up to power itself. My mother sees how each patch makes us drowsy some more than others. She realizes this when Pete goes only seconds after his patch is placed on his skin. He doesn't even have time to get under his sheets. He just flops on the bed. Lakuna covers him up hiding his bandaged chest.

"I brought this for you," she whispers. She pulls a brown leather ball from her back. It's the football my dad had bought me on my tenth birthday. CAM MALROOK is engraved in gold letters on the side.

"Thanks. Where's Griff's baseball?" My dad bought Griff a baseball instead of a football because that's his favorite sport. It has his name engraved along the red stitching. She holds out her other hand; I take it from her and toss it to Griff's side. "I'll let him know you brought it."

She nods her head, and her strawberry blonde bangs fall on her face. "I love you," she says. "Okay, Mom." Salt water spills out of the blue pools on her face, and she leaves our room.

Ezzard and Kanga finish their medical procedures. "Have fun tomorrow, kid," Ezzard says, turns the lights off, and shuts the door.

I push the On button on the TV and try to watch, but I'm restless. I throw the football at the ceiling for a little bit until it comes down, slips through my fingers, and smacks me in the face. I hear a small giggle. Thinking one of the younger girls saw me, I stand up to see which one it was, but none of them are awake. Ariel's smiling face goes still and then frowns. Sweat beads form on her forehead and water runs from her eyes. Her breathing quickens. She jolts upward and sees me staring at her. "She really is dead, isn't she?"

"Yes," I say, she tries to wake Pete up, but he's too far gone.

She crawls to the corner of the room and curls into a ball. "I don't understand," she says. "She was my best friend. She's not coming back? Ever?" She looks at me, expecting me to say she'll walk through the door in two seconds.

"No."

"You're lying," she accuses. "I'm not lying to you, Ariel."

"Yes, you are! Lying is wrong. She is coming back! She not dead! She can't die . . ." She sobs more than the other girls, so much so that I have to bring her into the hall so she won't wake anyone up.

I feel older than I am when she crawls into my lap; I feel like a father figure, one she never had, the one Pete took place of. But since Pete isn't here, it's my job to help her through something she can't get through alone, like my father used to do, and no one was there for me when he died, but I'll be here for her. I use questions to try to get her to stop crying. "Why was she your best friend?" I ask her.

She answers in no time, "Because we grew up together. She understood everything I told her. She never left me out or put me down like Tinley does. She liked the way I acted. She didn't want me to change, and when I tried, she wouldn't let me.

"But now I can," she continues and cries harder. Her body starts shaking.

That worked. I sit and listen to her cry; I become familiar with the sound. High pitched and breathy, two quick ins and two quick outs. It stops as her body falls limp in my chest. I carry her back in the room and lay her on my makeshift bed. I head back in the hallway where the air is less stuffy and lean against the wall.

"Feel bad yet? I heard Ezzard gave you that shot. Without my permission," Yanish says. "Were you gonna let me die?" I ask.

"Hilarious."

He carries around a clear bottle and takes a swig every few minutes. If he's drunk, it's not noticeable. He tosses my football with me down the hall, and every time a guard tells us to go back to our room, he tells him to layoff.

"So, Cam, I've seen the tape. Your mother and Hayden's mother brought some photo albums here from your old homes, but I still feel like I don't know you." I notice how he puts an emphasis on the *s* in homes.

"There's not much to know. I'm sixteen. Griff Malrook is my twin. Our birthday is February 1. My dad is dead, and I like to play sports." That pretty much covers the basics.

"Well, what kind of sports do you play?" he asks.

"I used to play football and baseball and run track."

He throws the ball harder. "What positions do you play? What events do you run?" he asks. He seems interested when I tell him about my positions and what difficulties come for me when I play them. I tell him what I run and how hard it is for me.

"Have you ever gotten hurt in a game?" he asks. "No, not seriously anyway."

He takes me to the weight room and lifts with me. He jots notes down as we go, such as how much I can bear.

"You like to go to the gym?" he asks.

"No. I hate going to the gym, but it helps me clear my head," I say.

"What are you thinking about?" "Just stuff."

"What stuff?" he asks.

"Why this happened to us. We're ordinary people, nothing special, and yet everyone seems to think we're amazing. And how Ariel cried over Ozalee or how much I want to sock Pete sometimes."

He raises his scruffy eyebrows. "Pete?"

I throw the ball at the ceiling. "Yeah, ever since he and Griff met, they've been best friends, and Griff hardly pays any attention to me anymore."

"Oh," is all he says.

"And I know he's Hayden's best friend too."

"Its 4:32 AM, kid. Get some sleep."

I push the door to our room open, move Ariel in the bed with Lakuna, and pass out on the sheet—covered floor.

I wake up when Bree accidently kicks me as she tries to step over me from going to the restroom. "Sorry," she whispers. I don't have time to say anything back before I feel my stomach flip inside me, and I run just fast enough to throw up in the toilet. This is how I spend my next three days, lying in my bed in my room. Every time I move, I puke, so I don't move. Yanish brought a huge bucket for me that Wyllie cleans out each time I vomit, which is a lot. Ezzard stops giving me any other treatment, my burns flare up in red blisters and my fever gets higher. He says it's only temporary, and he told me I wouldn't feel good for a couple of days. He got that right. They ask me to eat but I say no. Other than that, I sleep most of the time.

CHAPTER FIFTEEN

A lot of people come and go from our room now, Ezzard, Wyllie, Kanga, Yanish, my mother, Hayden's mother, the younger girls, and Hayden. In the times I am awake, Hayden's mother is working on me. She was promoted to doctor once Chipolaux learned that was one of her three jobs back in Villa. Ezzard observes her to make sure she does everything right, but she's as good a doctor as him or Kanga. Hixel sticks around a lot, I think anyway. One afternoon, she's there dabbing an ice pack on my face and soaking up my sweat with a rag.

"That feels good," I tell her.

"Yanish told me you'd appreciate it. You're so sick."

"I do and I know." Her brown hair is slightly tousled today, a common way she wore it back in Villa, but her eyes, usually orangish hazel, seem almost black now. "Is there something you want to talk about?" I ask.

"I don't fit in here, Cam. I don't like it here."

"Why would you say that?"

"Ever since I got here, all I've heard is bad news, and all I've seen is sick people. Like you. You never used to look like this. You were always so big and strong. Now I think I might be able to beat you in arm wrestling."

"Maybe that's the one thing you can beat me in now?"

She smiles a fake smile. "I want to go home," she says.

"Me too, more than anything, but you're not safe at home."

"Why not?" Hixel is only eight; too young to comprehend the entire concept of if she goes back to Villa she'll be taken and most likely murdered by the Duxians.

"You'll understand when you're older."

"They won't even let us play soccer," she whispers.

"Have you told Pete? He could probably have that arranged?" I tell her because I'm not as fond of Chipolaux as Pete is and he will go to any measure to get the girls whatever they want whereas I'm just here for support.

"He's too busy."

"Busy? With what?" I ask.

"The crowds, that's why we can't play soccer. They're everywhere. You guys are famous."

"We're famous?" I ask. Maybe my fever is skyrocketing again; the lamp next to me is talking.

"Ever since the base has played the video of the island, you guys are all everyone's been talking about. And you got especially popular when you guys chose for us to be sent over here. We're just as famous as you, and Chipolaux won't let us outside until the crowd dies down a little."

"Isn't that what you've always wanted? To be famous?" I ask.

"I'm not Tinley. So no. Ariel and Broppin are always together now because Ozalee is gone, and Tinley wants all the attention and then there is me."

"I'll tell you what. After I get better, we'll do something together, all right?" "Just you and me?" she asks.

"Just you and me." Then she is ordered to leave the room so I can rest and make a full recovery.

When I wake up the next day, I feel amazing, better than amazing. I don't know a word for it, but it's miraculous. I get in the shower and dress in my normal maroon shirt and black shorts. I head down to the cafeteria by myself and show the lunch lady the bracelet on my wrist. She gives me a tray with milk, one banana, and one pancake with a tiny cup of syrup. The sweetness of the syrup explodes on my tongue, and the banana's crystal sugar melts in my mouth. I savor every bite until my meal is gone; when I dump my tray, a giant bald-headed man and a younger guy approach me.

"Cam Malrook?" the baldie asks. "That's me," I say.

"How is that possible? You don't look any different than the rest of us. Are you extraordinarily smart or something?" the younger one asks.

"What? No. What are you talking about?"

"I don't think he knows yet," the older one says quietly so I'm not supposed to hear it, but I do.

"Knows what?" It's irritating that I don't understand what they're talking about.

The bald one pats me on the back. "Good luck, son."

Good luck? Good luck on what? Not throwing up for a day? I stomp through the base until I run into someone I recognize. "Fallon! Do you know where Yanish is?" I hiss at him.

"Oh, no, no, no! Do you not check your teletalky?" He laughs at me. "No, now where's Yanish?"

"You are to report to the Council Room. Come, come, and follow me!" He leads me to the Council Room where everyone is waiting for us. Chipolaux stands in the middle of the table with his new charcoal grey suit. He had it made just a week ago—he told me yesterday. Every one I've met since I've been in the base is here. President York is in the center of the table too. Everyone else lines the walls. Our mentors sit next to us. None of the younger girls or parents are in the room though, and I can already guess what this is about.

"Ah, Hayden. Good to see you here." He smiles at her. She doesn't make eye contact.

"As you can tell, this meeting is very important, so I'll get right to the point. You knew from the beginning all of you might have to go to battle. You will not be going into direct confrontation of soldiers from Duxia. We have a mission for you."

What kind of talk is this? "We have a mission for you." Ooh, scary.

"We want you to disable a machine," he continues.

"A machine? Our 'mission' is to disable a machine?" Lakuna asks. "You kept us here to disable a machine?" Brint tests in disbelief.

"You don't understand. We've sent troops in to deactivate it before. None succeeded. They were always killed or taken. We've been close to it, but they have a very strong force to guard it," President York says.

"Why can't you get someone else to do it?" Griff says.

"We've tried, but none work as a team like you nine. Your tape was miraculous. I honestly think you can put it out of action without all of you getting killed," York says.

"You mean to tell me you can't find anyone else but a bunch of teenagers to send to disable a machine?" Spence says unconvinced.

"They've tried," Yanish says. He pulls his shirt down, revealing a long scar. "They've sent you?" I ask. He nods his head.

"They sent all of us," Bronte says pointing to the scar on his head. "It didn't work." "Why?" Mazi asks.

"Our commander was killed. We didn't know what to do," Gibson says. "Why haven't you sent anyone else in then?" Bree asks.

"We did a couple more times, but they were blown up or executed or captured. The troops who were guarding the machine began to suspect the people we were sending, and they were always ready for them. So we waited, and now we're sending some again. You."

CHAPTER SIXTEEN

We are not allowed to tell the younger girls or our parents. The news didn't come as a shock to any of us; we knew there was a reason for the good treatment. It's not news that you'll get over though; it's the kind of news that automatically stamps "Hi, my name is dead" on your forehead. We are taken by Ezzard and Kanga for a complete physical examination. He takes us and our mentors to a special room with gym equipment and a full-on doctor setup. First, he takes my height and weight.

"Five-eleven and 172. That special diet seemed to have worked," Ezzard says with a smile on his face. He shines a light in my eyes, checks my ears, nose, and throat for any infections, and then he takes my blood pressure and a blood sample. I don't let him touch my neck to check my tonsils, so he moves on to my more serious injuries. He says the ointment he put on my burns will heal them up for good in less than a day then takes measurements of the guys' heads, necks, arms, shoulders, chests, hips, waists, legs, and feet. That's all of the treatment I need.

The doctors give Spence, Griff, Pete, Hayden, Bree, Lakuna, and Mazi pain pills to remove stitches and casts and whatnot. It makes them say weird things. Ezzard says it will knock them out eventually. He takes over two hundred stitches out of Spence's calf, removes Griff's cast and stitches from his leg, applies burn ointment to both of them, and puts like a gallon of the burn ointment on Pete's chest and then wraps it in tight bandages. Kanga rubs burn ointment on the girl's skin. She gives Hayden and Lakuna a pill to help with their concussions and then gives Hayden a morphine pill since the drip has been removed. She takes out the stitches from Hayden's calf, back, and arm. Even though the wound on her arm was small, all feeling from her forearm down is completely gone. Kanga removes the stitches from Lakuna's chest and shoulder; we have to leave the room for that one because she had to take off her shirt. When we come back in,

Bree's stitches from her hip are gone, and Mazi's back and hand are being worked on. Once they finish, our mentors escort us back to our room.

Our room has nine beds in it now; they finally put Hayden's in. We get most of them to the room before they go down, but Bolt, Gibson, and Simone end up carrying Mazi, Hayden, and Lakuna back. Brint and I are supposed to go to lunch and then see Rae for questioning. This time we're allowed to be questioned together. We lock our door behind us so the younger girls can't get in. Our lunch today is grilled cheese and tomato soup.

"Why'd you lock the door?" Hixel asks.

Because the stupid doctors here won't stop drugging us up and we don't want you to see it, I think.

"People are napping," Brint says.

"That's all you guys ever do," Tinley says.

"I know. Trust me, it's not our fault," I say. We finish our lunch; the younger girls say they want to go to questioning with us so we let them tag along.

"What are you afraid of?" Rae asks.

"Nothing really. Severe storms maybe?" Brint says. "I would rather not get in water," I say.

"Ah, I see. Can you think of anything handy that you're good at?" By *handy,* she means something we can use in war.

"I can swim pretty well. I know CPR," Brint says. "Um, I'm not good at anything important," I say.

"Tomorrow you begin prepping and training. I'll get more information then." She releases us to see Edna. And that's when I learn what pure torture is. Edna takes the younger girls away from us and leads us into the Makeup and Dress Room.

A tall, slim man takes Brint and I into a room across the hall labeled the same thing. He doesn't have an accent nor does he talk a lot. His name is Jack. His skin is a dark caramel color that matches his eyes. His hair is short, cut down so you can see all of his face and ears. He strips Brint and me to the skin and observes our bodies, then he sends us to the showers. At first, the water stings my skin, and then it becomes silky and smooth. I lop unscented shampoo in my hair and then wash my face. Jack yanks us out of the shower.

"The first phase was to remove dead or dying skin." He points to my burns, which are now a baby pink color. "The second was to moisten and renew." He dries my dark brown hair and likes the fact that it flips over my ears and the burn on the top of my forehead. He compliments Edna for trimming my hair so it falls to my mid-forehead. He tries spiking Brint's bangs, up but he doesn't like it, so he washes it out again and lets it dry in the usual triangle form over his forehead. We don't have circles under our eyes anymore, so we need very little makeup on our faces. "It's a good thing all of you have dark eyelashes because otherwise we'd have to apply mascara," he laughs quietly. I'm guessing he's somehow already seen the other guys because he said "all of you."

"Do you know what we're doing?" Brint asks as Jack slips a yellow long-sleeved button-up shirt on him. He unbuttons the top two buttons and steps back to observe him. Yellow shirt, black belt, black pants, black shoes.

"Chipolaux wants formal pictures in addition to recreational pictures to put in the persuasive tapes," Jack says, unbuttoning the top two buttons of my brighter green shirt.

"Persuasive tapes?" I ask. Jack looks at his work. Green button-up long-sleeved shirt, black belt, black pants, black shoes.

"The military base knows you'll be performing what they couldn't. Gipem doesn't," he says this, but it's confusing to me.

"Huh?" I ask anxiously.

"He is making videos to show Gipem how serious this war is and how they have resulted in sending you nine in to stop it." That explained absolutely nothing.

"What?" I ask again.

"He will be presenting these tapes in front of Gipem. It will be mandatory to watch. He is trying to get sponsors, charity per se. We are trying to keep you as safe as possible when you're down there because we truly believe you have potential," Jack says patiently.

"So he is showing our videos to the whole country to get money to support us?"

Jack nods. I don't even know why we're in war. I don't know why we're being sent in to stop a machine. I don't know what this machine does. I ask Jack. He says those questions are not his job to answer. His job is to make us look good and listen when we have something to say. I have a lot to say, but I keep my mouth shut.

Jack leads us through the base and into the field we came from. The fence has been torn down, letting my eyes soak in the Center. The military base and President York's mansion are easily the tallest buildings in the Center. The other houses, shops, and buildings are tall but not nearly to the extent of the place we're staying, and their shapes are like nothing I've ever seen. Every building is a different shape and color. It ranges from spheres to shapes I don't even know, from crimson to bright yellow. Every color I've ever seen or imagined is right in front of me. I stand in a small meadow of various flowers, exactly like the one on the island. Thank goodness there are no butterflies.

First, Chipolaux has the camera crew do single full-body shots of Brint and I, and face shots, then he has us put one knee on the ground and place our elbow on the other knee and our face in our hand, no smiling in this one. He takes some serious pictures and some of us having fun like us patting each other on the back or giving each other a high five.

Yanish and Cyrus pretend to sound trumpets when the younger girls enter the field. But they don't look like the "younger girls" anymore. Ariel and Hixel look like the "younger, younger, younger girls," and Tinley and Broppin look like girls our age. Ariel wears a soft pink dress that stops at her knees. It hugs her chest, bunches in a bow at her back, and poofs out at the bottom. Her shoes and headband are silky pink to match her dress, and her usually straight hair is in ringlets. Hixel is dressed in the exact same thing as Ariel except its orangish gold to match her eyes. I think the designers like to make our eyes pop or something because everything they dress us in corresponds with our eyes or brings them out. Tinley's silver satin dress hugs her body all of the way to her mid-thigh. Her hair is straightened, and her bangs are pinned back in a diamond-studded barrette that blends with her heeled shoes. I'm taken aback when I see Broppin. I can completely see the bloodlines that run between her and Hayden. They look almost dead on, other than the fact Broppin's eyes are brown and Hayden's are the color of the sea. Broppin is even shaped the same way as Hayden. Broppin is wearing the same thing as Tinley but in a deep purple.

"You girl's look beautiful," Cocoa says. It's clear Cocoa is fonder of kids than teenagers. They curtsy in front of her. Her face lights up with optimism.

Chipolaux has the camera crew take full-body shots, face shots, fun shots—they don't get serious shots. He is delighted when I scoop Hixel up in my arms, and she kisses my cheek. He has Brint and I do this with each of the girls, and we even get photos of us with our mentors. They give us a break to eat a dinner of onion soup and bread, and as soon as the sun starts to set, we're pulled back out for more pictures. They get shots of us lying in the flowers looking at the stars, and they get a shot of Ariel and Hixel holding hands and laughing. That one's my favorite.

Chipolaux is ecstatic with our performance and ends on a good, "That's a wrap, everyone. See you tomorrow." Exactly like Coach said the day we got kidnapped.

I unlock our door with the key Yanish gave me and peek my head in to see if everyone is to their senses before I let the younger girls in. They are just the younger girls now; Edna and Jack took our apparel back to be washed and restored for tomorrow's photo shoot and made us get showers, which rinsed our makeup away. The glitter and eye makeup from the girls' eyes is gone, and they look like their normal nine-year-old selves again, well, two nine-year-olds and two eight-year-olds. Ariel and Hixel are still eight but not by much. Some people are still in the dreamy drug land of the pain pills like Bree and Spence. Most of them are awake though. I'm not sure how here they are, but I guess I'll find out.

Ariel squeezes around my arm and jumps on my bed, the one Hayden went down on. "Hayden," she squeals and gives her a gentle hug.

"How are you?" she says tiredly.

Tinley and Hixel tell Lakuna about the photo shoot. It looks like everyone has already got a shower. Pete and Griff don't have shirts on. They're ready to hit the sack. I'm going to follow right behind. "Put a shirt on, Griff. You don't want to blind anyone, do you?" I joke.

"Ha ha, hilarious," he laughs at me; he knows I'm only kidding.

I go into the bathroom, slip off my shirt, and put on the shorts I wear to bed. By the time I get out of the bathroom, Ariel is already bugging Pete for a snack.

"What do you want?" he says, without getting out from under his covers. "Food," she says.

"Me too," Broppin adds. "Me three."

"Me four."

"All right." He pushes himself out of his bed, revealing the bandages on his chest. "Petrie? What happened to you?" Ariel cries.

"Oh, nothing you need to worry about," he smiles reassuringly. "But what?" she whispers.

"We were in a fire." He asks Lakuna to sit up, and he moves her hair from her back, showing the unbandaged burn that is baby pink.

"His was way worse than mine," Lakuna says.

"But I'm fine, I promise." He walks over to the box on the wall and presses a button.

"Yes?" Wyllie's voice answers.

"Can we get some cheese crackers or something? And extra blankets?" he asks.

"Of course," she says, and then there's a knock on our door. Broppin gets the crackers and blankets.

Pete, Brint, and I carry Ariel, Tinley and Hixel back to their room; they fell asleep on our beds.

"Did someone order trouble?" Pete says to Cocoa as she opens the door.

She steps aside and lets us put the girls on their beds. "Thanks, boys." Cocoa says, rubbing Broppin's back. We head back to our room for what I hope is a long night's sleep. Mazi crawls under Spence's limp arm and tucks her head into his chest, the same way Hayden did to me in the winter island. I flick the lights off and sit at the edge of Hayden's bed. Her back and ribs are wrapped so tightly in bandages, it cannot be comfortable. The scars from her wounds are scarlet and bright against her skin, and the bruises from Brint are clear as ever. I touch my finger to the back of her soft eyelids and kiss her cheek.

"Can you get me my medicine?" she whimpers. I give her the morphine pill and crawl into her bed.

I blink my eyes awake and find a red camera light flashing in my face. "What are you doing?"

"Videos. It's compassionate," Chipolaux says.

"Whatever." I push the camera out of my face and go into the bathroom.

"What is this? Like a reality TV show or something?" I say when I see the camera crew still filming in our room.

"Quite so, more like an infomercial or persuasive broadcast."

I throw my football at Griff's head. "Get up, dude. We have a photo shoot to go to."

He groans and literally rolls out of his bed. "What kind of guys go to photo shoots?" "The important ones," I say.

Chipolaux smirks. Griff nails Pete in the side with the ball. "Ow."

"Photo shoot," Griff says all frilly and girly.

"Oh my gosh." Pete's a little nicer than Griff and me; he uses Chip's bullhorn and tells everyone to get their butts up.

Chipolaux leads us down to the prep rooms, no teeth brushing, no hair combing, and no food. Jack and Edna take us separately. Yesterday just Jack worked on Brint and me, but today we have our own stylists. Jack sticks with me; he sits me down in a chair and wheels me into a private cube for my personal makeup and dress. He closes the curtain that says CAM and tells me to take off my clothes. He studies my body figure. "I'm glad I got you. You'll be easy to prep." He takes a brush to my hair and lets it flip as it usually does. He flicks skin-colored powder on my face and buttons my shirt up, leaving two undone. I wear the same clothes I did yesterday. Lastly, he puts a strip on my teeth that whitens them in a matter of minutes, and then I'm allowed to brush them. Jack shows me to the field we were in yesterday, the field where I can see the Center and the awkward buildings that come with it. The younger girls are out here, in the dresses they wore the day before today. The guys are out, Brint in his yellow shirt, Pete in a royal blue shirt, Spence in a grey shirt, and Griff has on a plain white one. We're all dressed the same with two buttons undone, a black belt, black pants, and black shoes. The camera crew takes the close-up shots of them individually and the full-body shots before the rest of the girls enter the field, but their time in the dressing rooms has without a doubt paid off.

Mazi garbs a full-length gown, a sugary white color with white shoes and a hair clip to match. Whichever stylist she was assigned decided to keep her natural hair in ringlets, pinned back from her face. The shoes she has on make her at least an inch taller than what she is; well, every one of them has heels on that make them taller. Bree has a brown dress on; it stops at her knees and hugs her chest. And surprise, surprise, her shoes are the same color as her dress. Her hair isn't pinned back; it hangs to the side of her face. Lakuna's flowing red dress is almost the exact same as Mazi's except it doesn't sparkle like hers. It has sequins on the part that covers her chest. But all I can look at is Hayden.

Her dress is aqua blue to match her eyes. The dress clings to her breasts and stomach and then flows down to just before her knees. The straps that hold the dress up are lined in sparkly silver; they go with her heeled sandals. Her normally wavy hair is straight, which makes it longer, past her ribcage, and her bangs are twisted behind her ear, pinned back with a sparkly silver clip.

"Whoa. That's a sight for sore eyes," Chipolaux says lifting up his sunglasses.

The camera crew takes the close-ups and full-body shots, and serious shots except the girls get to stand. I notice the citizens of the Center have stopped to observe the photo shoot. Chipolaux has to use yellow tape and some soldiers to keep the citizens back. They scream our names and hold posters of our pictures up. Our mentors make us go back inside and sit in the main office while they, along with Cocoa, Chipolaux, and President York, have a meeting about what to do.

We sit in our chairs patiently. We wait in the main office, Wyllie brings us our lunch, some kind of meat sandwich and a cup of fruit, something light so it doesn't show in the girls' tight clothes.

Chipolaux opens the door for President York. "You all are a bunch of lookers, aren't you?" he laughs at his own joke.

"Well, to sum it all up, we were going to wait to show the videos to let the people know you are going to Duxia, but we told the citizens outside. I doubt the news will spread to the blocks, but as of right now, the whole Center knows about it. So go out there. Talk to the people. Try to be nice."

He looks at Hayden and Griff and points his fingers. "You two, no attitudes. Mazi and Spence, you may present yourselves as a couple if you'd like. Pete, the entire country knows you and Ariel are siblings, and you and Hayden took in the younger girls."

Mazi grabs Spence's hand. Pete whisks Ariel up in his arms, and she buries her face in his hair shyly. We walk into the field of flowers; the citizens of the Center become quiet as we come closer to them. We stop in front of a group of middle-aged people; it's Hixel who gets them to smile. "Wait for me, fellas!" she says as she prances through the flowers and to Griff's side. I hadn't realized her shoe came off, and she stopped to fix it. Griff holds her shoulders. "Hi," she says in her sweet voice to the people standing in front of us.

"Hello, Hixel, isn't it?" an older man asks.

"Yes." She leans over to me. "I told you we were famous." The crowd asks questions about our time on the island and how we've made such a quick recovery when nearly all of us were close to dead, especially Mazi, Hayden, Pete, and I.

Ariel doesn't say anything, and Hayden speaks very little. When a question is asked, she answers and smiles, but it is the rest of us who carry the conversation. "This is my sister Ariel," Pete says. She shows her face to the crowd and tucks it back in his shoulder.

"How old is she? Six? Seven?" they ask with horrified looks on their faces.

"She's eight, just small." Very small, she only comes up to the bottom of my ribs.

"And she's going?"

Hayden and Pete's eyes grow big. "Absolutely not. No! We had them brought here for personal reasons," Hayden says.

"Anyway," I interrupt. "Pete and Hayden adopted them, Broppin, Hixel, Tinley, and Ariel. Well, Ariel and Pete are brother and sister, but when their parents died, he cared for her," I say.

"And Broppin and Hayden are sisters?" a woman asks.

"No, cousins," Broppin says. "Hayden had a sister, but you've seen the video."

The crowd drops their eyes to the ground. Pete puts Ariel in the flowers, and they see how small she really is. She hides behind Hayden. Hayden whispers something in her ear. At first, she shakes her head no, and then she warms up to the idea. She starts out quietly but gets louder. She sings Ozalee's song in her young beautiful voice.

"I sang this song to my sister the night before she died. That's why they're here," Hayden says. "So they won't face what she did."

"You were lucky Mr. Donovan and his crew found you," one of the men from the crowd says. "Yes, but you know what happened before they found us," Hayden says. The crowd utters sorrys and bless yous. "They killed my sister. She was only nine," she says.

"She was my best friend," Ariel whimpers, a tear rolls down her face. She reaches her arms up to Pete. She buries her head in his hair again, but this time she doesn't come out. Hixel tugs on Griff's shirt. Griff holds her in his arms. Tinley hides from the crowd and tucks her face into my back. Now that the crowd pleasers are scarred and crying, the crowd pushes forward. They shout things about Duxia that no one under the age of fifteen should hear. They push on the caution tape. Our mentors make us go back inside but to sweeten things up a little, I whisper my plan to Spence, Griff, and Pete. We run to the top of the hill with our group. Spence and I pull Mazi and Hayden close to our chests, look down at them for a long moment, and we smash our lips to theirs. The crowd breaks the tape. Pete and Griff set Ariel and Hixel in full sight of the citizens from the Center.

"This is what those people do to us. Look at them." He pushes sobbing Ariel and Hixel closer to the crowd, "What did they ever do?" he yells. We slam the door behind us just as the crowd reaches the top of the hill.

"Well done. Without practice either," President York says. He pulls a handkerchief from the white suit he wears and dabs Ariel's face with it.

"Why don't you girls come with me?" Cocoa leads the younger girls out the door.

Jack and Edna get us to the dressing rooms. We break apart, and Jack brings me into my cube. He strips me of my nice clothes, and I hop in the shower. I sit in my chair and yawn.

"Long day?" he asks.

"Yeah, I feel like I need sleep. I slept all night last night, but it's not registering."

"Do you want me to tell Yanish you need some rest? I heard you weren't going to get some for quite a while," Jack offers.

"No, thanks though. I think I can handle it," I say. Jack says I've already missed my supper, so he tells me he'll have dinner with me.

"What would you like?" he asks.

"Hmmm. Steak? Is that okay with you?" I say.

"Divine," he talks into the bracelet on his wrist, and the food is delivered to my curtain. We eat in silence, which is just fine with me; I relax into the back of my chair and am almost asleep when my teletalky beeps.

I listen to the voice message, "Report to Training."

But it's not training I go to. It's a tolerance test. Our mentors are there, and the buff guy who I backed into the day I got taken off the island. We are put in our maroon shirts and black shorts and taken into a small white room with metal chairs for us to sit in. Three of the walls are blank. One wall is all window. The window looks into another white room, but this one has all kinds of gadgets and gizmos I can't put a name on. We go one by one into the room, the girls first and then the guys. Our first test is breath holding—hold your breath as long as you can. This isn't that bad. I get one minute and six seconds.

For the next test, our mentors bring a circular target into the room and have us shoot a bow and a small .22 gun. They give us three shots with each. Hayden hits the bull's-eye almost every time, and the two shots she misses the bull's-eye with the arrows she hits right next to it. Spence hits the bulls—eye once, hits the target three times, and misses twice. Other than those two, we suck at aim. The buff dude puts us through a hand-to-hand combat test. It's like a tournament. The order we go in is by size. First, Mazi and Hayden. Mazi gets her shoulders pinned in only a couple seconds. Then Hayden and Lakuna. Hayden beats Lakuna by taking out her feet with a slide tackle. Next is Bree and Hayden. For such a smallish girl she can sure fight—Hayden effortlessly pins Bree down by the throat. I'm sure that hurt Hayden's ribs or spine or head, and I'm positive it hurt Lakuna because Fallon gives her an icepack for her head. First up for the guys is Spence and Griff. Spence gets him out with no effort at all as he does with the rest of us. He wins. Then it's him versus Hayden. He has her by the waist in the beginning until she kicks him where no male should be kicked, and she dives on his back, pushing his shoulders to the ground, but he can lift two hundred, and the most she weighs is 135. He flips her off and pins her shoulders down.

The last exam is why I know it's called a tolerance test. Since some of us don't have any severe physical injuries, we are forced to watch those who do go through their test and see how they handle it. The buff ties our hands and feet together and chains us to the wall of the room this test is in. First up is Lakuna. The buff dude picks her up and shakes her then throws her to the ground, smashing her head into the floor. She lies on the floor until Fallon picks her up and takes her away from our view. We thought he was going to try to wrestle her or something, not hurt her.

Next is Griff. The guy doesn't throw him on the ground or shake him. Instead, he ties his hands behind his back and presses on his hurt leg. At first, Griff's face is calm. I see the muscles in the guy's arm ripple, and his expression turns upside down into complete and total pain. When he yelps, his back curves in agony. It infuriates me; I struggle to free myself from the chains, but I can't and I yell loud for someone to help him but no one comes. When Griff gives up and slumps to the floor, the buff guy stops pushing. Fabien and Fallon put his arms around their shoulders and drag him out. Lastly is Hayden. Before the guy even starts the test on her, Mazi and Bree push their bodies closer to the wall, cringing. The guy picks Hayden up the same way he did with Lakuna, and he shakes her. I see her blinking, trying to get the world to stop spinning. I think she thinks it's over because she relaxes in the guy's arms, and he flexes his muscles again. He squeezes her ribs; I hear her breath catch, and then the excruciating pain washes her breath away. A blood-curdling scream works its way up her throat and out of her mouth. All of our chains start pulling. Her body goes limp in his arms, but he keeps squeezing. Now all of us are yelling. Slowly Spence's chain is ripping out of the loose bracket with the force of his pull. He slams her to the ground, and I'm pretty sure her head cracks the floor.

"Hayden!" I shout her name; I don't want her to leave me again, ever.

Her eyes open, the guy goes to pick her up again, but Mazi jumps in front of him, blocking Hayden's body. Somehow Mazi slid her hands out of the chains. The guy raises his hand at her. I hear metal ripping out of concrete, and all of the sudden, Spence is standing in front of Mazi. "That is enough," he snarls. His fists clench so hard, the veins in his arms pop out.

The buff guy leaves the room with Hayden in his arms, locking Spence and Mazi in and keeping us chained to the wall. I would never think it would be that hard to watch a brother or friend be tortured, but it is nearly unbearable. Our mentors come in and unchain us from the wall; as soon as my hands are free Yanish gets a bloody lip. "How can you make us watch that? How?"

Simone gets a deck to the jaw too. "You are unbelievable!" Pete shouts.

We run out of the room, leaving our mentors there. Lakuna is sitting in a plush chair. Fallon is talking to her in a hushed tone, but I can see the tears in her eyes. He gives her medicine for her headache, the nondrowsy kind; apparently, it's going to be a long night. Griff is in a wheelchair. They gave him medicine, a little too much. Hayden is lying on a couch. Kanga checks her eyes for any blood or following, but she hit the ground hard. I don't even think I've been hit that hard, and if I have, I had pads on. Griff gives in to his pills and zonks out in his wheelchair.

"Darn. I wanted you all awake," Chipolaux says as he pushes the door open and sees Hayden and Griff.

"Maybe if you didn't have that guy beat them senseless, they would be awake," Pete snarls.

Our mentors and Chipolaux take us to a new room called Tactics and Film. This is where the troops are commanded, procedures are planned, and videos are created. The room is big, filled with computers and monitors and televisions and holographs and buttons and maps and so on and so forth. A giant wood table is pushed against one of the walls, and the rest of the room is lined with black couches, chairs, beanbags, and love seats. Someone moves Griff to a beanbag. Hayden's head lies in my lap on a sofa. A large purple bump swells above the back of her ear. What have they done? Kanga wraps Mazi's wrists in tape and cotton. The chains around them were too small, and she actually sprained them when she pulled them out. Everyone else takes a seat on something soft.

Our mentors and Chipolaux go to work planning the broadcast of us. Each time they ask us a question, we purposely give them a one-word answer. Somewhere around one in the morning, Gibson comes and checks on Hayden. He lifts up her shirt to assess the damage; her ribs are purple and blue.

"She doesn't need your help," I say to him.

"Then who do you think is going to give her the pain pills?" he says.

"When she wants them, she'll ask for them," I say through clenched teeth. He waves me off and wakes her up; he gives her the chewable kind.

She sits up and moves to the other side of the couch next to Pete. "Can I have a blanket?" she asks. I give her the one behind my head. "Where's Lakuna and Griff?" she asks.

"They're fine, a little beat up. They're sleeping," Pete tells her.

"Oh." Pete pushes a strand of her hair behind her ear and wipes the tears from her cheeks. "That hurt so bad," she says.

"I could tell. I couldn't get my hands free or I would've helped," he says.

"I know." She becomes unreachable for the rest of the night. We all lose it, me around four. I didn't want to give in in case Lakuna, Griff, or Hayden needed anything, but I was tired.

Yanish wakes me at six; everyone else is sitting around the wooden table. The coffee has been broken out. Bree hands me a cup of the black liquid, and I drink it down—I need a boost. Yanish gives me pictures from my old houses for me to pick from. Chipolaux wants to put them in our video. I pick one of me sliding into home, taking out the catcher, one of me tackling Pete during football practice, one of me in my swim trunks holding a water gun, and one of Griff and I together. They give us breakfast. None of us eat, and they immediately take us to the makeup room. I get a hot shower with no stinging stuff this morning. Jack brushes makeup on my face and slips me in a pair of cargo shorts and a black tee shirt. He takes me to the now fenced-off field and sits me in a chair Chipolaux put out here. My friends sit in the other chairs, and we wait until the younger girls come out to get going with the pictures. Chipolaux brings out the horses I wanted here. Everyone is excited and happy to see them. We get pictures by the horses, not on them, too unpredictable in a new environment. That's bull. Pretty much all of them are calm.

Chipolaux wants the younger girls to model for some kind of beauty pageant thing so he can show Gipem how cute Gipem's Girls, the nickname the crowd stamped on the younger girls yesterday, really are. But while Tinley was getting her makeup put on, her stylist poked her in the eye with the sparkly mascara, and she has a temper tantrum.

"Nooo!" she screams, moving her head side to side.

"Please sit still." Her stylist was getting frustrated with her, and she grabs Tinley's cheeks. "Get off!" She turns her head so her stylist couldn't put anymore makeup on her.

"You're being a brat," her makeup artist says.

"I don't care!" she screams.

"Just stop. Do it another day," Hayden says as she picked Tinley up, pushes around Chipolaux, and leaves the room. They gave her a thick brace for her ribs and back and stuck extra painkillers in her pockets for training today.

Chipolaux has the camera crew film the other girls in their poufy, foo-foo dresses, and then they leave with Cocoa to do who knows what all day. We report to the real training room, and it looks painful. The whole room is camo painted. The ceiling holds real or what look to be real trees, vines, and leaves, kind of like a huge jungle gym. Parts of the floor are a squishy trampoline material, and parts are normal plastic. A giant pool takes up half the room. The other half contains a shooting range, treadmills, ellipticals, stairs, benches, weights, and everything else I can think of that relates to fitness. Our mentors are instructed to teach us everything they know about the war. It's safe to say they know more than even the commanders of the troops. They take us to the cushy part of the floor and, for the rest of the day, teach us gymnastics. Well, that's what I want to call it. They say it's not, but I think it is. Our mentors pack years of flips and moves into one day. We learned how to do front tucks and back tucks, punch harder, kick faster. Lakuna is already phenomenal at everything we learned today, so she helps teach us. Of course, all of the guys have trouble at this; even Bree and Mazi need assistance in the flexibility part. Hayden is reluctant to do any flips, but when it comes to the flexibility stuff, she goes above and beyond. Lakuna only needs to show her everything once, and then she copies it.

She can even do the splits. Gibson and Fallon take Hayden and Lakuna out of our view for more advanced training.

After we've conquered a tight back handspring, I have no freaking clue what I would need that for, but whatever it is, they lead us up the spiral stairs and to the entrance of the ceiling jungle gym. "Get through this without falling off. Try not to hurt yourselves. You have five minutes."

We climb in the jungle. We're a good forty feet off the ground, actually water. The jungle is located directly over the pool. As soon as I get far enough in to where I can't see out either way, my hand finds a thorn bush. I stop to pick the thorns out of my hand but am pushed off my branch by a falling log. I barely catch hold of a vine before I tumble out of the jungle and into the pool. The vine snaps, and I splash into the water. This is going to be a long day. I swim to the other staircase. Hayden waits with our mentors. I raise my eyebrows questioningly.

"I don't do heights," she says. Yanish picks the thorns from my hand while we wait for everyone else. Once they are through, some still in the jungle and others drenched with water, our mentors force us to run just one mile, and by the time we're done, we are sucking wind big time. Massively out of shape.

At midnight, we're allowed to stop training. My legs feel numb, and I'm positive my lungs shriveled up like prunes. My feet are dragging when I reach my room; I get a quick shower and flop on my bed. My body sinks into the mattress, and my muscles turn into jelly. I open my arms for Hayden, and we fall asleep, only to be woken up at six for more training.

BOOK THREE

Hayden

Over the next four months, we throw ourselves into training. I live, breath, and sleep workouts. Occasionally, we get to do something fun or at least easy, like questioning or swimming, but that's rare. Between being pushed out of patience by Gibson, who I now call Gibbs, I've grown extremely close with my friends. I never thought it was possible to get to know them more, but surprisingly, I have. The younger girls call us one big family. Other than the love connections, we are. Cam and I aren't or never will be official; I refuse because of simply one problem—Pete. But they are both mine, and everyone knows that, even the rest of Gipem. Chipolaux has broadcast many videos of us, Gipem's Glories. That is our moniker. We aren't called that by choice. After the first video was shown, which was mandatory to watch for all citizens of Gipem, they have nicknamed us. I don't know why. We aren't anything special, just a bunch of teenagers. But we do have a reputation. All of Gipem knows and loves us, some of us by name, others not. They call me Hayden or HD, a short for High Def'. They got that from one of the interviews Rae did with me, and Chipolaux put it in the video.

Today is the last day of only four months of training. Yes, we just got our evaluations; it's a paper that tells us what we're exceptionally good at and what we need to work on.

Name: Hayden Kolter   Eye Color: Blue
Age: 15   Color: Brown Hair
Birth Date: 3/13/5013   Weight: 138
                              Height: 5'5"

Pros: Shooting Accuracy
Flexibility
Common Sense

Leadership
High Tolerance For Pain
Drive, Passion

Cons: Fear Of Heights
Sensitivity
Temper

Well, that is definitely a better evaluation than I thought I would get. Gibbs pats me on the back. "Good job, girlie. You deserve it." He tells me he and the rest of the mentors have a special surprise for us, so he sends me to Edna, my assigned stylist. Every time I hear her accent, it brings a smile to my face. She is one of the very few people that can accomplish that nowadays.

"Darling, let me see!" She snatches the evaluation from my hand and pushes her glasses down to her eyes. "Ah, very good! You, my dear, are worth my time." As usual, I pull my maroon shirt off and slip my shorts past my ankles. She inspects my body for the first time in four months, my new healthier, more muscular body. She runs her fingers over the four-pack I now have when I flex, which I have been doing the whole time just to show them off. I'm kind of proud of them. She pinches the inch she can on my stomach and side. "Perfect," she says.

I step in the shower. The coconut-scented water stings my skin. I scrub the old dead flakes from my body, and then the shower spills a rich milky lather on me. I guess I'm going coconut-scented tonight because the shampoo and conditioner I massage into my scalp smells of the large nut. As soon as I step on the floor mat outside of the shower, a hot puff of air blows me dry. Edna leaves my hair in waves and pins my bangs back with a white flower. She strings shell-bead jewelry around my neck and clasps matching bracelets on my wrist and ankle. The first time I saw Edna, the moment when Gipem learned who I was while I was doing a photo shoot in the field, I got my ears pierced. Edna pokes coordinating earrings into my ears and starts with my makeup. A shimmery bronze dust covers the parts of my body that will be visible in my dress, which is most of me. She paints light blue eye shadow on my eyelids and lines my lips with a clear gloss. I am not in need of blush since my cheeks are already rosy pink, and Edna slips white sandals on my feet. She pulls the dress over my head; it curves under itself at my mid-thigh, the top being the same blue as my eye shadow and the bottom a mixture of beach and flowers.

It takes me a long time to realize the girl in the mirror is me, so natural . . . and beautiful. But I'm never beautiful, not like Lakuna or Mazi;

it's a different kind of pretty. The kind you get when you want to feel like a model but know you'll never be one.

"Do you like it?" she asks.

"It's perfect. I mean, it fits me."

She sprays coconut perfume on my wrists and tells me to wait outside the door for my escort. I sit on the chair by the door of the Makeup and Dress Room until Gibbs appears and links us by the elbow. It is obvious he was forced into the black suit he wears; all I've ever seen him in is torn-up jeans and a raggedy tee shirt with a jacket.

"Where are we going?" I ask.

"It's a surprise," he says in the gruff voice of his, but I can tell he's excited about it. We meet my friends and their mentors outside a pair of fancy white doors that can only lead to the lobby of the president's mansion. I hear music blaring inside the mansion, one of my favorite songs to be exact. I notice my friends are wearing nicer clothes and their mentors are all in suits. I don't know whether to be happy or weary about this "special" occasion. Waiters pull the doors open from the inside, and our mentors escort us into the party.

"Happy birthday!" the people inside shout and clap for us. I look around to see who they're talking to, but no one has a birthday hat on or anything. Gibbs leads me down a red carpet, up three stairs and sits me on a love seat next to a podium. Yanish pushes Cam's shoulders down next to me, and Pete is placed on my other side. The rest of my friends are seated in love seats and chairs next to us. President York mounts the stage and adjusts the microphone so it points toward his mouth.

He silences the crowd of people I don't know and begins to talk, "As you all know, these young people will soon be attempting to help end the war between us and the country of Duxia. They have been training so hard for this, and we are all very welcome!" The crowd cheers for us. "We are not certain if they all will be able to celebrate their next birthday, so Mr. Chipolaux Donovan and I have decided to throw them one last birthday party." Small fireworks explode into the ceiling, and orange sparks float to the ground. All of this is really nice, but the translation of President York's words is "You most likely won't live to see your next birthday, so enjoy your last party."

"Would you like to say a few words, Mr. Donovan?" President York asks.

Chipolaux walks to the podium. His suit is different than the ones he usually wears. It's brighter. He pulls off the blacks and greys just fine, but tonight, he styles a happy pink color to match the rest of the contrasting hues the audience flaunts. "I am very proud of all of the work the Rescue Squad has put into their training. And we will try extremely hard to get them out of Duxia safely, but for every squad to work, it needs a commander. In this case there are two squads, the male squad consisting of Pete Girth, Cam and Griff Malrook, Brint Turner, and Spence Leadmen and the female squad consisting of Hayden Kolter, Lakuna Crest, Mazi Seedar, and Bree Uley. Each of these will need a commander. Through the videos of their training and the tape of them on the island, you and we have voted for the commanders. This is a majority vote. The commander for the male squad will be Pete Girth. The commander for the female squad will be Hayden Kolter."

Lakuna for commander, that's what I thought. She has everything to be in that position. "Do you have anything to say about that?" Chipolaux smiles, wanting the new commanders to take their place and comment on the audience's decision. Pete rises from his chair. Lakuna doesn't move. She just has a quizzical look on her face.

Cam elbows my side. "Go," he whispers. "What?" I ask confused.

"Say something, Chief," he teases.

I stand up and smooth my dress out. Chipolaux hands me the microphone. I just look at it. What am I supposed to say? "Uh, um . . ."

Pete gently grabs it from my hand. "What she means to say is thank you for giving her this opportunity. I second that."

But I do have a question; I take the microphone from him. "Why?" I ask. The crowd says nothing. "Why did you pick us?" I say louder.

"You two are the ones who kept everyone alive more than everyone else. It stands out!" an older man yells over the other people's answers.

I stand out? I've never stood out a day in my life. How is this any different? "Stand out?" I ask. The middle-aged man I talked to the day Gipem found out about us going to war yells, "Everything useful is rolled into one person!"

Before I can pile the questions on the crowd, President York pulls the microphone from my grasp. "Now you have it. Enjoy the party," he says.

I dismount the stage with Cam and Pete flanking my sides. The crowd engulfs us, asking for pictures and autographs. Soon I lose both of them and stand in a bunch of people I don't know. I don't recognize anyone I've met in the Center, and the people I can put my finger on are already drunk. As the hours go on, the crowd disperses, and I can move again. I wander over to the food table, a table filled with delicacies from the whole country, most of which I've never seen. Fruit-stuffed duck, lemon yellow sauce topping a lobster, a white cake on fire. I fill my plate with sushi and pineapple chunks, the first good meal I've had in months. I find a seat at a white table drizzled with rose petals and shove every piece of food possible in my mouth.

"That's attractive," Griff says. He plops down next to me with a plate piled high with I don't even know what.

I swallow my sushi. "You know it," I say.

"I haven't seen a familiar face all night. Dang, people won't get off my back," he says.

"Yeah, they all want a picture with the pretty boy," I joke. He flashes a ridiculously flattering smile and plants a wet sloppy kiss on my cheek. "Griff, that's disgusting!" I push him out of his seat, and we laugh at each other. Ariel somehow finds Griff and I through the crowd. "What are you doing up so late, baby girl?" I ask playfully. She climbs in my lap and takes a bite of my pineapple.

"I brought you a birthday present," she says. She pulls a bag out from behind her back.

"You didn't have to get me anything," I say. She pushes it closer to me. I tear the silver paper out of the top. The first thing I see is my soccer jersey, with a large number thirteen written on the back. The next thing is a picture of all of us, my friends, the younger girls, and Ozalee. "Oh, Ariel, I love it." My throat gets the tight feeling it does before I cry.

She throws a bag at Griff. "Open it. It took me all night to find you people. I had someone else's presents, but when I saw you two, I didn't want to go searching again, so there you go," she says.

He looks inside the bag, and his face instantly lights up. He pulls his baseball jersey from the bag and the same picture. "Thanks."

The party ends around three in the morning. The younger girls cried when Cocoa made them leave. They begged to stay for our last birthday party, but they have to get up early for school tomorrow. They started school the day after they found out we were going to war. Chipolaux and Cocoa planned strategically to get their minds off things. They saw the rest of the video of us on the island after they knew we will be going to Duxia; there were too many tears that day.

I leave the mansion before the crowd does and go to my room; I wash the makeup off my body and face and throw my hair in a ponytail. I order a pair of sweatpants and a sweatshirt to sleep in tonight. The fuzzy material is soft on my skin; it makes me feel at home. Chipolaux allows us to do whatever we want for the last two days before we are shipped off to Duxia, so I can wear what I please. My friends enter the room at different times. Lakuna orders sweats and jumps in her bed. She folds her soccer jersey at the bottom of her mattress and puts the picture of us on top. I love sweatpants. If I could, I would wear them all day every day. Lakuna likes them too. Half of our closets at our home in Villa were filled with sweats. My mom always made fun of me for wearing sweats around the house. "Why don't you put on something else for a change?" she asked. But that's all in the past now.

As late as it is, I can't sleep. I carefully remove Cam's arms from my torso and crawl out of the covers. I crack the window in our room, letting the breeze flow onto my face. I remember when I was back in Villa, the last night I was at home. The air conditioning wasn't working, and I was wishing so badly wind would blow on my face then. I remember what I did that day; I played my last soccer game. We won by one. I scored our only goal. I had track straight after school. That night, I listened to the news. "The fifteen missing teenagers from Lakota were found dead in Riverelli early this morning. The children were suspected to be kidnapped and abused until their death. The killers are still loose and could be anywhere. It isn't likely they will find you, but take extra precautions. This is Heather Launter, Channel 8, saying good night, everyone." That would be terrible to die in Riverelli, the poorest block in Gipem. President York told me the Duxians killed those kids. They were on the list. It's weird though because York said the only list left was the one from Villa, and everyone on that list was killed except us. But the kids that died were from Lakota. Duxia killed those kids, so Duxia must've had another list. And there has to be more lists out there than just Villa's, or those kids wouldn't be dead. But they are. And that means we've been lied to.

CHAPTER SEVENTEEN

I wake Pete and yank him into the bathroom so none of our friends hear our conversation. I tell him what I figured out. His face flushes with red. I can almost see the steam coming from his ears. We run out of the room and know exactly where to go. I push the door open to the Tactics and Film Room and find our mentors and Chipolaux sitting around the wooden table. "You want us to be commanders when we don't even know the real story?" Pete snarls. They look at him like he had a little too much wine. "We know the other lists weren't destroyed. How did the Duxians get those kids from Lakota, huh?" he asks.

"Finally figured it out, girlie?" Gibbs asks me. I thoroughly consider coming across the table but manage to keep my feet planted firmly on the ground.

Chipolaux's head drops, and he shakes it sorrowfully. "You aren't going on one mission. You're going on three. The guys go on one by themselves. The girls go one by themselves, and then you go on the most dangerous altogether."

"No," Pete says.

"Yes. The lists are held in two different places. Guys go to one place, and girls go to another so the Duxians don't get suspicious. We need you to blow the buildings where the lists are held. We need you to destroy the lists."

This time I say it, "No."

"Yes. Do you want more innocent kids to die, like your sister, Hayden?"

And that decides it; we are going on three missions.

Pete and I are told not to tell our friends. They will find out in a meeting tomorrow, a meeting Pete and I will not be attending. We will be given special orders, directions crucial to operate by.

167

I close our door behind us quietly. Pete sits on the windowsill; I sit with him for a little bit, wondering how many days I have left to see all of my friends alive. Tomorrow I will write good-bye letters to each of them, the younger girls and my mother just in case I'm the one who won't be coming home. My toes get the annoying tingly feeling you get when you keep them in one place for too long, so I pace the floor.

"Hayden, get some sleep. We have a long day tomorrow," Pete says.

I can't resist. I walk over to him and hug him. His body feels different than Cam's does when it's pressed against me. He hugs me back; I can feel his stomach tensing with the building anxiety. "If you ever need to talk, I'm here," I say.

"You always have been." He squeezes me tighter. "I'm all ears for you too."

I slip into my bed and snuggle my head under Cam's chin, where it fits so perfectly. His arm falls over me in his sleep, and his breathing is reassuring in my ear. After all of the times I've slept next to Pete and Cam, now I have a feeling those days are numbered. If either of them die, I don't think I could handle it. Not being able to see Cam smile again or have his arms wrap around me . . . But what about Pete? It is unspoken and completely obvious I love them both. It's just they are so different. Two totally opposite people. I wouldn't even consider them friends. They just get along because of the rest of us. I can tell Pete anything, unlike Cam who would go directly to Griff. I couldn't cope if I didn't have Pete to tell my secrets to, the secrets Lakuna can't hear. And if he left Ariel all alone in the world, with just me to look to, I couldn't do it. I just couldn't. A hot tear runs down my cheek and into my mouth, and tonight is one of those nights I cry myself to sleep.

I went to bed around six. Even though I've only been sleeping for four and a half hours, I feel obligated to get up at the 10:36 mark. Pete and I are the only ones in the room. I get in the shower and pull a sweatshirt over my top and tie a pair of athletic shorts to my waist. I wake Pete up, and we grab a granola bar at the cafeteria before we proceed toward the tactics room.

When we get there, Chipolaux sits us at the wood table. Gibbs informs me on the girls' mission, and Simone gives Pete his mission. The lists the girls need to destroy are in the middle of the desert. All we have to do is land a bomb within five feet of the base. The wing we land it on will be blown sky high, and we make sure we get the heck out of there before the bomb goes off. The bomb we will use will explode over a three hundred yard radius within one minute that the trigger is pushed. So be smart and don't blow myself up, he tells me.

Gibbs lays a map of the area on the table for me to study. When he said it was in the middle of the desert, he's not kidding. There are no other buildings, no trees, no water sources just sand, cacti, and the Duxian military base. "The base is easily 1,200 meters long. Bomb the east wing. The entrances, floors, and ceilings are heavily guarded, so don't get within shooting distance of their guns." I'm given the direct order to use my bow to bomb the base, attach the microchip-sized explosive on to my arrowhead and let it fly. "Got it?" Gibbs says.

"Yes."

Pete and I are released to go wherever. But we made plans last night, and both of us keep our place sitting at the wooden table. We ask for paper and pencils. I start on the letter for my mom.

Mom, I tried. I promise I did. I'm sorry I couldn't save Ozalee. Having got this letter, you know I'm not coming back. If Pete doesn't make it either, please, please take Ariel, Tinley, Hixel, and Broppin. Keep them safe. Stay in touch with my friends. Ann will help you with the younger girls. Try to be happy.

I love you, Hayden

I move to the letter for Cam and Griff's mom.

Ann, you have two amazing sons. They have helped me in so many ways. Saved my life even. Please help my mother with the younger girls if Pete doesn't live through this either. Thank you.

Hayden

Ariel, you are so special to me. I love you just like I loved Ozalee. I know I'm not here for you anymore, but stay strong. Don't let my mom sell Girl. Keep her and Fancy for yourself. This is such a huge weight to put on your shoulders, I'm sorry. Remember, have fun, live life to the fullest.

I'll love you forever, baby girl, Hayden

Tinley, you are definitely something else. Stay that way. You're a little sister to me. Try not to grow up too fast. Trust me, being a kid is great. Help Ariel care for the horses I left her. I want you to have Edna, my stylist. You can't own her, but I know if I die, you will get publicity, so I'm passing her to you. Don't think I tried to die. I was just doing my job.

I love you, Hayden

Hixel, don't put yourself down. You're just as good as everyone else. Remember that. Cam told me you miss home and felt alone. Well, don't. I'll always be here for you no matter what. You have an amazing personality. Try to spread that around. By the way, Pete and I have been coming to your track meets since you started. It's an awful, awful sport with all that running. Haha! But you seem to take after Lakuna and Mazi in being good at it, so I think you should take Lakuna's track spikes. If she knew I told you to take them, she'll hand them over. They are lucky. She's a three—time block champion in those spikes. You can do the same. I believe in you.

You're you, not anyone else. I love you, Hayden

Broppin, I'm still here for you. Please don't ever think I'm gone forever. I'm not. You have things that other people don't have nor will ever possess. Take my soccer stuff. You have a lot of potential in that area. Get a scholarship if possible. I think it is. You're the best cousin I have ever had.

I love you like a sister, Hayden

Lakuna, you're so much like me. Our personality's just mixed together. I loved it. I want you to have my clothes. I've never met anyone that was the exact same size in everything. It's special. Train Hixel in track. She has it, and she can do it. Help her. You are my best friend and a beautiful person. You were special to me. Don't feel bad for saying you hated me on the island. I know the bubble in the tracker let the liquid out. It wasn't your fault. I can trust you with everything. Remember all those good times we had? They always made me smile—soccer, swimming, hiking, boys, suffering through school. Good times. Thank you for making it worth it.

I love you, Hayden

"Pete, I don't know what to write to Brint. I haven't known him for as long as everyone else." He scrapes his fingers across his face. "Hmm. Do you love him?"

"As a friend," I say. "Tell him that then."

Brint, well, I don't really know what to say except for thanks. I've seen videos of the island, and I vaguely remember you were the one who kept me company after the flood, and saved Pete and kept me from freaking out. Thanks again.

Love you, Hayden

Spence, you're a good person. Always trying to make everyone smile and being a big protector. I think you should show Chipolaux how you can play your guitar—let Ariel sing. That would be nice. Treat Mazi right. Don't hurt her. You make a great couple, and to tell you the truth, I see marriage. Don't tell anyone—that's a little weird.

Love you, Hayden

Griff, all I have to say is . . . I love you, kid! Me and you are like a brother and sister. You were never afraid to tackle me when we played football, and every time you did tackle me, you never hurt me, thanks. Your personality is just like mine but in male form. If Pete and I both don't make it, remember Ariel has a fondness for you. I don't know why, but help her out. And thanks for everything. You're always there to make me laugh, and it always works. I'll never forget how you saved my life.

Love you, bro, Hayden

Bree, I'm telling you these things because you'll do them right. The younger girls have bright futures. Ariel can sing. I know she can. She's only eight and she's already famous. Hixel could be a block champion for track. It is a definite possibility for Broppin to get a soccer scholarship. Tinley is exceptionally good at basketball—work with her. Hiding in my dresser in Villa is money. I'm attempting to save money for the girls to go to college. I want them all to go to college. I'm glad I can trust you with this. Thank you so much. My jewelry is in my desk drawer. Some belonged to Ozalee, so treat it right. I'm giving it to you. I know this is a lot to hand you at once, but remember, I'll always be with you. We had some amazing times together, and you were one of the very few people that made my life worth living.

I love you, Hayden

Cam, you saved my life. I will miss you. A lot. There is nothing I need to say to you because you already know it all. You were mine and always will be mine. As long as you want me, I'm yours. Forever and always. I want you to be happy no matter what it takes. If I don't make it back, I want you to know Pete was special to me, so please don't do anything stupid. Take care of the girls.

I love you so much. I feel something with you.
Love again, Hayden

Mazi, you're one of the nicest people I've ever met. No doubt. You're always there for me, through everything. And you put up with my attitude. Thank you. This letter should be a mile long. I know I don't have to say anything though because you understand. You'll never lose me. I'm still here for you. I can't tell you how much you mean to me and how much I will miss you. You were my other half. I want you to have all of the books on my shelf and my collage. Add to it over time. Make it more memorable.

I love you, Mazi, and by the way,
Spence is a good choice. Love, Hayden

Pete, you have to take care of the younger girls. I won't be here to pick up your slack anymore, so look at Bree's note. I left directions. If they have girl problems, tell Lakuna, Bree, or Mazi. They will help. I owe you my life for saving it before. I would've died if you didn't know how to stop blood from flowing. I am forever grateful you saved Mazi, Lakuna, and Bree. I'll never be able to repay you. But remember, Ariel, Tinley, Hixel, and Broppin are a top priority. They have to have a good life. They've been through too much already. You are my best friend, and you have to remember how much I loved you. You were always there for me even though half of the things we went through weren't your burden to bear. So keep your head and be smart. I always knew I could trust you with everything.

Love forever and for eternity, Hayden.

And that is it. My final good-byes to everyone I care about. I seal them each with a kiss. I can't just go handing them out. Should I store them under my bed? No, they might never find those. I need to give them to someone. My friends are out of the question, not my mom or the younger girls, not Gibbs. He would tell me not to have that attitude. Hmmm. Rae would show Chip. Chipolaux would put them on TV. Cocoa scares me, so not her. Kanga and Edna are too close to me to show. So that leaves Wyllie.

I leave Pete sitting at the table with his hands buried in his curls. I search every possible room I could before I find her in the laundry room. "Can you keep these for me?" I ask.

"What are they?" she wonders reaching for them.

"Letters for some people, the names are on the back of the envelopes. If I don't make it through the missions, give them to the people the envelope says."

She shoves them in her blouse and gives me a reassuring squeeze. "I'll be sure to deliver them, honey," she says quietly. Even she thinks we won't make it.

I go to the cafeteria and order an ice water with a bendy straw; I sit in a hard plastic chair at a table by myself. Now I know how soldier's wives feel, scared. Not for themselves but for their husbands. I don't care if I die; I would actually like it more if I did. I'm afraid one of my friends will die and leave me here alone. Especially Pete. If he dies, I get the girls. I will be a single parent with a red-eyed nanny. I feel my cheeks burn. My face breaks to sweat. I put my face on my arms and watch the condensation fall from the glass.

"Hayden, come with me," Mazi says, not in her normal sweet voice but a serious tone I rarely hear. Without question, I follow her out the door. She puts her finger to her mouth and tiptoes to the Council Room. The door is cracked open. She silently tells me to look inside. Chipolaux and our mentors are standing in front of Cam, Pete, and Spence. We listen in on their conversation.

"We just can't do that Pete," Chipolaux says.

"You know you're risking the lives of four of the most famous people in Gipem, and if they die, you are to blame," Pete replies.

"It has to be done this way," Chipolaux says.

"Please, please. Keep them here, please." Spence falls out of his chair and to his knees, begging.

"I'm sorry. We can't risk anymore children dying," Byron, Spence's mentor, says.

"Send us on two missions then, and don't send them on any alone!" Cam bursts, but our mentors aren't breaking.

"Too risky for you," Yanish says.

"I don't care about us," Pete says.

"We do. End of discussion, get out," Simone says.

Spence throws his chair across the room, and they head for the door. Mazi and I book it around the corner so we won't be seen; we act like we were just passing through. We pretend like we're talking about the party last night when the guys run into us. Pete instantly turns and whips around the corner.

"You chose this?" Cam asks. He doesn't want it to be true.

"Yes." He closes his eyes and leans against the wall. I stretch on my toes to reach his lips and softly kiss them. Not for me but for him. He doesn't want me to get hurt. And then there is me who is hurting him by my own option.

For the rest of the day, Chipolaux lets us play outside, such a childish thing to do since we are now labeled highly trained soldiers. Not only soldiers but threats as well. If I wanted to, I could easily kill a male citizen twice my size, but that's not what I was trained to do. Keep Gipem safe. Destroy Duxia. We play football, soccer, and baseball. I ride Girl; we race with the other horses and their riders. Wyllie prepares a picnic for us. We sit in the meadow and eat. I take a bite of my banana sandwich. Girl who was in the field trots over to me. She pushes her nose into my shoulder. When I ignore her, she stomps her foot into the flowers and nuzzles her fuzzy mouth into my hand. "Here," I say and give her a whole sandwich.

She has grown in the past five months. Her legs got taller, and her muscles got bigger. Maybe they put steroids in the food here or something.

The sky gets dark, and the stars shine bright in the blackness. It's a long day tomorrow. The guys leave at 4:30 AM sharp in time to make a night attack on the military base in Duxia. We head in at ten. The younger girls are allowed to sleep in our room tonight. It's crowded in here. Pete and I have decided to not wake them up in the morning; the guys don't need to be sad when they need to concentrate. Mazi lets me use her camera. I get pictures of every guy with every girl and each other. It's hard for the younger girls to say bye to Pete. It was like me saying I love you to Ozalee for the last time. He swears to them he'll come back, but they don't believe him. I wouldn't either. Once they fall asleep on his bed, he pulls me outside the room and goes over everything I need to know about them. I already know everything he tells me, but I listen just to make him feel secure.

"Hayden, you and me are all they have. We're it. If I die, you'll be it," he says.

"Pete, I know. I wrote it all down today. It will be fine," I say. We reenter our room and get ready for bed.

Spence and Mazi won't let go of each other. They get in his bed and stay there, talking quietly to each other. Brint doesn't say as much as usual. Neither does Griff. I lay with Cam, my face in his chest. We don't say anything, and eventually he falls asleep. I lie in our bed. It floats in the ocean. My father's boat sails past me. Cam waves to me from the deck. I smile at him, and then the boat crashes into a reef that juts out of the water like a mountain. He jumps in the water and tries to swim to me; the mast breaks off the boat and smashes into him, knocking him unconscious. He sinks below the surface; I dive under the water just in time to watch him get eaten by the fish that killed my sister.

I jolt upright, my body covered in sweat. I change into new clothes and put my hair in a bun. I return to my bed. Cam's eyelashes are long, sticking out from his face. His hair covers half his forehead. I love his hair; it's one of my favorite assets about him. It's obviously brown but not as dark as Mazi's and not as light as mine. His jaw bone is angled, more angled than most guys', and the skin over it is flawless. I can't help but miss him even though he is right in front of me.

Chipolaux wakes us in the morning. The guys go to the prep room, and we wait in the launch area. The aircraft they are taking is small but packs a lot; supposedly, it's the same one that got us off the island. We aren't allowed to accompany them on their mission, only them, their mentors, Chipolaux, the doctors, and some other people I don't know. They come out dressed in Duxia military uniforms. Just their appearance makes me want to put a bullet through their head, but I know who they are and shooting them is not a possibility. We say our final good-byes with hugs and kisses. It's not right, the feeling I have. My stomach feels like it's squirming inside of me, the way an inch worm does when you poke it.

Pete comes close to me and puts his lips next to my ear. "Keep them safe. Remember the letters." He hugs me, kisses me on the cheek, and disappears into the plane.

Cam presses his forehead to mine. When he smiles his dimples pop. "I love you," he says; his breath smells of icy pine. I take in the scent and look up to find him, but he's already gone.

Cam and me. The boy loves the girl. The girl loves the boy? I'm stuck on this question for a long time, through half of their mission. I sit in the Tactics Room on a beanbag, staring into space while the rest of my friends are glued to the screens showing the guys' every move. I like him as a significant other, yes. I love him as a friend but not in that way. It's a different love for sure. I don't know.

The younger girls bang on the Tactics door. "Please let us in." They are not allowed in; I push myself off the beanbag and crack the door just wide enough to slip out.

"What's happening?" Ariel panics.

"They are on the plane home," I inform her. "Are they okay?" Tinley asks.

"A little banged up but nothing too bad," I say. I hope that's a good assumption because I have no idea what is going on.

Just then Mazi, Lakuna, and Bree bust out of the door. "They're back."

Tinley asks the same question again, "Are they okay?" "I don't know. They cut the tape!" Lakuna says.

"They what?" I shout. We pick up a sprint and hurl ourselves through the launch room door.

CHAPTER EIGHTEEN

They are stripped to the waist with their heads between their knees. Their bodies drip sweat. Ezzard and other doctors swarm around them, closing up small gashes with butterfly bandages. They have oxygen masks strapped to their faces. The younger girls run to Pete and literally knock him flat on his back. He doesn't get up. Ezzard shoos the girls away; they take a few steps back and watch as he shines a light in Pete's eyes. I gently pat Griff's back, not wanting to confront Cam at the moment.

"It's really hot down there," he says.

"How'd it go?" I ask knowing I won't get much information.

"We got in, went through the town, and blew the building up. Not just one wing, the whole thing. I wasn't ready for it. To see all those people die, I mean. It was bad."

"Oh," I don't know what else to say.

"They sent in reinforcements, and we beat it out of there, under orders that is. We wanted to help the Duxians out of the base, but they told us to come to the plane."

The guys have to stay in the hospital tonight just to make sure they breathe fine, and well, I don't know exactly why they are in the hospital, but when I go down after supper, they are all sleeping. I guess they forgot we are being shipped out tomorrow because they would stay up with us. I give each of them a kiss on the forehead. As I step out of the room, I hear one of the hospital beds rattle. I turn.

"Sorry, that was rude," Pete says.

I cross over to a stool by his bed. "It's all right. You've had a long day. Well, at least for now the girls will have someone," I say.

"For now. Are you dreading tomorrow?" he asks.

"No. we've been training for so long. Anyway, Ozalee died because of them."

"Just remember, don't let your hate get in the way of your duty," he says. I kiss his forehead. "Good luck. I love you," he says.

And to him I say it back, "I love you too."

I walk to my room for an early night. I take a long, hot shower and relax into my mattress with a pair of sweats. Lakuna, Bree, and Mazi enter our room and head straight for the showers. The younger girls follow them in and climb on my bed. "Are you scared?" Broppin asks.

"No. I was scared for the guys but not for us," I say. "Why?" Tinley asks.

"Because I'll be with them, and I won't let anything bad happen to them if I can help it. Plus, everyone knows girls are more talented than guys." They giggle reluctantly. I braid their hair across their heads and tie it with a bow, just to comfort them, but I know it's not working. They shake slightly, and every time one of them talks, their voices crack. Lakuna, Bree, and Mazi come out of the showers.

"Well, we have to get to bed. We'll see you tomorrow night. We promise," Bree says. I hug them and kiss them, hoping Bree is right.

"Okay then, night. You can go talk to Pete. He's awake. I was just there," I say, and they run out the door.

I spread out under my covers; the other side of my bed is cold without Cam or Pete's body heat there to warm it. I put my hands under my pillow for a more comfortable position but am stopped by a feeling I don't recognize. I pull the object into the open, a blue flower. I don't remember much about being on the island. I know my sister died, and we had plenty of close calls, but other than that, I don't recall anything. I know what happened through the video we watched, and the video must be right. Cam gave me this flower when we were in the meadow and now again. I put the flower on top of my jersey and picture and go to bed.

Again Chipolaux wakes us in the morning, just us, not the guys. Edna takes my hand and leads me to my dressing room. "You'll do great, darling," she says. She zips up my new uniform and shoves my feet into perfect-fitting shoes. She sits me down in my makeup chair and applies a natural-looking coat to enhance my facial features, then she braids my hair down my back. I stare at myself in the mirror. My suit is jet black, a comfortable but tight fit. It covers me from foot to neck; my boots are light, made for running, and go up to my knees.

She tightens a black belt to my waist and points to each pouch. "This holds a knife. This one a gas mask. This one has extra bullets and arrowheads, and this one extra water. Make sure when you get close enough to the base, press this button." She points to a button on my wrist.

I press it just to see what it is. A hard helmet forms over my whole head. It leaves an opening over the front of my face. "Thank you, Edna, for making me look beautiful," I say.

"I don't have to make you look beautiful. You already are."

We load the plane for the nine-hour flight. I don't really say much. I don't have anything to say. I just stare out the window trying to remember what happened on the island. It's irritating to me, I don't know.

"Why can't I remember?" I ask Lakuna in a hushed tone so no one thinks I'm crazy. "Remember what?"

"Being on the island," I say.

"Oh, I honestly can't tell you. The concussion maybe . . ." she trails off and gets louder again. "I don't remember either, not a lot anyway."

"What do you know?" I ask.

"Um, being in the meadow, the flood, being taken off, the badger attack and that's about it. Oh, and the panther attack. You?"

"Ozalee and the fish, panther attack, Pete and Cam being sick. That's all," I tell her. "You hit your head hard when that tree crushed you."

Gibbs pulls me aside and goes over the game plan with me for like the thirtieth time. "I think I got it," I say.

"Think isn't an option," he says. "I got it!" I hiss.

"As a direct order," Chipolaux says, "listen to Hayden. Don't do anything without her permission." Great, completely under *my* command.

Gibbs sticks an earpiece in my ear and a small microphone on the collar of my uniform. "This piece will connect you to me. Listen to what I say. I know what's happening all around you while you only know what's happening near you."

"All right," I say.

"Okay, you'll do great, girlie," he says. The door to the plane opens, and already the temperature rises a good ten degrees and the floor of the aircraft is covered in red sand. My friends form a triangle behind me, and we march into the desert.

Chipolaux and our mentors have planned this perfectly; the plane was able to land about a mile away from the base because of a blinding sand storm. We have to put on our gas masks just to keep from breathing in sand. Even though the hike to the base is not far, by the time I get within shooting distance, I am dripping sweat and panting like a dog. The storm has died down, leaving a dusty but see—through area.

"You don't have much time before you're totally visible," Gibbs says. "Don't get any closer to the base, or you'll be within shooting distance of their guns." I load my arrow on to my bow and tape the microbomb on the arrowhead. I pull back on my bowstring and aim at the east wing of the base.

"Wait!" Bree yells and rips the bow from my grasp. "The arrow won't make it there. It's too far away," she says.

"No, no, we measured it," I inform her. "The arrow is weighed down because of the bomb."

The first major decision I have to make as commander. Get closer to the base and send an arrow in that might not make it or tape the microbomb to a bullet and hope it works. I would really love a coin right about now. Flipping is so easy. Arrow or bullet. Bullet or arrow.

"Hayden, you're visible," Gibbs says. I yank the bomb from my arrow and attach it to a bullet. "Don't you dare!" Gibbs snarls. "When you pull that trigger, the bomb will go off."

"Scoot back," I tell Bree, Lakuna, and Mazi.

They don't know what I'm doing. They can't hear Gibbs. I put the bullet in the barrel. "I have to." I look through the scope and put the crosshairs on a door that leads inside, and I pull the trigger.

CHAPTER NINETEEN

I throw the gun away from my body, turn and run. I hear the gunshots being fired at us and then the burst of the bomb. The heat of the explosion hits me the same time I'm blown to the ground. I turn over and watch as the center of the base goes up in flames. Smoke fills the air. The only thing I can see are the shards of brick and metal falling around me, some on fire, others not. I feel around me for any sign of my friends, but none are there. I click the oxygen button on my gas mask and wait for it to fill with clean air. With each breath I take, my throat burns from the smoke. Every time I cough, my mask turns grayer. "Where are they?" I gasp.

"Go right," Gibbs says.

I crawl to my right, stretching my limbs to find them; my hand grazes the silky fabric of Mazi's leg. "Are you guys hurt?" I ask.

"No."

The smoke clears quickly. Now it looks like a dark fog substance. "Pick us up," I tell Gibbs. It's more of a plea than an order.

"Change of plans, the base was expecting an attack as a result of the guys' mission. They have sent in reinforcements and patrol planes circling the area. We are unable to get in."

"So we're stuck here?" I ask in disbelief. "We're doing all we can," he says. "How many days?" I ask.

"Four."

We won't make it four days. It's too hot. "We don't have water?" I ask Gibbs. I can almost see him rubbing his temples through the plane.

I don't have to tell Bree, Lakuna, and Mazi. That's what their mentors are for. We are ordered to get farther away from the base and deeper into the desert. After a short while, we have to stop. The temperature flies over 122 degrees, according to Gibbs. The cactuses provide some relief from the sun but not enough. My water bottle is already half drained; I didn't even think to save some because I thought we would be out of here in no time. Wrong. The clock reads 2:33 p.m., and my head hurts.

To pass the time, I watch the soldiers from the base pulling bodies out of the burning building, wishing I could help those people. I shouldn't have done that. I regret it. Yes, I saved other kids, but I know I killed more than I saved. Even if they are fighting against us, my heart tightens with guilt.

Sweat drenches my clothes and steams up my oxygen mask, which I am so grateful to have. The cool air filling the mask helps me; it helps me remember I will get to go home. My tongue is dried up and scratchy. My saliva is bubbly in my mouth. By nightfall, I give in to my thirst and sip a small amount of my water. My eyelids get heavy, and I fall into a restless sleep. I switch between sitting and curling into a ball. I listen to the screams that continue to come from the base and the echoing howls of the wild dogs. Someone is connected to me at all times, Gibbs or Cam or Griff or Pete.

At one point during the night, I just want to talk. I press the button on my microphone. "Are you all right?" the voice says. It's Gibbs.

"As good as I can be," I say.

"Okay, what do you want?" he asks. I wish he wouldn't talk as loud.

"The first year we played soccer for the high school I was amused at how Lakuna slide-tackled people. I knew how but not as well, so I asked her to teach me. She made fun of me for it, but she taught me. It took a week or so before I got it down. I asked if I could test it on her. She pretended to run, and I came at her from her left side and took her out. She taught me well. It was not a foul. Her ankle broke in two places. She was out for the rest of the season, but she came to every game and every practice, and to top it all off, she cheered for me the most. Just a story I thought I'd tell someone."

"Thanks for sharing," he says.

"Oh yeah, we were at my house when I broke her leg. Her excuse for breaking it was she fell down the stairs. She didn't tell on me."

He seems more interested after that. He asks about different times in my life, good and bad. When he asks about Ozalee, I pretend I fall asleep, and he believes it.

As soon as I open my eyes the next morning, a wave of dizziness rushes over me. I can hear my pulse in my ears, and my tongue feels like sandpaper. I take a drink of my sixteen-ounce water bottle. Now the amount of water I have left is barely three ounces. A sheet of sweat covers my forehead, but as the day goes on, my sweat disappears, and by nighttime there is none left in me. My water is gone, leaving me with nothing to hydrate me for the next two days. Luckily, lack of water drains you of all energy and sleep is easy.

Every other hour during the night, the person connected to me wakes me through my earpiece; they just say my name until I talk back and then the earpiece clicks off.

The twisting of my stomach brings me to reality today. I haven't eaten anything in two days, and I feel like my belly is eating itself. I lick my lips with my dry tongue, but the pressure hurts. I gently feel my lips and find them blistered. I put the gas mask over my nose and mouth and press the oxygen button. The cool air feels good on my burnt cheeks. It is incredibly difficult for me to sit up, but I do. I have to use both arms to steady myself.

Bree is more responsive than Lakuna or Mazi, maybe because she is bigger. In biology last year, I learned the bigger a person is, the longer they can go without water. They will have negative side effects but they can live longer. Lakuna's skin bubbles with sunburn, I tell her to put her mask over her face just to reduce the amount of sun soaking into her skin. I unstrap her belt from her waist and place it over her eyes.

My earpiece clicks on. "You have extra water in your belt," Gibbs says.

Feeling stupid, I unzip Lakuna's pocket that holds the extra water but find it empty. "I already drank it," she says. I let her and Bree have a small sip of mine. I give Mazi the rest of my water, which is not much, considering the bottle isn't even half the size of my other one, but she needs it.

Grownups always say television is bad, and you shouldn't watch too much. Every night before bed, my friends and I would watch TV, the Animal Channel or the Reality Channel. I personally liked the Animal Channel. I learned plenty from it, and I was always interested in animals. Sometimes reptiles burrow under the desert sand to keep cool. I dig a shallow hole and use the sand around me to cover my body, instant relief.

Heat makes you crazy. Or am I already crazy? Regardless, the water bottle sitting next to me turned out to be a rock, and now my lip is bleeding. And what I thought was a snake slithering by me was just Mazi's fingers. When I flinched, my shoulder jammed into the cactus I use for shade, and I spent the next hour or so digging barbs from my body. The headache I have is relentless. If there was any water left in my body, I would be crying. With that, I fall asleep.

Bree shakes me awake when it's dark out. At the movement, I begin to gag. As soon as I'm partially aware, my earpiece clicks on. "I tried to wake you up, but you didn't wake up." It's Pete's voice.

"Sorry," I say.

"I got Gibbs. We've been trying for a while now." The microphone goes static, and then Gibbs talks to me.

"You need to stay awake," he says. "I'm so tired," I tell him.

183

"C'mon," he urges.

"I know," I say and close my eyes only to be woken the next morning by the ground erupting with an explosion of dirt. It takes me a long time to get on my feet. Blackness covers my eyes, but I don't fall over. I don't have the strength to lift my gun or bow.

Click. "Hayden, we're here. We're getting you out. Duxia planes are attempting to take you out."

I help Mazi to her feet and tell her to leave her gun. I can see the plane from where I stand, but it's in my farthest vision. The ground explodes all around me. I recognize Gipem's plane circling the base and the sky above us. I also recognize Duxia's planes, bombing the ground and trying to hit us.

Instinctively, we run, attempt to run, struggle. The bombs they release don't explode; they penetrate into the ground. As we get closer to the plane, I see our people with machine guns shooting at Duxia planes. The metal balls the planes are dropping get closer to us, but we can't run any faster. A smaller plane drops a ball right behind me, skimming my heel and knocking Mazi and me over. As we fall, I push her farther away from me. The pain in my heel is instantaneous. I can feel the hot blood trickling into my boot. I try to get up, but putting pressure on my foot hurts.

The bombs are raining all around us now. Bree catches up to us, dragging Lakuna in her arms. It doesn't seem Lakuna can go any further; her skin is scorched so bad, she is unrecognizable, and I cannot bear to put any weight on my foot.

"Bree, just go!" I shout. She drops Lakuna on the ground and hoists Mazi to her feet. "Lakuna, help me," I whisper. She looks up at me with my foot off the ground and pushes herself up. She gets on my bad side and helps me just enough to where we can get up the ramp of the plane. Lakuna lets go of my body. My knees give out, and I sink to the ground. I see the feet of people boarding the plane and then the noise of them latching the door closed.

Someone lifts my chin, Pete. He gives me a half gallon jug of chilled water; I drink it all down within minutes. He helps me on my feet, but I can't walk another step. He picks me up and sits me in a chair. Gibbs and a doctor I don't know take seats next to me. Immediately the doctor sticks an IV in my arm and strips my left boot off my foot. Blood spills onto the floor and splatters the bottom of his pants.

The room starts spinning around me. I lean my head against the window; the glass is cool against my skin. Someone reclines my chair and spreads a blanket over me. I feel like my head is going to burst. Everything is so loud and bright. I can see the white of my bone on my heel. Pete touches my face. I have chill bumps on my skin from the sudden change of temperature, but waves of heat keep flowing to my insides. The doctor comes at me with another shot. It quickly turns into the tail of a scorpion, and I scream. I try to push out of the chair, but my arms feel like spaghetti. The scorpion stings my heel. Its venom is thick and makes my foot tingle. Gibbs shoves a quail egg in my mouth, and I gag it back up at the mere thought of eating a raw egg. The doctor pulls another shot from behind him. The needle grows to be at least a foot long. I kick his hand with my numb foot. Pete holds my limbs down. My stress turns into a mix of crying and screaming. The doctor sticks my stomach with the huge needle; the plane spins faster and faster. I start gagging, but nothing comes up, and I can feel my body shaking. The doctor says something foggy to Pete, and he places a mask over my face. Sweet air fills my lungs, and my eyelids get heavy. Then heavier. Heaviest. I'm scared of the scorpion venom pulling me under that I'll never wake up. "Pete," I cry, but he just tells me it's going to be all right.

CHAPTER TWENTY

I feel a weight on my pointer finger; it makes my pulse beat there. I open my eyes to see what it is, but my vision is blurry with tears.

"You gave us quite a scare," Kanga says. My leg is hoisted up by a sling descending from the ceiling. The thing connected to my finger is gray. When I yank it off, the heart monitor next to me stops beating. Kanga removes the finger thing from my bed; Pete is sleeping in a chair next to me. "They've been switching on and off," she says. I hear more heart monitors in the room. I try to get up, but she pushes me back down. I reach for the glass of water on my bedside table. My sheet falls from my hand, and I notice red bumps all over my skin. I touch my fingers together. The bumps itch. I scratch it with the other hand. "No, no. Don't do that."

"What is this?" I ask.

"That is your allergic reaction to the anesthesia we gave you on the plane." My whole body is covered in the itchy red rash except my face, palms, and feet. I take a deep breath. "That heel of yours was definitely a challenge."

"Where are the other girls?" I ask.

"Still here, Mazi and Bree are just overheated and exhausted, a lot of smoke inhalation. Lakuna's kidneys were actually failing, but they are stable again," she says.

"What time is it?" I ask then lean over the side of the bed and puke in the garbage can beside the nightstand.

"3:07 am."

In the morning, Kanga rubs me down in thin pink anti-itch cream, and she puts a soft cast on my foot. It's hard getting used to the crutches; they make the bumps on my underarms bleed and my fingers itch. Mazi and Bree were released from CCH earlier this morning. Lakuna, on the other hand, was put on something to make her sleep so her brain function would go down and her kidneys would heal quicker. I hobble to the elevator and press 13. I knock on the door to our room, and Bree opens, helps me in, and sits me on the bed.

"How's your foot?" she says. Bree, Mazi and I are the only ones in the room. "It hurts. That's just part of the job, I guess."

"We found out what that machine was," she says. "What is it?"

"It's a cloning machine, not like a baby clone but a full-grown clone. The Duxians are making more and more soldiers." So that's why they want us to destroy it so bad because it's making more of the enemy. And that's why they want us to go altogether; there will be a lot of guards, and there will be more of us to take them out.

"I'm not gonna lie, Hayden. When you speared your shoulder on the cactus because of my fingers, it took all I had not to laugh," Mazi says.

"You can't tell me you weren't seeing things too?" I question.

"I was," Bree says.

"Where are the guys?" I ask.

"They had to go to school today." Mazi sort of giggles. "Do we have to go?"

"No."

All I feel like doing is sleeping. I don't have any meds in my system, and I'm not even sleep deprived, but Kanga told me this would be a side effect of surgery. My body doesn't hurt when I move. It feels heavy. Mazi wraps a garbage bag over my foot so I can shower, and then I get in. The bumps swell in effect to the heat of the water and begin to pop.

When I exit the bathroom, I press the button and ask for Wyllie. When she arrives, she massages the pink anti-itch cream into my skin. "Hayden, I need you to come with me," she says. "Mr. Donovan and President York planned some type of party in a week or so. They want all of you to look very nice. Mazi and Bree already got them." They open their mouths and showed me their teeth. There were bands braided together across their teeth. "They will only be on there for two days, but it will hurt."

Great. She takes me back down to Kanga and sits me in a chair. Kanga straps the braids on my teeth, and I instantly feel the pressure of straightening.

On my way to floor 13, I see one of the lunch ladies who serves me food every day. She struggles with a heavy load of dirty dishes. I ask her if she needs help, really hoping she says no. "Why, thank you, sweetie," she says and points to the direction of the kitchen. "Can you just start washing the dishes until the others get off break?"

I dip a plate in the scalding water and start scrubbing. Almost 120 plates and two hours later, the other lunch ladies come in and relieve me of my dishwashing job. I go to the cafeteria and ask for my lunch, but the fish is too painful for me to eat, so I go without. Frustrated, I crutch up to my room and lie on my bed. Someone knocks on the door.

"Come in," I say.

My mom walks over to my bed. "How do you feel?" she asks.

"Fine."

"How's your foot?"

"It hurts," I say.

"How's your teeth?" she presses. "They hurt," I snap.

"Have you eaten?"

"No, Mom! What am I gonna eat?" I almost scream.

She orders Mazi, Bree, and me chocolate ice cream with hot fudge and caramel on it and gives me a small painkiller. She says she needs to go help in the hospital. Something went wrong with a tank's engine, and it caught fire. Long story short, people got hurt.

Bree clicks on the television, and Mazi gets in the shower. I relax into my bed. The pain in my heel subsides, and I attempt to zone the world out.

"Ariel, you're stupid. It's C-E-L-A-B-R-A-T-I-O-N!" I hear Tinley yelling from down the hall. They bust into our room and throw their books on the floor.

"Bree, tell Ariel there's an A after the L in celebration, not an E." I can tell Tinley is annoyed.

"Why does it even matter?" Bree sighs.

"Because we have a spelling test tomorrow, and I don't want her to miss it, and she thinks I'm wrong and I'm not!" she says.

"It's an E," I say.

"Whatever. I'm spelling it how I think. I don't care if I miss it." "Told you," Ariel says.

Broppin and Hixel sit in the corner and work on a small paper their teacher gave them about World War One. I quiz Ariel and Tinley on their spelling, and I help Hixel with her math. They don't talk about our mission at all, and since they don't bring it up, neither do I. I know I owe them an apology though. I broke a promise.

"Hey, guys, is it okay with you if we take a nap?" Mazi asks as she opens the bathroom door. "Do we have to leave?" Ariel asks. Mazi just smiles. "Aw, see you at dinner then," she says, and they leave the room.

Bree closes the blinds and turns out the light. I wrap the warm covers around my body. Before I even close my eyes, I hear the guys outside our door. I put the blanket over my head, hoping they'll think I'm not in here.

They open the door and fling their books to the side. "Mazi, when did you get released?" Spence asks and walks over to her.

"After you guys left for school," she says.

"Where's Hayden?" Cam asks. Someone must have pointed to the blanket because he tries to lift it up. I hold it tighter.

"Stop, I look ugly."

"C'mon, let me see," he says. I loosen my grip on the blanket, and he peeks his head under to look at my allergic reaction.

"It's not that bad," he smiles.

"You're just being nice."

He pulls the blanket down all the way, and I sit up. "Our stylists want to see us." He hands me my crutches, and once again I have to leave floor number 13. Ugh.

Edna is happy to see me. "Oh, poor darling," she says as she evaluates my poor body condition. She examines my rash and says she has an antidote for it. She digs through her drawers and pulls out a tube of white cream; she twists off the cap and rubs it over my body. The cream smells like pure bleach. My bumps begin to burn, and I feel my muscles tense up.

"This is burning my skin," I say painfully.

"Yes, yes, get in the shower and wash with this." She gives me baby soap. I turn the water to hot and scrub my body and face with the gentle soap. I rinse my hair with flower shampoo and conditioner and dry off with a towel; by the time I am water free, my skin is smooth rather than itchy.

Edna once again takes measurements of my body, how wide my hips are, what shoe size I need, how tight she'll have to make the clothing around my chest. "That is all I need, darling. Did you forget your teletalky?" she asks.

I check the pockets of my sweat suit. "Yeah, I don't have it." "Gibson wants to see you at supper, so you better shoo!" she says.

Mazi and Bree meet me outside my dressing room. "Well, you look better," Mazi says. "Yeah, she had some medicine for it."

Our mentors have us sitting at one large table tonight at dinner while everyone else eats lobster tail and carrot chips with ranch. Mazi, Bree, and I are stuck eating mashed potatoes and pumpkin crème brûlée.

"Lakuna was taken out of CCH today and put in the nurses' unit. She'll be back in your room tomorrow," Gibbs tells me from across the table.

I nod. "How long do your teeth hurt for after you get these off?" I ask Pete quietly.

"They don't. They make you brush with something that heals and whitens." He shows me his teeth, perfectly straight and brilliantly white.

"I guess it's worth it."

"A show is playing on the Rescue Squad tonight. I would like you to watch it," Chipolaux says. He leads the younger girls in through the double doors.

"Do we have to go to the theatre?" Mazi asks tiredly.

"No," Chipolaux answers.

Hixel hugs me from behind. "Where were you?" I ask.

"Mr. Donovan took us to the Center's soccer academy so we could watch them play. He says we could sign up if we wanted, but we'd have to get your and Pete's permission," she says and squeezes a little harder.

"Where is it?" I ask.

She turns to Chipolaux for the answer. "It's about six miles from here." "I'll think about it. What did Pete say?"

"He'll talk to you," she says. "Have you eaten yet?" I ask her. "Yeah."

The younger girls go with my mom to their room, and we head up to ours. I put on shorts and a tee shirt. Everyone changes and gets ready for the video which shows at 8:45 pm, and its only 8:30. The guys get showers and come out one by one; all of them have grown in mass since we've been here. They look so muscular and built compared to the starving boys on the island. They look like they have matured; the youngest in looks is Brint, but even he looks older than he should. Brint may be the smallest guy, but he is still bigger than any of us girls.

"Okay, guys, the younger girls want to join some kind of soccer academy. All I know is it's about six miles away," I say to everyone to get their inputs.

"I don't see why not," Griff says.

"Well, my only worry is someone from Duxia will try to get them since we won't be there," I say. "Will they be under supervision?" Mazi asks.

"I don't know," I say.

"I talked to Chip. He said there will be guards around the perimeter but not in the complex," Pete says.

"How will they get there?" Spence says.

"Cocoa will take them and stay with them, but she can't protect them," Pete adds.

"I don't know guys . . ." I say reluctantly.

"Is it bad this decision is a big deal to us?" Mazi says sarcastically. "I know. It's ridiculous," I say.

"I think it will be fine, and if something happens, we can just pull them out," Pete says. "Me too," Cam says.

Cam and I sit on his bed. My head on his shoulder, his fingers tangled with mine. Griff turns the lights off, and the show begins. The screen is black, then waves crash through and a dark voice booms, "On May 13, nine teenagers and one child were abducted by the Duxian military and put on an isolated island to die. The Duxian leaders put many treacherous obstacles on this island . . ."

Images of our time there flash on the screen, the fiery tree separating Mazi, Lakuna and I from the rest of the group, Lakuna and I being shot with darts by the Uglys, the panther attack, and the flood.

"The teenagers did everything they could to survive . . ." More pictures, Griff saving Lakuna from the cliff and falling himself, me putting Cam in the ice-cold creek to break his fever, and Griff bashing Brint with a shell to save Lakuna and me.

"But one of them wasn't so lucky . . ." The video of Ozalee's death and her funeral plays. Hot tears trickle down my face.

"Now the teenagers are risking life and limb to avenge the child's death and save our country." A picture of Ozalee and I sticks to the screen.

"Pete Girth, Spence Leadmen, Brint Turner, Cam and Griff Malrook, Hayden Kolter, Lakuna Crest, Bree Uley, and Mazi Seedar are thinking the impossible for us . . ." It shows the guys getting shot at on their mission and us getting bombed on ours.

"And now we are going to thank them. On October 13, we would like to have a celebration in their honor. It will be held in the Center's square, the indoor area, and we hope to see you there." The pictures that we picked the night of the tolerance test play, and then the program fades to black.

By the time a regular show comes on, my insides are shaking, and I'm holding back sobs. Cam studies my face. I can feel myself cracking. I don't even use my crutches; I run out of our room and burst into my mother's.

She wraps me in her arms. "It's okay. It's okay." "I miss her. I can't do this anymore," I cry.

"I know." She lets me cry in her arms. Cry about Ozalee, cry I don't have the life of someone normal, and cry I don't know what to do anymore. In the end, I'm back to where I started, confused and hurt.

She walks me back to my room. I'm glad mostly everyone is sleeping. My mother makes me take a painkiller for my foot. I already know before I take it that it would make me sleepy. Cam wraps his arms around me when I sit on the bed, I push them off. I don't want him right now. I want Pete. Pete knew Ozalee more than Cam; he grew close to her because of Ariel.

He looks at me sadly. "I don't know what I want anymore," I say to him. "I want you. I do, but then sometimes I think I need someone else."

He thinks for a while. "Well, I'll always be here for you. Whenever you need me, I'll come." I look deeply into his soft green eyes. I try to think of what to say, but my mind is foggy, he knows.

"Do you love me?" he asks patiently. "Yeah," I say.

"Do you love Pete?" he pushes. I lie down and nod.

"What about Griff, Brint, and Spence?"

I can't keep my eyes open anymore. "Mm-hmm." I move my hand to put it under the pillow, but I find the hot skin of Cam's cheek. The rest of my fingers fall there. I don't have the energy to move them, and the painkiller pulls me under.

I am woken in the middle of the night by a crack of thunder; my hand still rests on Cam's cheek. My heel throbs invincibly; I take the small blanket on the end of our bed and wrap it around my shoulders. I hop to my crutches; I am just about to push the button on the panel between the bathrooms when I remember everyone else is sleeping. I get on the elevator and push the Lobby button; it takes me only a few minutes to get to the cafeteria. They have an all-night food buffet set out, but there is a certain thing I want. I pour the creamy chocolate in a cup and squirt whipped cream on the top. Through my teletalky, I ask Wyllie to give me some more painkillers. She meets me in the cafeteria and stirs some powder in my drink. I give her a questioning look.

"I'm sorry. I don't want to overdose you. It's a knockout powder," she answers. "Wow, I feel like there is a lot of medicines and stuff here that makes you sleep," I say.

"Yes, they do that on purpose because of all of the psychological damage." She leaves me in the cafeteria.

"Hayden?" Pete says.

I look around and see a figure sitting at a table in the corner. I go to him. "What are you doing up?" I ask.

"Psh, I haven't really slept recently," he says. I can tell he's tired, and by the shine of the emergency lights, there are shady circles under his eyes.

"Have you taken medicine?" I ask. "No."

I drink half the cup of my hot chocolate and give the rest to him. The effects are immediate; he grabs my hands across the table. "Are you scared?"

"Yes."

"Me too."

He kisses my knuckles and pulls my chair closer to him; I put my head on our hands. He doesn't say anything for a while, and I drift of in the chair. Before the powder takes full effect, he helps me to my feet. He takes one of my crutches so we can give each other support as we walk. By the time we get to the thirteenth floor, I'm pretty sure he's holding all of my weight, and I have all of his. He puts my crutches against the wall and goes to his bed; I fall asleep as soon as my head reaches the pillow.

When I wake up, Dr. Ezzard is looking at me. "What are you looking at?" All of my friends are standing around me except Pete. Ezzard shows me the empty syringe in his hand. "What is that for?" I ask.

"This is for when a young nurse gives you the wrong type of knockout medicine and you won't wake up," he says.

"Oh, well, she's young," I say.

"It could have been much worse," he snaps.

Cam helps me up and steadies me. I'm a little wobbly. We move on to Pete, and Ezzard injects the stuff into his arm. A couple seconds later, he opens his eyes and asks the same stuff I did.

Chipolaux walks into our room. "There was a tornado last night. It tore down the orphanage. We already have Troop 415 out looking for the missing children." Troop 415 is the squad with search dogs. "We need all of you to get in your uniforms and we want to film you searching for the children."

Mazi helps me into my uniform and gives me back to Cam. It's hard for me to stand by myself without falling over. I think it's because the sleeping powder is still in my body and the wake-up meds are present also. Our mentors enter our room with our breakfast of a bacon, egg, and cheese biscuit. Gibbs give me a walking boot and takes my crutches from me. We pile in a Hummer with the Center's logo on it and drive to the orphanage.

As soon as we exit the car, camera crews swarm us. They separate me from Cam and Pete. I sway on my feet. "Ms. Kolter! Hayden!" the newscasters shout. I fall backwards into the arms I recognize as Gibbs.

"A little shaky there?" he says sternly. Bright lights of the cameras flash in my face, making it even harder for me to get anywhere. "Excuse us!" Gibbs shouts. We meet the rest of the rescue squad in front of the crumbling orphanage. Chipolaux starts giving orders, but I can't focus. Screaming children are running everywhere, bloody and telling the people of 415 where they last saw their friends. Medics, including my mother and Ann, Griff and Cam's mom, are caring for the injured. Search dogs are running in and out of the place, some bringing back evidence and others nothing. The wind is crisp and the rain is blinding. In some of the puddles on the ground is the redness of blood.

"Everyone got that? Go!" Chipolaux orders. The squad runs in every direction except for Pete and I who are stuck shaking on the rubble.

"You take my arm, and I take yours?" he asks. We grab each other's shoulder and wrap our hands around the other's ribs.

A camera crew follows us everywhere we go, but that isn't as distracting as the bloody children running around. Pete and I walk the perimeter until we see one of the search dogs crawl through a space in the building an adult wouldn't fit through. We drop to our knees and crawl on the sharp edges of broken brick and glass. The dog leads us through a winding path until we arrive in a room large enough for us to stand. The room is blocked on all sides. Cracks run up and down the walls, flooding the room with rainwater.

The whistle of the wind is so loud, I can barely hear Pete's voice. "What?" I scream.

"Follow the dog and listen!" The water is up to our ankles; I feel my adrenaline surge through my body. The dog is barking at the wall with water seeping through. I pet the animal on its head so it gets the feel I'm nice, and then I clamp its muzzle shut.

The noise is faint, but I hear it. "Pete, we need to get over there." The dog tries to dig under the tile floor, but it doesn't budge. Pete and I start hitting the wall, and a few crumbs fall but not enough, then I get an idea. I take my walking boot off and give it to him. "You hit harder than I do." He bangs the boot on the wall, creating little holes until we can get our fingers through. He stills chops with the boot as I scrape the stuff away with my hands, and soon all of my fingers are bleeding heavily. Finally the hole is big enough to get our bodies through.

We smash into the other room as water spills into ours; the water is higher in here. Now we can hear their shrill cries easily. Four cribs are still standing, each holding a hysterical toddler. Two more cribs have tipped over, and two more toddlers are on the ground in the high water. The little girl is standing in water up to her thighs; Pete scoops her up in his arms. Her foot is gushing blood. I tear my sleeve off of my uniform and tie it around her cut, and Pete sets her in a crib. The baby boy is pinned under the crib, not crying and not conscious. Pete lifts the crib up, and I grab the child. His leg is twisted weirdly and so clearly broken. The child's lips are a light shade of blue.

"He's not breathing," I say. I hold my arms out straight, forming a table, and Pete proceeds with mouth to mouth. Minutes pass and the boy doesn't show any signs of life. The little girl with the bleeding foot is screaming, "Bubby!" as she watches Pete. Pete gives one last big breath and pats the child on the back, and then the boy coughs. Water spills from his mouth, and his chest rises and falls by itself, but his eyes never open.

"Okay! Grab a kid. Let's go," Pete says. He hands me the baby boy, and he takes the bleeding girl. The dog leads us back through the tunnel and pops out in the open; we climb out carrying the wounded toddlers. The camera crew must've got Gibbs and Simone because they are there with my mother and Ann. We hand the children to them and run back to the tunnel. Someone yanks me back, "You're not going back in there!" Gibbs says.

"No, let go of me. There are more kids in there!" I scream at him. I pull as hard as I can, and his hand slips from my shoulder. I dive in the hole before he can catch me again.

The water is now flooding the tunnel. There is no way we can come back in this way without drowning. We're going to have to take all four children at once. When we stand, the water is at our knees. Pete unzips my suit and positions the smallest baby in there and rips off one of his sleeves to tie my suit back in place. We each take one in our arms, and the dog is just helpful enough to drag the other by its hood. We send the dog down the tunnel before we go. I get on my knees and start to crawl.

"Hayden, wait," Pete says.

I back out of the tunnel and listen carefully, and I hear another noise. "We'll come back," I say. We crawl through the tunnel and scrape our way out the other side.

My mother takes the baby from Pete, and Ann gets the children from me. Gibbs grabs my arm and tells me he's not letting go this time.

"It's fine. We got them all." I comfort him. He lets go of my arm, and I make a bolt for the tunnel. Pete and I press our noses to the top of the tunnel just to breath; the water is now at our waists. We go into the room where the toddlers were and listen again. I can hear a noise, but it's not a cry. It's a thumping sound. We use a broken piece of wood from one of the cribs to smash through another wall. Water pushes us over, and it takes all of our strength to stand up. We look around the large room, but no one's in here. All it is a bed with a bunch of chairs and a closet. But we can tell the thumping is coming from this room. I open the closet, and a young girl jumps out at me.

I scream at the fact I didn't know anyone was here, but she is no more than four years old. She hugs my leg, and Pete plucks her out of the water. Her hair is dark and her skin is tanned. She has eyes the color of crystal.

"We're going to get you out," I tell her. She doesn't say anything. Her face is in the crying stage, but nothing is coming out of her mouth. She shows me her fingers, swollen and purple, her pinky bent out of the socket. Pete loses his other sleeve to stop the child from seeing her mangled hand. The child points to a door, and we run through it. She continues to lead us out of the rubble. Pete ends up putting her on his shoulders to keep her from getting wet. She points to a door with golden handles, and we push it open. The water from the room behind us floods out into the open floor. We get to our feet and see we are still under the roof of the building. One of the walls leading to the street is missing. That gives us a clear passage to safety.

I see a black-haired boy digging through the crushed bricks of the orphanage. "Griff!" I shout. He looks at me then looks up at the roof. Pete takes the girl off of his shoulders and extends his arms to give her to Griff, but he doesn't come in. I hear a cracking noise on the ceiling, and the walls groan.

"Get out!" Griff screams. I see the camera crew run at him and point their cameras in our faces. That's when the walls give, and the roof crashes down on us.

Chapter Twenty-One

I expected us to be crushed like the way I was on the island, but we aren't. When I look around, it is dark. We are in a tight space, not big enough to move. Somehow I ended up sitting with my back leaned up against the wall. My feet are jammed into the insulation of the ceiling. The young girl is lying next to me. Her long hair wrapped around her neck. I gently put her on my lap and move her hair into place. I can feel the bump on the back of her head, and her hot blood runs onto my fingers and mixes with mine. Her head slumps to her chin. When the wall crashed down, Pete must've dropped her. There is enough room to lay her all the way down. I use my emergency pack to prop her head out of the trickling water. Pete's upper body is in the space, but another piece of wall or ceiling or something cuts his legs off from our space.

"Pete?" I wave his hair away from his eyes. He's knocked out. I move his face so its toward me. I can't see any bumps or swelling. Other than a busted lip and a cut cheek, he looks fine. I wipe his lip and cheek with my good sleeve and fix his hood so his ears are out of the water.

I hear his teletalky beeping, but I can't reach it. "Pete? Hayden? Are you there? Can you hear me?" It's Chipolaux.

My teletalky beeps next. "Pete? Hayden? Are you there? Can you hear me?" I hear it, but it's on the other side of the wall. I try to reach Pete's by pressing my feet against the wall and leaning. That's when I feel the intolerable pain in my left heel. I pull my foot closer to my face. All of the bandages have been ripped off, and the stitches are snapping because of the new swelling. I can see the white of my bone again. With every beat of my heart, more blood spills from my foot. Very quickly, my adrenaline disappears.

Pete's teletalky rings again. I press my good foot to the wall and pull his body closer to me so I can reach in his pocket. I grab it in one quick painful motion. "Pete? Hayden? Are you there? Can you hear me?" Chipolaux says.

My fingers are twitching trying to find the right button. "Ye-yeah."

"How many people are trapped?" he asks.

"Thr-three." My voice is shaky; I've never felt a pain like this before. "Are you hurt?" he presses.

"Yes." Thump . . . Thump . . . Thump . . . I feel my heart beat in my temple.

"How bad?" My breathing gets heavy as the seriousness of our situation settles in. My throat goes numb. "Hayden, how bad?" he repeats.

"The little girl has a broken hand . . . She's out cold," I say. I have a large amount of pressure on my lungs, and my vision is starting to go out of focus.

"Hayden, I'll take it," Pete whispers. I hadn't noticed he came to. I drop the teletalky in his hand. "Hayden's foot is bad. The stitches are ripped open. I see her bone. There's a crack in it."

"Is she conscious?" Chipolaux asks.

Pete looks at me and I open my eyes. "Barely." The girl is clearly not a priority. "Can you bandage it?" he asks.

"I'm not going to," Pete says.

"Is she losing blood?"

"Yeah," he says. The stream coming from my leg is red and flowing. "Pete I need you to knot it," Chipolaux says. "Are you losing blood?" "Not that much."

"Does the child need her hand set?" Chipolaux continues. "Her pinky."

"Do it while she's out."

I rip off my other sleeve and pull the girl into Pete's view. I hold her arm out to him, and he pushes her pinky back into place. I wrap her hand in the sleeve she had on and mine just to give her extra cushion. Pete strips his belt off his waist and tells me to move my leg closer to him. "This is going to hurt," he says. He wraps the belt around my ankle, and he yanks one knot through. I scream in pain.

"Only one more," he says. He wraps it around one more time.

I hear Pete talking on the teletalky. "The girl is awake now. Hayden is awake."

"Let me talk to her," Chipolaux says. I shake my head no, and Pete doesn't answer the rest of the calls.

"I'm sorry," he says.

"I don't know what a bandage will do other than make it hurt more. I'm still bleeding, so it doesn't matter," I say.

"I was just following orders," he says.

"I know." The girl is using my lap as a pillow; I brush her hair out of her face. "She can't speak," Pete says.

"What do you mean?"

"She's mute." She puts her thumb in her mouth. "What time is it?" I ask.

He looks at his teletalky. "4:43 pm."

"Are they even trying to get to us?" I ask.

"Yes, they are, but they are scared if they move something they'll flood us out only we won't be able to get out." Something is different about his voice. It quivers when he talks.

"You're hurt," I say. "No," he protests.

"You can't trick me. I'm no idiot." "I never said you were."

"Then sit up." But he can't.

"I hurt my shoulder. A little," he says. "Pete! Why didn't you tell them?" I ask. "It's not a big deal," he says.

"Is it cut or broke?" I ask.

"It doesn't matter." I lean over and poke it just hard enough. He winces. "It's broke." "Guess what we're going to be doing when we get out?" I ask.

"I don't know what?" he says.

"In surgery. I bet you. Only because they'll need to fix my heel, and if there are splinters in your shoulder, then they'll need to fix that too," I say.

"It's a bet then because I'm fine," he says. "Whatever."

I move the girl to my spot and take hers, lying down by Pete's hair. I lay my head on my hand; I notice the crimson liquid on my skin before I realize what it is. Now that I'm on the other side of him, I can see the large cut on his head. I put my hand on top, and it comes away red. He seems to have fallen asleep. I want to wake him up to make sure he's all right, but I know sleep is the only way to ease the pain at this point.

Pete and the girl wake up when his teletalky beeps loudly. He picks it up with effort and presses the Answer button. "We are coming in," an unrecognizable voice says. The rubble around Pete's waist loosens, and I try to pull him into our space, but I can't do it without using my feet. I press my feet to the wall, knowing he would do it for me and push. It feels like a thousand needles embed themselves in my heel.

"Thank you," he says drowsily. The wall tumbles down, and shards of brick and glass sprinkle over us. I cover the girl's head and receive a sharp piece of glass down my face. It scrapes past my eye, down my cheek, and over my lip. Four guys with hard helmets and plastic body armor hoist Pete and me up by our arms, and another carries the girl. They drag us out of the rubble and into the wide-open street. Cold water chills my spine and the temperature has dropped dramatically because of the complete darkness.

They lay me by Pete. The girl holds her arms out to me and I reach for her but the guy won't let me have her. I stand up desperately and take a step to get her. Gibbs uses only one arm to hold me in place while I push for her with all I have. The red from my foot blends with one of the puddles on the ground. The girl signs something to me. Pete turns to me and smiles with grey lips, "She said thank you both." Then his eyes roll to the back of his head. His smile disappears, and his body goes limp on the ground. Medics put the sweet-scented gas on his face, the kind I got on the plane after the mission.

"He's having surgery?" I ask Gibbs.

He pushes my hair back like I did the girl's. "Yes." They pick up our stretchers and load us on an ambulance.

First, they clean his head wound with strong antiseptic and put a butterfly bandage over it. They use a cotton ball for his lip and cheek. "His shoulder is broke. The left one," I tell Ezzard, examining the rest of him. Ezzard feels around his shoulder and says a couple incomprehensible things to his assistant. They sit him up and feel the back of it and then they pull the cutting knife out. They make and incision right on his shoulder blade. I start to choke on the blood coming from my face; I sit up by myself and notice the camera crew filming us.

"Gibbs, Pete can't feel anything, can he?" I ask.

He smiles, "Not at all."

The doctor flips Pete over on the operating table. One of the nurses wipes the blood from my face and pinches it together with bandages. "Ow," I push her hand away. She has me extend my arm while she inserts the numbing medication in through a needle. The meds quickly freeze over my veins and reach my foot where she begins giving me stitches, and this whole time I can't take my eyes off of Pete the way, even under sedation, his body seems to lean toward me.

"You swear he can't feel anything?" I ask.

"Positive," Gibbs says. "Don't worry, girlie. He'll be fine." The nurse attaches a bag of blood to my IV. The camera crew videotapes silently from the corner of the ambulance until we reach the military base. Maybe they know we aren't in good enough shape to be answering questions right now because surely if they didn't, we'd be surrounded by reporters and cameras. Gibbs lifts me off the metal table and out of the ambulance doors, drenching both of us in rainwater, and into the base's air conditioning. Ezzard and his assistants lug in Pete's stretcher while the camera crew gets trapped outside. Other mentors are there waiting for us with thick wool blankets and hot broth.

Yanish wraps me in a blanket and give me a cup of broth. "Sip this. It will get your body heat up."

Gibbs carries me down to the clinic, and Yanish holds my blood bag steady above my head. Kanga strips my sopping uniform and replaces it with my freshly dried base-issued clothes. Chipolaux bursts in the room. He sees me sitting on the hospital bed and Pete getting stitched up on the bed adjacent to mine. Yanish hangs the blood on a metal stand beside my bed while Kanga wraps my foot in thick gauze and slips it into a metal brace.

Chipolaux and Gibbs plant their feet in front of me, and Chipolaux says with jaws clenched, "We'll talk about this in the morning." Kanga tucks me in the hospital bed, but I am, in no way, sleepy. Ezzard props Pete up on two pillows and wraps a cushioned black shoulder sling around his left shoulder. He then removes the IV from Pete's skin and tells me he'll wake up soon. Everyone leaves the hospital room except the unknown nurses that walk around, silently checking on us and filling out our medical reports.

"How do you feel?" the male nurse asks me.

"Cold." He wraps another wool blanket around my upper body. "You did a great thing for those kids," he says.

"I told myself that. Gibbs and Chipolaux don't think so."

The nurse looks at me. "They told the cameras they were proud. As soon as the building collapsed, Griff Malrook, Gibson, and Chipolaux were interviewed."

I squeeze my dripping hair with a towel. "Does Lakuna know what happened?" For some reason, I want her to be here. She'd probably tease me and say, "You don't even like kids, Hayden. You're crazy." And I would laugh.

"Yes. Griff told her. She was worried."

Pete takes a big breath and straightens himself out hesitantly. He looks at me through glassy, drugged eyes. "You win the bet."

"What do I win?" I joke. He closes his eyes and gives a little laugh. I click on the television and let him sleep off the rest of the anesthesia like I wanted to do the first time I got out of surgery.

Later that afternoon, I make him get up. He doesn't want to, but we need to get the day started. I steady him at first; he leans on me with the arm not in a cushioned sling. We head toward the main entrance of the base so we can go outside to get some fresh air; we open the doors and sit on the benches outside. Citizens strolling by the nearby shops begin to glance our way; they get closer as they realize who we are. I see some people pointing at us, and only seconds later, news reporters run around the corner. We hurry to get inside, but we aren't fast enough.

"There they are! There they are!" one of the men says as he grabs me by the arm. "What were you thinking when you followed the dog into the building?" a woman asks. "Uh, uh, um . . ." All I can do is stare at the light in my face.

"We were thinking there are children inside who needed us and we were the only people who could save them," Pete answers.

"So you would risk your life for a child you don't even know?" a woman asks.

"We know who we are, but these children, you never know what they'll become. If we save them, they could do the world better than us. It just depends on how everything turns out," Pete answers.

"How do you think the war will turn out?" shouts the guy with the camera.

I finally come up with something good to say, "I won't quit until I get what I want, and I want it to end," I say.

"And what do you want to end, Hayden?" asks the guy latched on my arm.

I say the only thing I really honestly want. "I want Gipem's Girls to be safe."

They press me for more answers. "And who exactly are Gipem's Girls?" A man I haven't spoken to yet asks. I feel like they are asking questions just to get me to say something to them.

"Ariel, Tinley, Hixel, and Broppin?" I ask. "Last names?" the guy urges.

"That doesn't matter," Pete says. I get a better look at the guy and notice how the dye in his hair is fading and the lightening makeup on his face is blotchy. He is a Duxian spy.

The reporters go back to the orphanage happenings. "There was one girl in particular you rescued and it got you trapped inside the building. Do you regret saving her?"

Pete looks at his shoulder. My face throbs. But that doesn't matter. "I've come to learn that with every bad thing that happens, a good thing comes along, and there's always that one moment that makes everything worth it. The moment when we were lying in our own blood and every muscle in our bodies ached, who cares? Because to understand someone needs you that much makes all the pain go away, and at that moment the girl was that someone," I say. The reporters fall silent and the cameraman can't seem to hold his camera up anymore. Pete just looks at me. Even two soldiers who were roaming behind us stop in their tracks. I feel the heat of my blush rush to my cheeks and call directly to the soldiers, "Can you tell me where the Rescue Squad is?"

It takes them many moments to find their voices again, "The orphanage."

We manage to escape the reporters and the soldiers take us to the field that holds the horses. I call Girl and she runs to me eagerly. She is no longer the small filly I had. Her muscles bulge, and her legs are longer than the last time I saw them. The soldiers put a saddle and bridle on Girl and help Pete and me up.

"You are a couple of brave ones," says the soldier with dark curly hair in his Southern accent.

"You would do the same thing," I say.

"We were trained for stuff like that. You did it because you felt the need to," the bearded one says.

"If you were in that situation, would someone had to have forced you to save those kids?" I ask and point Girl in the direction of the orphanage. As her hooves hit the printed pavement of the street, more and more people start to notice us, but then again how can they not? Two of Gipem's Glories riding down the roads of the Center on a giant horse. On top of that, two of Gipem's Glories riding down the roads of the Center on a giant horse with bandaged faces. The shops around us are high class with flowers around the doors and windows and decorated manikins showing through the glass. The citizens roaming the town are dressed in furs and satins and velvets, materials that would be unaffordable in Villa. I used to think President York took all of the money for himself and the Center, that he was being selfish, and I wasn't wrong. My heart goes out to the people of Riverelli or Wikasha, the blocks that struggle every day to keep from starvation, and yet I'm living the high life here.

My dad always said stuff like that, things that would try to make me feel guilty. It never worked—it just annoyed me. But now, with him dead and me living here, I understand what he was talking about. I rub Girl's glossy fur, the last living thing I have to remember him by.

We reach the orphanage in haste. The crowd behind us has dispersed to talk to the rest of Gipem's Glories and more camera crews show up. It is bright today; I can see where the sun dried Pete's and my blood to the pavement. I gently slide off Girl and help Pete down. I lead her to Lakuna sitting on a boulder and sipping hot cider. When she looks at me, her face instantly furrows. "You two are in so much trouble."

I give her the reins. "Taking it easy?" I ask. She sips her drink. We ease down on the ground next to Lakuna; Wyllie offers us cups of cider.

She's in a white medic's uniform, still tending to the injured children whose caretakers can't afford medical attention. Her teletalky beeps. She turns on her heel and rushes away.

Rescue dogs still crawl in and out of the battered building, coming up with nothing. I notice a dog pushing through a recognizable tunnel. Its fur is sandy and scruffy with a clipped ear and brown puppy eyes. I find the soldier who owns the dog from Troop 415. "What is your dog's name?" I ask.

The women's appearance and the dog's traits are alike, yellow and welcoming. "Blue."

"Why Blue?" I can't quite comprehend why I want to speak to her or even acknowledge her. "It reminds me of someone," she wisps.

"And you are?" I think I might know this woman.

"Beverly." She acts like she is scared to communicate with me. Maybe it's the bandage covering half my face.

"I like your dog," I begin with a certain politeness I don't normally use.

"He's a good boy." The dog comes when she whistles for him. I scratch his ears, and he licks my hand.

"He is older?" I can tell by the coarseness of his fur.

"Yes, I'd say about nine years or so."

I remember nine years ago, Ozalee was only a baby. I was in the first grade, my favorite year in school. Mazi and I sat at the same table together; we had only known each other for two years then. The teacher always used to make us come to the board to present our work because we were above average students. She was by far my favorite teacher; with blonde curly hair and a rough voice, she taught me the essentials. The alphabet, addition, subtraction, even cursive.

"That was the time." I offer her my cup I never drank from; she takes it with a bony hand.

Five fingers grip my shoulder. "This time you can't run away." I sense the agitation in Gibbs' voice. His nails dig into my skin as he leads Pete and me to Chipolaux. His suit is black at the moment, with a white undershirt and black tie. His shoes were shiny, but a layer of dust covers them. He whips off his sunglasses, revealing deep circles and stretched skin.

"Do you two understand how much stress is building up in my body?" Pete opens his mouth to talk. "Don't say anything! Just listen." Chipolaux scrapes his fingers down his face. "Do you know what would happen if you two were hurt beyond repair? Killed?" My eyes float to the ground. "Let me tell you what would happen. Do you see those people out there?" He points to a camera crew, to the citizens staring at us, to the children. "Those people wouldn't have the life they have. And would you like to know why?" Gibbs is really hurting my shoulder now. "Because those people"—he pokes his finger at Cam and Mazi and Lakuna and Bree and Griff and Spence and Brint—"they would be ruined without you. Can you two even imagine what they would do without you?" Chipolaux is way past yelling. "If you two were killed, they could not." He emphasizes could and not. "Duxia would obliterate us. The cloning machine has to be destroyed and without you two, that can't happen. The Rescue Squad needs leaders and we have none without you." He pauses for a slight second.

"What about Lakuna or Griff?" My words slip over themselves because I speak so fast.

"It's a mental thing, Hayden! They can't do it!" I've never seen Chipolaux so angry. "What you did was thoughtless and irresponsible. You disobeyed obligatory directions." In my defense I didn't hear a word Chipolaux said.

"We saved lives!" Pete yells.

"Your lives are more important than anyone's at this point in the game," he says blearily. "Go back to camp. You no longer need to be here." Gibbs pushes me in the direction of the military base.

"We did the right thing," Pete barks behind us. Rather than going back to the base, Pete and I stay and assist Troop 415 and our squad in digging through rubble. I can't seem to keep my eyes off of Beverly; I sneak peeks at her, memorizing the features I swear I've seen before. The focus I have on this woman has an effect. All of my energy ebbs and then vanishes. A wave of exhaustion rolls over me, and the back of my head begins pounding from where I banged it on a wall when the roof gave in. I sit on the ground; I have a clear view of the women giving commands to her dog.

"What are you looking at?" I bring my head up slow, making an attempt at not sending my vision in a flurry. Mazi smiles at me with bright straight teeth. I had forgotten I still had the braids on and I haven't eaten all day.

"That woman," I point at her.

Mazi parks herself next to me. "Oh," she sighs with a hint of recognition. "I know her." Mazi's eyebrows dip as she recollects her past. "Ms. Florence," she utters.

"Our first-grade teacher?" I ask, but then it dawns on me, nine years ago.

We stroll up to her, Ms. Florence. She recognizes Mazi right away, showering her with hugs. "Why are you here?" Mazi is confused; she asks the question I was thinking.

"After you ten were kidnapped, all schools closed, and all teachers lost their jobs. Rumor had it the government took you for guarded purposes. Nonetheless, we lost our jobs, and I was in desperate need for money to support me and ol' Blue here." The dog comes to his name. He licks my hand again. "As it turns out, Blue is a decent search dog."

"Didn't you say you named him after someone?" I ask, interrupting their conversation.

"One of my students, she always used blue construction paper on artwork." Without her saying, I know Blue is named after me.

"He helped Hayden and Pete save those toddlers." Mazi indicates, bringing them back to the discussion.

"Yes, that was him. He was also the dog that led us to find them after the ceiling collapsed. I was on break at the time. How are they doing in recovery?" Ms. Florence questions.

Now I am confused, "What?"

"How are Hayden and Pete doing?" she repeats. "I am Hayden."

Chapter Twenty-Two

Her expression is blended with glee and misunderstanding and then horror. She absorbs my torn body, my flushed cheeks, the twisted cut running down my face, my metal-lined foot. She takes my neck in her hands. "You used to be so healthy and strong, but now . . ." Her voice dwindles. "You're burning up, honey."

"It's just a fever."

"You should see your mother," she says.

"These kids need more treatment than that. I'll be fine." I push off her sympathies.

"I'll get her some medicine." Cam's arms wrap around my waist. His breath is hot in my ear. "Cam Malrook? Oh my goodness! My, have you grown."

He beams my smile. "How are you, Ms. Florence?" "Dear, I am doing quite well, and yourself?"

He laughs a little. "As good as I can be."

Cam and I say our good-byes to Ms. Florence, and he leads me away, placing me on the concrete.

"Cam, it's small, just a fever probably from the wet clothes." My attempt at comforting him is dull and worthless.

"The party is tomorrow. We are departing for Duxia in three days. We can't have you sick. We'll have to delay the mission." He's on his teletalky before I can debate anymore. In moments, Gibbs and Kanga whisk around the other side of the orphanage. Gibbs is visibly unsatisfied.

"I thought I ordered you back to camp," he growls through his nostrils.

"I don't have to listen to you." I am so sick and filthy tired of getting told what to do.

"The heck you don't! When I tell you to do something, I expect you to do it." His teeth clench so tight, I can almost hear them crack.

This is a type of fight my father and I used to have. I was a free spirit then. I hated listening to him and talking to him for that matter. Even his presence got under my skin. Every conversation we had ended in a fight and this is exactly what one of them sounded like. Only one thing is different. Gibbs is not him. "You're not my dad! You don't know what's best for me! You don't even know me!" I scream so loud, everyone in the front of the orphanage gawks at us.

"Hayden, you have two choices," he says as he steps closer to me. "One, you get your pretty little behind back on that horse and ride there. Or two, I take you back by force."

Yes, I remember those fights. The fights where he'd yell at me for nothing, the ones that ended in me crying myself to sleep because I had bruises on my wrists from him grabbing me. The time I asked myself why he hated me and only liked Ozalee because she was so perfect and everything was wrong with me. And the fights where my sobbing was intensifying the situation and my mom would come to my defense. Those were the kind that my house went into complete chaos, with everyone loud and desperate as I am now. There were periods when another person would yell at me or give me unreasonable orders and my dad would go haywire in the persons' face. "This is my kid, not yours. If I ever catch you talking to her like that again, I swear on everything I have you'll be sorry." Then he would yank me away and flip them the finger.

I have to remind myself over and over while I stand here with Gibbs's cold eyes piercing through me that my father, no matter how many fights we got into, isn't here anymore, and he's never coming back. Ever. I will never see him again. Or hear him. He'll never take me hunting. He'll never teach me how to pick the correct screwdriver. Pick anything. I could make a wrong decision, and he isn't here to make it right. I feel my throat tighten as Gibbs says, "Your pick." My chin trembles and I can't seem to swallow.

All I can get out is, "You're not him." My voice cracks at the end of the sentence, making my point facetiously weak. Kanga takes my temperature, 102, and gives me some medicine. I don't give Gibbs the time to say anything else before I jerk out of Cam's arms, mount Girl, and ride her back to camp.

I hadn't noticed Pete or Lakuna were being pulled by Girl in an attached wagon until we get to the base and they assist me in untacking her. "Did Kanga tell you guys to rest some?" I ask. That is the only logical explanation I have for them to come back with me.

"Yeah, a little under the weather," Pete says. I hand the tack to the stable guard and lead Girl back into the pasture. As we reenter the building, we are handed more glasses of cider to warm our chilled bones.

My bed is cozy. My aching body relaxes into the comforter; I spread a fuzzy blanket over myself. I cannot comprehend why I've been ill so much. My theories are this: the medication from surgery weakens my immune system, submerging my body in subzero water from the orphanage and being stuck in those same clothes for so long, or just irrevocable stress. All of them probably. I don't feel sorry for myself because I can't seem to get well. I feel sorry for the kids who died from the lists. I feel sorry for the soldiers who were lost trying to destroy the machine while all this time I've been in Villa living the "high life" or what most people would consider anyway. But now, with my sister dead because of Duxia, all I want is revenge. Bitter and sweet, payback for what they have put me through. Not just the president of Duxia will die, but the one guy who has not only supported his idea of kidnapping but altering it into a reality. Foryark Dranken.

It was approximately three months ago when I first heard his name. President York, Chipolaux, all of our mentors, chiefs of Gipem's different military forces, and everyone important to bringing down the Duxian military were meeting in the Council Room. I overheard a conversation I know was not for my ears to perceive. It was late. I was restless. I freed myself of Cam's warmth and lumbered aimlessly through the hallways until I heard Chipolaux's voice I've never before, or since, heard him sound like that. It wasn't angry or scared; it was the most intensity revving, thrill-seeking tone I've ever experienced. "We have him sighted?" I peeked through the cracked door; Chipolaux was clenching the tip of his seat to keep from jumping up.

"Affirmative," one of the chiefs I hadn't met before said.

"Are you confident he is confined and incapable of leaving?" I noticed how when the adults were talking only to each other their speech is more sophisticated. Chipolaux wrenched the maps and charts out of another chief's hand and held it out so President York and he could see.

"Our troops are surrounding the city. Their guards and troops are plenteous in the center of the town but dilutes as the city ends. We are at least thirty miles away from the perimeter of Xil"—Xil is Duxia's capital—"They have us on radar and recognize we have them confined. Their troops have multiplied, flying in on planes and hovercrafts. We are struggling with terminating their air travel."

Chip's tone becomes more serious. "All I want established is Foryark Dranken will not be able to escape."

"As long as he doesn't fly out, he's as good as dead."

I ran back to my room after that, immediately typing *Foryark Dranken* into the search bar on our computer. Links after links appeared and click after click I made. That whole night, I filled my head with data about this man and how he was the one who ordered the Duxians to capture us and all of the other children; he was the one who called the shots on which ones of us died or how. He was the one who designed the cloning machine. He was the one who killed Ozalee, and he was the one who etched himself as number one on my personal kill list.

I can only imagine what I will do to him first—chain his hands and feet and have him dipped in a pool of monster fish or turn him into a human torch like he did to us. Maybe I'll even sick a panther on him and let him slowly bleed to death. Some might think a fifteen-year-old girl dreaming about how to kill a man is weird or psychotic. I honestly don't care what anyone thinks in this category. He took something of mine I'll never get back, and I'll do the same with him.

"Hayden, wake up." His breath smells of icy pine, the same as it always has. He runs his fingers across my cheek and up to my forehead where he places his whole palm. His sigh is despairing. I can feel the air from his lungs as his face gets closer to mine and then our lips softly press together. I wrap my arms around Cam's neck and he lifts me to my feet. The sheets are drenched in cold sweat; even though my skin feels hot, my insides are frigid.

"You're going to get sick," I tell him.

"I don't care, I'd get sick a million times just to kiss you once," he says quietly. His note rubs me wrong; I push away from him and shut the door to the bathroom. He made it sound like that's all he wants to do is kiss me or keep me for how I kiss. I don't want that. I want him to like me, not just my kisses.

I turn the water hot in frustration. The steam feels good in my sinuses; I scrub the sweat from my hair with shampoo that has an aroma of ginger and cinnamon. I lather my body in a spice soap and rinse. I am thankful for the automatic blow-dryer—my wet hair would've given me chill bumps, but instead, it floats down to my chest warm and dry. A clean maroon shirt and sweats have been laid on the toilet for me to change into. I flip my bangs to the right side and Cam is still waiting for me in the room. We rouse Pete and Lakuna and then go to the cafeteria for the mandatory supper.

I hadn't noticed how hungry I was until I pushed the doors open and the tang of orange chicken and rice fills my nostrils. I get in line to accept my meal and am disappointed when Lakuna and I are given only a sandwich and peaches. I slap my tray on the table and sit in my seat between Griff and Cam. "Why do they get that when Lakuna and I have to eat this?" I ask Bolt from across the table. I am not going to talk to Gibbs, and since it is required for our mentors to eat with us for these last days, Bolt is an easy alternate.

"Don't you still have your braids on?" he questions. His accent is different, English maybe? My forgetting about my braids and empty stomach is nonstop. I take a bite of my sandwich. The taste startles me. Creamy and sweet with a hint of tartness.

"What is this?" I ask, trying to get the sticky stuff off the roof of my mouth. "Peanut butter and jelly!" Bolt says.

I raise my brows curiously. "I don't know peanut butter and jelly?" He stares at me like I have four eyes, but my friends' give him questioning looks also.

"You don't have this in Villa?" He seems shocked. "Um, no?" Spence says.

"It's gluey," Lakuna says, making a clacking noise swallowing the peanut butter.

"It's a common thing here. The peanut butter is made from peanuts and the jelly from grapes," Bolt says. Lakuna and I split our sandwiches with our friends so they can enjoy the new and delightful taste of peanut butter and jelly.

After dinner, we return to our room. Our mentors are very stern about us getting an adequate amount of rest now. I've just changed into my nighttime sweats and tee shirt when there's a knock on the door. Gibbs and Chipolaux step in.

"May we see you?" Chipolaux asks in an innocent voice.

For an instant, panic sprouts in my intestines. Pete gives me a reassuring squeeze on my shoulder and Cam shoots me an encouraging look. I sulk into the hallway and they shut the door. I lean against the wall in the hall. What are they going to do now? Make me sleep in a room alone? Ban me from the party or the mission? But I'm not saying sorry. Pete and I did the right thing by saving those toddlers, and Gibbs is not my father.

"Hayden," I start to object, but before I get anything out, Chipolaux speeds up, "We're sorry." Shock. "What?" I ask in disbelief.

Chipolaux apologizes first, "You had every right to save those children, after watching your sister die." I feel like someone just socked me in the stomach. My forehead breaks to sweat, and my hands turn clammy. "I can't believe we were dumb enough to even bring you along. We knew you weren't good with orders, much less not going to save a bunch of trapped children inside an orphanage. I am truly, deeply sorry. Do you forgive me?"

No, I don't forgive you. You made me look like a fool in front of everyone, and you went against what I knew was right. "Yes."

He kisses my cheek and disappears around the corner.

My eyes memorize the tiny pattern on the floor by the time Gibbs starts to speak. It's white tile with sparkles flecked in. "I know I'm not your dad. I shouldn't have talked to you like that. Just remember, I'm always on your side, no matter what. I'm sorry I let my anger get the best of me." He holds his arms out for a hug and I slide right into them.

"I do forgive you." Because I do, and as of now, I need the most support I can get.

"Get some sleep," he says after he gives me my pain meds and pushes me back in my room. I climb in bed with Cam, but turn my back; I notice how someone has changed our sheets. He lays his cheek on mine. "What's wrong?" I debate with myself whether I should tell him the truth or not. I want to know.

"I don't want you to love me only for my kisses." I peek up to see his expression. He just smiles.

Why is he laughing at me? "What?" I snap. He kisses my neck. "I don't."

"You could have any girl you want and you chose me?" I ask, skeptical about everything he's saying.

"No. I found you. Somehow."

"But what if you find someone else?" I ask.

"That won't happen."

The next morning, we aren't woken by an alarm or cameras. We have the privilege of sleeping in. Spence plays his guitar like he did on Sunday mornings in Villa, before church. I used to hate going, having to sit through an hour and fifteen minutes of service, but now I miss it. They don't offer any religious sermons in the military base, and the Rescue Squad was denied permission to go for fear of a religious brawl starting at our choices. At noon, when we all awaken, Wyllie and a couple of maids bring in our brunch. Hot eggs, honey bacon, and fluffy biscuits with butter and jelly. The minute we're done, eating we're split apart and taken to Makeup and Dress.

Edna puts me in a stinging bath this time instead of a shower, and she personally scrubs me raw with a horsetail brush. By the time I'm done stinging, rewashing, shampooing, conditioning, and lathering with cleansing lotion, my skin is smooth and glowing. She leads me to my chair and spins me to face her; she looks distraught at the sight of my metal-lined foot.

"Darling, you just had to get yourself into trouble." She gradually runs her hands down my hairless leg and on to my brace. She unclicks the latches and slides it off my foot, then she unwraps the waterproof bandages.

The mere sight of my foot makes me gag. Swollen to twice its size, purple, and over forty stitches wrapped from my heel to my toes. "Ohhh, darn, I thought you could go without for a night, but that isn't likely." Edna gently puts my brace back on my foot and zips me back around to face the mirror. She runs her fingers through my saturated hair and digs something out of her styling fanny pack, straightening spray.

I gasp; I rarely ever see that. "You didn't use that the last time you made my hair straight?"

"It's an essential when hair is wet, doll!" she laughs. She spritz the spray in my hair and pulls the blow-dryer out. The warm air sends chills up my spine. When she's through drying she pulls my hair off my neck, leaving some of my bangs down and wrapping the rest in a diamond band. She spirals the hair pulled up and the strands left down. When she's happy about the styling of my hair, she turns me to face her again. She pads my face with some type of powder to cover the scab from the glass cut I received in the orphanage and then applies all of my eye makeup, which I don't even know if it has a name. She files my nails into perfect ovals and puts french tips on all twenty of them even though only fifteen will be showing. I know what french tips are because my mom used to paint her nails like that all of the time. Edna opens a velvet pouch and lets me examine its contents, a diamond necklace and diamond earrings. She clicks the necklace around my neck and pokes the dangly earrings through my ears. She smiles at her work.

"Just one more thing," she squeaks, apparently excited about what I will look like. She snaps the braids off my teeth and asks me to brush them with a minty-smelling brown goop. As soon as the paste touches my teeth, the pain eases out swiftly, leaving them with a clean scent. I rinse and look at my teeth in the mirror, snow white and flawlessly straight.

"Close your eyes, darling." I hear the wrapper to my dress hit the ground, and she steadies me with one arm as she slips on my gown with the other. I can feel only one strap. She puts a shoe on my braceless foot and faces me towards the mirror. "Open."

Once again Edna has done the unimaginable—transformed me into something gorgeous. My royal blue dress swoops around my breasts and meets with a diamond clip in the center. It hangs over one shoulder and fits me perfect all the way down until it drags the floor and touches my diamond heel. My makeup is natural with shimmering tan eye shadow and shiny lip-gloss. "Oh, Edna, thank you so much. I . . . I don't even know what to say."

"It's a privilege to work with such an amazing young woman." She sprays me with perfume that owns a fragrance of what I can only describe as sexy, walks me to the front entrance, and hands me off to Gibbs.

"You look too old. Go back and change," he says.

I stare at him uncomprehendingly. "Seriously?" I thought I looked good. Apparently not. "I'm just kidding."

I smack his shoulder and he escorts me to the limo. As soon as I sit down, I am awestruck with how amazing everyone looks. Lakuna in a full-length gold dress, Bree wearing soft grey, and Mazi in satin white. Her dress makes her look more to the elegant side rather than beautiful even though she fulfills that also. Spence is in an original tux, and other than him, they all wear different-colored shirts with black pants, ties, and shoes. Cam wears a yellow shirt and Pete a pink. They look stunning. Almost the whole ride to the Square I silently argue who looks the best Cam or Pete even though Griff blows both of them out of the water.

The limo driver reels the window that separates him from us to the top of the ceiling. "Hayden?" Chipolaux gets my attention.

"What?" Pete takes my hand. Uh-oh. Everyone is looking at me except Cam and Lakuna who keep their downcast eyes on the window.

"I sent some of my men to the island yesterday and they discovered something," he states.

There is only one thing they could've found. "Ozalee?"

He nods. "Tonight," he whispers, "This is not only a party for your departure but also a funeral for her. Your mother is already speaking. Would you like to speak too?" This would be a good time to have a one-on-one talk with Pete and Lakuna.

"I don't have anything prepared," I say.

Pete hands me a small slip of paper. "Done. Lakuna and I wrote it."

Of course you did. "What if I start crying? I'll mess up my makeup."

Mazi smiles, "It's waterproof." Decisions, decisions.

As the limo pulls up, the camera flashes begin. The door to the limo opens. The cheers of the people enter my ears and I step into the bright light. I'm blinded by the cameras as we walk into the Square. "And now presenting Gipem's Glories!" a voice booms from the hidden speakers and citizens flock us. My head spins as hundreds, maybe thousands, of people ask for my autograph or picture or just to touch me, appreciate I'm actually here. I hadn't realized how much I was adored until now, how much the people need me. Hours tick by, and individuals continue to flood around me, overloading my mind. Eight to nine, nine to ten, ten to eleven, this is the time I can actually keep track of before I am able to escape from most of the people. By the period it takes me to get to the table labeled Gipem's Glories, my cheeks ache from smiling.

"Do you want me to get you something to eat?" Cam offers. Out of the hundreds of tables of appetizers, entrées, and desserts, I highly doubt he will pick foods I actually like, but I let him go because frankly I don't want to get up. He comes back with a plate of Caesar salad, crab, veal, and a slice of seven-layer chocolate cake.

"Good enough?" He smiles his perfect smile; I get a tingly feeling in my stomach. "Perfect." He takes a seat next to me and helps me eat my food. There is no way I could've finished it by myself anyway. Spence pulls Mazi to the dance floor and Griff grabs Lakuna. "May I have this dance?" Cam asks and offers his hand.

The song is so memorable, so unforgettable I lose myself in it. We twirl slowly to the lyrics. "Walking alone is hard to do, so take my hand I'll stay by you. Forever and always I'll be here. Never worry I'm always near. You're so precious, little dove. I'll never leave my sweetest love." His hand rests in the small of my back. My fingers touch his hairline.

"You look beautiful," he says. I search his eyes for any sign of insincerity, but find only pleasure. I push up on my tiptoe and kiss him, just a small peck but some kind of déjà vu yanks on my memories and suddenly I want more. He pulls away for just a second and studies my face, then he comes back to me and kisses me with such longing that time stops. The only two people in the world are him and me. And then I remember one small portion of something I thought was lost forever, and so far only this boy has made me really recognize any moment that happened on the island.

"Cam," I whisper, gulping in a huge breath of air, "in the meadow on the island we kissed?"

He grins the grin I love so much. "Yes."

I feel a tap on my shoulder. "Can I steal her away from you?" Pete asks modestly. Cam squeezes me tighter, not wanting me to leave him again and lets me go.

Pete is shorter than Cam, easier for me to get my hands around his shoulders. Easier for me to study. When he blinks, I swear I can feel a puff of wind from his lashes. After a while he says, "You know, I'm jealous of Cam." Why would Pete be jealous of Cam? Certainly not for looks or athletic ability, especially not leadership skills. I can't think of anything Cam has that Pete lacks.

"You shouldn't be."

He looks at the floor; the blush on his cheeks is unmistakable. "That's where you're wrong." "I'm not following you?" I ask.

He gazes at me with those blue eyes, the no longer drugged or glassy eyes and says, "Because you love him, not me."

I almost laugh because of how evidently wrong that it is. He obviously doesn't realize he is the one person that helps me hold myself together in the times I think I'm losing my sanity. The day when Pete and I found out we were going on three missions, the words he said to keep me calm still ring in my head, and "*I'm all ears for you too.*" Just the one sentence helped me miles. At my father's funeral, I stood at the front of the church staring at his casket. At the nothingness, I knew was in there. They never recovered his body. There were exactly 1,472 guests at his funeral, mourning his death. Out of those 1,472 people, I got 1,472 hugs. I only wanted one shoulder to cry on at that funeral. Only one person out of 1,472 people really mattered to me that day. Him. I remember how he kissed each tear that fell from my eye. "You know, each tear you cry, multiply that by a million, and that's how much the person you're crying for loves you," he said.

"Loved," I corrected between sobs.

"No, Hayden, *loves*. He wouldn't have died if he didn't want to. Do you know why he decided he wanted to die?" My hands started to shake and I could feel myself crossing into some line of insanity. He pulled my chin up, forcing me to look at him. "Hayden, do you know why he decided he wanted to die?" he repeated. I shook my head hopelessly, thinking there was no point in living either. I just couldn't handle myself. I couldn't go through life with no father figure, no one to guide me when my mother couldn't, no one to help me set an example for Ozalee. "He knew he could watch over you all of the time. And now he can." I stopped crying instantaneously and hadn't shed a tear since. Until the nightmares began.

"Pete, don't say that," I tell him.

"No, it's true. The way he looks at you," his voice trails off.

In my opinion, Cam doesn't look at me any different than anyone else, but apparently I'm blind. Or just plain dumb. "Pete, you don't understand how important you are to me."

He laughs a little. "Then show it."

The only thing I can register in my mind, "I can't."

The small signs of humor in his voice disappear. "Why?"

There is only one thing in my life that keeps me from showing my love for Pete. "Cam. I can't hurt him." I look around the Square, realizing the song has changed, and many eyes are trained on Pete and me, including Cam's.

"But you can hurt me?" he asks. *Yes, I can hurt you, but I don't want to, not at all.*

"What choice do I have?" I ask. A Center boy taps on Pete's shoulder asking for a dance with me. "That's something you have to figure out for yourself," he smiles, kisses my forehead, and hands me off to the stranger boy.

For two hours or so, I dance with different boys from the Center, under the careful eyes of Pete and Cam. We dance and make small talk until President York asks the Glories to come up on stage. As we mount the stage, applause roars up. Chipolaux lines us up. Spence, Mazi, Brint, Bree, Griff, Lakuna, Pete, me, and then Cam. "And now, Gipem's Girls!" President York cheers. The younger girls run onto stage from a hidden side door, dressed in light purple dresses and flat sandals. Their hair is in ringlets held by a light purple barrette.

"Everyone here knows why we are having this festivity, to celebrate these kids"—he points to us—"accomplishment in completing two successful missions!" The crowd cheers louder, and massive pictures of us on our missions roll down from the walls; in between each of us is a younger girl in their pageant dresses. In my picture, my hair is braided to the side, and small wisps blow in the wind. I'm looking straight at the camera, which I didn't even see, with cracked lips. My brows are creased, and I can tell that was my first look at the plane the day of our rescue.

"But this party is for something not everyone knows. Spence?"

Spence steps up to the microphone. *What is he doing?* I look down our line. The guys all have weird smiles on their faces, and the girls just look confused. *So the guys know a secret that we don't? Wow.*

"Mazi Seedar," Spence says, "for as long as I've known you, you have made my life more fun and easier to live. You have helped me through the good times and the bad. I don't know what I would do without you. I love you more than life itself and I would love to spend the rest of mine with you." He holds his hand out to Mazi and she steps to him. He gets down on one knee. *Oh my gosh, is he doing what I think he's doing?* "Mazi Seedar, will you marry me?"

CHAPTER TWENTY-THREE

My jaw drops before Mazi's does; I look at Cam and then Pete and mouth the words, "Why didn't you tell me?" They just laugh.

"Yes," Mazi says. Spence jumps up and spins Mazi in a circle. *What the heck just happened? She's only fifteen!* Even though fifteen through seventeen is the normal age to be married for the inhabitants of Villa, she's still too young! The crowd goes ballistic; our mentors have to be escorted by security just to get on the stage. I don't even know what to think. Should I be happy for them, or should I be against it? Nonetheless, everyone seems excited but me. I don't want Spence to make Mazi and me grow apart. I want her to be mine forever. Even though she's a girl, she's still one of my good friends and that can't be taken away. Can it?

Before everyone even begins to congratulate them, the marriage papers are already signed, and they're officially a married couple. I'm glad they decide to have the wedding after the mission. At least it gives me time to get used to the new arrangements. I use the foot pain excuse to get off the stage and go sit at our assigned table. The younger girls come to the table with huge plates of food; I pick some off of Tinley's.

"Hayden, Mazi said we could be in the wedding. Flower girls and junior bridesmaids," Broppin says enthusiastically. I smile and purposely shove my mouth full with food.

"Will you take me to the bathroom?" Ariel asks. I grab her hand eagerly and lead her toward the hallway. We pass at least thirty more tables of food and a monstrous fountain of champagne before we reach the hallway. I push the doors open and lead her into the bathroom.

Through my makeup, sweat is working its way through the satin of the dress. I hold on to the countertop trying to make sense of what just happened and allow myself a split moment of panic. When I hear the bathroom lock to Ariel's stall click open, I compose myself and tell her how pretty she looks.

"Our stylists put us in this color on purpose," she says. Of course they did. It's Mazi's favorite color.

"So how do you like it here? In the Center I mean?" I ask, changing the subject.

She wraps her arms around my waist. "I like it, but I feel like I barely get to see you and Pete anymore."

"Ariel, I promise as soon as we get back from the mission, we'll spend more time with you," I say.

"But what if you don't come back?"

If I don't come back, you'll have Pete. If he doesn't come back, I told my mother to adopt all of you, and Ann will help her take care of you. I don't tell her that. "I promised I would, didn't I?"

"Well, yeah, but last time you said you'd be gone for only one day and you were gone for four. You almost died."

She's scared, terrified actually, of losing someone else she loves. An eight-year-old should never have to go through this; it's messing with her, I can tell. She's lost a lot of weight. Cocoa told me she cries herself to sleep almost every night. In my spare time, which I rarely get, I search for her and find her in the same spot each time, sitting in the pasture with Fancy, Ozalee's old horse. My mother, who keeps an eye on them when Cocoa is working, says she spends countless hours just sitting there watching the horse.

"Ariel, I will not leave you alone. I'm not going to die. I promise and this time I won't break it. How can I make you believe that?" We're standing in the hallway now; she buries her face in my dress.

"You can't." And that's when I realize she is scarred, too deep for medicine but not enough for meltdown. I used to have a scar right through my chest where my heart used to be. But hers is different. Hers is all over. Every body part that any of us ever touched is ruined. Any good memory destroyed. Because as much as I've been through, it's nothing compared to her, just sitting by and waiting for news on whether her brother and I are alive or dead. Watching her best friend's gruesome death on television, even being taken out of Villa and brought here upon our request. I've finally realized no matter how hard I try for her and the others to have a normal life, it will not happen. It's too late. And as much as I long for her to be whole again, I have to face the fact that scars too deep never go away. They only get deeper.

The only thing I allow my brain to say now is, "Let's get back to the party."

I'm just pushing open the door when I hear a whistle from behind us. "Hey, there are some pretty ladies," a slurry voice says. I turn around just to see it's a group of six of the guys I danced with tonight. All holding champagne, all incoherent. I yank the door harder, but they slam it shut again. "Aw, going so soon?" the tallest one says.

I shove Ariel behind me, hiding her from their view. "Leave us alone," I say defensively. I could easily outrun them if there was a place to go, but the bathroom just happens to be jammed in a corner, and they have us surrounded. Two of the darker-skinned ones step closer to me, so close I smell the alcohol on their breath. "You know if you hurt us, you'll be arrested and put in jail for so long, you'll never see the light of day," I spit at them.

"You've got yourself a nice body, don't you?" the tall one says, pulling something from his pocket and pressing a button. A three-inch blade pops out from the handle. Two of them pull Ariel out from behind me and the dark ones slam me against the wall. I could effortlessly take out at least two of them, but strong with drink and outnumbered, all I can do is use my social status as a threat. The two dark skins run their hands over my body and around my chest.

"If you try anything with that blade, you'll be executed, and if you touch the girl, I'll make sure the rest of your lives are hell," I snarl.

The tall one steps to my throat and holds the knife against my skin. "What if you're not here to protect her?" He presses harder, cutting only a little. Ariel screams.

"I'll always be here for her. And I can assure you, you will get caught." His lips get closer to mine. This is how I'm going to die, getting raped by a drunken stranger and then stabbed to death. I want to tell Ariel how sorry I am for everything, how much I love her, but I keep quiet because that's just one more promise broken. I kick him with my metal foot, and he crumples for just a second but returns quickly. He orders the dark skins to pin my hands and feet against the wall. Now I am completely and utterly defenseless. I close my eyes and wait for the worst to come.

"If you make one more move, I'll kill you," Griff's voice surprises me; I open my eyes and find him standing right behind the tall kid with a pistol pointed at his head. Spence and Brint position themselves a little farther back. More muscular than the drunken kids and with deadlier weapons, they too hold pistols. The kids drop the knife and haul themselves out the exit in the hallway. Spence and Brint follow them out into the street, but I don't hear gunshots.

"How'd you find us?" I ask, trying to contain my tears; Ariel isn't as good as me at that because she's on Griff's shoulder bawling.

"I saw you two go out and when you didn't come back, I assumed something happened. Good thing too," he says. Spence runs back into the party room, leads out two security guards, and points them to the six Center kids.

"Ariel, it's alright. You're fine. I'm fine. We're safe now." I comfort her until she stops crying.

Griff puts her on the floor, "Ariel, we're not going to tell anyone about this, okay? Not Pete, not Cam, no one. Got it?" She shakes her head. I raise my eyebrows at the guys and they nod sticking their guns back in their belts. I wipe the tears from her face.

"Now then, we need to get this checked out," Brint says, examining my neck and taking Ariel in his arms. They lead us back to the party and take me to see my mom.

"What happened to you?" she asks.

"Oh, I just slipped in the bathroom and cut it on the counter."

She doesn't believe a word I'm saying. "It's a long story?" I nod. She pulls an antiseptic wipe out of her purse and cleans the wound, leaving a mass stinging sensation behind and puts a large bandage on it.

"That brings the whole outfit together." Brint laughs at me. "Now you're just a mess, Band-Aid and brace, good combo." He laughs more and walks away.

As soon as I get back to our table, we are called to the stage once again. Last time, I felt beautiful and only a slight bit worried. Now I feel a mess and very—well I don't exactly know a word for how I feel—fidgety, agitated, concerned, and anxious. All at the same time and it's only been an hour. Seats have been set up for us. Chipolaux positions Pete and me conveniently on the same couch.

"As you know a few days ago, two of our Glories, the commanders of our squads actually, disobeyed direct orders from the military leader Chipolaux Donovan." President York gives a small laugh showing the base has put off what we did, and Chipolaux waves to the crowd. "Pete Girth and Hayden Kolter got themselves in a world of trouble for that one." Another laugh. "But it was all for a worthy cause. These two risked their own lives and followed one of our search dogs"—Ms. Florence and Blue gait out of the door and stand on a spot marked with duct tape—"Blue, into the fallen orphanage. Luckily they didn't go in there for nothing. They found something we missed. Seven young children. Thanks to the knowledge and heart of our commanders, seven lives were saved." So the boy Pete gave mouth to mouth to, the one the girl called Bubby, did survive. Cocoa and some other people come out of the door with seven children.

The eldest girl, the one with the dark hair and bright eyes, runs to me. I scoop her up in my arms. She shows me her pink cast on her no-longer-mangled hand. Pete and I are ordered to stand. She holds her arms out to him and he takes her willingly. "She says her name is Kahlua," he tells me. He learned sign language when he was young because one of the landlords of his old foster home was a mute also. The toddlers are not as swift as Kahlua and need assistants to reach us, especially the two I recognize as the ones trapped under the cribs. The boy or girl cannot walk. Both have casts on their feet. Only now can I see the family resemblance in the two.

"We thank you so much for saving our children," the women holding the pair says.

President York starts speaking again, "Another surprise for the Glories tonight, all of the children that attended the orphanage, rescued or not, have been adopted."

Astonishment. Amazement. All good though. There were like four hundred kids in that orphanage. Pete and I, a pair of normal people, helped every single one of those children find a home. Kahlua finds a man and a woman in the crowd and waves them forward. "Those are her new parents," Pete says.

The man takes Kahlua from Pete. "You have given us the best gift we could've ever asked for. We will be forever grateful." The woman hugs us both.

"You have a beautiful daughter," I tell her. "My sister had skin like hers." Bronze and natural. "Thank you. I'm sure your sister was very beautiful as well." The woman kisses my cheek and disappears back into the crowd; all I can think of is how I have to use past tense when I'm speaking about Ozalee now.

We sit back on the couch, and the interview, the one that none of our mentors knew about, plays. They must've found it. After the interview plays, the footage of Pete's surgery plays. How Kahlua said thank you and Pete passed out and then me telling the doctors about Pete's shoulder when he couldn't. And last but not least, me choking on my own blood, trying to get away from the doctors cutting up Pete's shoulder because I couldn't bear to watch.

"You crazy girl," Pete whispers in my ear. "Do you know how much that could've hurt you?" I ignore him.

President York hushes the crowd. "Thank you for everyone's support. Now on to some more serious business." The lights dim down, and everyone takes their seats at their assigned tables. Pete, Cam, Griff, Spence, Brint, and Gibbs disappear out the back door and reenter the room with her casket. Small and baby pink with gold letters that write "Ozalee." They place her casket on the metal poles positioned on the stage to support it. I scoot closer to Pete on the sofa. "I don't think I'm ready for this."

He squeezes my hand. "You don't have to do anything you don't want to." Chipolaux moves Pete and me by my mother and the younger girls to watch the video of her death play for the audience. I don't cry like I used to.

My mother steps to the microphone to say a few words. She wipes a stray tear from her face. "As daughters go, Ozalee was the best." Of course she was. "She was such a bright, beautiful child. So full of life and love. Who would've ever thought her end would come so soon? Not me for sure. She didn't deserve to die like that. She was a child that was supposed to live a long life, but I guess the end is unpredictable. She always loved to play with her friends and ride her horse and follow her older sister around. She was a joy to have around, and I am so incredibly proud I can call her my daughter. Thank you for listening."

Ariel tugs on my mom's dress. "We prepared something too." The younger girls stand at the microphone.

Tinley clears her throat. "As long as I can remember, there have been five of us, me, Hixel, Ariel, Broppin, and Ozalee, but on May 15, we lost one of our best friends."

Tinley steps aside and Hixel begins to speak in her sweet sugar voice, "We had so many good memories together and they were all shattered. Can you even imagine what we felt when we first saw the video? We never thought something so terrible could ever happen to one of us. We thought stuff like that only happened on television."

Ariel takes the microphone. "After we found out she wasn't coming back, we didn't know what to do. I can't remember a time there was no Ozalee. I'm still lost. Of course I would be. She was my best friend in the entire world."

She hands Broppin the microphone. "Ozalee was not only one of my best friends. She was my cousin. I grew up with her from birth. We shared things no one else could know, not even Hayden. Her death had a huge impact on all of us, and I, all of us, just wanted to let her know we still love her and we'll see her again someday. It might not be soon but we will and until then we'll be missing her."

Broppin turns toward me. "Did you want to say anything?"

I rub the piece of paper in my pocket. My throat tightens. I take the microphone, unfold the paper, and bring into being Lakuna's stretched writing. "Ozalee was not only my sister, but my best friend as well. It's hard to envision the pain of your baby sister dying in your arms. It's like killing yourself over and over again. I tried so hard to save her. I tried. I may come across strong right now, but I do fall asleep crying, and at times I act like nothing is wrong, but as my friends have come to know, I am good at lying. And although I'm standing here making a speech about my dead sister, that doesn't mean I'm letting her go or releasing the fact the Duxians killed her. It means I can finally feel like I gave her the funeral she deserves. I still can't comprehend she's really gone. She's never coming back. Sometimes I have dreams about her that seem so real, I can't help but say her name. That's according to my friends anyway. Other times, I watch the younger girls and see how Ozalee's personality is reflected in each of theirs, like Broppin's love for soccer or Ariel's loyalty or Tinley's drive and even Hixel's kindness. Ozalee is all around. And I wanted her to know I loved her more than anything in the world and I would do anything to get her back. Thanks."

Pete, Cam, Griff, Spence, Brint, and Gibbs take her casket to the helicopter where it will land in Villa and be buried next to my father's under an old weeping willow tree beside the red barn my father built. And that's it. Ozalee is really truly gone.

Chapter Twenty-Four

It's dawn when we finally return to the base from our party. Exhausted and sore from dancing, smiling and illness. Everyone we knew, other than our mentors and Chipolaux, came back around three last night, but we had the honor of staying out all night and socializing with guests. After we're finished undressing, returning our formal attire to our stylists, and bathing, we drag ourselves back to our room and climb into bed. Mazi and Spence have been issued a new room to themselves just down the hall, but I can already feel the emptiness of their absence. Cam wraps his arms around me, but I can't help but feel endlessly guilty about Pete. "Chipolaux said he had us stay all night for a reason," Bree says. "Since Xil has an eight-hour time change, he wants us to get acclimated. It works perfect for us."

Cam's fingers lightly touch the bandage on my neck. "What happened?" I make sure Pete is asleep before I tell him the story of how Ariel and I were in the beginning of the process of the rape murder duo before Griff, Spence, and Brint had saved us.

"You weren't going to tell me if I hadn't asked?" His voice has a hint of unhappiness in it.

"I didn't want you to freak out. It's all good now though," I say in my defense. I didn't want to tell him because there is a high chance he would have told Pete not because they are close friends, but he knows that will be another pair of eyes to make sure I'm safe. My lie isn't cutting it. "I didn't want you to tell Pete. He might not think I'm responsible enough to watch over Ariel if he doesn't make it back from the mission." Relief crosses his face; I think that's a good enough excuse. He gets closer to kiss me, but I move my lips. "Cam, I'm not going to get you sick."

I endure my sore throat, fever, nausea, and headache for most of the night, rolling around trying to find a cool spot on my pillow or leaning over the bed into my bucket until I realize Cam's breathing has been the same speed for the entire time he's been sleeping. "Why didn't you tell me I've been keeping you up too?" I ask.

He turns to face me. "If I could take that away from you and give it to me, I would."

"I know." Someone must have been actually watching the security cameras in our room tonight because there's a knock on the door. Cam gets up to open it and Kanga and Wyllie walk in. Wyllie helps me sit up, and Kanga takes my temperature, which is still 102. Wyllie has to swab the back of my throat with a long stick and I gag. After five minutes, they tell me I have something called strep throat. They give me an antibiotic that will not make me feel any better tomorrow but almost normal the next day. They move me out of bed with Cam so he can get some rest and into Mazi and Spence's old bed. I don't get much sleep tonight.

The next day, well, night technically, I can hardly move. Every little touch sends a wave of discomfort through me. I want to throw up so I can get all of this phlegm out of me, but of course that is too much to ask for. Kanga gives me a bag of lemon mint lozenges and they numb the soreness in my throat, but nothing, not the sore throat or the nausea, can compare to the intolerable headache I have. I've asked for complete silence, and everyone but Kanga leaves the room for the rest of the day. My room is completely dark with only the light of the hushed television shining in my face. Even that is too much and I switch from moving my covers over my face to hiding under my own arm. Occasionally, I doze but not often. Around seven in the morning, Kanga manages to persuade me to eat a bowl of chicken noodle soup and it actually doesn't taste too bad.

Later that night I lay in our bathtub filled with steaming water. The bath is virtually heaven to my body and after two hours, Kanga is afraid I'll shrivel up like a prune and makes me get out.

Before bed, Griff and Lakuna walk in the room with a bag of ice. Lakuna sets it on my head. "Here, I hope this will help. I want you to feel better."

I smile, "I know you do because without me you're having absolutely no fun, right?"

She laughs. "Yes, zero fun."

I catch Griff's hand before he turns to his bed. "When did you start carrying a gun?" I ask. He smirks and lifts his shirt, revealing the pistol tucked in his belt. "Ever since Chipolaux and President York began thinking there would be a lot of Duxian spies out trying to kill us before the mission."

The next day, I'm able to move around almost like normal, still not one hundred percent but better. Tomorrow we depart for our mission, and tonight is the only time left we have to spend with the people we're leaving behind. Today we are called into Dress the moment after breakfast ends. Edna takes measurements of every part of my body, even my eyes and nostrils. After measurements, Wyllie takes all of us to a large wooden room with nine leather beds with a hole where your head would go. The room smells of lavender and vanilla, my least favorite smells. Nine people in black open the door to the room. "Please remove your clothes and put these over yourselves," one of the men says. They hand us each a thin white robe. I change into the robe in a fitting room filled with warm air and, to Wyllie's surprise, get on the table when directed.

One of the men in black begins to move his fingers in circular motions around my toes and then he starts scratching and pinching. He moves his hands over my body, unknotting muscles and relaxing tightened tissue. He tells me I have too much tension and stress and I need to try to relax. It's obvious he hasn't been in the Center for long; he thinks I'm just another rich girl wasting my money on a $500 massage. He has a Wikasha accent; he most likely worked at one of the best Wikasha spas and was recruited here.

Wyllie laughs at him and tells him who I am. "Oh, that would be hard for you then. I'm sorry I said anything, Ms. Kolter."

"You don't have to say sorry. Treat me like everyone else," I tell him, hoping he actually will. But after two hours of massaging, I can tell he has the certain respect for me that many people of the general public do.

Chipolaux, along with every troop leader, will not let us into the pasture to see the horses. For some reason, I seem to get the most upset by this and find myself arguing with Chipolaux as we enter the cafeteria for lunch, which is actually a midnight meal. "Today might be the last time I get to see Girl, and you're not letting me go?"

"That's right," he says and turns for the door.

"No! She is the last thing I have left of him. I have to see her." I yank his shoulder back, so he is forced to face me.

"I said no and just to make sure you don't see her or any of them as a matter of fact, I am putting round-the-clock guards on the doors and the field's fences." His voice isn't ordering at all. It's like he's mocking me or trying very hard to make me mad.

I fill my plate with a tuna lettuce tortilla, almonds, and whipped cream. I sit at the table and twirl my hot tea around with a spoon, trying not to cry. It's just been one of those days where I can't seem to win and nothing goes right. I mean, nothing has gone incredibly wrong, but I have a feeling. A bad one, a sense something will go wrong, way wrong. I have these occasionally but rarely this strong.

"Hayden, you'll come back. You'll see her again," Mazi says.

How do you know? I think. She can't see the future; she doesn't have the power to predict what happens. "I know," I lie. "It just irks me he thinks he can boss me around."

At four in the morning, it is hard to find something to do at a military base. Mazi and Spence said they had to go get checkups because they've missed our most recent ones and they leave the rest of us to our own business. Lakuna, Griff, Brint, and I find ourselves at the shooting range while Cam, Bree, and Pete rewatch the video of us on the island to get a feel of what each individual is good for, the video I am too much of a coward to relive for a third time. I train with my bow and once I've mastered hitting the bull's-eye one hundred times in a row, I switch to my assigned gun. I feel bad for the person who gets in my way when I have this thing loaded. After my target is completely annihilated and only a pile of feathers is left, I give my gun a full on cleaning until I can see my reflection in the barrel.

Gibbs, who shouldn't be up at this hour, calls me on my newly issued teletalky. I lost the old one when the roof collapsed. "Will you and Pete come down to the hospital? The doctors need to evaluate how much longer you'll need the brace and the sling." I get Pete from the theater; his face is red from crying.

"I told you not to watch it again," I tell him.

"One of us had to and there is no way I was getting you in there," he says. I am not really the comforting type, so instead of saying something consoling or mean to show him how right I was, I just hug him.

When we reach the hospital, Kanga and Ezzard are all too ready to evaluate our conditions. They sit us on a cushioned grey table with paper covering the majority of it. Ezzard asks Pete to take off his shirt. He has almost as many stitches as me and they're just as swollen. "You're going to have to wear your sling on the mission. Your stitches are not ready to be taken out yet." Ezzard presses on different spots on his shoulder. "Do you feel any pain here?"

Pete winces and pulls away quickly. "Yes."

Ezzard moves to a new spot. "What about here?" Pete gasps in pain. "Stop!" I snap. "It obviously doesn't feel good."

Ezzard turns to Yanish. "You'll have to get him a one-handed gun."

Yanish groans, "You just had to get hurt." Gibbs isn't at all happy when Kanga tells him I'll have to wear my brace and not only that but we will both be on pain medication. I mean I'm used to it by now. It's not anything new.

It's seven in the morning now, our dinner and everyone else's breakfast. It's being served early today because the Rescue Squad was ordered to be in our room alone in three hours, no younger girls or parents allowed. Our parents, mentors, and the younger girls meet us at our dining table, which is oversized tonight. While they eat waffles, black beans, and pineapples, we eat a high-carb meal of lobster-stuffed ravioli, with steamed broccoli and chocolate lava cake served with a scoop of vanilla ice cream and raspberries. Hardly any words are exchanged during our last meal. They know we are not all coming back. I know we are not all coming back; we all know we are not all coming back. But the question that haunts me is not the one everyone else is worried about. The question they dread is who won't be returning. The question I wonder is who I can't save.

CHAPTER TWENTY-FIVE

Back at our room, I have one hour left to muster the audacity to say good-bye possibly forever. Mazi and Spence have to stay in our room tonight; it's easier for Chipolaux and President York to keep the base calm. I say good-bye to Brint and Mazi's parents first. That is rather easy—I don't know them very well. They thank me for keeping their children alive and tell me to keep it up. Next comes Ann. First, I thank her for giving me her sons. She's already teary eyed.

"You are such a pretty girl, and brave. I could never do what you have done. I owe you for saving Griff and Cam." She has no clue I don't even remember saving them. The only reason I know I did it is from the tape.

"It's my job. I love your sons."

Now for my mom. She squeezes me so tight, salty water leaks out of my eyes. "Please come home to me," she cries.

"Mom, I will try everything I can. I won't leave you alone. I will do everything in my power to stay safe," I reassure her, but I can't see the future either. "Mom, if I don't come back, you know how much the younger girls mean to me. They mean everything, especially to Pete. He can't raise them by himself. If I don't come back, you and Ann need to take them in," I say sternly.

"I . . . I won't. I can't. You have to come back." She shudders under my palms; I try to shake some sense into her.

"Mother, I might not come back. You just have to accept it. I will try, but I won't promise. And you have to take care of those girls!" I order.

"Okay-o-okay," she whispers.

"I love you, Mom," I tell her. "I love you more."

I give her one last hug, kiss her cheek, and then she's gone.

Everyone leaves the room other than the four girls. It breaks my heart to say farewell too. Everyone else says good-bye, with sobbing and hugs and kisses, of course, but Pete and I just sit. We sit next to each other, his body heat rubbing off on mine. On the tip of his bed is where we say what could be our last "I love you" to our four children. Ariel sits on one of my legs and on one of Pete's. Broppin hugs my shoulders, and Tinley and Hixel are on our backs. "Girls, listen to me. No matter what happens to us on this mission, remember we will always be with you." I pause a second and wait for Pete to chime in, but he doesn't seem like he's functional enough to talk. They cry harder than they were.

"Please don't leave us," Broppin whimpers.

"No, don't say that. We will come back." It only makes them tremble. I notice how Pete's stomach has tensed up and realize he's crying too.

"I want you girls to know you mean more to us than life itself, and we would never put you through something you couldn't handle. We can do this. You can do this."

Pete nods. "You know I would never do that. I will not leave you alone."

I hurry and grab the letter Pete and I wrote together while Pete talks to the younger girls in his quiet soothing voice.

To: Broppin, Ariel, Hixel, and Tinley

Girls this letter is from Pete and I. Although it's in my handwriting, we thought of it together and sat down together to write it. We just want to make it clear we loved you girls more than anything in the world, and nothing—I repeat, nothing—can change that. Of course the only way you'll be reading this letter is if both Pete and I do not return from the mission. You girls have to remember we tried with everything we had to come back and be with you, but something must have happened to us that was uncontrollable. You have to realize we'll always be here for you no matter what, and nothing that happened is your fault. When you miss us, think of all the good times we had and our lives before the island. Don't hang on to the bad things. And most of all, know we'll always be here for you.

Love with all our hearts, Hayden and Pete

I give the letter to Broppin. "Only read this if something happens to me and Pete, all right?"

She looks at me with big brown eyes that resemble Ozalee's almost exactly. "Stay." "Hayden, I don't want you to go," Hixel weeps. She squeezes my chest.

"I don't want to leave you, but I have to for Ozalee." "I'm coming with you," Tinley says.

Pete's head flies up from Ariel's neck. "No, you're not. It's not safe for you there. You're staying here and we'll come back."

They cry on our shoulders and in our arms until the clock hits ten, then our mentors come in. "You girls have to leave now," Chipolaux says.

"No, no!" Broppin screams. Gibbs rips her off the bed and drags her toward the door. Bolt and Yanish grab Hixel and Tinley, and Simone steals Ariel out of Pete's arms.

"Petrie! Hayden!" Ariel's voice catches between sobs.

"No! Please no!" Tinley shrieks. They are almost out, and I can feel my brain telling me to run after them and not ever leave them.

"We'll be all alone," Ariel whispers.

Pete and I break for the door. We grab on to the door with our fingers and yank it, trying to oppose the force someone else is exerting to keep the door shut. "You won't!" Pete screams down the hallway.

I can feel us losing the pulling competition. "We'll come back! I promise!"

"I love you girls," Pete cries.

"I love you too!" I yell through the crack. Another person pushes on the door, crushing my and Pete's fingers and shutting the younger girls out of our lives, maybe for good.

Pete and I sit on my bed in tears as Ezzard and Kanga scold us for trying to open the door in the first place. Chipolaux has had to make emergency changes to our uniforms and add extra padding to one hand of each uniform. Gibbs and Simone look at us in disgust and watch as we wince when our doctors wrap our broken hands. But I don't care about the pain. I don't care about the disappointed looks from everybody. Ariel, Broppin, Hixel, and Tinley have been taken away from me. Those girls are what took the spot of my real sister, except this time, it was multiplied by four. And now I've lost Ozalee plus four.

Chipolaux shoves a pain pill down our throats and the Rescue Squad is left alone. I've not only made myself more upset, but I've managed to make Mazi, Bree, and Lakuna cry too. This time everyone has someone to comfort them; Mazi has Spence, Bree has Brint, Lakuna has Griff, and I have Cam. Pete is alone, huddled in the depression of losing four sisters, the hardest thing he's ever had to face, and he has no one to help him. I look at Cam and kiss his chin softly. He holds on to me willingly and then let's go. I can only think of how many times he'll have to let me go before my body slams against Pete's and our lips smash together.

He takes me and we fall on to his bed. The room grows silent. I've never, not once, kissed Cam the way I have Pete. Long, sorrowful, and ardent. He doesn't loosen his grip on me, and I don't think I will ever let him leave my grasp. Our tears mix together on our cheeks, the tears we've shed over four young girls. My chest tightens, remembering why I was crying, and I start again. After I've drained Pete's lungs of air, we need to take a breath. Cam takes the time to turn the lights out and everyone gets into bed. Pete and I help each other under the covers. He uses the sheets to wipe my face and then I clean his. He pulls my broken hand above the covers and kisses every finger. I can't keep my body from feeling the instantaneous pain and I flinch.

"It does hurt you."

"I don't care." I kiss his fingers until they recoil from the ache. "You too," I say. "It doesn't compare."

"I know. I've done this before."

He pushes my hair from my face. "They didn't die?" "Saying good-bye," I whisper.

After a while of talking and crying, Pete does fall asleep. The others are long gone. I kiss his lips, his forehead, and the tip of his nose. I take his bandaged hand and press it to my face. "I do love you, you know?" I say to no one. I get out of his bed and sit on Cam's. "Cam?" I say. I trace the outline of his jaw.

"Hm?" He asks drowsily.

"Cam, I don't want you to be mad."

His eyes flutter open. "Hayden, I understand you don't know what you want. Pete needs someone now."

"I can't lose you though," I press. If life was easy, I could have them both and not worry. If life was easy, I would only have feelings for one of them. But life is never easy.

"You won't lose me." He sits up and touches his forehead to mine. "I will love you no matter who you pick." And that's the thing—I don't think I can pick. I kiss Cam and run my hand down his arm until he drops off and go back to Pete.

Chipolaux bangs on our door at four in the morning, telling us it's time to get up and report to Makeup and Dress. With only four hours of sleep, I somehow gather enough energy to walk down to my dressing room.

"Oh, darling, hard night?" she asks as she observes the deep purple circles under my eyes. "Yeah, I . . . I cannot seem to make up my mind."

She strips my clothes off swiftly and pushes me into another stinging hot shower. "Boy troubles?" she asks. The soothing water covers my hairless body now.

"Life troubles." For as much as I want to stay under the hot water, she yanks me back out and gives me my fuzzy robe. She spins me to my mirror and pulls my hair back into a ponytail, and before I can resist, she slices her scissors across my hair and takes out the hair band. I gasp. "What? Why did you do that?" A puff of hot wind blows my brown waves, which now only fall to my breasts, dry.

"I can't quite say I know what you're going through, but I had to cut your hair. Mr. Donovan's orders." She files my unbandaged nails into ovals and paints them jet black along with my toes. She applies a quick coat of makeup that she says will last up to three months. It's sort of like a comfortable tattoo that enhances the look of my eyes. "Darling, how can you break something in so little time?" she asks and turns my hand gently.

"Trying to see something for a last time," I say.

She gives me a breakfast of goetta, eggs, and banana slices and tells me to brush my beautiful teeth while she gets my uniform ready. I push my food around my plate. "You have to eat," she says.

"I'm really not hungry." She takes my tray from me, and I brush my teeth. "Why didn't you sleep?" she asks.

"Pete doesn't think he'll see the younger girls again and he's spacing out. I'm not going to tell you, I'm not, but I stayed up with him, and then I talked with Cam." She is careful not to touch my hand when she puts on my thermal uniform. Once again it's solid black with a special helmet that fits tight over my head in case of emergency. The suit covers my neck and, this time, has built in boots, which are comfortable and good for running with extra room on the left to fit my brace. My whole suit is highly heat conducting. Apparently it's going to be very cold in Xil.

This time, I have six extra pouches around my belt instead of seven. Edna points to each pouch as she explains its contents. "Water, bullets and arrowheads, gas mask, first-aid kit, gloves and socks, and your picture you got at your birthday celebration."

My teletalky beeps violently, my reminder to myself it's time to board the plane. "Edna, thank you again for making me into something pretty. You are one of the only people I feel like I can trust here. Thanks."

She hugs me and kisses both of my cheeks. "It has been my pleasure." I mope out of the room and fail at an attempt to find the transportation unit without Spence's sense of direction. I end up sitting in the middle of the hallway until Gibbs comes and finds me. He grabs me by the arm and tows me to the plane where everyone, our mentors, Chipolaux, and my friends, wait. All of my friends and I wear the same thing except Mazi. She's in the clothes that were issued to us and she's crying on Spence's shoulder.

"All right, everyone ready?" Chipolaux asks. No. Not at all, especially not ready for a twenty-one—hour flight. Xil is only five hours away, but Chipolaux and our mentors have decided to circle the globe so our plane isn't shot down by any Duxia bomber planes.

We begin to load the plane, but Mazi just stands there and sobs while Spence lets her go and boards before me. Then it dawns on me. "Mazi, you're not going on this mission, are you?"

She shakes her head. "It was an accident, a last-minute change. I mean, when we got our checkups . . . they told me I can't come anymore."

It takes me a second to process I'm saying good-bye to her too. "But why?" I ask in disbelief. Gibbs is getting impatient and pushes me away from Mazi and onto the steps of the plane. Mazi doesn't say anything; she just looks at her torso and holds a spot where a baby would be. Gibbs shoves me onto the plane in one hasty motion and latches the door shut. Just as the engine of the plane revs, I realize why Mazi is not certified to come on the mission anymore. And in a matter of five minutes, Mazi Seedar is thrust out of the spot of friend. Because in only one night, two nights before the most important event of our lives, the occasion that could save a whole country, Mazi has gotten herself pregnant.

CHAPTER TWENTY-SIX

Crrrshh. Crrrsshh. Crrrsshh. The lights on the ceiling of the plane crunch as I kick my soccer ball at the roof of our bare cabin. I cannot even bring myself to look at Spence. All of my friends think she's sick. Only our mentors. Chipolaux, Spence and I know the truth. While everyone else is doing something productive such as surveying maps of Xil or conversing about what to do if one of us gets captured, I drill the soccer ball I was given, upon request, at the wall. I don't understand how Mazi could do this to me. First marriage and now a baby? How can that be possible? We haven't had our periods since the island. Kanga said it was some drug the Duxians gave us. Anyway, her hips aren't even wide enough for a baby to fit through there! She knew how much I would need her on this trip; this was going to be the only chance to get revenge for Ozalee's death. And she went and did this.

Someone knocks on the door. "Come in."

Gibbs walks in with armfuls of blankets and comforters; he drops them on the floor. Now we at least have something in our cabin. "Thought you all would need something to sleep on," he says.

"Thank you," I whisper.

"Look, girlie, I know this is all of the sudden. We should have never agreed to have them stay in a room alone."

I would love if we could go back in time and make them stay with us, but we can't, and now no one can help what has happened. "What's done is done, "I whisper so quietly that he has to cup his hand over his ear to hear me.

"And please quit breaking lights," he says and leaves the room.

I order some hot tea with lemon and sit out in the open of the plane sipping it. I watch the ocean fly by under the window and I'm pretty sure a pod of whales swims through the waves. The clouds are in an array of

236

shapes, hearts, crosses, horses, flowers. My cup is taken from my hand; I look up with tired eyes.

Spence plops down next to me and chugs the rest of my tea. "Would you like to play?" he asks, pulling up a checkers board.

"I would prefer if you would just leave me alone," I snap.

He sighs and stands up again. "I'm sorry." Just to keep myself from crying, I pull my hood up over my head and close my eyes.

When I wake up, our cabin is pitch black. The sky outside the window is dark. I'm cosseted in a cocoon of blankets. I hear a faint conversation through my blankets. "No, I'm not happy about it! What do you think?" Cam hisses. All of the sudden I can feel a red-hot tension in the room.

"I can't control how I feel, Cam," Pete says calmly.

"You couldn't just find yourself a new girl. You had to take mine?" he snarls. "I didn't steal her. We don't know what she wants," Pete says.

"She will choose one of us eventually," Cam says.

"Until then, what do we do? Act like nothing is going on between us?" Pete asks. He is now trying desperately to keep his voice calm.

"Exactly, and then she will pick who she thinks it better for her," Cam hisses.

Pete clears his throat. "I've been her best friend since first grade. That will be hard to compete with."

Cam's fists clench in the dark, "I can more than manage that."

I take a deep breath and push myself up. The room silences, and Pete and Cam act like they are sleeping. I trudge back to the seat I fell asleep in and ask for my meal. Cam thinks I need him. I do need him. Pete thinks I need him. I do need him. I need so many things. If a normal teenager needed as much as I do, I wouldn't consider them normal. I'd consider them crazy. Maybe I am. I am a fifteen-year-old mad girl who Gipem stumbled upon and then put her through so much she got confused and was never able to understand again. That is me. That's why people think I'm going into Xil because I'm crazy and confused. It's sad to say I am.

The captain's voice announces on the radio, "We'll be landing now. Everyone, prepare for descent." The windows automatically close, so we can't see out of the glass. We've only been on the plane for sixteen hours, but the ride was typically supposed to last twenty-one hours. But at this point, I'm so mad at everyone, excluding Lakuna. However, I haven't seen her since we took off. I don't ask any questions.

The plane grounds and the door opens. The sunlight shines on my face, and the scent of the ocean waves sucks into my lungs. You've got to be kidding me. I step onto the white sand. Gibbs appears behind me. "Why are we here?"

He pats my shoulder. "President York, Chipolaux, and the mentors decided we should show you how the Duxians plotted your island experience before you begin your mission." I shake his hand off my shoulder and take shade under the wing of the plane. It's not a surprise they didn't tell me or any of us we were coming here. But now that we're here and I can't do anything about it, I strip off my uniform and change into the more appropriate attire of tank top and shorts. It's around eight in the morning now, so they will probably start the explaining soon. They have to be done by nightfall so we stay accustomed to the time changes and whatnot.

Chipolaux gets the Rescue Squad together and rounds our mentors up by the area where our old shack burnt down. This is the place where I supposedly kept Brint from being struck by lightning and where Cam saved me from the panther. Lakuna and Bree flank my sides. I nudge Lakuna's ribs. "Where have you been?"

She licks her lips and presses her hands on her hips the way she used to stand in a soccer game while waiting for the right time to make a run. "You know," she whispers, "after we destroy this cloning machine, Gipem can handle the war by themselves. They won't need us anymore. Maybe we'll be able to go home and go back to the way things used to be."

I think back to the way things used to be, actually to the last soccer game I played the night before we got kidnapped. After an easy track practice, Lakuna, Mazi, Bree, and I hiked back up to the soccer field where we had a high school game versus our toughest rivals. We changed into our purple uniforms, put our silver sparkles on our eyes, and headed to the field to warm up. As I was kicking long balls with Bree, I glanced over to the sidelines and saw everyone sitting there, Pete, Cam, Griff, Spence, Brint, Ozalee, Ariel, Tinley, Hixel, Broppin, and my mom. With only five minutes left in the game and the score tied at zero, our team was dying because of lack of subs. The other team got the ball down by our goal, and just by chance the referee called an offensive foul on me, the sweeper. I passed the ball to Lakuna at outside midfield left side, and she crossed it to Bree at stopper, then Bree sent a long ball to Mazi over their defense's heads. Mazi ran on to the ball but couldn't get the shot off at the angle the ball was stopped, so she crossed it to Lakuna again, and I made a run all the way up the field for a wide—open shot. Their defense didn't even know I was there. But I couldn't shoot with my left foot, so I was forced to drop it back to Lakuna, the handy left, and the ball was put in the back of the net. We won that game one to zero, and not only did Lakuna score our lone goal but we also all helper her do it.

"Yeah. We could do some crazy stuff at my house like the old times, and even better, we won't have to go back to school just yet. Did you know school has been called off until the war is over? You don't know this because you were still in the hospital, but Blue, Ms. Florence's dog, found Pete and me after the orphanage collapsed. Ms. Florence is here as a soldier in Squad 415."

Lakuna looks at her feet and then at me. "Griff told me. That's horrible actually." Ever since we've been put on the island, Lakuna and I have had a rocky relationship. She's still one of my best friends, but I haven't spoke to her directly to her in weeks. We've both been so bombarded with training and work and everyone else that we haven't had time for each other, and by the way we're speaking to each other now, we both miss it.

"There are only a couple of things I needed to show you," Chipolaux says. He leads us down the sloped peak to the small pond where Ozalee was bitten. The forest has regrown its flowers and leaves from the fire. I can see how the sand from a small hole has been packed down after they removed Ozalee's body. I can't do this. Chipolaux turns to me. "Hayden, look." I glance at the pool where he's pointing. The water has been drained, and I can clearly identify the cages where the Duxians kept the monster fish. "Each fish was bred to crave the scent of a certain individual, Hayden. The Duxians saw how much you cared for Ozalee, and they needed to see if her death would break you."

"Break me?" I ask.

"See how far they could push you until you did something crazy like commit suicide." Great, so now I know the story of my sister's death. Thank you, Chipolaux, I could've gone on perfectly fine without knowing that.

Next Chipolaux takes us to the forest area where Lakuna, Mazi, Bree, and I got attacked by the panther. This is the place I saved their lives, and this is the place I got the massively evident scars across my calf, back, and ribs. Chipolaux picks up one of those poison flowers. "Only if you knew." He laughs. "This flower helps clot blood." Well, that would've been nice to know considering all four of us passed out from blood loss. The guys told me how difficult it was for them to carry us back to the shack without our ripped skin falling off our blood-slick bodies.

Chipolaux lets us go back to camp for lunch. He said he was done explaining anyway, but Lakuna and I aren't done listening.

"What about the Uglys?" Lakuna asks. The Uglys are the things that shot me with the spear that cut the feeling on my forearm.

"Oh, those. The Duxians told them if they killed you nine, they could live in Xil, and the Duxians wouldn't modify their tribal ways."

"Where did they come from?" I ask.

"The Duxians captured them and told them if they killed you, not only could they live in Xil but the Duxians would let them live as well," Chipolaux says.

"Where are they now?" Lakuna questions. "When the flood happened, they drowned."

That night, our cots are scattered all over the perimeter our mentors set for us. Lakuna and I built ours right next to each other. She said she's worried about me. Haha! A lot of people are worried about me. We lie next to each other on our cots until Bree decides to come over and join the conversation, so Lakuna climbs on to my cot and Bree lies on hers.

"What is bothering you, Hayden? You haven't talked once today," Lakuna says.

"Don't tell anyone. But last night after someone moved me into the cabin, I woke up in the middle of the night, and I heard Pete and Cam fighting over me."

Bree shrugs. "What did they say?"

"They want me to decide which one of them I want to be with." Lakuna's eyes drop. "Do you have any idea what you're going to do?" "None at all."

The bushes rustle beside my cot. I stretch my limbs, shining my flashlight in that direction, "Who's there?" Pete and Cam tumble out of the greens, bleeding heavily and heaving at one another with their fists. "Guys! What are you doing?" I scream. The mentors gather around them and watch. No one helps.

Griff chuckles at my side. "Idiots."

"Griff, stop them! They are hurting each other! We have the mission tomorrow! They won't be able to go!" He crosses his arms like he can't even hear me. I push them apart from each other until I'm standing in the middle; they rest their hands on their knees while their sweat drips off their faces. "What are you two thinking?" I yell.

Chipolaux snickers. "I knew this would happen soon enough."

"Why didn't you stop them?" I hiss. He ignores me. "How can you guys do this to each other?" I ask.

Pete and Cam look past me at each other. "You should have let me have her," Cam snaps. Pete pulls the gun from his belt. "I told you, I'd win this fight." He aims at Cam.

Cam whips the pistol from his waist. "You told wrong." Their guns explode, and the bullets enter each of them in the heart.

I fall in the sand with a thud and struggle to free myself from my blankets. Sweat pours down my face. Just a dream. I put my head between my knees, letting the night air into my lungs. When I stand up, every one is silent on their cots. How could Lakuna not wake up? I just about took our bed out with me. I shine my flashlight at Pete and Cam; they are bloodless, weaponless, and utterly peaceful. How can I dream of something as awful as that? Well, my dreams are almost always disturbing, but what bothers me even more is sometimes one comes true. Like how when I was in the hospital after I had surgery on my back, I dreamt Mazi was pregnant and now look at her. I board the plane in search of water. Why didn't we just sleep here? I look through the cupboards on the plane—guns, ammo, food, blankets, more ammo, extra sports balls, television equipment, and no water.

"What are you doing?"

I throw my flashlight across the room. "Ah! What? You scared me." Brint smiles. "What are you doing?"

I grab my light again. "Looking for a drink."

He grabs a cup from the counter. "Try the sink." I take the water. "What are you doing?"

He sits on the floor. "I don't know looking for something to do. I can't sleep."

"Me either."

The rest of the night, Brint and I sit like ghosts by the water, letting the sea wave's trickle over our toes until the sun rises through the clouds. We fold up our cots and load them on the plane before our mentors tell us to; I don't even want to hear Gibbs voice right now.

Chipolaux grabs the bullhorn from his bag. "Everyone up! Be on the plane and ready to takeoff in five." The Rescue Squad runs around like a bunch of chickens with their heads cut off, trying to fold their makeshift beds and throw their uniforms back on. Lakuna and Bree get me to eat something although I refuse; they sit me down and give me the fruit.

Lakuna looks at me. "I was talking to Griff. He said Pete and Cam are not acting right because you won't talk to them."

"I can tell too," Bree says. "They've hardly talked to anyone either, and Spence hasn't said one word to anyone this whole time. He feels like it's his fault for getting Mazi sick."

I throw my hands in the air. "It is his fault she's pregnant!" "What?" they gasp.

"That's the only reason she couldn't come. Did she look sick to you? No!"

They turn and look at Spence who's gasping air while trying to carry six cots at once. "It would make sense," Bree says.

"Great, so now almost everyone is upset with each other?" Lakuna smirks. "Sounds right for everything to fall apart before the real deal begins."

Chapter Twenty-Seven

Three meals and no sleep later, our plane lands forty-five miles outside of Xil. As soon as my feet touch the snow-frosted ground of Duxia, I realize I am in for more than I bargained for. Thousands of Gipem soldiers are wondering around everywhere. Tents are set up as far as the eye can see and big metal heaters are in the center of the circular tent patterns. The thermometer built in my suit reads only twenty-eight degrees; white specks flutter down from the sky. Edna has done a fabulous job at making my uniform; the cold has no effect on the covered parts of my body. I pull my hood up over my head and put a glove on my unbandaged hand. I bend down to cover my feet with extra socks when a polished black hoof plants itself right in front of me.

I know exactly who and what is standing there before I even look. Girl has a large saddle on her and a saddlebag that would hold over forty pounds of supplies. Ms. Florence hands me her reins and Blue licks my cheek.

"Were you forced, or did you volunteer?" I ask.

"Volunteer," she says. "We are proud to do our duty. We're on your squad actually." "The Rescue Squad?"

"No, well, your squad needs security, and that includes me and a few others."

Now, with so much lost, I am more glad than angry to have Girl here. I know she might get hurt. She knows she might get hurt, but she doesn't care. My horse is happy to be with me, and I realize with her here, I am one step closer to keeping Broppin, Ariel, Tinley, and Hixel safe.

Gibbs helps me onto Girl's saddle and throws me the reins, then he helps Pete up. Pete and I have to share Girl since she is the gentlest horse here and we are the two that need the most care. The two commanders are the ones with the most injuries, Pete with his left shoulder in a sling and me with my left foot in a brace and a slit in my throat. Then both of us with our left hands in black casts. Our left side seems to be an unlucky side. Mostly all of the horses are here, even Fritz and Liberty, Tinley's and Broppin's horses. I am thankful Chipolaux had the heart to leave Fancy back with the girls.

Our trek to the base camp is fifteen miles in which we will ride and the rest of the troops will walk by foot. The Rescue Squad, our security, and twelve other troops are setting out to destroy the machine the day after tomorrow.

The scattered trees get denser as we grow closer to Xil and as the trees get more plentiful, our troops' tents are more dispersed. Huge heaters are placed in random areas, melting the snow-tipped tree branches. I can feel the temperature dropping and the wind picking up; when I check my thermometer, it reads only fourteen degrees. My suit is designed for cold but is ineffective against this. At dusk when we finally reach our camp, I'm chilled to the bone, shivering uncontrollably and exhausted. We tie the horses by a water trough near a heater and put down hay for them to eat. Our tents are already set up for us and labeled with our names.

The Rescue Squad's camp is set up under what has to be done to keep us safe. Our tents encircle the heaters. In the back of our tents are our mentors, and surrounding them is the security troop. I grab my stuff out of Girl's saddlebag and spread it out on the floor of my tent to see what Gibbs has packed me. A thick sleeping bag with a built-in pillow, a portable heat pad to put under my sleeping bag, a water bottle, my soccer jersey and ball, and a bag of my favorite candy, chocolate mints. I situate everything so it's exactly how I want it and crawl out of my tent. People are lighting fires all around our camp; the heater doesn't do very much. It makes the outdoors feel a smidge warmer, but the heat doesn't penetrate the thick plastic of our tents. Ms. Florence must've let Blue off his leash because he's running around playfully, rolling in the snow with a baseball in his mouth. I wish everyone could be that happy. Blue's ears perk up and he runs around the heater. Griff crashes out of the trees. "Give me back my ball, you stupid mutt." Griff gets closer to Blue and just when I think he's going to catch him, Blue runs away. Griff huffs in frustration. "I hate dogs."

"Come here, Blue." I pat my leg, and he jumps on me. I'm careful not to land on my hand when I fall. I grab the slobbery ball out of his mouth and hand it to Griff.

He yanks me to my feet. "I need to talk to you anyway."

I follow Griff to his tent, which has his stuff thrown everywhere. "I have two things," he says. "Shoot." I sit on the frozen floor.

"First. I think I might like Lakuna. What do you think?" he asks.

They would make a cute couple; they're like the prettiest people in Gipem. Only if Brint liked Bree, then everything would make sense. Spence and Mazi, Griff and Lakuna, Brint and Bree, me and . . . ugh. "I think she might like you too. I mean you two did dance the whole night at our farewell party, and didn't you kiss? You sleep together all the time and tell each other everything."

He nods. "I know, but I really like her." "What are you going to do?" I ask.

"I want to ask her to be my girlfriend," he says.

They would be good together, but they only started thinking about it a week ago. But if they get together, then I don't have to worry about her stealing Pete or Cam. I know that sounds sly, but I like the thought. "Isn't that a little quick?"

He stares at the floor. "If it's what I think it is, no." "Then go for it."

"Next. What are you going to do about Cam and Pete?" He drops down next to me and raises his eyebrows. To even think about telling him is an absurdity. He is Pete's best friend and Cam's twin brother for crying out loud! But then again, Griff has never told anyone anything I said before.

"I have no idea," I whisper.

"Even though Cam is my brother, Pete is my best friend, so I'm speaking for the both of them when I say they love you," he says.

I know they both love me and I love them. But I can only have one, and I'm not ready to choose. "Are they on speaking terms?" I ask.

Yes, they are cool. Everything is fine. That's what I want him to say, but instead I get a quiet "Not even close." Someone bangs in the tents zipper and tells us to come to the heater.

We sit on logs surrounding the device giving off heat and Gibbs wraps a wool blanket around my shoulders. Chipolaux stands in front of us. "Well, it's nice to see we got most of you here safely." I laugh. That has to be a joke—we're going to freeze and Mazi isn't even here to experience it. Chipolaux shoots me a look. A camera crew of four and a woman trudge out of the trees behind him. "You remember Rae, your interviewer. She's here to do her job and they're just going to get some footage of you. You don't have to do anything spectacular, but please try and not hurt yourselves before you leave for your mission." The camera crew and Rae are bundled in heavy snow gear, clearly way overdressed. "Oh! Hayden and Spence, we've seem to have forgotten to bring a meal for tonight. Would you mind going hunting?" Chipolaux asks. My face lights up before I can stop it. But it furrows rapidly. That is a lie. They would never do that. Chipolaux and Gibbs are trying to get me to forget about Mazi and their not telling me about the horses coming.

"I will go but not with him." I am handed a bow loaded heavily with arrows, and a necklace is put around my neck. It's black with a small button on the bottom of the *H* dangling from the chain.

"If something happens, press the button," Gibbs says and I go.

I go deep into the woods, stopping every couple seconds to listen for prey. After a mile or two I come across a frozen creek that has many animal tracks traveling across. I sit ten feet up on the first branch of a small tree; there is no way in heck I'm getting any higher because I don't plan on falling out of a tree today. I pass on some of the smaller animals that come to drink such as a fox and a raccoon and wait to see a deer, which never comes. I am just about to get down when I hear scraping across the icy creek. I can't see what is crossing; I bring my bow up and draw back an arrow. I can hear the animal sniffing the air and knows it has my scent. The scraping stops and the snuffling of the animal comes to a halt. I gently let the string of the bow loosen and assume I must've scared it off. Then a stick breaks in front of me and a deranged badger, the type from the island movie, jumps at me from the bushes. I don't have time to draw my bow; I point my arrow at its throat just as the weight of its body knocks me off my branch.

I cover my face to protect my head from the attack, but it never comes. I try to catch the breath that was knocked from my lungs. I lie gasping on the hard ground with blood on my face; I can't tell if it's mine or the creatures. I pick the necklace off my chest and start to press the button; I turn my head to look for help that might be coming. Badger teeth are only inches away from my face. I jolt backward and wipe the blood from my face, realizing it's not my own. My arrow is jammed in the open mouth of the badger, and red is staining the ground, now layered with a thin blanket of snow. I yank my arrow free and wipe it on some leaves. I shove my arrow in the sheath and throw the bow over my shoulder.

I manage to drag the badger halfway back to camp with my right hand until the animal gets too heavy and I have to switch. As hard as I've tried to keep from hurting my hand, again it didn't work. When I was knocked backward off the tree, I had no other choice to catch myself on my hands. My soft cast has cracked in half and my hand throbs sorely. The badger is twice my size and it takes longer than an hour to drag it the rest of the way to camp. As soon as I enter the clearing, people pour around me, Chipolaux, Gibbs, Cam, and Pete. They wipe the snow from my face and ask me questions to see if I'm okay, but I can't focus. I see past all of them. Lakuna looks at me with horror and then at the badger. Her face flushes red and she instantly starts crying. And then Griff is there behind her, hugging her. She turns to him and buries her face in his shoulders. I remember why

Lakuna is so scared. She was attacked on the island and I'm the one who let her. I'm the reason why.

The badger's feet are ripped from my hands. I reach my head around to see Lakuna again; she looks at me with water cutting down her cheeks. "I'm so sorry," I mouth; she smiles a crooked, broken smile. This is why I'm different than my friends. They all know what happened on the island; they actually know what they fear. All I remember is how Ozalee died and a few minor details. A doctor I don't recognize steps in front of my view and shines a light in my eyes. He pushes me down on a log.

"No headache? Do you remember anything?" he asks. "Yeah, I'm fine," I say.

"You're hours late!" Chipolaux worries.

"I didn't see anything, so I waited and that thing attacked me." I show him my wrist and the cast. He groans and rubs his hand down his face; they step aside so the doctor can examine my hand. He probes my bones and wrist. I yank away reflexively.

"Well, there doesn't seem to be a new break, but it definitely needs rewrapped."

Gibbs gives me my medicine and Chipolaux hands me a stick of roasted badger meat. The meat is tough and gamey, but it's food, so I don't complain. The doctor wraps my hand in thick black bandages and tells me to be more careful. I take the old bind off my neck and patch a fresh one on. I sit on the ground with my shoulder pressed up against the heater; I play with my bowstring until everyone retreats to their tents for the night. The thought of me being capable to save a whole country. To save my mom and Ann, Broppin, Ariel, Hixel, and Tinley. They will be safe, away from the people of Duxia who want to kill me so bad and therefore are a major threat to those I love. I want to be the girl who can do that. I want to feel special for my ability that so many other people can do. The good thing is after we destroy the cloning machine, which will make it a thousand times easier to defeat Duxia in a war I don't even know why we're fighting, I will be.

I sing Ozalee's song to the wind that whispers through the trees and to the wild squirrels Blue continues to bark at. I crawl over to Ms. Florence's supplies and dig through her pack until I find a muzzle for her four-legged friend, then I strap his mouth shut. A stick cracks behind me. I'm on my feet with an arrow drawn and pointed toward the noise faster than I could even blink. "Well, don't go killing me," Gibbs whispers.

I drop my bow to my side. "I'm sorry. I thought you were a badger."

He takes my weapon from me. "We have stealth bombers surrounding our camps; they have reported the Duxian military releasing many of them. They have your scents."

"You mean they're specifically after us?" I ask.

"Yes, like the fish. We should've never let you go off by yourself. But don't worry. We have this place surrounded with guards." I lean against the tree and wipe the cold sweat from my forehead. "I just came to tell you how proud I am of you," he says awkwardly. I smile my now-beautiful smile. "Get to bed."

I can't bring myself to sleep in my own tent tonight. I don't think it's healthy anyway. It's way too cold outside. I open the zipper to Cam's tent, but he's dead to the world, no blanket on or anything. I feel his forehead to see if he's sick. His temperature is normal. I take his sleeping bag and leave my thin blanket in case he gets cold and move on to Pete's tent.

I knock on the thin plastic. "Come in." He's huddled in the corner wrapped in his sleeping bag and heat pad tracing the picture we got for our birthday.

"Pete, I don't want to stay alone tonight," I say. I can feel my blush of shame. He holds his good arm out and I crawl in his sleeping bag with him. His body heat encases me. My intense shivering slowly turns into a small shake. He yawns with blue lips. "Pete you should get some sleep."

He traces the outline of the bandage on my neck. "I like when you sing." We press our bodies closer to the plastic and I spread my heat pad over us.

"It calms me down," I say.

"It calms everyone down." I turn to face him and put my arms under his back, then I sing to him until his arm falls over my body and his head touches my cheek. I know he's asleep.

The bright light of the morning sun wakes me. I check the thermometer on my uniform, one degree. I leave Pete and crawl out of the tent to get my breakfast. The cooks have started a bonfire near the heater. They hold sizzling metal pans over the fire; I can smell the black beans and bacon. One of them hands me a plate. I savor the steaming warmth running down my throat. I climb up on the heater and spread out letting the hot air blow through my uniform.

"May I ask you a few questions?" Rae sits on a log next to me. Without her suit on and hair neatly crafted, Rae looks ten years younger. She looks like a normal woman, not some high-class lady from the Center.

"Yes." I shove in a mouthful of beans. "Are you scared to go on this mission?"

I wonder how many times I've been asked that question. "No."

She presses the Record button on her high-tech teletalky. "After you got rescued off the island, why didn't you refuse to come?"

I didn't want the Center or the Duxians to come after me and kill everyone I knew because I know they have the power to do so. I don't dare say that. "I didn't have a choice. The people of the Center had done so much to get me and my friends home safely. I need to repay them somehow." That is bound to get me plenty of publicity. After all, so much lying in one sentence might be a real record for me.

"What will you do to protect the rest of the Rescue Squad?" she asks. "Anything."

Chipolaux makes me wait to film until everyone is up; he says we need as much sleep as possible. "Keep yourself busy," he says and gives me Girl's grooming box. I brush out her winter fur, which is now a soft down of fuzz. I pick the ice out of her frozen hoofs and run a comb through her silky mane and tail. She presses her nose against my face, and after a while of feeling guilty, I have to untie her from her post. She doesn't deserve to be chained up. Gibbs helps me on her, and I just sit there, staring at the fire.

He hands me my gun, and Rae puts lip gloss on my lips. "We're just going to get a few pictures. Just act normal."

I look up at the trees in front of me and then I hear Lakuna and Bree. "This stupid zipper is stuck. What the heck?"

I can't help but giggle. "You gotta wiggle it a little."

They fall out of the tent. "Hey, guys, how many idiots does it take to open a tent?" They laugh at themselves. "Apparently more than two."

They walk to me from the other side of Girl. Her ears pull back against her neck. Girl hears it. I hear it. Lakuna and Bree hear it. The soft paw pads on a tree limb behind us. Once again, I know exactly what is behind me. I whip around just as Rae screams and shoot the badger descending on Lakuna and Bree right through the heart. Blood spews everywhere, and the dead horror lands on top of Lakuna and Bree with a thud. Spence, Pete, Brint, Griff, and Cam bolt out of their tents with their knives drawn, and people swarm in from out of the woods. Lakuna screams while Bree pushes the badger off of them.

"You know they can climb too!" I yell at Gibbs. He mumbles something into his teletalky and heavily armed guards scurry up into the trees.

Girl stands there serenely while all of the commotion sets in around her, highly trained. I slide off her. "Lakuna, it's dead," I say trying to calm her down. But the sight of it, teeth barred, fangs dripping with blood is too much for her. She runs for the trees, I push myself up and trip trying to catch her.

"Griff, go!" I order, but he's already gone. Just before Lakuna hits the tree line, Griff tackles her into the snow and whispers something in her ear.

Chipolaux smiles ear to ear. "That was fantastic! Hayden, I am so glad you actually put a little thought into your training."

"Um, yeah, I did," I say a little offended. Griff leads Lakuna back slowly, and for the first time in two days, I want a hug from Cam.

He leans his head on my shoulder, "I can't wait for this to be over." "Me too. I just want to go home." He kisses my forehead.

They eat breakfast while I groom the rest of the horses and then we're lined up for filming. Pete and I sit on Girl while they photograph us in many different poses and positions. I feel like a movie producer's puppet. The camera crew asks if they can get a shot of Pete and I kissing. I reach my head around and he leans forward. I pull away quickly, hoping Cam didn't see. Gibbs helps me off Girl and onto Fritz, Tinley's horse, with Cam. Then they ask me to kiss him. But this pose is different; he dismounts and reaches out for me. I jump into his arms and he holds me above his head with my arms on his shoulders, and in the picture of us, I'm actually smiling.

They line us up with our guns pointed at the snow and our heads facing the ground, feet shoulder-width apart and wind blowing through our hair. After they take the pictures they want, they line up burlap bag dummies and have us blow their heads off for the entertainment of the troops. Then they ask us to have a fake death battle. They want us to fight each other until we can get the other person in a death hold. For their enjoyment, typical.

"I'll do it. Whatever," Griff says.

Lakuna elbows him in the ribs. "What? It's something to do at least." "We're in," Brint says, indicating him and Spence will play a match. "So that decides it then!" Chipolaux says clapping his hands.

The troops gather around our ring constructed of loose sticks. They have a large pile of betting money in the center. First up is Lakuna and Bree. They look at each other playfully. Bree steps forward and Lakuna attacks. She swoops down acting like she's going for the feet. The second Bree leans down, Lakuna pops up and grabs her shoulders, throwing her to the ground. Bree lands right on her back, the wind knocked out of her. Lakuna has Bree's shoulders pinned down with her knees, and as she's acting like she's going to bury a knife through her heart, Bree flings her off and quickly puts her in a sleeper's hold. Bree wins.

Now I'm up, me versus Bree. I stare at her with her short hair and brown eyes. I can see myself feral and rabid, slitting her throat while she stands there and begs me not to. What if she was on the other side, a Duxian, and I killed her like that? Would I know not to if I've never seen her before? Would I know she'd be one of my best friends? I close my eyes and take a deep breath. Think of Foryark Dranken, the man who killed my sister. And all of a sudden, I am facing someone whose life I would take in a heartbeat. I attack her with ease, yanking her by the hair to the ground and pretending to stab my elbow in her jugular. I win.

Now Cam against Griff. Brother against brother. Twin against twin. Cam's face is hard, Griff's joking. Griff's knee comes up to his chin and his hands rise above his head. He holds a ridiculously inaccurate karate pose. He laughs. "Now seriously, seriously." But Cam is already on top of him with his arm locked around his throat. This match goes to Cam.

I know why Cam wanted to beat Griff so bad. He and Pete are going to fight now, but I have a feeling they're not only fighting for bragging rights. They are fighting for me. What they don't realize is no matter how long they fight or how hard they try, I will always love both of them. What I don't realize is how much I'm hurting each of them. I can't make a choice. I do not have the mental strength to choose. I'm always going to be a coward and they don't even care. They'll love me no matter what I do. I want to run in between them, hold out my arms, and tell them to stop. But they've already started.

Cam kicks Pete in his rock-hard abs and he flies backwards. He back-rolls to his feet. Cam lunges forward and Pete takes out his feet. He rolls to his side just as Pete slams his foot where Cam's head was. Cam grabs Pete's ankles and yanks himself between his legs, but Pete was expecting it and falls on top of him, elbow to his cheek, crushing his skull. And Pete beats Cam.

Pete and I are in the circle, his eyes on mine. The troops quiet down as a lover fights a lover to the death. I put myself in that place again and allow Pete's face to transform into Foryark Dranken's. I have an idea; love comes before death even if I'm looking at Foryark. My hands fly up to my ribs, and my knees buckle under me. My scream is so loud, birds fly away from the nearby treetops.

Pete's hands catch my head before it can bash into the ground. "Hayden, what's wrong?" The troops stand up and look for any attackers; I know my plan has worked. I summersault backward and take his throat with me, pinning it to the ground. I kiss the tip of his nose. "I win." The troops clap in amazement, and money flutters down from everywhere.

Pete grins. "Devilish."

Now it's me against Spence. He easily has eighty pounds on me and is almost a foot taller. But I have one thing he doesn't. I have the thought of him taking my friend from me and saving her for himself. Making Mazi his with his child. All I need is one arrow, one shot, and she would be mine again. I'm not heartless though and I do not want to fight him. He runs at me. I duck under his arm and pull one of his knees back while I push his opposite shoulder forward. His head hits the ground with a thud, and I act like I break his neck. There. Done. I win.

They crown me champion and give each other the money they owe. We've missed lunch by many hours. The sun is falling under the hills, and everyone is ready for supper. The cooks fry our meal while we sit around the fire in blankets. As much as I want to sit by Pete and Cam, Cam got to me first and my head is in his lap rather than Pete's. He sits across the fire with his face down and a stick in hand drawing pictures in the snow. A cook passes out plates filled with hot bread, potatoes, and pot roast. The meal warms my insides and ends up giving me chills on the outside. Gibbs makes me swallow my unnecessary pain medication and sends us off to bed.

I take my sleeping bag from Pete and leave him my heating pad. I kiss his cheek and tell him I'm sorry for what I'm putting him through. He brushes a strand of my hair. "It's nothing."

I crawl into Cam's tent and situate his stuff so both heating pads and sleeping bags are on top of me instead of him, but he doesn't mind. "So champ fighter, huh?" He laughs.

"No. I mean Bree was easy, and I could get Pete to do anything, but I have a reason for doing so well against Spence." I pull the covers over my head.

"Which is?" he asks.

"I can't tell you," I say.

He never makes me tell him; instead he lets me fall asleep in his arms.

The ground is dusty and cracked where I stand. My lips are dry and bleeding. Behind me, everyone is dead; in front of me is a metal cage, big with barbs. Ariel, Broppin, Tinley, and Hixel are pressed against the fence with the points poking through their skin. Their flesh is sunburned and peeling. Foryark Dranken smiles wickedly at me with his red eyes on blackened skin and spits on a golden button in front of him. I put the scope of my gun on his head and pull the trigger. Nothing happens. He snickers through his teeth, and his hand slams down on the button. Gates open on the other side of the barbs and sickly oversized panthers step into the bright sunlight. "No! No!" I scream. The panthers look at me, and I swear they smile at me before they attack the younger girls, and they fall to their knees dead in front of me.

"No. This isn't happening . . ." I shoot out of my sleeping bag.

"What is it?" Cam whispers.

It was just a dream, I reassure myself. *The younger girls are safe in the Center.* "A nightmare." I struggle to catch my breath. He scoots closer to me; I rub my fingers through my hair.

"What was it about?" he asks.

"Everyone I knew was dead and I was all by myself," I say.

He grabs my shoulder and pushes my chin up. "That will never happen."

"Cam, if something happens tomorrow, they could do anything to anyone," I say.

He wipes a tear from my cheek. "I won't let that happen," he says. But he might not be able to. The second nightmare materializes only seconds after I close my eyes. I cannot move. I am held in place by my own fear, for if I move, they will kill each other. Pete and Cam are staring into each other's eyes, knives drawn and held to the other's throats.

"Stop! I will never choose."

They turn to me and step closer. "But we love you," they whisper. Their knives are lured to my throat and hold there.

"I'm sorry. I don't want either of you," I say.

"Then you shall have no one." They look at the other's knife, switch blades and stab me through the heart.

I jolt upright and scoot away from Cam, examining him closely to make sure he's not armed and he isn't in the mood to kill me. His fingers are curled innocently to his palms and his head is turned away with absolutely no death look on his face. I trace the muscle in his neck, thinking two things. One, I might lose you tomorrow. Two, why can't I get one of these?

CHAPTER TWENTY-EIGHT

The next morning when we are woken for our early departure, no one looks well rested, especially not Cam and I. Bruises run up and down his legs and his arm is rubbed raw from my cast. I had been kicking and hitting him all night. Rae and other personnel try their best to make us look our best for the cameras, which will be tagging along, but we are all a torn-up mess. The cooks give us a high-protein, high-carb, high-energy shake type thing. To me it tastes like spaghetti and meatballs mixed together in a blender but I don't ask. Gibbs, in his grey uniform instead of black, helps Pete and I onto Girl. Everyone other than the Rescue Squad wears grey; we are dressed differently so we're easy to pick out in case of emergency and are the first to be saved.

The journey to Xil is long and exceedingly heart stopping. Every stick that cracks, every branch I see move, or every person's breath that stops, I want to draw an arrow and send it flying in that direction. But there is no need. Even though I can't see them, troops from Gipem have the perimeter of Xil surrounded and only when we get close enough can I see the full extent of what I got myself into.

Millions upon millions of soldiers stand on the outside of the external city of Xil. They hold their guns in their arms, pointed at the barren city before them, waiting for the signal. The external city is small with only metal ceilings and thin sheets of plastic holding it all together, but this is not what we're after. We want what is on the inside. The slums are pressed against a thick wall of shining bullion and inside that wall holds the cloning machine and Foryark Dranken.

I have a bad feeling about what lies inside the wall. Like I want to go in but then again if I go, someone will get hurt. But this is what we've been training for and there is always a chance we're ready for what's inside. A hovercraft appears over the wall and opens its hatches. Fire bombs drop on top of the wall and spill over both sides. The people from the slums scatter out of the city and toward us. No one shoots at them. The idea that the bombs were the signal digs its way into everybody's brain and the thousands of people we have fighting for our country charge forward. It has begun.

CHAPTER TWENTY-NINE

The rescue squad is in the shape of an arrowhead with our security on the outer limbs, the rest of the Rescue Squad on the interior, and Pete and I as the arrow's tip, leading the whole expedition. I tap on Girl's armored sides, press the button that brings my helmet over my head and we hike forward into the smoke ahead.

The wall has melted down dramatically and our horses easily jump over it. Bullets ring through the air and dead bodies of Gipem soldiers and Duxian soldiers lie everywhere. I hear the guns of our security firing and bring mine around my body just in time to shoot a guy who had his barrel aimed at Girl. That was the first person I've ever shot, but he was going to kill Girl, and that would just postpone my revenge. I slide off Girl and yank Pete down. I will not let her be slain. My friends get off their horses and quickly lead them to the wall and push them over into a safer place. One less thing to worry about.

We get back in our formation with Pete and I side by side at the tip. We cannot see anything through the smolder of the bombs. "We need to go this way," Pete says. He pulls my arm to the right. Our speed picks up to a run. The grey disappears as we get closer to the innards of the city. The smokeless Xil finally comes into my view, golden buildings encrusted with emeralds, rubies, and sapphires. It's beautiful.

"Blue," Ms. Florence calls. The dog runs to her from Pete's side. So much good we are, a newly trained dog leads us out of the smoke, not the commanders who've been training for almost five months.

Pete holds his teletalky up to his mouth. "Enable map."

A holographic image of Xil pops up in front of me. The blinking green dot, indicating where we are, is extremely close to the machine. I look ahead into the streets of the city and find one not burning or flooded with Duxian soldiers. I point straight ahead and wave my squad forward. Just as we reach the entrance to the street, Pete whips his personally crafted gun out of his belt and aims it at my head.

"Duck!" he yells. I slam to the ground and a body with a hole through its head falls beside me.

I press the button on my earpiece that allows everyone in my arrowhead to hear me. "Drop!" I yell. My friends scrunch to their knees while our security breaks off from the group and begins to shoot at the invading Duxian soldiers. I was too oblivious to see them hiding in the doors and windows of the evacuated building.

"Hayden, get moving! You are so close," Gibbs says. Chipolaux and our mentors stayed back at camp so they can see our every move and all of our surroundings from the video camera's placed around our suits. I shoot up, adjusting my gun so I can use my broken hand as well. I help Pete up and we continue forward until we reach a four-way intersection. We stop for a quick second, analyzing which direction to go.

Pete brings his teletalky to his mouth, "Enable—" His voice cuts off and he whips around to face the others the same time I do.

More and more Duxians march on to the street; they've encased our security and are now firing their guns at us. Bullets bounce off my vest. While I don't feel any pain, they are pushing me off my feet. Blue limps to me from another direction; Ms. Florence is nowhere to be seen. Bree quickly wraps the dog's paw. Pete must've been given an order because he starts yelling for us to run.

"We can't just leave him here?" Bree says. Spence grabs Blue in his arms and pushes her forward. We turn right at the intersection and run halfway down the road before I get an idea.

"Give me your bombs," I order the back line consisting of Cam, Brint, Spence, and Griff. They hand them over willingly. They have different things in their belts because of their positioning on the mission. I press the panic button on the bombs and throw them into the intersection. In seconds, I'm blown off my feet.

CHAPTER THIRTY

The street goes up in flames, cutting us off from the advancing attackers. We stand assessing our injuries. I flex every muscle in my body, but nothing seems hurt. "Is anyone injured?" Pete asks. They get off the ground, deliberately dreading the pain that will come, but none does. That is officially the first good thing that has happened on this mission.

"Well, let's go then." We hurry down the rest of the road and turn on to what the teletalky says is the road the cloning machine is kept.

Pete and I recognize it first. No sound I've ever heard was more twisted and ghastly as the one making its way into my ears right now. How someone has managed to evoke them into making this noise is a quiz to me, a sure form of death. They are safe in the Center. Ariel, Broppin, Hixel, and Tinley are out of harm's way. They shriek again even more monstrously.

"Stop them!" Lakuna shouts before I even move. I throw my gun over my shoulder and easily dodge Griff's arms. I spin around Cam and hurl myself into the tiny side street leading to my sisters. Pete runs so fast, he barrels over me and skids to a stop right in front of the electric barbwire fence holding them.

Ariel, Broppin, Tinley, and Hixel are huddled together, fighting against the cold. Their bodies are bare of clothing, and I can see their frostbitten fingers and toes from here.

"It's a trap!" Gibbs screams in my ear. "Get out of there!" The girls hold their hands out to us for help; I step closer to the fence. I am reliving my dream from last night but in a different sense. Frantic, I search for Foryark and the gold button.

"Pete," I utter as my eyes skim the rooftops and find the golden button with a hand descending on it.

"Chipolaux!" Pete screams. "Don't press that!"

Chipolaux looks down on us; his smile wicked and pushes the button.

258

Doors behind the electrical thorny fence open, and four panthers, black as the night itself, stalk out. They stare at us; they're eyes piercing through me and their fangs dripping. They smile the smile I saw in my dream space out in a flurry of murderers. The girls stumble to us and grab the fence just as the panthers reach them. Their hair stands on end and spittle falls from their mouths. Their skin instantly blackens as the fence electrifies them. Their blood splatters the golden pavement of Xil and their bodies freeze in midair. They look at us one last time before their heads tweak in odd ways, and the panthers deliver a death blow.

And just like that, I have nothing left to work for. Someone pins my arms behind my back and shoves me to Pete's side. I feel a barrel of a gun in the back of my head and I can see the black tip of the gun threatening to kill Pete too. I don't care.

"Do it," I say. "Shoot me. I don't want to live like this anymore."

Gibbs comes into my head so fast, I can barely understand what he's saying. "It was a trick. They are alive and in the Center." I just saw them die; they are not alive in the Center. I'm sick of being lied to; Chipolaux Donovan just killed my sisters. I no longer want to work for Gipem or anyone.

"I'm not going to hurt a hair on your pretty little head," the guy holding me whispers in my ear. "You're too valuable to throw away."

Then Gibbs is talking to me again, "Don't get taken prisoner. The squad knows what to do!"

The men detaining Pete and I turn us toward our friends. They stand there, mouths gaping, guns drawn.

"If you kill us, we kill them," the guy holding Pete snarls.

Lakuna looks at me through her purple blue eyes and I know this is the last glimpse I'll get of her for a while, if ever. I wave good-bye to her as her gun drops to the ground.

"Cam," I cry. I feel the hot tears streaming down my face. "Shoot us."

I can tell Cam is being given orders from his earpiece because his gun dips for just a small second and he whispers to Yanish on the other end, "I can't."

He aims his gun at Pete, "No! No! Me first!" I cry because I know he will actually shoot Pete and I cannot bear to watch it. He inches the barrel toward the direction of my head.

"Cam . . ." He looks through the scope and his finger finds the trigger.

A single tear drops from Cam's eye and drips to the ground with a small splash. His gun slips from his grasp, bangs to the road, shutters, and then goes still. He can't do it.

"All you have to do is leave. We won't harm you on your way back to your country," the man behind me snaps. He sounds like he's losing patience.

"Cam?" I beg.

Out of one thing in the entire world, I want death. I have finally chosen between Cam and Pete. My pick is to die. He looks at me and then at the man behind me. He steps close to me and ever so gently kisses my forehead as if not to break me. Then he digs in his belt and pulls out a newly bloomed blue flower. He places the flower on top of his gun. Griff grabs him and yanks him farther away from Pete and me. He looks over Griff's arm and, with defeated, hunched shoulders walks away, leaving Pete and me in the hands of the Duxian killers and alone forever.